Healing Notes

By

Beth Hope

Cover Art by Illustrator-Anna Bovi Diamond

Contents

Dear Reader,

Before you begin this book, I want to take a moment to give a heads-up about the content. This story deals with some topics that I know may be triggering. If you aren't concerned about that and/or don't want spoilers, I would suggest going ahead and starting chapter one.

Spoilers ahead.

You've been warned.

Okay, here we go.

This is a story about trauma, much of which is tied to a character's religious background. Other things that come up in the story are body dysmorphia, ADHD, and sexual abuse of minors by a religious leader (this is not graphic; I have kept it as vague as I possibly can). I have done my best to be very careful as I tackle difficult/delicate subjects. I have tried to balance the hard stuff with humor and sweetness. There is R-rated sexual content that is consensual between two adults in a loving relationship.

And with that, on to the story!

-Beth

To Tom for seeing me.
To Lindsey for being there.
To RTBS for changing my life

One

Zoe

Nine-thirty to noon, every Saturday morning, was the best part of Zoe's week. For two and a half glorious hours, she didn't have to think about her awful job, Fred (her awful boss), or any of the other things that made her miserable. She got to sit and read the newspaper live on the air at Nebraska Reading Service (NRS). A radio station that provided both live and pre-recorded content to people living with vision or other disabilities that would prevent them from reading. She'd been volunteering at the studio for a little over a year, and it had quickly become her favorite place in town.

Most Saturdays, listeners could hear Zoe and her reading partner, Moira. She was a few decades older than Zoe and had volunteered at the studio for years. The woman was kind, patient, and incredibly encouraging. Zoe adored her.

It was a chilly November Saturday when Zoe arrived at the station. She tapped out a quick text, letting Dante, the producer, know that she'd arrived so he would unlock the door. While waiting for him, she wondered who would be subbing for Moira. The previous Saturday, the older woman had informed her she would be out of town for the next two weeks. The news didn't faze Zoe. Moira's mother lived in Minnesota, and Moira was typically gone one weekend every month to visit her.

The only downside to Moira's absence was working with a sub. Early on, Zoe had discovered that the subs tended to be a bit hit or miss. There were a few she loved working with, but there was never a guarantee that one of them would be filling in. It wasn't always easy, but she did her best to roll with whoever her partner was. She always tried to remember that they were all volunteers doing their best.

The door opened, revealing Dante. While he was taller than Zoe, he was a little shorter than the average man. Always cheerful, he greeted her with a huge grin, "G'morning!"

She returned the smile as she stepped inside, "Hey! How are you? Love the shirt."

Dante had a seemingly endless supply of geeky t-shirts. The one he was wearing was a mashup of *Doctor Who* and *Back to the Future*. "Thanks!" he replied as they walked back to the studio. "I'm good. Bit nippy out there this morning."

"Yeah, but at least we haven't had any snow yet."

He chuckled, "You're right about that."

She stepped into the booth, and as she pulled off her hoodie and dropped her purse on the floor, she asked, "Any idea who's subbing for Moira this morning?"

Dante leaned against the door frame, watching her, "Yeah."

"Someone I've worked with before?" she asked as she set up her area.

"Nope, new guy. This will be his first time doing a live read."

"Cool. Well, hopefully, I won't scare him off," she joked as she sat in front of the computer. Notebook open, pen in hand, she navigated the mouse to open the obituaries in the paper's e-edition. As she began jotting down the information she needed for the broadcast, she asked, "Have you met him before?"

"Yup. Our moms were friends when we were little."

She paused her notes and turned to Dante, "So, what's he like?"

He didn't immediately answer, seeming to search for the right words. Finally, "He's got a great voice. I think you'll enjoy reading with him."

That was a strangely vague reply, and Zoe asked, "That's great, but what's he like? Nice? Friendly? A complete ass?"

Before Dante could answer, his phone dinged with an incoming text. He headed down the hallway, telling her, "I gotta go let in one of the other readers. Be back soon."

Zoe turned her attention back to the computer. There weren't many obituaries, but that was normal for a Saturday. She rolled her chair over to the computer her sub would be reading from. The papers they read from were published by the same company and tended to have crossover in both obits and articles. Occasionally, she or Moira would slip up and accidentally start reading a story the other person had already read. Fortunately, that happened rarely. To Zoe's relief, there was only one crossover in the obits, and she removed the duplicate in her notebook, leaving it for the sub to read.

Rolling back to her computer, she began to browse through the paper. They had a schedule to follow, and she needed to figure out which stories would fit each category. While she skimmed, she found herself wondering about Dante's evasiveness. That wasn't normal for him. It made her wonder just what kind of guy she'd spend the next two hours with. A glance at the clock told her she'd find out within the next twenty minutes.

Sure enough, ten minutes later, she heard Dante call out, "He's here. I'll be right back."

Working through the sports section, she heard Dante's voice floating down the hallway, "You've got a great partner this morning. I think you're really gonna enjoy working with her."

Behind her came the sound of people entering the booth as Dante said, "And here she is." Zoe turned her chair, and Dante made a quick introduction, "Zoe, this is Liam McPherson. Liam, this is Zoe Callahan.”

Good lord, the man was tall. It took everything in her not to stare with mouth agape. Reminding herself to smile, she lifted her hand in a small wave, “Hi!”

Liam watched her, his gaze intense. There was no smile anywhere as he nodded, “Hello.”

“So, you’ll be sitting here, and I’ve already got the paper pulled up for you.” Dante directed Liam to the other chair, then asked Zoe, “You got this?”

She nodded, “Yup, I’ll talk him through it.”

Dante left for the production side of the booth, and Zoe was alone with Liam. She was finding it difficult not to stare. He was quite a bit younger than the volunteers she usually worked with. His face wasn’t traditionally handsome, but there was something pleasing about it. A well-defined jaw, full lips, and large dark eyes were complimented by some of the most beautiful hair she’d ever seen in the real world. She didn’t know anyone could have hair that gorgeous. Her hair was frizzy with faded purple that had partially grown out to reveal mousey brunette roots. She nearly always kept it up in a ponytail and felt self-conscious about how bad she was sure it looked. Meeting his eyes, she asked, “You’ve been in to observe a live read, right?”

He nodded, “Earlier this week.”

“Okay, so Saturdays are pretty much the same as what you saw. The biggest difference is we have no editorials to read on the weekend. Typically, we just read more local stories to cover that part of the schedule.” She gave him a quick rundown of the schedule and showed him the signal she and Moira used to let each other know when it was their turn to read. Pointing to the headset and the container of wipes, she told him, “If I were you, I’d clean them before putting them on. Some people forget to do it when they finish.”

He took her advice and began wiping his pair down. She gave him a few more instructions and wrapped up with, “That’s basically it. Any questions?”

He shook his head. She glanced at the clock, “We’ve got a few minutes. If you need a drink or the bathroom, now's the time to take care of that."

"I'm fine," he replied, picking up the black travel mug he'd walked in with.

She watched him take a drink and asked, "Dante said you're one of the newer volunteers. Do you like it?"

"It's fine," he answered.

That wasn't much to work with, and she wanted to ask for more details, but she noticed Dante moving to the board and knew that was their cue. Rolling her chair a few inches to the door, she shut it, rolled back, and quickly cleaned her headphones before slipping them on. Meeting Liam's eyes, she offered what she hoped was an encouraging smile, "You're gonna do great."

Dante's voice came through the headset, and after doing his usual starting spiel, he introduced them, "With us this morning are our wonderful volunteers, Zoe Callahan, and filling in for Moira is Liam McPherson. So, if you don't have anywhere else to be, sit back and spend the next couple of hours with us. Zoe, Liam, what's in the news today?"

As she'd instructed, Liam introduced himself first, "This is Liam McPherson, and I'll be reading the Gazette."

"And this is Zoe Callahan, and I'll be reading the Tribune. As always, we're starting with national and international news, beginning with a story from Sydney."

As she reached the end of the story, she lightly tapped the space on the desk between her and Liam. He began his first story, and Zoe took the opportunity to listen to him. Dante was right; the man had an excellent voice. He spoke clearly and concisely. His voice was deep. Really deep. Listening to him, she decided she wouldn't mind hearing him read pretty much anything. He could read her microwave instruction manual, and she'd gladly listen to every single word.

The first half hour went smoothly, but trouble began as they moved into local news. She was partially through a story about a drug bust when her ears were assaulted with the sound of loud breathing. It had slipped her mind to remind him that the mics were incredibly sensitive. She would bring it up at the break. Unfortunately, the rest of the hour, every time she was reading, all she could hear in her ears was the steady sound of inhales and exhales. It grated on her like nails on a chalkboard.

Finally, it was eleven, and she said, "That brings us to the end of the first hour, and we're gonna toss it back over to Dante."

The producer spent the next five minutes covering the weather forecast, and Zoe turned her attention to Liam. "You doing okay?"

He nodded but said nothing.

She smiled, "That's good. You sound great. Just remember that the mics pick up everything, so don't forget to use the mute button. And try not to breathe into it when you're not reading, okay?"

He nodded again and still said nothing.

Standing, she told him, "I'll be right back. We've got a couple minutes, so now's the time to stretch, or run to the bathroom, or refill your coffee."

Not waiting for a response, she dashed to the bathroom. She was quick and returned to the booth in less than two minutes. Dante was winding up the weather as she slipped her headphones back on. Liam was watching her with that same intensity he'd had since he'd walked in the door. She gave him another encouraging smile as Dante said, "Looks like our readers have returned to the booth, so I'm gonna send it back to my friends on the other side of the glass."

The second hour went as smoothly as she could hope. Liam mostly remembered to use the mute button, but she heard him drinking his coffee loudly a few times. She reminded herself that he was new and doing his best to follow instructions. There were plenty of subs she'd worked with who were far more experienced and made way more mistakes. As far as subs went, Liam was decent.

The hour wound down, and they signed off. Dante took over with a few final remarks, and Zoe pulled off her headphones. She turned her attention to Liam as she cleaned up and said, "Good job. You did well. Did you have fun?"

He raised an eyebrow, "Fun?"

She nodded, turning off the equipment, "Yeah, fun. I know it can be a little overwhelming at first. I promise it gets easier. I was so nervous the first couple weeks I did this. I love it, though, and now it's pretty much the best part of my week."

He cleaned his side without saying anything. Zoe picked up her hoodie and purse and left the booth. Stopping at the door to Dante's side, she began chatting with him. Liam left the booth a minute later, and a few strides had him walking past her. She quickly said, "Hey, Liam, thanks for being here."

Dante added, "You guys sounded great together. I'm sure people enjoyed listening this morning."

She smiled up at Liam, "Have a great week!"

He nodded, "You too."

Before she could say anything else, he was out the door, and she was alone with Dante. Fixing her attention on the producer, she asked, "Is he always so...so..."

"Sunshiney?" Dante supplied.

She laughed, "Yeah. Kind of has a Dark Lord of Darkness vibe."

He grinned, "I dare you to call him that to his face." She snorted at the suggestion, and he added, "Give it time. He may warm up to you."

"How much time are we talking?" she asked lightly.

He chuckled, "Can't tell you that. Maybe he'll be better next week."

"He's subbing again?" In her experience, most subs didn't do multiple weeks in a row.

"Yeah."

Knowing what to expect the following Saturday was a relief, "Alrighty, then. Sounds good." Pulling her keys from her purse, she told him, "I'll see you next week. Thanks as always."

"Thanks for being here. Have a good one!" Dante said as she headed out the door.

There were only three cars in the lot. One was hers, and one was Dante's. The third was unfamiliar. Liam was sitting inside, and after a few seconds, he seemed to sense that she was looking, and his eyes met hers. She smiled and lifted her hand in a wave. He looked away, and she finished making her way to her car. As she pulled out of the lot, he was still sitting there.

Driving home, she couldn't shake the feeling that Liam McPherson was a very unhappy man.

Two

Liam

He took a seat on the grey couch, overstuffed throw pillows on either side of him. It was the last place he wanted to be. At the same time, it was the place he needed the most to be.

"So, Liam, how was your week?"

He studied the woman seated in the armchair not far from him. Pen in hand, she held a notebook open and watched him with a curious expression. She was an older woman with a bob of auburn hair streaked with silver. The lines on her face told a story of a woman who loved to laugh.

He'd been seeing Dr. Constance once a week for the past five months. She claimed they were making good progress, but he wasn't sure he agreed. All the reasons he'd started therapy were still just as present and problematic. Nearly every week, she told him, *Healing takes time, Liam. You're here, that's the important thing.*

Shrugging, he replied, "Same as always."

"Do you want to talk about what you mentioned in our last session? The news reading? How did that go?"

He looked away from her, voice flat as he replied, "It was fine."

"I'm curious what that experience was like. Would you be open to sharing a little more?"

He clasped and unclasped his hands, his thoughts fixed on the previous Saturday, "It wasn't what I was expecting."

She jotted something down and looked back at him, "What were you expecting?"

He ran a hand through his hair, "When I went in to observe, the people were old. Pretty much every volunteer I've seen there is older. I figured I'd be reading with someone in their sixties or seventies."

Zoe's lovely heart-shaped face and bright hazel eyes filled his mind as he chewed the inside of his cheek. He hadn't been prepared for her. Not even a little.

"Liam?" Dr. Constance interrupted his thoughts, and he realized he'd been silent for well over a minute, possibly longer.

His eyes moved around the room as he forced himself to continue, "The woman I was reading with...she was young. Probably in her late twenties. She was..." his eyes shut, and he could see the soft smile of her pale pink lips, complete with cupid bow. He remembered how she had spoken to him, "She was cheerful and kind. I think I might've...might've annoyed her a little...but she didn't get mad."

"Did you enjoy working with her?"

He sighed and leaned forward, elbows on his knees, resting his forehead in his hands. "I...I..." he couldn't figure out how to answer the question.

"Liam?" Dr. Constance's voice was gentle.

He swallowed hard, "She was so beautiful."

The scratch of the pen on the paper sounded so loud in his ears. After a moment, Dr. Constance asked, "How did that make you feel?"

It took him a long time to finally admit, "Confused."

"Do you know why you felt confused?"

He sat up straighter and looked at the doctor. His thoughts were a swirling mess as he tried to figure out how to express them in a way that would make sense. "I wasn't angry." That was a good place to start. The anger he'd felt his entire life, a near-constant presence, had evaporated while sitting in the booth with Zoe. Her happy, calm demeanor had done something to soothe the rage inside. "She was so patient with me."

Dr. Constance considered what he'd said. "How did you feel after working with her?"

He didn't immediately answer. He'd spent nearly all Saturday and part of Sunday feeling strangely mellow. "Okay. It didn't last, though. There's something about her..." he shook his head, "I don't know."

She was quiet a long time before asking, "Liam, is it possible you're attracted to this woman?"

He squeezed his eyes shut and pinched the bridge of his nose. She'd hit upon the question he'd been wrestling with since Saturday morning. "I don't know."

"That's okay," she reassured him.

He opened his eyes and stared at her, "Even if I was, what's the point?"

Her head tilted to the side as she watched him with curiosity, "What do you mean?"

He leaned his head against the wall and stared at the ceiling, "We both know why I'm here. I'm a monster. Someone like her? She deserves far better than the nightmare that I'd bring into her life."

"I'm not suggesting that you jump into a relationship with her. In fact, I can't advise that it would be a good idea at this point. That said, I do think it's good that you had such a positive interaction with this woman." There were a few seconds before she asked, "Do you remember what we talked about a few weeks ago regarding how you speak about yourself?"

He met her eyes, "I can't lie to myself. I'm a monster."

There was a hint of sadness in her voice as she told him, "Liam, you're healing from trauma. If your friend was recovering from what you went through, would you be okay with them saying things like that about themselves?"

"I know you want me to say no, but I can't." He couldn't keep the frustration out of his voice.

She leaned forward, "That's okay. We'll keep working on it. You deserve to be able to be kind to yourself."

His eyes shifted to the clock. They still had twenty minutes left in the session. Annoyed, he informed her, "I don't want to keep talking about this." He might scream if he had to spend one more minute talking about being kind to himself.

Anyone else likely would've quailed at the edge in his tone. She didn't even bat an eye; just took it in stride and asked, "What do you want to talk about?"

It was a relief she was willing to let him shift the conversation. Taking a drink of his coffee, he told her, "I'm subbing again on Saturday. I'll be in that booth with Zoe for two solid hours."

"Zoe is the woman you worked with last Saturday?"

He nodded.

"How are you feeling about that?"

Eyes fixed on his travel mug, he answered, "Anxious."

"Is there a specific reason you feel that way?" she asked.

Memories of how tongue-tied he'd felt the previous Saturday morning flitted through him. "I don't know how to talk to her."

He left therapy feeling wrung out. It was how he always felt at the end of sessions. When he'd started therapy, he'd had the idea that going would make him feel better. Instead, his emotions got put through the wringer, and he always spent the rest of the day barely able to function. Dr. Constance had assured him that, eventually, it might not be so bad.

You're working through trauma, Liam. She'd told him that countless times.

Trauma. He wasn't even sure it was the right term. Trauma seemed like something other people experienced. People who had actually gone through serious shit. What he'd been through had been rough, but did it really qualify as trauma?

You can't compare your experience to that of others. Someone will always seem to have it worse, but that's their journey, not yours. Another thing she'd reminded him of several times.

He wished he could believe her.

Driving home, he thought about Dr. Constance's advice regarding Zoe and the upcoming Saturday. She'd suggested that if Zoe asked him questions, he try giving answers that weren't the word *Fine.* She'd encouraged him, if he felt comfortable, to try asking Zoe some questions of his own. Basic things like, *How was your week?*

Communication had never been his strongest skill. It had been easier when someone was telling him what to say. Trying to think for himself and behave like a functioning human was far more difficult. It was what he wanted, though. He was done being used as a tool by other people. That was part of why he kept going back to therapy week after week.

Saturday morning, he found himself pulling into the studio's parking lot, his insides twisted into about a thousand anxious knots. Over and over, he repeated the advice Dr. Constance had given him.

Dante let him into the building, saying, "Zoe's running a few minutes late, but she should be here soon. Go ahead and get yourself situated."

Liam pulled up the obituaries and began making notes the way he'd been instructed. A few minutes in, he heard Dante call out, "Zoe's here. Be right back."

Less than a minute later, he heard Zoe's voice. She was talking fast and sounded frazzled, "...and you'd think that after a year, they'd know not to block my car in on Saturdays. Trying to get them to wake up so I could get my car freed was such a pain in the ass."

He turned a little and watched as she stepped inside the booth. Her eyes met his, and he noticed dark circles around them, making her look a bit like a raccoon. She gave him a weary smile as she dropped into her chair, "Hey, Liam."

The studio phone rang, and Dante disappeared into the hallway. Liam remembered Dr. Constance's instructions about talking to Zoe. He tried, "Hi. Rough morning?"

She was already opening the obituaries on her computer and nodded, "I overslept, and by the time I showered, I was already running late. And I'm sure you heard me talking about my roommates blocking my car. Kind of a shitty way to start the day." She took a deep breath and glanced at him with a weak smile, "But I'm here now, and it's going to be better."

Her eyes returned to the screen, and she pulled an elastic band off her wrist. He watched as she put her still-damp hair up into a ponytail. The faded purple from the week before was gone, and now she sported a deep blue. She opened her notebook and began scribbling down information as she asked, "How about you? Been a good morning?"

No vague answers. He turned back to his screen; it would be easier to talk if he didn't have to look at her, "Yeah. Nowhere near as exciting as yours, that's for sure."

"Lucky," she laughed. "Oh my god. Do you have the obituary for Felix Sedlacek?"

He looked through his list, "No."

"C'mere, you have to see this."

He hesitated for a moment before rolling his chair a foot closer to look at her screen. She pointed to the obituary, and his eyes scanned it, "That's a bit long."

She replied, "It's insanely long, but that's not the craziest part. Look at this," she pointed to a paragraph, "Why would anyone put that in their obituary?"

His eyes went wide with surprise, "He hopes his family rots in hell?"

"I've seen some crazy obits in the last year, but this might take the cake." She laughed, "I can't believe his family actually let that get published."

Liam almost replied, but his brain had grown very scrambled. He was much closer to Zoe than before, and his senses were getting overwhelmed. The scent of coconut and ginger filled his nostrils, and he quickly rolled back to his side of the desk. Zoe was beautiful, and she smelled good, and her laugh made something inside him feel warm. Suddenly, everything was too much, and he got up, mumbling, "I'll be back."

The bathroom was an easy escape. He knew he couldn't stay in there long, but at least he'd be able to try to pull himself together. Practicing the breathing exercises Dr. Constance had taught him; he got his heart to stop racing. Splashing cold water on his face, he looked into the mirror. *Get ahold of yourself, McPherson.* It wasn't much of a pep talk, but he was running out of time, so it would have to do.

Zoe already had her headphones on when he returned. "You okay?" she asked.

He nodded but didn't trust himself to speak.

"Good. I checked your obits; we don't have any crossover today." Her smile was bright, and it was hard to keep looking at her as she added, "Just remember to breathe, but not into the mic. Don't forget to use the mute button if you need to cough or take a drink or anything like that."

He grabbed the wipes and quickly cleaned his headset before slipping it on. Next thing he knew, Dante was starting the broadcast, and they were off.

Zoe had the first story, and he listened as she read. Her voice was pleasant. She was a decent reader, though he noticed she occasionally tripped over words, and sometimes, there would be names she would struggle to pronounce. Still, he liked listening to her. She spoke very animatedly, and he remembered how she'd told him that doing the news was the best part of her week. He didn't doubt that; she very obviously enjoyed the work.

He remembered her instructions regarding the mic. Just to be safe, when he wasn't reading, he kept the mute button pressed. Roughly halfway through the first hour, he realized there was something pleasant about how he and Zoe volleyed the reading back and forth. There was a rhythm to it that he liked. She was easy to read with. It was more than that, though. She was just easy to be with. He liked being with her.

He didn't like being with anyone.

Maybe Dr. Constance was right. Maybe he *was* making progress.

When Dante took over at the end of the broadcast, Liam pulled off his headphones and began cleaning them. Zoe did the same and asked, "How did today feel?"

Wonderful. He almost choked on the thought. That was not the kind of thing he felt about anything. Instead, he told her, "Better than last week."

"Good. Think you'll want to sub in the future?"

Yes! Okay, he really needed to get his thoughts under control. "Probably."

She smiled at him, "That's great. You're a good partner. I like reading with you."

Feeling his cheeks warm at her compliment, he looked away and mumbled, "Thanks."

She finished turning everything off while telling him, "Moira's back next week, but she's usually gone at least once a month. Hopefully, they'll ask you to sub next time she's gone." Standing, she pulled on her hoodie, slung her purse over her shoulder, and fished out her keys, "I wish I could stick around longer, but I have to run. Today is just kind of crazy. Have a great day!"

And then she was gone.

He got up and began to leave as well. When he reached the door to Dante's side, he found the man was leaning against the doorframe. Dante grinned at him, "You got a sec, or need to dash out of here as well?"

Liam wanted to leave but hesitated, "I can spare a minute."

"How would you feel about doing this every Saturday?"

Liam froze, "What are you talking about?"

Dante shrugged, "Moira sent an email this morning. Her mom had to have emergency surgery yesterday, and Moira's not sure when she's gonna be back in town. She asked if we could find a replacement for her. You and Zoe are good together. Would you be interested in being the replacement?"

Three

Zoe

She had Wednesday off and headed to the studio to do some recording for the Bookmarks program. Unlike the news, Bookmarks was prerecorded. This meant that if she made a mistake, all she had to do was back the track up and fix her blunder. She was slowly working her way through a YA fantasy novel. Bookmarks was an hour-long program, and she'd gotten quick enough that she could usually get the material recorded in an hour and a half.

Stepping into the studio, she stopped at the office and greeted Will, the program director. He smiled when he heard her greeting and responded, "Zoe! How's everything in your world today?"

"Good. You?"

"Also good. Listen, I'm glad you're here. Was going to send you an email, but now I can just tell you in person."

She rested her shoulder against the doorframe, "What's up?"

He leaned back in his chair, "Dante said he didn't get a chance to talk with you on Saturday."

"Yeah, Saturday was kinda nuts," she acknowledged. Anxiety flooded her,

"Did I do something wrong?"

Will laughed, "Always so worried you've messed up." His face softened, and his voice was kind, "You need to go easier on yourself. You do a really good job."

She shrugged, "I try." For some reason, no one else ever seemed to understand the pressure she had to put on herself. No one else seemed to get the need to do everything perfectly that had run her life for as long as she could remember.

Maybe Will sensed her unease since he didn't dwell on the issue and instead said, "Moira let us know this weekend that she's not going to be able to continue doing Saturdays."

Zoe's face fell, "Is everything okay?"

"Her mom isn't doing well; had to have emergency surgery. Moira's gonna be staying there to take care of her for a while."

She shouldn't have been surprised. Moira had mentioned before that one of these days, her mom would probably require her to be more available than she currently was. "That's too bad. I love working with her, but I understand. I assume this means I'll be working with subs for a bit?"

He shook his head, "Possibly, but hopefully not. We asked someone to consider taking over the role, and they're supposed to get an answer to me by the end of the day."

Her curiosity was piqued, "Is it someone I know?"

"That new guy, the one who's been subbing the last two weeks." He snapped his fingers, and his face took on a look of concentration, "Damn it, his name just left my head."

"Liam?" she offered.

He relaxed and nodded, "Yeah, that's it. Dante said you guys work well together, and after listening, I have to agree."

She smiled, "He's easy to read with."

"So you're okay with this?"

She nodded, "Yeah."

He grinned, "Great. Well, like I said, I should have an answer by the end of the day. Think you'll be in again before Saturday?"

She shook her head, "I wish, but I'm working the next two days."

He nodded, "In that case, I'll shoot you an email once I've heard back from him. Just want to keep you in the loop."

"I appreciate that," she told him. Standing up straighter, she added, "Anything else?"

"Nope, go read." He waved her away.

She made her way down the hallway and entered Booth Two. It was her favorite of all the booths. The equipment in Two seemed to work better than in the others. Shutting the door, she let herself relax in the quiet of the small room.

Much like on Saturdays, she had a routine for setting everything up before beginning to record. There was a specific spot where she put her e-reader, a specific height her chair needed to be set at, and specific spots for the computer mouse and the pad of buttons she used when making her recordings. Once all that was arranged, she pulled out a wipe and cleaned off the headphones. Satisfied that everything was ready, she took a seat and moved the microphone to the perfect angle.

A few taps of buttons, a click of the mouse, and she was ready to go.

Overall, it wasn't one of her better days of reading. It felt like she was stumbling over a word in nearly every sentence. She knew others might let small mistakes stay, but the perfectionist inside her couldn't stand to do that. There was a lot of rewinding and re-recording before she finished.

The thing she loved about being at the studio was that no matter how rough her recording might go, she never left the place feeling bad. Everyone there was always kind to her, and she always walked away feeling better than when she'd arrived. The place was peaceful, and she desperately needed that peace in her life.

Late that afternoon, Will emailed her that Liam had agreed to do a trial run.

Zoe was pleased with the news, and it was what helped get her through the next two days.

"You're late," growled Fred Pluto when she arrived at work the next morning. "You know, I don't have to keep you employed. I do this out of the kindness of my heart."

Zoe resisted shooting back with *You only keep me employed because you'd have to pay anyone else a living wage*, and explained, "Sorry, there was an accident, and traffic got backed up."

He narrowed his eyes at her as if sensing her traitorous thoughts. Gruffly, he informed her, "Got a pile of laptops back there to get cleaned up and repaired. Get to it."

She was relieved he wasn't going to make her work the counter. He knew how much she hated it and seemed to thrive off the evil delight he got from forcing her to do it as much as possible. However, he also knew she was far quicker and better at cleaning and repairing electronics than he was.

In the back, she hopped onto the stool in front of the workbench. She slipped her headphones on and pulled up the playlist featuring metal covers of Disney songs. Music in her ears, she set to work.

Her fingers worked dexterously, muscle memory taking over. Meanwhile, her thoughts turned to Liam. They'd only met twice, but after the previous Saturday, she'd been even more certain that he was incredibly unhappy. There was deep sadness that radiated from him...and something else. Regret?

It was strange. He was handsome, wore clothes that probably cost more than she made in a month, and she didn't even want to think about how much he probably spent on his hair. His car was a newer model. It seemed unlikely he had the vaguest idea of what it was like to experience financial insecurity.

And yet, for all that, he was miserable. Proof positive that money didn't buy happiness.

She wondered if he had friends. Did he even know how to make friends? Would he let her be his friend? Maybe that's why the universe had let their paths cross.

A box of phones was dropped on her bench. She jumped in surprise and looked up, lowering her headphones as she did. Fred glowered at her, "Fix these, too."

She just nodded and moved the headphones back on her ears. Fred stomped away, and she went back to work.

Dahlia and Alex, her roommates, had been telling her for months that she needed to find a different job. They were right. She knew they were right. Pluto's Pawn was a dead-end job. She'd been there longer than she wanted to think about, and she hated the place with every fiber of her being. And yet, she kept going back, day after day, year after year. That probably said something about her mental health that was easier not to think about.

At least she didn't have to live with Fred anymore. Before moving out, she'd had to spend every day working for him at the shop and then spend every evening doing the same at his house. He'd always treated her like a servant rather than the child he was supposed to care for as a guardian.

Maybe that's why she couldn't leave the job. The man, odious as he was, had put a roof over her head and food in her belly from the time she was five. She owed him for that. It was a debt she'd never be able to repay.

She hadn't been sleeping well. For weeks, she'd been waking up between two and three a.m. and couldn't get back to sleep. It didn't matter when she went to bed, either. By three a.m., she would be wide awake.

Saturday morning, she was completely exhausted. If she hadn't loved doing the broadcast so much, it would've been impossible to get out of bed. Using the largest travel mug she had, she filled it with coffee that she'd made extra strong and hoped it would keep her alert enough that she wouldn't mess up too much while reading.

Liam's car wasn't there yet when she pulled into the lot. That didn't surprise her. She always arrived far earlier than necessary. It was nice to have time to get comfortable before the broadcast got underway. She didn't like to feel rushed the way she had the previous Saturday.

Dante let her in and asked, "Did you hear about Moira?"

She nodded, "Yeah. Will filled me in on Wednesday. He said Liam's gonna do a trial run taking over the spot."

"Yup. That okay?"

She sat down in front of her computer, "Of course. I like reading with him."

Dante's phone rang, and he stepped out of the booth to take the call. He returned a few minutes later, and Zoe took the opportunity to ask, "Does Liam have any friends?"

He shook his head, "I don't know. He's not exactly the most social person."

When he didn't offer anything else, she shifted the subject, "Still planning to come over on Thursday?"

He nodded, "Yup. Need me to bring anything other than pie?"

She shook her head, "As long as you make sure to bring a ton of whipped cream, too, we should be good."

His phone dinged, and he glanced at the screen, "Looks like Liam's here. Be right back."

She turned her attention to the paper, and less than a minute later, Liam was sitting in front of the other computer. "Morning." she greeted him, turning her head slightly from the monitor.

He looked at her, "Hi."

His attention shifted to his monitor, and she let him work. After ten minutes, she asked, "Mind if I see your world news section? We've got time and can figure out which stories we've got that are the same and divvy them up."

He clicked through a few screens, and the requested page populated. Zoe scanned the headlines, "Well, it looks like we both have that story about Congress, but I think you have the longer version. You want to take that? I've got a longer version of the story about the strikes, so I'll do that one."

"Okay," he nodded.

"Any stories sticking out that you really have your heart set on reading?"

He raised an eyebrow, "Is that something I'm supposed to feel?"

She laughed, "Not necessarily. Sometimes there are stories that are too fun to give up the chance to read. I just don't want to rob you of the opportunity."

"I assure you, I feel no attachment to any of these articles." He wasn't smiling, but his voice wasn't as morose as usual.

She yawned and took a swig of her coffee, "God I hope this keeps me awake. If I start snoring mid-program, you're welcome to throw something at me."

He tilted his head, studying her, "Trouble sleeping?"

Another yawn, and she nodded, "Yeah, the last few weeks haven't been great. The joys of being an adult, am I right?"

Somehow, she managed to get through the broadcast without falling asleep, though she had to hide multiple yawns. About halfway through, she had a thought and sent a quick text to her roommates.

Okay if I ask the new guy from the studio to come to Friendsgiving?

It was entirely possible that Liam had plans, but there was no harm in asking. She knew how much the holidays could suck when there was no one to spend them with. The replies arrived while she was reading. The first was from Dahlia, and the second was from Alex.

Go for it. We'll fit him in.

Sure.

While Liam was reading a story, she quietly flipped her notebook to a blank page. She wrote a few things on it, and when the broadcast ended, she removed the page from her notebook. Looking at Liam as he cleaned, she asked, "Do you have plans for Thanksgiving?"

He shook his head, "No."

Holding out the paper, she said, "If you want, you should come over for Friendsgiving. Dante's coming, so you'll know two of us. Plus, my roomies are super nice. It'll be very chill, and the food will be good." He stared at the paper for several seconds, and she began to feel awkward, "Take it. It's my address and phone number. We eat at one, but you're welcome to come over before that and watch the parade."

A few more seconds passed before he finally took the paper from her.

Four

Liam

He was stumped. Why had Zoe invited him to Friendsgiving? The question bounced around in his mind for days, and he grew more frustrated the longer he went without being able to come up with an answer. By the time he sat down with Dr. Constance on Wednesday morning, he was in a terrible mood.

She was quick to pick up on his mental turbulence, "Want to tell me about it?"

He sat with his arms folded across his chest, his thoughts whirling around like a tornado. "It's Zoe."

"Did something happen?" The question was asked gently.

Through gritted teeth, he replied, "She invited me to Friendsgiving tomorrow."

"Are you going to go?"

He shook his head, "Haven't decided."

Dr. Constance studied him, "Do you know why you haven't decided?"

Liam was silent for a long time. The truth was something he wasn't sure he wanted to admit, but it was also driving him crazy. "Why would she do this? What's her game?"

Dr. Constance considered his questions, "You're worried she has an ulterior motive?"

"She's met me exactly three times and then up and then invites me to this? It doesn't add up."

"Have you considered the possibility that she is nice and wants to make sure you're not alone for the holiday?"

Liam's laugh was bitter, "No one is nice without wanting something back."

Dr. Constance gave him a few seconds, waiting to see if he would say something else. When he didn't, she asked, "Is there any chance you would be willing to consider the possibility I suggested?"

He sighed and raked his fingers through his hair. A long time ago, he would've gladly believed that someone could be nice just because. But that had been decades ago. He'd learned the hard way what happened when he trusted someone because he thought they were nice. How many times was he supposed to get burned? Despite all that, something deep inside wanted to believe that maybe Zoe wasn't looking to get something from him. It was a faint hope at best. Probably a fool's hope.

He shook his head, "I know this song and dance. I've been put through it over and over my entire life. I won't be used like that again." Not even by Zoe. Beautiful, funny, sweet Zoe. Unlike the fake saccharine personalities that had surrounded him for so long, she was genuinely sweet. Given his history, he knew it was too good to be true. It was impossible that she was as wonderful as she seemed.

Dr. Constance sat forward and held his gaze, "Liam, I know that because of your past, it's easy to want to isolate. Giving another person a chance means giving them a measure of trust. It means being willing to be open and vulnerable. That's a big step, and I understand if you're not ready to take it yet. I hope that one of these days you're able to. You deserve to have people in your life who genuinely care about you simply because they like you and not because they have an ulterior motive."

Late Wednesday night, he sat on his couch, holding the paper Zoe had given him. He'd been picking it up and setting it down repeatedly for at least three hours. Every time he looked at the paper, he would change his mind. Each time he would start writing a text accepting her invite, he'd immediately back out of the message, fighting the urge to write *Thanks, but no thanks.*

Vulnerable. Open. Trust. The words chased each other through his brain like a dog chasing its tail. All were words that made him completely uncomfortable. He had no idea how to be any of those things. What he did know was how to protect himself. He'd spent decades learning how to read between the lines and see what people actually meant, what they actually wanted. A life skill he wasn't comfortable having but one he excelled at anyway.

He wished he could believe Dr. Constance. Someone liking him just because? That was nothing more than a pipe dream. No one ever had, and no one ever would.

An ache formed deep in his core. The thing he wanted more than anything in the world was the one that felt the most out of reach. He wanted to belong somewhere. Belong with someone. To love someone, give them his everything. He thought he could do that if he met the right person, but then he would remember all the shit in his past, all the things he'd done that had hurt people...anyone with half a brain would realize keeping their distance from him would be for the best.

What if someone was out there who could accept him, like him, maybe even love him? Someone who could hear every awful detail of his past and still see him as someone they wanted to be with.

He stared at the paper. Traced his finger over the rough penmanship. If someone like that was out there, he'd never find them if he continued to isolate.

He very nearly turned around and went back home at least five times as he drove to Zoe's address. Even as he parked outside the small house, he was still debating the wisdom of telling her he'd be there. He sat in his car for nearly ten minutes before finally getting out and walking to the front door.

His finger was barely off the doorbell button when the door opened, and Zoe stood there with a huge grin, "Hey! You're here!"

Her curly blue hair was up in a high ponytail. She wore black leggings, a baggy Wonder Woman sweatshirt, and Stitch slippers. God, she was adorable. His brain completely stopped working for at least five seconds.

She stepped back and said, "Come on in."

He stepped inside and shut the door. Glancing around the room, he noticed that absolutely nothing matched, but there was something strangely charming about it. The ceiling was a little low. His head wasn't bumping against it, but he still fought the urge to slouch.

"Okay, so if you haven't guessed, this is the living room. Down there is the bathroom." She inclined her head toward a hallway. "And straight ahead is the kitchen slash dining room.

"If you want, you can hang out here on the couch or go to the kitchen. I'll warn you: it's a little cramped back there. At best, it's a one-butt kitchen, and right now, there are three in there."

He almost laughed at her words. The corners of his mouth definitely twitched. "Sounds like a tight fit. I'll stay here for now."

After a moment, he sat on one end of the couch. Zoe plopped down on the opposite end. It caught him a little off-guard. She was acting as if she wasn't completely uncomfortable around him. In fact, he wasn't sure it was an act. She genuinely seemed to be comfortable. It was unsettling.

"I should warn you," she spoke in a low, conspiratorial tone, "Dante and Alex, my roommate, are going to be flirting all throughout lunch."

"We heard that!" A voice drifted out from the kitchen.

"I apologize for nothing!" Zoe called back.

He started to smile in amusement at the exchange, but then a man appeared in the kitchen entryway, and Liam's entire body froze. The man looked at Liam with confusion, and his face grew dark. Liam tried to mask his own emotions by letting his face go blank. Zoe followed Liam's gaze and turned to look at the other man.

She started to make an introduction, "Liam, this is Alex, my roommate. Alex, this is–"

"I know who he is," Alex's voice was ice cold as he cut her off. His eyes were fixed on her as he curtly asked, "Zoe? A word alone?"

She stood from the couch and looked at Liam, "I'll be right back. Remote's there if you want to watch the dog show." She followed Alex down the hall and into a room. The door slammed shut.

I should leave. I shouldn't be here. Any second, Zoe would come back, and she wouldn't look at him the same. She'd tell him to leave. Saturdays would suck because she wouldn't be able to be nice to him anymore. It would probably be best to tell Dante to find someone else to cover Saturdays. Liam wouldn't be able to handle sitting there week after week, having Zoe despise him. Deciding to leave, he stood but froze as the door opened and Zoe returned.

He held his breath as she reached the couch. She didn't look angry. Her eyes had a little sadness, but he could handle that. It was far preferable to the anticipated hate and disgust. She looked up, and her smile was surprisingly gentle, "Alex has promised to abide by a truce for today if you decide to stay. You don't have to, but I hope you will."

Nearly every part of him was screaming to run away. But a tiny part focused on the fact that, even after whatever Alex had told her, Zoe wanted him to stay.

He slowly sank back onto the couch, and she rejoined him. Rather than making him talk, she grabbed the remote and turned on the TV.

Dogs pranced around on the screen, and she made little comments about how cute they were and squealed in delight over some of the breeds. He relaxed a fraction but quickly tensed again as Alex reappeared.

The other man barely looked at Liam, but at least he didn't seem quite as hostile as he had fifteen minutes earlier. Liam wondered what Zoe had said to convince Alex a truce was a good idea.

Zoe wasn't wrong. Dante and Alex flirted shamelessly throughout the meal. Dahlia, Zoe's other roommate, didn't say much of anything. She seemed a little intimidated by Liam. He wished he could say that was unusual, but most people seemed to respond that way to him. His height and dark mood typically sent people scurrying away from him as quickly as possible.

Once the meal finished, he decided it was probably time to leave. No need to put Alex through any more discomfort than he already had. But when he got ready to tell Zoe he was leaving, he couldn't do it.

The table had been cleared, and Zoe dropped a box on it. "Who's in?"

Several minutes later, Ticket to Ride had been set up, and as the only person who didn't know how the game worked, Liam found himself reading over an instruction manual. Zoe cheerfully informed him, "It's pretty easy. We can do a practice round so you can get a feel for it."

He'd always had a knack for strategy and picked the game up quickly. The little plastic train cars filled the board. Cheerful colors intersected with other cheerful colors. One game ended, and they reset the board to go again.

Engrossed in the game, a few hours quickly passed. By the time the sun was setting, the group agreed it was time to take a break and eat some pie. And once they had the pie, Dante suggested putting on a movie.

I really should leave. But he didn't. He found himself on one end of the couch, with Zoe on the cushion next to him. The lights went off, and the movie played.

Alex and Dante were curled up on the loveseat, wrapped in a blanket, almost oblivious to the rest of the group. Dahlia sat in the recliner and spent most of the time staring at her phone.

Zoe made dumb jokes, and he loved it. It was so tempting to reach out and drape an arm along the back of the couch behind her, but he resisted. They barely knew each other, and something like that could cross a boundary. The longer they sat there, the more he longed to reach out and hold her. Another boundary he was wise enough not to cross, reminding himself *I'm nowhere near being healthy enough to be anything more than friends with anyone.*

When she leaned her head against his arm and asked, "This okay?" something inside of him came to a decision. He didn't know her, not really, but he wanted to. She was treating him with a small amount of trust that he knew he didn't deserve, and it kindled a tiny spark of hope inside him.

Maybe he wasn't as much of a monster as he'd let himself believe.

Five

Zoe

A lex's face was tight with anger as he pulled her back into his bedroom. Shutting the door with a little more force than was necessary, he turned on her, seething, "How could you invite *him*?"

Confusion flooded her, "I asked if I could. You said sure."

His eyes narrowed, "I didn't think I'd have to ask for details about who you were inviting."

Trying to diffuse some of his anger she quietly said, "Okay, breathe. What's your problem with Liam?"

Alex sank onto his bed, and Zoe sat on his desk chair facing him. His eyes were fixed on the floor as he said, "Y'know how I told you that things went really shitty when I came out?"

She nodded, "Yeah." In truth, she didn't know anything more than what he'd just said. She'd never pressed for details, and he'd never offered any.

His eyes lifted. Her heart ached as she saw just how much pain was there as he said, "He was there. He watched the whole thing happen and didn't do a fucking thing to stop it. I thought he was my friend."

Oh. Zoe felt awful and moved from the chair to sit beside him on the bed. Alex loved hugs, and she wrapped her arms around him, explaining, "I'm so sorry. I didn't know." She bit her lip, "He just seems so sad and lonely, and he didn't have anyone to spend today with. I know how much that sucks, and that's why I invited him."

Alex sighed, patting her arm, "You've got a good heart."

"Do you want me to ask him to leave?" she dreaded that, but she wouldn't make Alex miserable.

He was quiet for a long time before shaking his head, "No, I'm not going to ask you to do that. If he behaves, I'll behave. But I reserve the right to kick him out if it gets to be too much."

"You sure?"

He nodded, "Yeah."

That night, after Liam had gone home and everyone else had dispersed, Zoe sat in her room staring at the empty Google search bar. She chewed her thumbnail, trying to decide if it was a breach of privacy to look up what she was curious about. Had it not been for Alex's reaction to Liam, she wouldn't even be considering it.

It would be so easy to look him up. Googling people was a pretty common thing, wasn't it? Her fingers hovered over the laptop keyboard. A quick peek wouldn't hurt, right? Her phone buzzed, right as she began typing. She picked it up and was surprised to see a text from Liam.

Thanks for inviting me today. I hope Alex isn't too upset with you.

I'm glad you decided to come. Don't worry. Alex & I talked. We're ok.

She assumed that would be it and set her phone down. To her surprise, it vibrated with another text.

Did he tell you what happened?

Not really. I know something shitty happened when he came out, but he's never told me anything else about it, & I've never asked. Today he said you were there & didn't do anything to stop it.

You've really never asked?

No.

Why not?

It's his story. He can tell me as much or as little as he wants. Would you want someone to force you to talk about your past?

...

...

...

What I want has never been much of a consideration. Google has plenty of evidence of that.

Do you want me to Google you?

You haven't?

Not yet.

You don't have to lie. I won't be mad.

I'm not lying. That said, I was debating it when you texted.

There was no reply for several minutes. She had just about given up on hearing anything when he sent another text.

If I ask you not to look, will you still look?

If you ask me not to look, I won't look.

Nearly thirty minutes passed before his next text arrived. During that time, she saw the dots on the bottom of the screen appear and disappear multiple times.

Go ahead. If you don't want to continue working with me, I'll understand and let Dante know to find someone else.

Sadness flooded her. He was automatically assuming the worst, which made her wonder what the hell he'd been through.

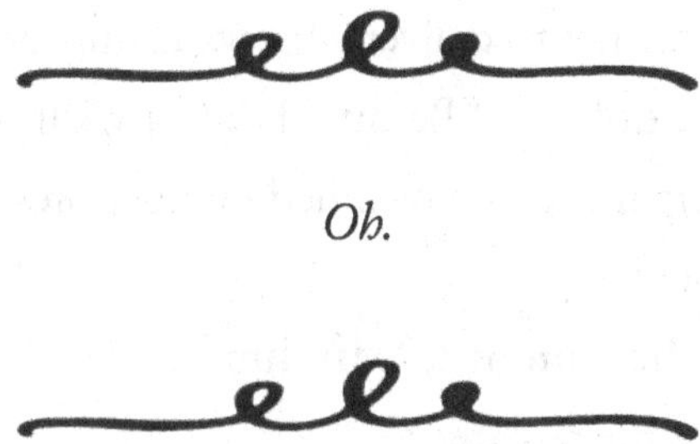

Oh.

Liam's car was already in the lot when she arrived at the studio on Saturday morning. Getting out of her car, she noticed he was still sitting in his. Hesitating only a moment, she walked over and lightly knocked on the window.

Given how he jumped at the sound and whipped his head toward the window, she assumed he must not have seen her approach. A few seconds passed before he opened the door a few inches. Though the car was off, she noticed one hand was holding on tightly to the steering wheel, and his seat belt was still buckled. Smiling gently, she asked, "You coming in?"

His eyes met hers and held her gaze. He seemed to be searching for something, and unable to find whatever it was, he finally asked, "You want me to?"

She opened the door a little wider and joked, "It'll be annoying if I have to read both papers by myself."

His eyes softened slightly, and there was the tiniest uplift of the corners of his mouth. Letting go of the steering wheel and undoing the seatbelt, he pushed the door open and got out, "Well, we wouldn't want that."

She texted Dante that they were there and walked beside Liam to the door. Two minutes later, they were in the booth getting set up.

"You didn't ask Dante to replace me." Liam broke the silence after a few minutes.

Zoe's pen paused as she looked up from her notes, "I did not."

"Why not?"

He wasn't looking at her, but she couldn't help looking at him. His body was tense as if waiting for her to deliver a blow. It hurt her heart that he was so convinced she would be unkind. "Because I didn't want to," she replied simply.

When he said nothing more, she resumed taking notes. A few minutes later, he asked, "Did you Google?"

Focused on an obit, she hummed, "Mm-hm."

"And you don't want me replaced?"

She set down her pen and saw him staring at her. Gently, she replied, "I think this is a conversation better had when we don't have to be on the air in fourteen minutes. But for now, try to relax because I don't want you replaced. It's not something I'll be asking Dante to do. Okay?"

He looked perplexed but replied, "Okay."

Six

Liam

"I don't know what I was thinking." He sat, slumped forward, hands clasped together. He could feel Dr. Constance's eyes fixed on him. She didn't say anything, which was a little frustrating. He knew she was waiting for him to continue. To dig deeper into what he'd just said.

God, he hated therapy.

He sighed, "I told her to Google me. Who the hell does that?"

"This isn't about what other people would do; it's about you. Think back to when you told her that. What was your goal in that moment?"

His mind went back to Thursday night. Why had he texted her in the first place? Because it was good manners, and he hadn't thanked her before he'd left her house. Why had he continued texting with her that evening? He wasn't sure.

That was a lie.

He knew exactly why.

"Liam?" Dr. Constance prompted.

He opened his mouth, and nothing came out. After a few deep breaths, he tried again, "I thought Alex had told her more than he had. I...I assumed she'd already looked me up and seen it all. When I..." he swallowed hard, "When I found out she hadn't..." His words trailed off into nothingness. He shook his head and found his voice again, "She probably lied to me."

"Do you really believe that?" Dr. Constance's voice held no judgment, just curiosity.

He glanced up and met her eyes, "I..." He ran his fingers through his hair, "I wanna believe she told me the truth."

Dr. Constance smiled warmly, "That's good."

"Just to be clear, I'm not saying I actually believe she told me the truth."

"But you're willing to consider the possibility that she did?"

He sagged a little more, "I...I think so."

"Liam, that is a huge step. I'm proud of you."

Confusion filled him, "What?"

"You're willing to consider the possibility that someone was honest with you. That's a good step towards learning to trust."

He wasn't sure he agreed but avoided saying that. If he did, they'd end up in a discussion he did not want to have. *Why did I do it?* He mulled the question over until the words felt like they had lost all meaning. "I expected her to Google me. When I found out she hadn't, it felt like...like maybe I still had some control over the situation. She let me make the call as to whether she would look me up or not. It was like she was waiting for permission."

"It sounds like consent is important to her."

He hadn't considered that before. In his mind, consent was typically tied to the word *sex*, but he had to acknowledge that it wasn't a sex-specific action. For most of his life, people hadn't asked for his consent about anything. They just made decisions for him, and he went along with them because that was what was expected. That had been what was easier. He'd told himself he was okay with it because he knew if he fought back, he'd ultimately end up on the losing side of the argument.

But he'd never been okay with it.

"Should I talk to her about what she found?" He searched Dr. Constance's face, trying to get a read on what she was thinking. It was nearly impossible. She was excellent at keeping an impassive face when necessary.

"Do you want to?"

Damn it. All he wanted was a simple yes or no. But he wasn't paying Dr. Constance to tell him what he should do. He was paying her to help him learn how to decide for himself what he should do.

He shrugged, "I'm not sure. Part of me does. I want to know what she knows, and if she has questions, I'd rather she ask them to me than someone else. But part of me wants to go as far away as I possibly can so I never have to wonder what she thinks of me when we're together."

She nodded, face still impassive, "These are normal things to feel, Liam. The kind of conversation you're suggesting is one that will require a lot of vulnerability and openness. That can be a very overwhelming or even frightening thing to face, and running away may seem like the easy answer. That's a very short-term answer, though. Running away tends to mean you'll face the same challenge all over again at some point in the future. So, you have to decide if you want to face this now or if you're going to spend your life running and hiding."

Her words were spoken kindly, but they were incredibly blunt. That bluntness was part of why he'd stuck with her, unlike the other therapists he'd tried over the last year. Too many of them tried to be nice without actually calling him on his bullshit. "What if she hates me?"

"What if she doesn't?"

That seemed a little too much to hope. Then again, she'd been just as nice after Googling him as before she knew the awful truth. She'd even gone so far as to reassure him that she didn't want him replaced. After what felt like an eternity, he decided, "I should talk to her."

He really should talk to her. That's what he told himself on Saturday when he saw her again. Yet, he hesitated. By the end of the broadcast, he was working up the courage when she threw on her hoodie and grabbed her purse, telling him, "I wish I could stay, but if I don't leave now, I'm gonna be late for work. I'll see you next week, okay?"

She was gone, and he was left feeling off-kilter. All morning, she'd still been nice. If it was an act, she was a phenomenal actress.

I'll talk to her next week.

Except, the next week came and went, and she ran out of the booth at the end of the broadcast again, claiming she had to get to work. "My boss will be extra pissed off if I'm late, and I just don't have the energy to deal with that today."

When it happened again the following week, he wondered if she was trying to get away from him. Trying to avoid him.

Paranoid. I'm being paranoid.

When he mentioned it to Dr. Constance, she encouraged him to look at all the facts. Zoe was still nice to him. It was the holiday season, and depending on her job, she might have to work when she normally wouldn't. He was making assumptions based on bad experiences from his past. Dr. Constance told him, "Your past will always be a part of you, Liam, but that doesn't mean that it should get to control your future."

Christmas Eve was on a Saturday, and he arrived at the studio before Zoe. He was determined to talk to her before she had a chance to run out again. It needed to happen before the worry and assumptions drove him completely crazy.

Zoe was late.

Really late.

In fact, he had to start the broadcast without her, and Dante ended up calling to make sure she was okay. Fifteen minutes into the program, she ran in the door.

Liam kept going, trying to give her a chance to get settled before jumping in, but to his surprise, she indicated she was ready after barely being there two minutes. She began to read, and he took the opportunity to look at her.

The dark circles were the worst he'd seen them. Her hair was lank, the curls limp and greasy. He wondered if she'd slept or showered in the last few days. She looked completely exhausted, and even her voice couldn't completely mask how drained she was. He had to give her credit; she was putting everything she had left into what she was doing, but it was impossible to ignore that something was very wrong.

When they reached the halfway point and took a break, she ripped off the headset and dropped her head into her hands, "I'm so, so sorry. I've never been late like this before. You have every right to be pissed off."

She sounded like she was on the verge of tears, and he felt a weird twinge hearing the misery in her voice. "Don't worry about it. Are you okay?"

Voice low, she replied, "No, not really."

They didn't have enough time to have a full conversation and he told her, "I'll take care of the obits for both of us, I already looked at yours and took notes. Catch your breath."

She turned her head a little and peeked at him from the side of her hand, "You don't have to do that, but I don't have the energy to fight about it. Thank you."

"Are you going to have to go running out of here when we finish today?"

Dante was finishing the weather, and she put the headset back on. Her face went dark, and her voice was curt, "No."

It wasn't the best way to end break, but he managed to get through the obits without trouble. Then he and Zoe were back to volleying stories back and forth. Normally, it was pleasant. Over the weeks they'd worked together, he'd grown to enjoy it, but she was in such a dour mood it ended up feeling like work.

When they finished, she slouched in her chair, staring at the monitor but not seeming to see it. By the time he finished cleaning, she hadn't moved. He focused on her, "Are you going to be able to get yourself home okay?"

"I..." a tear trickled down her cheek, quickly followed by another. She wiped her face with her sleeve. Reaching behind the monitor, she retrieved the box of tissues. Tears continued to fall, and he felt helpless. "I'm...sorry..." she managed to get out.

"It's okay," he reassured her.

She blew her nose and coughed before saying, "You...you should go. Don't...need...to see my...meltdown."

"Zoe, what happened?" He was surprised that he managed to sound as gentle as he did. Gentle was not something he had ever been very successful at before. Zoe's distress was bringing out a side of him he didn't know existed. He wanted to protect her, wanted to fix whatever it was that was wrong, wanted to pull her close and let her sob every single tear into his chest. He knew better than to do that and settled for trying to sit quietly and patiently. Two more things he'd never been particularly good at.

She wiped her eyes again, "Just a shitty week. A really, really...shitty week."

Grabbing the canister of wipes, she began cleaning, sniffling the entire time. It was killing him watching her be so completely miserable. She finished, tossed the wipe in the trash, and grabbed her purse. Standing, she yanked her hoodie over her head before walking out the door saying, "I'll be better next week, I promise."

It took him a moment to register she was actually leaving. In an instant, he snatched his coat, stood from his chair, and followed her out to the parking lot. She walked fast. He jogged to catch up with her before she got into her car. "Zoe, wait," he called out.

She startled and looked at him, seeming to have only just realized that he was there. "What?"

"I don't think you should be driving."

She wiped hard at her face with the heels of her palms, leaving her cheeks momentarily red. "I'm fine, Liam."

He folded his arms and looked sternly at her, "You're clearly not. You need someone else to drive you."

Her laugh was bitter, "And who do you suggest? My roommates, who are out of town? My parents, who dumped me when I was five? Or maybe my asshole of a boss...make that ex-boss."

There was so much pain in her words, and he hated it. "I'll drive you." he offered before he could let himself remember the pile of reasons why it was a bad suggestion.

She hesitated. He could see the inner-debate raging inside her. After almost a minute, she slowly nodded, "Fine."

Seven

Zoe

Work had been hell. It was normal for work to be awful, but Fred had managed to be an even bigger asshole than usual. The majority of December was spent dealing with him yelling at her, demeaning her, constantly finding fault with every damn thing she did. She tried so hard to hold it together. To do better. To give him no reason to complain.

But it wasn't enough.

The Thursday before Christmas, she reached her breaking point. Fred had forced her to work the front counter, and she was in the middle of dealing with a customer when Fred was suddenly beside her, completely livid. He berated her right in front of the customer, who was watching with a look on their face that matched the panic she felt inside. Her brain could not process what Fred was bellowing about. It was all a jumble of words. Frantically, she searched her mind, trying to figure out what she had said or done that could possibly have merited such treatment.

He continued to rage, and an eerie calmness settled over her. Rather than try to defend herself or apologize for something she hadn't done, all she could think was *I don't deserve this. I don't have to take this. I won't take this.*

Without a word, she stepped away from the counter, grabbed her purse and hoodie from where she'd tucked them, and walked to the front of the store. She started to open the door when she heard Fred's roar, "Where the fuck do you think you're going?" As she pushed the door open wider, she heard him add, "If you leave, don't bother coming back!"

Without turning around, she assured him, "Don't worry, I won't." Stepping out into the cold December afternoon, she let the door swing closed behind her and hurried to her car.

Relief surged through her as soon as she was out of the parking lot and headed home. She was free. Finally, she was well and truly free of that bastard. She never ever had to go back. Never ever had to see Fred Pluto again if she didn't want to, and she couldn't imagine ever wanting to.

By the following morning, her relief was replaced with overwhelming guilt. She'd quit her job without notice. She'd left Fred in the lurch. That wasn't like her. It wasn't the first time he'd treated her so abominably, which left her wondering why this time had pushed her to her limit.

Her phone began to blow up five minutes past when her shift would've started. As fast as possible, she blocked every single number she knew Fred might try calling her from. She should've done it when she'd left the day before, but it hadn't even occurred to her. Glaring at her phone, she decided that no matter how badly she needed the paycheck (and make no mistake about it, she needed it desperately), there was no way in hell she was ever going back. She would never spend one more second in that man's presence.

As the day progressed, her guilt began to mix with anxiety. She doubted that Fred would ever send her final paycheck, and it was a fight she didn't have the energy for. Without that check, she wouldn't be able to cover her bills. Alex and Dahlia might float her for a bit, but they didn't have much money either. She might be lucky and find a new job immediately, but she knew better than to lie to herself about her prospects.

That night, sleep evaded her until nearly four a.m., and what she did manage to get wasn't restful. She was plagued with nightmares that tormented her until she was pulled from them by the ringing of her phone. Her eyes opened to see the sun was up. Looking at her phone, she blanched. Hopping out of bed, she answered, "I overslept. I'm so, so sorry, Dante. I'll be there in a few minutes!"

"Are you okay?" Dante asked calmly.

Cradling the phone with her shoulder, she grabbed a pair of leggings from the floor and sniffed them. Deciding they were at least clean adjacent, she pulled them on, saying, "Yeah, yeah. Just a bad night. I'll be there as soon as I can." Before he could say anything else, she hung up.

Somehow, she managed to make it through the morning. At break, Liam asked if she would have to leave for work as soon as they were done. The question only reminded her of what a mess she was in, and she felt like she was about to fall apart. She held it together through the second hour, but Dante mentioned it was Christmas Eve as he was signing off and that was the final straw. Thanks to her stress, she'd completely forgotten what day it was.

The pieces began to crash around her like an upended jigsaw. She had no job. Her bank account was dangerously close to empty. Her roommates were out of town. She was going to be completely alone for Christmas. Something that had never bothered her before was suddenly too much.

Liam sat quietly the whole time she melted down. She wasn't sure why he wouldn't leave, and when she finally got herself mostly pulled together, she ran out of the studio with one goal in mind. Get home and hide under the covers until December twenty-sixth.

If Liam hadn't called out to her, she wouldn't have realized he had followed her. He informed her she shouldn't drive, and she had a minor explosion. To her shock, he didn't flinch at her harsh words. She was fully prepared for him to walk away and leave her alone.

But he didn't.

Instead, he offered to drive her, and she had no fight left. Wearily, she agreed and followed him to his car. He assured her that he'd bring her back to retrieve hers once he was convinced she could drive without being a danger to herself and others.

The drive to her house was quiet. She was relieved he didn't press her to talk. The closer they got to her address, the more she felt the cold fingers of dread clutch at her as she knew what was coming. He would let her out of the car, drive off, and she would be alone.

She didn't want to be alone.

He parked in her driveway, and she knew she should get out of the car. She should tell him to have a good holiday and thank him for getting her home safely. She should not, absolutely should not, ask him if he wanted to stay and hang out. It would be an incredibly dumb thing to ask.

"Zoe?"

His voice broke into her racing thoughts. She turned to look at him. The worry she'd seen in his eyes at the studio was still there. Over the last few Saturdays, she'd noticed that he had begun to soften around her. Grown friendlier. Didn't seem quite as sad and withdrawn. She still hadn't seen him smile, but there had been a few moments where she'd seen the corners of his mouth lift slightly, and she'd known he was close. Looking at him, she desperately wanted him to stay. Instead, she forced that desire down deep, reminding herself she needed to let him leave.

Opening the car door, she unbuckled, telling him, "Thanks for getting me home. If you celebrate Christmas, I hope you have a good one."

"You're welcome," he replied in a voice so tender she would've melted if she hadn't felt so broken.

Forcing herself out of the car, she closed the door between them and headed for the house. Barely five feet from the car, she stopped. Turning back, she saw

Liam still sitting there, watching her. Her feet began to move back toward him, her mind screaming, *What the hell are you doing, Zoe? Just let him go. Don't do this. He'll say no, and it'll hurt.* And yet, she stopped in front of the window he'd lowered when he saw her coming back. Biting her lip, she said, "Um…listen…I don't want you to feel like you have to or anything. Trust me, it's totally fine if you say no. I promise." She was scrambling, trying to find the courage to ask for what she wanted.

"What am I saying no to?"

She squeezed her eyes shut for a moment. Opening them again, she asked, "You want to come in? I really don't want to be alone right now."

Without a word, he raised the window. Her stomach sank. He was going to leave. She'd known that's what would happen. *It's for the best. Why would he want to be here with you?*

To her surprise, the car didn't back out of her driveway. Instead, the ignition turned off, and Liam opened the door. Regret filled her, and she panicked, "Wait, no. You probably have plans. I'm sorry, you don't have to stay. I—"

He held up a hand, stopping her mid-babble, "Zoe, it's fine. I have no plans."

"Are you sure? I know it's Christmas Eve. You should go hang out with your family."

There was that twitch at the corner of his mouth as he asked, "Are you always this stubborn?"

It wasn't a funny question, but for some reason, it was the funniest thing she'd heard in days. Starting to laugh, she fished her keys out of her pocket and said, "Come on."

Liam followed her quietly. Once inside the house, she belatedly began to wonder if she should feel anxious about being alone with him. Wasn't this the stuff *Dateline* episodes were made of? Well, if he murdered her, that would be the icing on the cake of a truly disastrous week. Month. Year. Life.

Her stomach growled loudly. She hadn't eaten breakfast and realized she'd barely eaten anything since Thursday. Walking to the kitchen, she checked the fridge. It wasn't exactly bare, but besides a few questionable containers of leftovers and several bottles of condiments, there wasn't anything to eat. Shutting the fridge, she turned to the pantry.

They never kept much in there and didn't have the finances to keep it stocked. There were some cans of green beans and a box of granola bars she was fairly certain had expired a year earlier. Leaning her head against the door, she considered the remaining options. Ramen or macaroni. Neither sounded good. *Merry fucking Christmas to me.*

"Zoe?"

She jumped at the sound of her name. Spinning around, she saw Liam leaning against the counter a few feet away, watching her. Willing herself to sound and look better than she felt, she asked, "Ramen or mac? Either of those sound good?"

He shook his head, "What do you want to eat? I can tell you're not thrilled with your options."

Pulling out two packages of ramen, "It's fine. Not the first time I've settled for something I don't want. Won't be the last. Sorry, but I don't have anything on hand to make it very fancy. It'll just be noodles."

Getting a pot out of the cupboard, she moved to the sink, intending to fill it with water. Before she could lift the faucet handle, Liam put his hand over it, stopping her. Looking up, she asked, "What?"

"What do you actually want to eat?"

Sighing, she set the pot on the counter. Resting her hands on the edge of the sink, she stared at the drain, "Out of my options, this is the more preferable. If you want mac, I'll make that instead." And then the tears started again. Maybe it would be funny later, but at the moment, she felt like she'd truly hit rock bottom. She was standing in her kitchen, sobbing over crappy food choices in front of a man she couldn't get a good read on.

And because she was making terrible choices, she moved closer to Liam and rested her head against his chest. Her tears quickly soaked the material of his black sweater. She clutched at the material, fisting it in her hands. Liam started to rub her back gently. He said nothing, just stood there calmly and quietly, letting her openly weep against him. The material of his shirt was soft against her skin, and some part of her brain realized that he smelled really, *really* good. She didn't even know what scent it was, but mixed with the salt of her tears, she found it weirdly comforting. Eventually, the tears slowed, and horror filled her as she realized what she was doing. Quickly, she released her hold on him and stepped away, "I'm so sorry. That was...that was..."

"Zoe, it's okay," his voice was just soft. There was no condemnation or judgment in it.

She frantically shook her head, "No, it's not. I probably ruined your shirt, and...and..." Oh god, more tears felt like they were on the way.

He assured her, "Pretty sure it takes more than tears to destroy a shirt." Saying, "C'mon, let's get you outta here," his hand went lightly between her shoulder blades, guiding her out of the kitchen to the couch.

She collapsed onto one corner, pulled the blanket off the back, and wrapped it around herself. He sat on the other end, eyes fixed on her. Her fingers found a loose string on the edge of the blanket, and she began worrying it.

"When are your roommates going to be back?" he asked after several seconds.

Blinking confusedly, she looked up at him, "Um...next week."

"Were you going to spend Christmas alone?"

It was too hard to look at him, and her eyes dropped back to the string, "It's not the first time. Pretty much the norm."

There was silence for over a minute before he said, "Okay. Will you be alright if I leave? It'll be less than an hour, and then I'll be back."

Eight

Liam

Christmas Eve was not a good time to be stuck in a grocery store line, but that's exactly where he found himself. Normally, he would've been incredibly irritated, but his mind was back with Zoe.

When he parked in her driveway, he'd watched her get out, and it had taken all his willpower not to ask her to let him stay. They'd gotten friendlier, but he doubted they knew each other well enough for her to feel comfortable being alone with him. He'd been relieved when she turned back and asked him not to leave.

He hadn't been prepared for her nearly bare fridge and pantry. Nor the way she had reached for him as she began sobbing again. Letting go of her had been the last thing he wanted to do, but he had released her as soon as she stepped back, dropping her hold on his sweater. He had no idea what had happened, but based on contextual clues, he suspected she had lost her job. Not something anyone should have to face at Christmas.

She was alone. Incredibly alone. No family. Her friends were out of town. As she tried to shrug off being alone for Christmas, he decided he couldn't let that happen. He'd never cared much about the holidays. For most of his life, they'd been nothing more than a stressful, scheduled event that he found exhausting. Still, he knew other people cared, and maybe Zoe was one of those people. Whether or not she was, she shouldn't have to face it alone, and she needed a break from trying to take care of herself.

He could do that much. He could make sure she was fed and didn't have to spend the holiday by herself.

And on Wednesday, he'd sit down with Dr. Constance and try to figure out why he felt the need to take care of Zoe.

Zoe let him in when he returned and followed him to the kitchen. He placed the bags on the counter and heard her ask, "Liam, what's going on?"

Opening the fridge he started putting away produce and meat, saying, "You needed more food options." Moving to the pantry, he asked, "Does any of this look good, or shall I go back out and continue foraging?"

"Wait, no. Liam, this is too much," she said, shutting the pantry door.

He stared at her, "Zoe, you're welcome to be as stubborn as you want, but that's not going to change the fact that I'm going to make sure you don't starve between now and Monday." Opening the pantry again, "Now, would you please decide what you want to eat."

She leaned against the fridge, quietly watching while he finished putting the groceries away. His attention shifted back to her, "Made a decision?"

Her eyes searched his face, "Why are you doing this?"

Resting against the counter, he held her gaze. Her eyes were wide and puzzled. Chewing on the inside of his cheek, he debated what to say. After a few seconds, he told her, "I'm not sure. It just seems like you need a break from whatever shit life has dumped on you, and while I'm not good for much, there are some things

I can do." He ran his hand through his hair, "I don't want you to be alone, but if you want me to go, I'll leave."

She crossed her arms, studying him. Her voice was tight as she asked, "Is there something you're trying to get from me? Is this some kind of tit-for-tat situation? Cause, I'll be honest, you're going to be disappointed. I have no job. My bank account is closer to red than I want to admit." Swallowing something invisible, she added, "If it's sex you're looking for, you might as well leave right now."

Of all the things he expected she might say, none of that had been on the list. She had managed to render him speechless. The growing alarm in her eyes managed to get him talking, reassuring her, "No, I promise I'm not expecting anything from you."

The alarm began to dissipate, but the puzzlement was still there, "Then why...?"

Open and vulnerable. Looking at her, the two words came to mind, and he wondered if he could do it. Could he open up to her? Even a little? He wanted her to trust him, and she certainly wouldn't do that if he didn't give her an honest answer. Making a decision, he told her, "I think this would be easier if I had something to do while I talk. You figure out what you want to eat?"

He watched as she browsed the options he'd brought back. After a couple of minutes, she pulled a jar of pasta sauce from the pantry and a package of ravioli from the fridge and set them on the counter. He filled the pot with water and set it on the stove to boil. "You have any spices?"

She opened a cupboard next to the stove. He pulled a few and set them on the counter. As he did, he began talking, "You've seen some of my past. I won't make excuses for what I did. I know...I know that I did harm. I hurt people."

He made himself turn and meet her eyes. *I have to keep talking.* Shame filled him as he admitted, "The few good things I did? It was all performative. Publicity stunts." Looking back at the water, he asked, "Do you have a colander?"

A handful of seconds later, it was placed by the sink. She leaned against the counter, much closer than she'd been, and her attention was fixed on him. He couldn't bring himself to meet her eyes, "I'm not a good person. I did things that I questioned, some things that I knew for sure were wrong, but the people I trusted...they told me I was doing the right thing. And it was easier to do what I was told."

Watching the water, the words felt sticky, like they were trying to lodge in his throat. "I can't...undo what...what I did. There are things...I can never atone for."

Little bubbles had begun forming on the bottom of the pot. His eyes were fixed on them for a long time. He could feel Zoe still watching him. She didn't say anything but didn't move away from him either. He released a shaky exhale, "I'm trying to do better. To actually do good when I can without it being something just for show." He made himself lift his eyes to meet hers, "I have no ulterior motive. I'm not expecting anything from you. I will never do to anyone else what was done to me."

Her eyes were misty. That was not the reaction he had anticipated. He had just admitted to being a terrible person, and it almost looked like she felt compassion for him. It made no sense. He added it to the growing list of topics for therapy.

Looking back at the water, he saw a boil had started. Dumping in the ravioli, he stirred the pasta, wondering if it would be too much food. He wasn't sure how much Zoe would eat, but he also suspected she hadn't eaten much lately. Better to make too much food than too little.

"I quit my job this week." He shifted his attention from the stove back to her. She was staring down at her hands, picking at her thumb cuticle. Sighing heavily, she added, "I'm not sure I should've."

"Do you have a job lined up?"

She shook her head, "Nope. I just...I just couldn't take one more second there. My boss freaked out on me, and I walked out."

Moving the pot off the stove, he drained the ravioli before returning it to the pot and pouring in the sauce. "Bowls?" he asked.

Zoe put two by the stove, along with forks. Turning it off, he portioned out the food, making sure to put a little more in the bowl he pushed toward her. Setting the pot on a trivet, he told her, "There's more if you're still hungry after finishing that."

She took the bowl and walked toward the table, "Thank you."

"You're welcome," he replied as he joined her.

Why did it make him feel good to see her eat? Why had he been able to tell her as much as he had? Why did he feel better just being around her? He would have enough to talk about at therapy for at least the next month, possibly two. Dr. Constance would probably be thrilled.

She finished her bowl and got up to refill with what was left in the pot. "You sure you don't want any more?"

He nodded, "Positive. Go ahead and finish it."

Zoe placed the pile of DVDs on the coffee table and turned her attention to Liam, "Which one do you want to start with?"

Sifting through the choices, he paused on one asking, "*Die Hard*?"

"It's a Christmas movie."

He looked up at her, raising an eyebrow, "Is it, though?"

She nodded emphatically, "Absolutely. It takes place at Christmas. It's filled with Christmassy things. It's a Christmas movie."

He shook his head, "Take Christmas out of the story, and nothing actually changes."

Picking up the case, she pulled out the disc and walked to the tv, "Well, you clearly need to experience it again." She returned to the couch and used the remote to start the movie. Curled up, wrapped in her blanket, she focused on the movie.

It was obvious she'd seen it multiple times. He was amused as she started quoting the lines as the actors spoke them. Normally, he'd find that annoying, but something about her made it charming.

Part of the way through, he heard her say, "Fred never really did Christmas."

"Fred?"

Bruce Willis was crawling through a vent as she replied, "Fred Pluto, the biggest asshole in the galaxy. Growing up, he was my guardian and my boss." The laugh that escaped her was harsh, "I'm twenty-eight, and I've spent twenty-three of those years with him being part of my life."

He hadn't been too far off regarding her age. At thirty-four, he was six years older.

Unsure if she was finished talking, he remained quiet, waiting to see if she'd say anything more. Several minutes passed, but eventually, she spoke again, "I'm not sure I should've quit. It was impulsive. He was being so awful, but he's always been awful. And he didn't pay me well, but it was a job I couldn't afford to leave."

"Did you enjoy it?"

She was picking at her thumb cuticle again. He had to force himself not to reach over and stop her. She shrugged, "Some of it. I liked fixing things. I'm pretty good at it."

"What was your job?" Why was he asking so many questions?

Her eyes shifted from the tv to him, "Fred has a pawn shop. I was his assistant. My job was to do whatever he told me to do. A good day meant he was in a foul mood, but I was allowed to hide away at my workbench and repair things. Usually, though, he forced me to work the counter. I hated it."

He held her gaze, "Then why are you questioning your decision to quit?"

Her attention returned to Bruce Willis, and nearly ten minutes passed before she answered, "He raised me. Took care of me. Gave me a job. I owe him." She shook her head and added, "I paid him back by walking out."

A young woman's face filled his mind, and he shuddered at the memory of her sitting in his office, clearly traumatized, saying similar things about the bastard who had just done despicable things to her. Hearing those words come out of Zoe's mouth made him feel sick.

She sighed, "Maybe I should see if he'll take me back. He probably would. He didn't have to pay me what he'd pay someone else."

"No," the word came out sharper than he'd intended.

Her head swiveled, "What?"

He tried to gentle his tone, "You shouldn't go back to him."

"I need a job," she stated.

"There are other jobs."

"What if I can't get hired?"

"What if you can?" Inwardly, he groaned. Dr. Constance was going to have a field day with this.

Zoe turned back to the movie. The rest of it passed without either of them speaking. When it finished, she switched out the disc. *Gremlins* filled the screen, and she returned to the couch. To his surprise, she didn't resume her seat on the opposite corner. Instead, she picked up the blanket and sat beside him. Looking up, she asked, "Is this okay?"

He nodded, remembering Dr. Constance's suggestion that consent was important to Zoe. He was perfectly fine with her sitting there, and if she decided to use him as a pillow, he certainly wouldn't complain.

He came to, and the room was mostly dark. The only light was from the tv screen, but *The Muppet Christmas Carol* had long since finished and returned to the menu screen. After a moment, he grew alert enough to realize he wasn't alone.

He was still sitting on Zoe's couch, and she was still right beside him. Except, her head rested against his chest, and his arm was draped around her shoulders. She was fast asleep. He stared down at her as the pieces slowly fell into place.

Earlier in the evening, Zoe had started leaning against him. At some point, his arm had grown stiff, and he'd asked if it was okay if he moved it. She'd said yes, and when he did, she moved even closer and rested her head against his chest, asking, "Okay?"

Even though he'd secretly wanted her to do that very thing, he was still caught off-guard when it actually happened. He'd assured her it was fine, and when his arm slipped around her shoulders, he'd checked to make sure she was okay with it. She'd nodded and yawned. The movie wasn't even half over before they had both drifted off.

This wasn't something he had planned on. Not that he'd planned on anything that had happened since Saturday morning. Holding her felt completely natural, which he found confusing. Even more confusing was how he dreaded letting go when she would eventually wake up. He would, though, if she asked him to because he would never force her to accept touch she didn't want. For the moment, he was a little greedy and glad she was asleep. It gave him a chance to memorize how this felt. He'd store it in his memory, and maybe it would help him cope when his thoughts got a little too dark.

She was lonely and needed a friend. That's all this was. Dr. Constance had been very clear on the point that she wouldn't recommend that he seek anything more than friendship at the present. He knew the doctor was right, but he also knew that Zoe wasn't like anyone else he'd ever met. Being around her gave him a sense of peace he'd never experienced. He could talk to her about things he struggled to discuss with anyone else, including Dr. Constance. Zoe listened to him without making him feel like she was constantly judging every single word that came out of his mouth.

They'd known each other for nearly two months. They didn't know each other well, but she already knew him better than pretty much anyone else in his life. That probably wasn't saying much, considering his lack of friends and family.

A whimper distracted him, and he felt her tense against him. The whimper grew louder, and he attempted to be comforting. "Shhh...it's okay...you're safe..." he murmured that and other similar things. He wasn't prepared for the whimpers to turn into full-blown screams.

Before he could react, she was on her feet beside the couch. She didn't move away; just stood there whimpering and screaming. Eyes wide open, but not looking at anything.

Cautiously, he stood and looked down at her, "Zoe?"

She was staring at his chest, but it was like she didn't see him at all. He wasn't even sure she was awake. Another scream tore from her lips, and the light from the tv reflected off the sheen of sweat that now covered her.

Words began to fly from her mouth, but they were gibberish. He couldn't make sense of any of it. Worried about what was happening, he slipped his phone out of his pocket and did a quick Google search.

Night terrors.

He'd heard the term before but had no idea what it actually entailed. Based on what he was witnessing and what Google suggested, night terrors were the most likely answer.

The screams resumed, and as terrifying as they were, he forced himself not to back away. The internet said to remain calm and be comforting. Stepping a little closer, he tried his best to soothe her. Gently, he rubbed her upper back. She'd seemed to like that when she'd been crying in the kitchen. He resumed his patter, "It's okay...you're okay...I'm here...you're not alone...you're safe..." Over and over, he repeated variations of that, and she kept screaming.

After what felt like an eternity, she jolted awake. Her eyes widened, clearing and focusing on him. He watched her face twist with confusion, and he immediately stepped back and dropped his hand.

"Liam?" she asked, perplexed. Horror quickly took over, and she began to shake her head, "Oh god. Oh god, please tell me I didn't...I'm so sorry...Did I..." she swallowed hard, "I didn't hurt you, did I?"

"No," he replied as she sank onto the couch. Joining her, he saw the panic that she was fighting. Trying to calm her, he said, "It's okay."

She groaned, "What did I do?"

"Screamed and gibbered, that's pretty much it," he replied.

Her head fell into her hands, "Fucking hell." Looking at him, she said, "I'm so sorry. You shouldn't have had to see that. You...you should probably go home."

Her words were the tiniest bit hesitant, as though she was saying what she thought he'd want to hear rather than what she actually wanted to say. Quietly, he asked, "Do you want me to leave?"

A mix of emotions crossed her face before he heard, "Honestly?"

He nodded.

"No. No, I don't want you to leave."

Nine

Liam

"I slept with Zoe. Twice."

Dr. Constance's mask slipped just a little at his words and he saw her eyes widen. It only lasted for a second and then she was back to her normal, impassive self. "You had sex with her?"

He very nearly smiled. Yes, he had chosen those particular words just to see if he could get a reaction. Yes, it had been an immature choice, but he didn't care. "No, nothing like that. Just sleep."

She nodded, "Tell me what happened."

He didn't respond immediately. His thoughts drifted back to a few nights before. He could still feel how Zoe had felt nestled against his side, wrapped in his arms, her head on his chest. She was so soft, and he'd loved every second he'd spent holding her. Christmas night she had slept better. There had been no repeat of the night terrors. He had been the one who hadn't been able to sleep. The whole situation had been incredibly intimate. The level of trust she'd given him had been staggering.

Finally, he began relaying the events of the weekend, starting with Saturday morning. He told Dr. Constance everything. Told her about buying groceries and about Zoe's night terrors. When he got to Christmas morning, he said, "We needed to get her car, and since my apartment is halfway between her house and the studio, I asked if it would be okay to stop there so I could change."

The doctor studied him, "You invited her to your apartment?"

He nodded, "Just so I could get changed. Plus, I had some ingredients I wanted to pick up from my kitchen. I left it up to her. Told her that if she wasn't comfortable with it, I could drop her at her car first, and then I'd return to her house after going to my apartment. She said she didn't mind stopping there, so we did."

"How did it feel having someone else there?"

He knew what she was asking. Since he'd moved in nearly two years earlier, he hadn't let anyone else inside. Hadn't even considered the possibility of inviting anyone there. Not that there had been anyone to invite, but even so, the fact remained that it was his space. Private. Personal. No one was allowed to be there. And yet, he'd invited Zoe with barely a second thought.

"Zoe's not just someone else," he admitted quietly, eyes dropping to the floor.

Nearly a minute passed before Dr. Constance spoke. She must have been waiting, giving him the opportunity to add more. When he didn't, she asked, "Liam, what is she to you?"

He closed his eyes, picturing his apartment. Remembering how, after he finished changing, he'd re-entered the living room and found Zoe standing at his piano. She was studying the open book he'd left sitting on the instrument. The fingers of her right hand were on a few of the keys, not pressing them down, just lightly stroking them.

"Do you play?" he'd asked.

She'd jumped at his voice, pulling her hand back, her cheeks turning a little pink as though she had been caught doing something naughty. Shaking her head, she'd replied, "No, but I always wanted to."

He'd stepped closer, "Do you still want to?"

Her eyes had been fixed on the keys, and her voice took on a note of wistfulness, "A little. Maybe one of these days I will."

Opening his eyes, he stared at the blue carpet of Dr. Constance's office and found his voice, "I'm not completely sure. She's important to me. I couldn't stand the thought of leaving her alone, of not making sure she had everything she needed." He raked his fingers through his hair and looked up, "I don't want to hurt her, and I'm terrified I'm going to."

Be careful.

Go slow.

Dr. Constance had seemed mostly pleased by what Liam had shared with her. She viewed the events of Christmas weekend as proof positive that he was making real progress. Still, she'd cautioned him.

He knew she was right, especially in light of what had happened Christmas night. Not that anything had actually happened. Not really.

The hour was late, and Zoe had been getting a little punch-drunk. A movie was running, but he only had eyes for the woman resting against him. She'd been very giggly, and he could tell she would likely fall asleep soon. Looking up at him, her fingers had lifted to brush the hair out of his eyes. The touch was delicate, and he hadn't been prepared for how it would make him feel. There was no fear in the touch; she was doing it of her own free will. Smiling, she murmured, "That's better. Your eyes are too beautiful to hide."

Her fingers had dropped, and her arm had gone across his abdomen. With a yawn, she'd snuggled against him and drifted off to sleep. Leaving him wide awake and overwhelmed.

Returning to his apartment after therapy, he sat at the piano. Thinking. He hadn't been completely honest with Dr. Constance. While he wasn't sure what Zoe was to him, he knew he was feeling things he hadn't felt before. Things he had honestly believed he was incapable of feeling.

He let his fingers move, and music played, but he didn't think much about it. Didn't need to. He'd been playing since he was five. His fingers operated on muscle memory. He couldn't stop thinking about how Zoe had looked standing at the piano. Couldn't stop hearing the wistfulness in her voice.

He didn't let anyone touch his piano. Didn't let anyone in his apartment. Didn't let anyone touch him. And yet, he'd let Zoe do all of that, and it hadn't bothered him.

What did that mean?

Saturday morning, he arrived at the studio a few minutes before Zoe. He was already in the booth when she walked in. Since Monday, they hadn't seen each other, only texted. Mostly, it had been Zoe sending him memes she found funny.

His heart beat faster when she walked in, smiled, and said, "Hey!"

"Good morning," he replied.

She didn't look very well rested, but some of the tension he'd sensed the last few weeks was gone from her. Sitting down a few feet from him, she went through the tiny routine he'd noticed she always followed. Drink would go on the right side of the computer monitor, notebook on the left. She'd pull up the obits and work on them for a few minutes, then skim the rest of the paper. Finally, she'd turn her attention to him and start going over the stories they'd be reading.

The first hour of the broadcast was going fine. They were twenty minutes from break, and he had just finished an article. Zoe began reading, and he was pulling up his next article when it happened.

She made a weird sound that pulled his attention back to her. He watched as she coughed, but it sounded very fake. "My apologies," she said into the mic before continuing, "The man bit..." her voice broke, and he watched as she squeezed her eyes shut, her body shaking. A smile on her face clued him into the fact that she was trying very hard not to laugh. Amused, he watched as she tried to speak again, "The man bit the security...security guard...and...and..." She snorted. Voice shaking with mirth, she gasped, "I'm so sorry...I can't get through this story. Liam?"

He took over with a story about a fish farm, and Zoe fled the booth. She returned a couple of minutes later as he neared the story's end. They made it through the rest of the hour, but he could tell she was on the verge of cracking up the entire time.

As soon as Dante took over for the break, Zoe's head dropped, forehead resting against the desk, and she laughed hard, managing to get out, "Oh my god. I can't believe I did that."

"It wasn't that bad," he told her, unable to hide how amused he was.

She rolled her head to the side and stared at him, "Didn't you hear me?"

"Would've been difficult not to," he teased.

She giggled, "Can you start the next hour? I need to collect myself. Not sure anyone would appreciate me laughing through the obits."

The second hour passed without further incident. Once finished, she asked, "So, big plans for tonight?"

"Tonight?"

"Yeah, for New Year's Eve." The look on her face suggested that she couldn't believe he wasn't registering what day it was.

He shook his head, "No. You?"

"Same. Dante's coming over, but he and Alex will probably spend the night making out, and Dahlia's stuck working the holiday at the hospital. You want to come over? I'd rather not spend the evening stuck in my room or being the awkward third wheel."

He barely thought about it, "Sure, if you think Alex will be okay with it."

She grinned, "I already asked him. He's fine with it. I think he's feeling a little less animosity toward you since you made sure I was taken care of last weekend. Though," she hesitated for a moment, but then plunged forward, "you two might want to talk one of these days. Clear the air, y'know?"

After a few seconds of consideration, he nodded, "You're probably right." If he was going to keep spending time with Zoe, it would be better if he and Alex could get along.

Ten

Zoe

She missed Liam. She'd spent all week missing him. After he left Monday morning, she felt more aware of her loneliness than usual. She tried to keep herself busy, but there were only so many hours a day she could spend job hunting. She thought about going to the studio to work more on Bookmarks, but she was trying to conserve gas. There wasn't much in her bank account, and she needed to be able to stretch the little she had as far as she could until she landed another job.

Monday night, her sleep returned to its pre-Christmas weekend awfulness. She would barely get a few hours of sleep before being wide awake. By Thursday morning, she was so exhausted she found herself tempted to text Liam and see if he'd consider being her sleep buddy. It was a genuinely terrible idea. Even in her sleep-deprived state, she knew how phenomenally bad it was and had no intention of actually asking. That said, sleeping beside him had been the best sleep she could ever remember having.

The good sleep wasn't the only reason she missed him. It was his presence she missed the most. Spending nearly two full days together had been lovely.

Though she had her roommates, being with them wasn't the same as being with Liam. And she couldn't quite figure out why.

Friday night, she approached Alex about inviting Liam over on New Year's Eve. Alex sat quietly, considering her request. After several long seconds, he asked, "Do you want him here?"

"I do, but not if you're going to be uncomfortable."

There was another long pause before he made his decision. With a nod, he told her, "Same rules as Thanksgiving. If he doesn't behave, I can kick him out."

She hugged him, "Thank you!"

"Y'know, out of everyone you could've fallen for, Liam McPherson would've been on the bottom of my list of guesses. I'm not even sure he would've made the list," Alex mused as the hug ended.

That brought her up short, "I haven't fallen for him. He's just a friend."

Alex laughed, "Sure he is."

"He is," she insisted.

"Whatever you say," came the amused reply.

She tried not to think about what he'd said, pushing it out of her mind. Unfortunately, when she woke in the middle of the night, it was all she could think about. Over and over, she reminded herself, *I haven't fallen for him. I can't fall for him. It's just a crush. He's been nice. We're friends. I CANNOT fall for him.*

She would have to bury her crush as deeply as possible. They were friends. That was it. There was no way Liam would ever be interested in her romantically. She needed to remember that.

"We've been over this. Pineapple does not belong on pizza," Alex stated flatly.

Zoe laughed, "I like it, and so does Dante."

"It's true," Dante agreed.

"It's an abomination," Liam interjected, causing Dante and Alex to swivel their heads toward him in surprise.

Zoe sighed in mock exasperation and met Liam's eyes, "Have you ever even tried it?"

"Unfortunately. My tastebuds will never recover," he informed her.

Dante snorted, "Don't worry, Zoe. I'll get us a pizza with pineapple, and they won't be allowed to have any of it."

She laughed, "Sounds good." To Liam, she added, "Sorry, but you can't have any."

He rolled his eyes in response.

The pizza order was placed, and Zoe turned her attention to the shelf of games. "You guys want to play something?"

Alex joined her. A few seconds later, he pulled a small green box and took it to the table. Zoe grinned, "Why am I not surprised?"

Liam read the title, "Zombie Fluxx?"

Zoe sat beside him, "It's easy, I promise."

The cards were dealt, they played a practice round, and she wasn't surprised that he picked it up quickly. He seemed to have a knack for games, and this was a far simpler game than Ticket to Ride.

Before they started playing for real, Dante suggested, "Let's make this interesting."

Zoe groaned, "Let's not. I'm broke."

Dante laughed, "Oh, I wasn't thinking about playing for money."

It was decided that whoever won a round would get to pick something for the other players to do. Things began quite silly. Alex got stuck eating a piece of a pineapple pizza. He gagged but did it. Zoe had to sniff the milk to see if it had expired. It had, and she vowed her vengeance would be swift. Everything continued to be ridiculous, and then Dante won a round.

He sat quietly for a moment, his eyes flitting around the table. His face was mischievous as his gaze settled on Zoe and Liam. "Hmmm...it *is* New Year's Eve, and you two don't have anyone to kiss at midnight."

"Excuse me?" she asked Dante. She didn't dare look at Liam but wondered if he was as red in the face as she probably was.

Dante grinned like the Cheshire Cat, "You heard me. You and Liam have to kiss at midnight on the lips for at least five seconds. That said, we certainly won't stop you if it goes longer than that."

"You can't be serious," she groaned.

"As a heart attack," he retorted with a laugh.

Zoe's mind raced as she tried to come up with a reply. Liam came to her rescue and said, "I won't agree to it unless Zoe does."

She snuck a peek at him, muttering, "You don't have to."

"I know," he replied.

Her attention swiveled back to Dante, "Fine. You want us to kiss? I'll only agree if you agree that when I win a round, I can assign you toilet scrubbing duty here for the next two months. Deal?"

He nodded, "Deal." Looking at Liam, he teased, "Want some mouthwash?"

A little while later, when Dante and Alex went to browse the game shelf, Liam leaned over and, in a low voice, told her, "If you don't want to, that's fine."

Watching the men picking a game, she replied, "I'd much rather kiss you than smell more expired food."

He made a noise that sounded almost like a laugh. Sneaking a peek, she saw a smile on his face. Not a big one, but it was definitely a smile.

10

Zoe looked at Liam.

9

Liam looked at Zoe.

8

He got off the couch.

7

He held out his hand to her.

6

She stared at his hand.

5

She stood and took his hand.

4

He led her to the kitchen.

3

Out of view of Alex and Dante, they came to a stop.

2

"They don't get to watch," he murmured, looking down at her and cupping her cheek.

1

"Okay?" he asked, face lowered to hers.

Happy New Year!

"Okay," she replied, stretched a little, and pressed her lips against his.

Liam's arm went around her back, pulling her a little closer. Her hands moved to clasp at the base of his neck. Her kissing experience was nonexistent, but feeling the softness of his lips against hers was rather nice. She liked how he was holding her. It was gentle and made her feel safe. The kiss was cautious, almost as if he was as unfamiliar with what they were doing as she was.

She leaned into him, and his hold tightened a fraction. The hand on her cheek slipped back and rested against her hair. His fingertips pressed lightly against her skull.

With a gasp, she broke the kiss, trying to catch her breath. They stood there, both breathing a little hard, staring at each other. "Um..." she couldn't form an actual word.

"Yeah," Liam breathed out on an exhale.

Her lips tingled, and she wondered if her eyes were as hungry as his. "Think that...was...five seconds?" she joked.

At that, he broke into a broad triangular smile complete with dimples. Her breath caught at the sight. It completely changed his entire appearance. He leaned forward and rested his forehead against hers, "I'm not sure. Maybe we should do that again, just to make sure."

She giggled, "Maybe we should."

This time, he initiated the kiss. They melted into each other as the kiss deepened. She sighed happily, loving how it felt. And then, a wave of reality crashed into her. Her heart clenched, and she pulled away, staring at him wide-eyed.

Liam's eyes were still hungry, but there was worry there as well as he asked, a little breathlessly, "Zoe? Are you...?"

Her voice was shaky as she asked, "What are we doing?"

Eleven

Liam

What are we doing?

He blinked, trying to process what she was asking. His brain was still stuck on their kisses. How soft and pliant she'd been in his arms. Her hands let go of where they'd anchored at the base of his neck as she staggered back. He didn't want to, but he released her from his embrace.

She was less than an arm's length away, still staring at him, her fingers lightly running along her lips. Her face was flushed and perplexed. He wasn't sure what to say and went with the first thing that popped into his brain, "This doesn't mean anything unless you want it to."

Her fingers stilled before her hand dropped to her side. She stood searching his eyes, something unreadable in hers. Her voice was barely more than a whisper when she finally spoke, "I...Liam...I...what if I don't know if I want...if I want it to mean something?"

He reached out and gently tucked a flyaway, letting his fingers brush slowly against the edge of her ear for a few seconds as he said, "We'll talk about it."

Her eyes slid shut at his touch. "Not tonight," she said quietly. "Okay?"

It was probably for the best. It was the middle of the night, and neither of them was probably in the best headspace for what would like to be a very serious conversation. "Okay," he agreed.

He left not long after that. Driving back to his apartment, he cursed the late hour. He needed to be able to sit and play, but it was quiet hours in his building. Even on New Year's Eve, the place enforced that particular rule.

So much for being careful and going slow. Maybe he should've refused to kiss her. It had been a risk to his heart. He'd known it and still gone through with it.

He couldn't lie to himself anymore. There was no point. No longer could he pretend he didn't know what he felt for her.

It was too fast. Dr. Constance would probably tell him that when he saw her on Wednesday. She wouldn't be wrong. Hadn't he just admitted that he was scared of hurting Zoe the previous Wednesday? Dr. Constance would probably point that out as well. Or maybe she wouldn't. Maybe she'd just sit there waiting for him to bring it up himself.

By the time he reached his apartment, he was exhausted from fighting the urge to turn around and drive back to Zoe. He almost laughed as he remembered how, just a month earlier, he'd struggled to resist the urge to stay home instead of going to Zoe's.

He lay on his bed in the dark, staring at the ceiling. As much as he wished that Zoe was there, he knew he needed to be realistic. There was a very real chance that once they talked, she would realize what a terrible idea being with him was. It was incredibly tempting to avoid, but if there was a chance things might work between them, they needed to be able to trust each other.

He spent the rest of the night mostly awake. Trying to stop his racing thoughts was impossible. By six a.m., he was a complete wreck. He needed to talk to Dr. Constance, process what had happened, and get advice on moving forward. But it was Sunday and New Year's Day, to boot. She wasn't going to be in the office. The office wasn't even open.

He didn't think he could wait until his regularly scheduled session on Wednesday. Maybe she could squeeze him in a day or two early? He scrolled through his phone until he found the office's phone number. He'd leave a message, and someone would probably call him back in the morning. He'd be a mess the rest of the day, but at least he'd know he'd been as proactive as possible.

Rather than going to voicemail, he was surprised when the call was connected to an answering service. He gave them his info and explained he was one of Dr. Constance's patients and was trying to reach her. The operator told him she would relay the message to the on-call provider.

Less than fifteen minutes later, an unfamiliar number populated on his phone. Hoping it was the on-call provider, he answered.

"Liam?" Dr. Constance's calm voice came through, sending a wave of relief crashing over him.

Relief that was almost immediately replaced with overwhelming guilt. He was interrupting her holiday, her day off, just because he didn't know how to handle a girl problem. "I'm...I'm sorry, I shouldn't have called. I didn't mean to bother you."

"Liam, it's okay. I'm on call this weekend," she reassured him. "What's wrong?"

He swallowed hard, "It's Zoe...there were...developments...last night. I'm worried I fucked up."

"Okay. I want you to take some deep breaths for me." He did as she instructed, and then she asked, "Are you alright?"

No. "I don't know."

There was silence for a few seconds before she asked, "Can you come to the office this morning?"

Her question surprised him, and he said, "I can."

"Good. Meet me there at eight, and we'll talk."

His insides twisted with the anxiety that had joined his guilt, "You don't have to do that. I know it's a holiday."

"You are my patient. Come to the office."

He chewed the inside of his cheek, "Are you sure?"

"Yes, Liam, I'm sure. See you at eight."

The call ended, and he stared at his phone. Relief had returned to join the swirl of feelings. He didn't care if Dr. Constance charged him double or triple her usual rate for seeing him that morning. It'd be worth it.

"On the phone, you said there had been developments. What did you mean by that?" Dr. Constance asked after he'd gotten settled onto the couch.

He stared at his hands, "She invited me over for New Year's Eve."

"Was it just the two of you there?"

He shook his head, "No, her roommate and his boyfriend were there too." With a sigh, he continued, "We ended up playing this card game, and Dante had this idea that whoever won a round would get to pick something for another player to do. Stupid stuff like smelling expired milk."

"You had to smell expired milk?" she asked when he didn't immediately continue.

He looked up at her and shook his head, "When Dante won, he wanted Zoe and me to kiss...on the lips...for at least five seconds...at midnight."

Dr. Constance's face was unreadable as she asked, "Did you agree?"

"I told him I wouldn't if Zoe didn't. I didn't think she would, and I didn't want her to feel pressured, but she agreed to it." His fists clenched, "I tried to give her an out. I didn't want her to go through with it if she really didn't want to, but she said it was fine."

"Did you want to go through with it?"

His voice was low when he finally replied, "Yes." His eyes immediately dropped back to the floor.

"Did you go through with it?"

"Yes." He could feel tears welling and pressed his palms against his eyes, trying to force them back. It wouldn't be the first time he'd cried in front of Dr. Constance, but he didn't want to cry at that particular moment.

She didn't immediately say anything, and when Liam opened his eyes, she was watching him. Her face was a little softer than usual. He grabbed a tissue and wiped away a few of the tears that had escaped. She spoke gently, "Liam, I can see you are dealing with many emotions right now. Are you able to tell me what they are?"

He balled the tissue up and held it in his fist. She waited patiently, and he tried to figure out how to explain what he was feeling. His words stumbled as he said, "You said to...to go slow and be careful. I tried...and I failed. She kissed me first...and...I kissed her the second time. When she broke that kiss..." He squeezed his eyes shut and rubbed his temples, "She looked so...so...upset, and she asked me what we were doing."

"What did you tell her?"

He opened his eyes, "It's stupid."

"You told her it was stupid?"

"No! What I told her was stupid. I...I told her that it didn't mean anything if she didn't want it to."

"And what did she say when you told her that?"

Liam sighed and leaned his head back, resting it against the wall behind the couch. His eyes stared at the ceiling, and he pictured Zoe's troubled face from the previous evening. "She asked me what if she wasn't sure if she wanted it to mean something. And...and I told her we should talk about it. She agreed but didn't want to talk last night."

He fell silent and heard Dr. Constance's pen making notes. After several seconds, she asked, "Did the kisses mean anything to you?"

"Yes." His voice shook with the tears he was desperately trying to keep from falling.

"Why did you tell her it didn't mean anything if she didn't want it to?"

He met the doctor's eyes, "Because I don't want her to be scared of me." Quieter, he added, "I don't want her to go away."

"Are you going to tell her it meant something to you?"

He shook his head, "I...I don't know. I don't want her to feel like she has to feel something for me that she doesn't."

"If your positions were reversed, would you want her to tell you?"

He was exasperated, "I don't know. Alright? She's the first person I've had a connection with in a really long time. I thought that the kiss would just be a quick thing. We'd get it over with, and that would be that...but that's not what happened. I'm terrified I've fucked up whatever it is that's between us."

Dr. Constance considered that and asked, "What happened was consensual, correct?"

He nodded, "I'd never do that without permission."

"That's good. Are there any other things you're feeling about what happened that you'd like to share?"

His lips trembled as he forced himself to tell her, "I'm a hypocrite."

"Why do you think that?"

He looked away from her and stared out the window, "I've never experienced this kind of attraction. I've never felt any of those things I'd hear other people describe."

"Liam, that doesn't make you a hypocrite." Dr. Constance said after a few seconds.

He shook his head, "I am because I stood by and let people be shamed for acting on their urges. I even preached about how premarital sex was a sin. Lust was a sin. I told rooms full of teenagers that they shouldn't let their hormones control them." He laughed bitterly, "I spent years judging people for doing the same thing that I now want more than I ever thought I would. Ever thought I could."

She gave him a few moments before asking, "Liam, how many relationships have you been in?"

"Romantic relationships?" he clarified.

She nodded, "Yes. How many romantic relationships have you been a part of?"

"None."

"Have you dated very much?"

"No. Why?" He wasn't sure where she was headed with this particular line of questioning.

She held his gaze, looking unperturbed by the clear irritation in his voice. "I ask because we've never really discussed that aspect of your life. When you first started with me, you told me you were straight and not in a relationship, never married or divorced. Until recently, you haven't mentioned anything about that. I'm curious. What is it about Zoe that attracts you?"

Some of his irritation melted, and he thought about what she was asking. He thought about Zoe. Her cheerful disposition. The way she had reached for him when she was crying. How it had felt to hold her while she slept. Her face after their first kiss. The slightly flushed cheeks. The bright eyes. Hearing her musical laugh. "Everything," he murmured.

Dr. Constance's eyebrows lifted a little, "Really?"

"Well, maybe not everything. I don't find her love of pineapple pizza attractive."

That earned him the tiniest smile, "Putting aside a controversial pizza topping choice, what else? Is this purely a physical attraction, or is it more than that?"

"She's...she's kind. Selfless. Life shits on her, and she keeps going. She's so incredibly beautiful." He swallowed hard, "She trusts me."

"Trust is important to you." It was a statement, not a question. "Do you trust her?"

He didn't immediately answer. The conversation he needed to have with Zoe would require trust. With his history of putting his faith in the wrong people, trusting anyone else was frightening. If he were going to do this, he'd have to take a leap of faith. "She's given me no reason not to trust her."

Dr. Constance nodded and asked again, "Do you trust her?"

Take the leap. "I do."

"Liam, are you familiar with the term demisexual?"

He shook his head, "What is it?"

"It's when a person doesn't feel attraction, especially sexual attraction, to another person without having a close relationship where trust has formed. What you're describing sounds quite a lot like demisexuality."

He was puzzled, "But I'm straight."

She shook her head, "It's not about the gender you're attracted to. It's about how you experience attraction. Does that make sense?"

He nodded. It did. In fact, it lifted the mystery of certain aspects of his life. He would need to think about that, but that would have to happen later. At the moment, he wasn't sure how this new knowledge would help what he was facing.

"Liam, the things that you're describing feeling for the first time, many experience those as teenagers. You're not a teenager, but that doesn't change the fact that these feelings are going to be complex and new. You may find it confusing or even frightening, but I promise I will help you process this."

Twelve

Liam

Leaving Dr. Constance's office, he found himself driving to a part of town that he'd avoided for years. He pulled into the lot across the street from a massive structure with its own lot that was completely full. It was hardly a surprise, considering it was ten a.m. on a Sunday morning.

The last time he'd been there, the add-on had only been a discussion. The place had been repainted, and the landscaping was impeccable as always. Appearances had always been an important part of the place, both of the building and of the people.

How different would his life have been if he hadn't spent so much of it there? Pain and regret coursed through him as he remembered who he'd become to fit expectations. Feeling sick, he headed back across town.

He stopped to get gas. After filling his tank, he pulled out his phone. No new messages were there, which disappointed him. He opened the texts with Zoe and tapped out a quick message.

Have you had breakfast?

To his relief, a reply arrived seconds later.

No. You?

Nope. Want breakfast? My treat.

Depends.

On?

Will this breakfast contain cinnamon roll pancakes?

It can if you want it to.

Then yes, I want breakfast.

I'll be there to pick you up in 20.

She must've been watching for him because she was out the door and headed toward him a few seconds after he pulled into her driveway. Sitting in the passenger seat, she looked at him, smiling shyly as she said, "Hey."

Seeing her smile brought a smile to his own lips. "Hi. Still want cinnamon roll pancakes?"

"Yup."

The restaurant he took her to was busy, but not as busy as it would be once the churches dismissed their morning services. Fortunately, they didn't have to wait very long to be seated. After placing their order, they sat staring at each other across the booth.

"So, how are you?" Zoe asked after a few moments of silence.

"How are you?" he tossed the question back to her.

She shook her head, "Nope, I asked you first."

"But I asked the more important question," he retorted.

She rolled her eyes, "Don't say that. Mine is just as important. Answer the question."

"Okay. You?"

"Same."

Were the dark circles around her eyes permanent? It was probably better not to ask. "Still having trouble sleeping?"

She sighed, "I just don't seem to be able to sleep very well without—" Her words cut off abruptly, and she immediately glanced away.

What didn't she want to tell him? He nudged her, "Without what?"

The server dropped off their drinks, saying, "Your food should be out in a few minutes."

Zoe sipped her orange juice, "That's good."

"Hmm?"

"The juice. It's good," she answered.

It was a little frustrating the way she was avoiding the question. He knew he shouldn't keep pushing, but he wasn't doing so great with his self-control. "You didn't answer my question."

"About the juice?"

He shook his head and leveled a pointed stare at her, "Zoe."

She matched his stare, "Liam."

"What is it you need to get better sleep?"

Her eyes dropped to the juice, "Can you just drop it? Please?"

Sensing how uncomfortable she was, he eased up, "Sure."

"Thanks."

She fiddled with her straw wrapper. He watched as she twisted it into different shapes, just to undo it and make more shapes. Her nails were painted a shimmery blue, and he realized it was the first time he'd seen her with nail polish on.

The server returned and set plates on the table, asking, "Need anything else?"

Zoe looked at Liam. He shook his head, and she said, "Nope, I think we're good. Thanks."

They ate quietly. Liam was distracted. He'd thought he might be able to ease into the conversation over breakfast, but there were too many people around. This wasn't the place to start a serious conversation. His options felt limited. It would be easiest if they went to his apartment, but after their kisses, he wasn't sure she'd feel comfortable there. What if she wasn't ready to have the talk yet? He wanted to have it sooner rather than later, but it was entirely possible she felt differently.

"Hey. You okay in there?" Zoe's hand waved in front of him, pulling him out of his head.

"Yeah."

She ate a bite of pancake and asked, "Something on your mind?"

He shrugged, "Just thinking."

"Something you'd like to share with the class?" Her voice was slightly teasing.

He finished his scrambled eggs before asking, "Do you have any plans for the rest of today?"

"Oh yeah. Big plans. Mostly involving the couch and *Power Wash Simulator.*"

He gave her a quizzical look, "*Power Wash Simulator?*"

She laughed, "Yeah, Alex has it on the Xbox, and I'm kind of addicted."

"I see. And how set in stone are these plans?"

She ate the last of her pancake before replying, "I could probably be convinced to put them off until later."

The server came back with the check. Liam handed her his debit card. She told him, "I'll be right back with this."

His attention shifted to Zoe, "Are your roommates home today?"

"Alex is. Dahlia's still at the hospital."

His card was brought back along with the receipt. "Need anything else?" the server asked. They assured her they didn't. She walked away, saying, "Have a great day. Happy New Year!"

He filled out the tip and flipped the receipt upside down, placing the pen on top. "Ready to go?"

Zoe nodded, "Sure."

In the car, he hesitated, not turning on the ignition, trying to figure out what to say.

"Liam? What's going on? Are you contemplating murdering me?" Her tone was light, suggesting she wasn't too worried that was what was happening.

He rolled his eyes, "I'm not going to murder you."

"That's good." She laughed, "The Netflix documentary would be super boring." Her tone softened, "If there's something you need to ask, just ask. I won't get upset."

A few seconds of deliberation passed before he asked, "Will you come back to my place?"

She looked slightly surprised, but to his relief, she nodded, "Sure."

"Want something to drink?" he asked when they arrived.

"Sure. What are my options?"

He waved a hand at the fridge, "Pick whatever you want."

She retrieved a bottle of tea and joined him in the living room, "Can I ask you something?"

"Yes."

Her eyes traveled to the piano, "Do you actually play, or is that your attempt at decoration?"

"Why would I have a piano if I don't play?"

She shrugged, "I've known people that have pianos that just sit and collect dust. Based on the books, I'm going to assume yours doesn't. But, you never know."

"I play," he assured her. "Been playing since I was five."

"And you're how old now?"

"Thirty-four."

She laughed, "So ancient."

He rolled his eyes, "Hardly."

"Will you play something?" she asked as she sat on the couch.

"Don't believe I actually can?" he teased.

She grinned, "Maybe. Maybe not."

He studied her for a moment, hesitating. It had been a while since he'd last played in front of anyone. Like his apartment, his playing was a very private, personal thing. Playing did help him gather his thoughts, and he needed that now. "What do you want to hear?"

She considered the question, "Whatever you want. I'm not picky. I just want to hear you play."

There had been a time when, if someone had asked him to play, he would've gravitated towards something difficult. Something that would show off just how skilled he truly was. That didn't feel right anymore. Hadn't in a long time.

Looking at Zoe, he thought about what he'd picked up from observing her. None of the books he had out were right. He headed for the bookshelf in his bedroom, "I'll be back."

It took him a minute to locate the book he had in mind. He'd purchased it a few years earlier when he got roped into playing for a wedding and hadn't touched it since. Flipping through the pages, he returned to the living room. Finding the song, he placed the book on the piano. His eyes scanned the pages as he sat down. Hands centered over the keys, he began to play.

It was a gentle tune, almost a lullaby. His fingers lightly danced over the keys, and he let himself get lost in the music. He was unprepared for the voice that began singing along with the tune. Zoe's soft mezzo-soprano joined with his playing. He had to remind himself not to stop. He hadn't known she could sing, though perhaps he should've guessed it, considering how pleasant she was to listen to when she read.

The sound faded as the song ended, and he rested his hands on the keys. He was lost. Zoe was everything he had ever wanted and more. Even if he had doubted it before, he certainly didn't now.

"You play beautifully," she complimented him, her voice soft.

Eyes fixed on his hands, he replied, "You sing beautifully."

He heard her move off the couch. Footsteps approached the piano, coming to a stop beside him. Looking up, he met her eyes. Her face was serious. Biting her lip, she hesitated. He waited, giving her a chance to find her words. She released a shaky exhale, "I think...I think I might want it to mean something."

Thirteen

Liam

O*kay.*

We're doing this.

Settling on opposite ends of the couch, they faced each other. "This okay?" he asked.

She nodded. He watched as she picked at the label of the bottle she was holding. By all appearances, she was as nervous as he was. Her restless fingers continued moving. His mind raced, trying to figure out how to start.

To his surprise, her eyes shut, and she began to speak slowly, "Last night...that...that was my first kiss." Her cheeks turned a lovely shade of pink as her eyes opened. They immediately dropped to the bottle. There was a slight tremble to her voice as she added, "You could...could probably tell. I'm sure you've...done that plenty of times before."

Was it really possible she was just as inexperienced as he was? His voice was low as he admitted, "That was a first for me too."

Her eyes flew up to meet his. Voice incredulous, she asked, "That was your first kiss?"

He nodded.

She eyed him suspiciously, "You're thirty-four. You honestly expect me to believe that was your first kiss?"

He shrugged, "You're twenty-eight, and it was yours. Why is it such a surprise it was mine as well?"

Baffled, she waved a hand up and down towards him, "Look at you. You're..." her eyes dropped, "you're ridiculously good-looking."

Taken aback by the compliment, he mumbled, "I'm really not."

Looking back up, her eyes scanned his face while her own scrunched up adorably as she asked, "Do you really think that, or are you fishing for compliments?"

He was well aware of how weird he looked. His nose was too large. It was his most noticeable feature, and it only added to his overall awkward appearance. "Have you actually looked at me?"

"Um, yes, I have. At least once a week for the last two months. You have the most expressive eyes I've ever seen. And don't even get me started on your hair. People would kill for hair that good." Her cheeks were pink again, but she didn't look away from him.

He shook his head, "If anyone is the good-looking one here, it's you."

She snorted, her reply dripping with sarcasm, "Yeah, right. Short and fat with frizzy hair is super attractive."

Was that really how she saw herself? She was short, but he knew from the few times she'd been in his arms that she wore clothes at least two sizes too big. She was curvy, and he liked that. He also liked her curly hair. It was a little dry, but that could easily be mended. His words stumbled as he told her, "I...I think you are."

The pink deepened, and a tiny smile graced her lips, "Oh...um...thanks."

He studied her quizically, "You never kissed anyone in your previous relationships?"

She burst out laughing, "What previous relationships? What about you? You're saying you never kissed your exes?"

He shook his head, "No exes."

Her eyes searched his face, trying to determine if he was telling the truth. "Okay, let's say you haven't had any relationships. You have dated, right?"

"Unless you're counting Winter Formal at college, the answer is no. And even that was just a group of friends. Hardly romantic."

She sat back, shaking her head, "Incredible."

"What?"

"I just assumed that you...had...experience, y'know?"

He shook his head, "Sorry to disappoint."

She chewed at her thumbnail briefly before saying, "I'm not. Disappointed, I mean."

Uncertainty seemed to fill the air around them as they both fell silent for a moment. *Leap of faith. Leap of faith. I have to jump, or this isn't going to go anywhere.* "Zoe?"

"Yeah?"

Inhaling deeply, he plunged, "What do you want to know about my past?"

Her brow knit in confusion, "What do you mean?"

"You know what the internet says. I'm sure you've got questions."

She shook her head, "You don't have to do this."

"Yes, Zoe, I do."

He watched her, his stomach twisting and churning. She slipped off her shoes and pulled her feet up to sit cross-legged. Still worrying the label, she finally said, "I know there are different sides to every story. I think...I think you should tell me your story, and I'll ask questions as we go along."

That wasn't what he'd expected. He'd thought she'd have a laundry list of things to ask with no interest in hearing more than fit those parameters. "Where do you want me to start?" he asked.

"It's your story. Where do you think it starts?"

It was the kind of thing Dr. Constance would say. It put him a little at ease. "We might be here awhile."

"Guess power washing will have to wait," she joked.

He smiled slightly as his mind processed her request. He thought about the things he was going to have to talk about, some he hadn't even discussed with Dr. Constance. Things he'd intentionally made a point of trying to forget because they hurt a little too much. Try was the operative word. The memories were still there.

"Liam?" Zoe's voice broke through his thoughts. He blinked, realizing that he had been quiet a little too long.

It shouldn't be so difficult. All he had to do was start, but figuring out where was nigh impossible. "When you looked me up, how far back did the info go?"

"Maybe your late teens?"

That sounded about right. He'd mostly flown under the radar until then. "You know that church over on Park and Main?"

"The giant one? Temple of Light or something like that?" She cringed, "Pretty sure I saw on Reddit that it's a cult."

He chewed the inside of his cheek, "I can't say that's completely wrong. You ever been there?"

She shook her head, "No, I'm not really religious. Fred viewed Sunday as just another day of business."

The way he slightly envied her was a little twisted. "My uncle is Mark King. He's the pastor of that place."

The way her eyes went wide told him that despite not being religious, she'd definitely heard of Mark. Likely, she had run across him on tv. "So, your family is famous, not just you?"

"Famous, infamous. Not much of a difference, I suppose," he replied with a shrug.

"Did you go there?"

He nodded, "Mom took me. Mark's her twin brother. I don't know how much of us going was because she actually wanted to and how much was because she was trying to be supportive. Dad wouldn't go. He's kind of a seeing-is-believing type of guy."

"Did you like it?"

"I think I did when I was little. There wasn't..." he searched for the right word, "pressure to fit a specific mold. And I hadn't been introduced to church politics yet."

Her brow furrowed, "Chruch politics? Like who to vote for?"

He shook his head, "No, though that is certainly something that many churches do." Pausing, he tried to figure out how to explain it, "It's a lot of networking. Keeping the right people happy."

"Who are the right people?"

"The ones with money," he replied flatly.

She took that in and asked, "How are they kept happy?"

He raked his hand through his hair and grimaced, "You give them positions of power. Let their pet projects take priority. Do what they want, and the money is pretty much guaranteed."

"Sounds like a business."

He sighed, "Yeah."

"How old were you when you realized what was happening?"

He considered that, "I'm not sure. I think I started to pick up on it pretty early on. I'd hear the things Mark would tell my mother."

"That doesn't seem like something a kid should hear."

"It wasn't." A bitter laugh escaped him, "I heard a lot of things growing up that I never should've." Standing, he informed her, "I need a break."

"Okay."

Moving to the piano, he looked back at her, "C'mere."

With a quizzical look, she stood and moved toward him. "Yes?"

He pulled out the piano bench, "Sit."

"Why?" she stared up at him, still confused.

"Please?" His voice had gone soft.

Hesitating a few seconds, she acquiesced and gingerly took a seat. He walked to the kitchen table and retrieved a chair. Making a quick detour to the bedroom, he grabbed another book. Returning, he set the chair beside her and placed the book on the piano lid. Sitting down, he lightly patted the instrument, "This is a piano."

She laughed, "And here I thought it was a saxophone."

He smiled, "Easy mistake to make." Pressing down a key in the middle of the keyboard, he told her, "This is middle C."

She looked from the key to him, "What are you doing?"

"You want to learn, and I'd like to teach you."

A soft look stole over her face, "That's very sweet." Sighing, she added, "You don't want to teach me. It would require a level of patience that I'm not sure you possess."

He raised an eyebrow, "Why don't you let me make that decision?"

A second passed, and then another. She looked back at the key, "Middle C. Does that mean there are other C's? Are all of these C?"

"Not all of them."

She groaned, "And I'm going to keep this straight how?"

He picked up the book, opened it, and placed it before her. "It's all about where things are marked on the staff." Pointing to five parallel lines on the page, "That's a staff."

"Why does this feel like a math lesson?"

He huffed out a laugh, "This is more fun than math."

She grinned, "I like math."

"Really?" He was surprised simply because he hadn't encountered many women who claimed an affinity for the subject.

She shrugged, "I enjoy putting together puzzles. Math is just a puzzle that needs solving."

He smiled, "You're right."

Looking from the keys to the book, she said, "Okay, middle C and staff. Seems easy enough." Her face scrunched in concentration, "What goes on the staff to indicate middle C?"

"That would be a note. We're getting to that."

"I don't know, we might be going too fast," she joked.

He rolled his eyes, "Were you like this in school?"

Her face fell slightly, and she glanced away, "Let's just say there's no such thing as no child left behind."

The pain in her voice saddened him. "I'm sorry," he told her quietly.

She looked at him, "It's okay. Her smile returned, "What's next?"

"Show me middle C," he instructed.

She chewed her bottom lip, staring at the keyboard. Her finger went lightly against one, "Here?"

He nodded, "Good." Pointing to an image in the book, "These are clefs. This one is the treble, and the one beneath is the bass."

The concentration scrunch returned. It was so adorable he couldn't look away. She didn't seem to notice, her eyes fixed on the page, "Squiggly thing is treble. Backward C is bass." Looking back at him, she asked, "What do they mean?"

"There are exceptions to what I'm about to tell you, but we'll get to those eventually. Right now, I'm going to keep it simple. Middle C and every key to the right of it are on the treble clef staff. Middle C and every key to the left are on the bass clef staff."

Nodding slowly, she said, "Let me see if I've got this straight. This," she touched a key, "is middle C." Pointing to different spots on the page, she added,

"Treble and bass clef, and staff. Is that right?"

"It is."

She grinned, "Okay, maybe this isn't that hard."

He chuckled, "I'll be sure to remind you of that when we get to scales."

"So, what's next?"

He felt slightly better and told her, "I think I'm ready to resume our talk."

Fourteen

Liam

"Mark's church isn't what it was when I was a kid. It was much smaller." He glanced at the water bottle he'd pulled from the fridge when they'd returned to the couch. "Before he turned into a televangelist, Mark was much more hands-on. There was no giant staff to deal with everything."

"So, no private planes?"

He laughed, "No, not back then." Taking a drink, he screwed the lid back on the bottle and told her, "When I was ten, I moved in with Mark."

"Why?"

Answering that question required admitting something that might upset her. Might send her running for the hills. "I...I've always had...anger issues." Taking a few breaths to center himself, he continued, "My parents didn't know what to do with me. When mom got a job in another state...it was...easier...to leave me behind."

Worried about what he might see if he looked at her face, he shut his eyes and kept going, "Mark had some experience with...*helping*...angry people. Leaving me with him was the..." pain at the memory of the rejection by his parents coursed through him as he finished the sentence, "logical choice."

Sitting there was too much. His eyes opened, but he still couldn't look at her. Getting up, he sat at the piano, resting his fingers on the keys. There was something comforting about the way they felt against his fingertips. "Mark's never been married and doesn't have kids. I became the de facto pastor's kid." His fingers ran up and down the keyboard, playing a few scales before he added, "Not a position I'd recommend for an angry kid. Then again, I'm not sure I'd recommend it for any kid."

He couldn't talk anymore. Memories were stirring up too much pain, too much rage. Letting muscle memory take over, he let his fingers be free, and music poured out. Exercises he'd learned years earlier filled the apartment. Slowly, he was able to bring the anguish back down to a bearable level. Stopping, he stared at the keys and said, "I had to learn how...how to hide what I felt. What I thought. God forbid that anyone in the congregation see I was a human being. I was just a kid who wasn't allowed to be a kid." The words were full of bitterness.

His elbows rested on the music stand above the keyboard. He pressed his forehead against his open palms, "The word *no* had to leave my vocabulary. I was told what I was going to do, when I was going to do it, and it was never optional. It didn't take me long to learn it was best to obey without question."

Sitting up straighter, his fingers dropped back to the keyboard. More scales played. When he stopped again, he continued, "Mark had this idea I was destined to follow in his footsteps and go into ministry. I found myself placed in leadership positions that I didn't want and shouldn't have been in. I...I coped by trying to be what he and everyone else expected. I did what I was told. Said what I was supposed to, even when I wasn't sure if I believed or agreed with what was coming out of my mouth."

Shame washed over him, "The more...more I parroted back what everyone wanted to hear...the more it became a part of me. I can't honestly say if I ever truly believed what I was saying. Mostly, I just felt...confused, and asking questions was unacceptable."

He played more. His fingers moved faster and faster as if the speed would somehow make it all better. A sound distracted him. Glancing to his right, he was surprised to see Zoe had moved to the chair he'd brought from the table. "This okay?" she asked quietly.

Having her so close didn't raise his anxiety like he would've expected. Rather, it was soothing having her right there. "Yeah."

"You don't have to tell me everything today. I can tell this is hard for you." Her voice was as calming as her presence.

One of his elbows rested against the music stand. Leaning his head against his fist, he studied her, "Is this too much for you?"

She shook her head, "No."

"You can tell me if it is."

Her hand reached out and pushed his hair back out of his eyes. "I know."

He felt the wetness on his cheeks before realizing there were tears. Another wave of shame crashed over him as he squeezed his eyes shut. He didn't want her to see how pathetically weak he truly was.

Her hand was soft against his face, and his eyes flew open. She swiped away some of the tears with her thumb. His voice was thick as he apologized, "I'm sorry."

Her smile was tender, "For what? Being human?"

He reached up and covered the one on his cheek with his free hand. When was the last time someone had touched him so comfortingly? He searched his memory and realized it had been his mother when he'd been a very small child. That was before his anger had grown so wild that every interaction with his parents was fraught with tension. He had scared them, a fact that was reinforced with every look, every leary touch they gave him. That had been his first indication that he was a monster. Completely unlovable and absolutely terrifying.

"Liam?"

He focused on her, realizing just how close she was. A shaky sigh escaped him, "I think I need a break."

"I think that's a good idea," she agreed.

He dropped his hand and turned away. Her hand left his face, and he missed her touch as soon as it was gone. She sat quietly while he rifled through the books stacked on the piano. Returning to the book he'd used earlier when she'd asked him to play, he flipped to a song and asked, "Know this one?"

"Kind of."

He placed the book on the stand, "Will you sing?"

"I can't promise it'll be good, but I will...if you want."

Beginning to play, he told her, "I do."

Her voice blended with his playing. It had been so long since he'd accompanied anyone, and he'd certainly never accompanied anyone that he felt he meshed with so well. It was as if she and he were meant to make music together. There was a purity to what they were doing. It almost made him feel like he could be a better person than he knew he was.

Questions flooded his mind. Why was she still there? How was she able to sit and listen to his pain and bitterness and not immediately make a run for it? What would be the thing that would be too much?

He kept playing. Though he didn't verbalize it, she figured out he would nod when it was time to turn the page. One song led to another. Tears still occasionally trickled down his cheeks, but he made no effort to stop them. Eventually, his fingers grew clumsy as fatigue filled him. Notes were missed, and he suddenly came to a stop mid-song.

Zoe's hand cautiously went on top of his, "What do you need?"

He gazed at their hands. How could she bear to touch him? The previous night's lack of sleep combined with all the emotional stress he'd been experiencing. His answer was short and simple, "A nap."

She stood and tugged at his hand, "You and me both."

He looked up into her eyes, "What are you…?"

She tugged again, "C'mon."

He stood and followed her the few feet back to the couch. Sinking onto it, he watched as she moved a footrest so he could stretch out. She settled against his side, just like she had on Christmas weekend. He wrapped his arms around her, holding her as tight and close as he dared. Yawning, his eyes slid shut, and sleep took over.

The girl's eyes were terrified. The older man shot him a dirty look. Liam took in the tableau in front of him. Horror flooded his entire being.

He'd been lied to.

How many times? How many people had been hurt because he'd believed that bastard's lies? Bile filled his mouth as the full weight of the truth plowed into him.

Liam's eyes flew open. His stomach was rolling. Bolting off the couch, he made a mad dash for the bathroom, managing to get there in the nick of time. He sank to the floor and let go. After, he brushed his teeth and washed his face.

Leaving the bathroom, he found Zoe leaning against the hallway wall, her face pinched with worry. She looked relieved when she saw him, "Are you okay?"

Looking down at her, his voice soft, he said, "I'm sorry. I didn't mean to frighten you."

She shook her head, "You didn't. Not really. Bad dream?"

Surprised, he asked, "How did you know?"

She walked back to the living room, and he followed, listening as she explained, "You got really restless, and then you were up and running for the bathroom. Sorry, but the sounds were kind of hard to ignore."

Retrieving the water bottle, he took a drink. Glancing out the window, he noticed it had grown dark. How long had he been asleep? He pulled out his phone and saw it was past six. Turning to Zoe, he asked, "Are you hungry?"

She nodded, "Little bit. Breakfast was a while ago."

"What do you want?"

"I'm open to suggestions," she replied.

He was too tired to even think about trying to cook. Tossing his phone to her, he said, "Order something. Go with delivery."

Her brow furrowed, "You sure?"

He collapsed back onto the couch, "Yeah. I don't care what you pick. Just get something."

A few minutes later, she returned his phone, "It'll be here in forty minutes."

Even with the nap, he was still exhausted. Therapy and baring his soul to Zoe all in the same day had taken far more out of him than he'd expected. He still needed to tell her so much, but it would have to wait for later.

She sat beside him, "Want to talk about the dream, or have you already forgotten it?"

He rolled his head to his shoulder, meeting her eyes, "I haven't forgotten it, but I'm not up for talking about it right now."

"Okay."

He was grateful she didn't push for more, "Thanks." Pointing toward the coffee table, "Remote's there if you want to watch something."

She began to browse her options and, after several minutes, settled on something he'd never have picked in a million years. He was indignant, "This is a show for toddlers."

Her sweet smile soothed some of his irritation, "Give it a chance, okay? I think it'll help."

Unconvinced, he raised an eyebrow, "How?"

Lightly patting his arm, she said, "Just watch. It's helped me. I wouldn't suggest it if it hadn't."

His attention shifted to the show. What could she possibly be thinking? He felt movement beside him as the theme song played. His eyes shifted to see Zoe bouncing happily while singing along to the music. Baffled, he alternated between watching her and the screen. Cartoon dogs were going to help? Help with what?

They'd watched a few episodes by the time the food was delivered. Calmness had settled over him. Even more calm than he felt just being around Zoe. He was re-evaluating his initial thoughts about her choice as he paused the show and joined her at the table.

"Hope this is okay," she said as he perused what she'd ordered.

A few boxes of Thai food sat there, and he assured her, "This is fine."

As they began to eat, she asked, "So, was I right?"

"About?" He knew exactly what she was referring to but wanted to buy time since he wasn't quite ready to acknowledge he'd been wrong.

"The show."

He ate a mouthful of mango-fried rice before replying, "It's not what I expected."

"Is that your way of saying that you like it but don't actually want to admit it?" Amusement radiated from her.

"If you tell anyone, I'll deny it."

"Ha! I'm right!" she giggled with glee.

"I will acknowledge that I may have misjudged it."

She shook her head, still laughing, "Yup, you like it. I bet Muffin speaks to you."

He rolled his eyes "In any other context, that sentence would make absolutely no sense."

"Can I call you Muffin?"

"If I say no, is that going to stop you?" he asked in mock exasperation.

She ate a spring roll, asking, "If I promise not to do it around anyone else, can I?"

He grudgingly gave in, "Fine."

"Yes!" she made a fist and pulled it in victory.

"You're five," he informed her.

"Whatever you say, Muffin."

Fifteen

Zoe

She watched Liam with concern. Even with the nap, he looked like he was about to drop. The emotional toll of the afternoon was evident, and whatever he'd dreamt had been bad. Saying he'd grown restless had been an understatement. His mumbling had woken her. It was a good thing it had. Otherwise, she wouldn't have been able to duck out of the way when he began to thrash.

He ate slowly. At one point, he paused and looked at her, "I'm not sure I'm up to driving you back to your place tonight. You can borrow my car if you want to go home."

There was no fucking way she was going to leave him alone in his current condition. She shook her head, "I don't think you should be alone right now."

Was that relief that momentarily flashed in his eyes? He nodded, "Okay."

"When do you have to be to work tomorrow?" They'd never discussed his job, which, in retrospect, was a little strange.

His eyes dropped to the box of food in front of him. Nearly a minute passed with him saying nothing, just staring at the fried rice. She finally asked, "What aren't you telling me?" When he still didn't answer, she nudged, "C'mon, Muffin, talk to me."

That finally got a response. He rolled his eyes, but she could tell he wasn't too annoyed. He was anxious, though, and she found that a bit odd. What kind of job did he have that would make him so cagey?

He replied stiffly, "I don't have a job." Sighing, he added, "I'll explain later. I can't get into it now."

"Okay."

He closed the box and pushed it away, "I think I'm done."

She was getting full as well, so she went ahead and closed her box, too. Picking them up, she put them away in the fridge. Closing the fridge door, she turned and found Liam standing, staring at the couch. He told her, "You can take the bed. I'll sleep out here."

"Don't be ridiculous. Sleep in your bed. Out of the two of us, I'm the one who can actually lay down on it comfortably."

He studied her for a moment, "You sure?"

She nodded, "Yes. Go to bed. We're screwed if you collapse 'cause I doubt I can move you."

He huffed out a laugh and wandered back to his room. She was filled with a mix of relief and loneliness as she watched him disappear. Apart from his nightmare, the nap had been wonderful. It had been the first restful sleep she'd had since Christmas. That morning, at breakfast, she'd very nearly admitted that he was what she needed to get sleep. That was too dangerous to tell him since she still wasn't sure where they stood with each other.

Hitting play, she dropped the volume, turned off the lights, and settled onto the couch. Her thoughts were racing. Liam had shared some very personal things with her. Surely, he wouldn't be doing that unless he thought something was between them. Something more than friendship. Then again, he didn't seem to have many, if any, friends. He'd certainly never mentioned any.

She was worried. It was entirely possible she was completely misreading his signals. Growing up, she'd learned quickly how to sense people's emotions. It was necessary to survive living with Fred. Unfortunately, there was a difference between sensing emotions and knowing how to read between the lines to know people's intentions.

Pulling the blanket from the back of the couch, she tossed it over herself and curled up on her side. Two days earlier, Alex had made that comment about her falling for Liam. Less than twenty-four hours earlier, she and Liam had kissed. It had been an intense, emotional weekend. No wonder Liam was exhausted. She certainly was, and she hadn't been the one sharing her life story.

Shhh...sweetheart...it's okay...you're not alone...I'm right here...I've got you...you're safe...

The voice pulled her toward the surface. With a gasp, she woke from whatever level of hell her subconscious had trapped her in. Blinking uncertainly, she rapidly tried to figure out what was happening. Arms were holding her. A broad chest was in front of her. She was in a room she couldn't quite place. The pieces started to come together.

Her body shook. Her face was wet, whether with sweat or tears, she wasn't sure. Possibly a combination of both. She leaned against Liam's chest, comforted by how solid, safe, and warm he was. Her voice trembled, "It happened again, didn't it?"

"Mm-hm."

She wrapped her arms around his torso. "Please..." the request faded to nothing. She couldn't ask it. He would say no, and she knew she couldn't handle that.

"Please what, sweetheart?" The words floated down to her ears from where he rested his cheek against her head.

She choked back a few tears, "Don't...leave...me alone."

"Never," he murmured.

"Please," she knew she was begging. The thought of being alone again was terrifying.

To her horror, he dropped his arms. She held on tight, even as he gently said, "Zoe, let go."

"You said you wouldn't leave me alone!" she couldn't keep the panic out of her voice.

"I won't. I promise. Give me your hand."

Slowly, she released her tight hold on him and let him take her hand. He gazed down at her, and she saw him swallow something invisible. Reaching out with his free hand, he tenderly stroked her cheek as he told her, "We both won't fit on the couch. Bed okay?"

She hesitated, chewing her lip, "Bed?"

He nodded, "You need sleep, not just little naps on the couch. Nothing is going to happen that you don't want, I promise. Do you trust me?"

She looked into his eyes. Did she trust him? He'd given her no reason not to, and all evidence led her to believe he trusted her. After a few seconds of hesitation, she nodded, "Yeah."

He shut the tv off and led her to the bedroom. "I'm gonna turn on the light, okay?"

"Sure." What the hell was she doing? Was she really about to crawl into bed with this man?

Yes. Yes, she was.

The light illuminated the room, and she glanced around blearily. She watched as he went to the bed and moved a blanket to make a barrier in the middle. When he finished, she crawled onto the nearest side. Slipping under the covers, she curled up under the warm bedding. The light was turned off, and seconds later, the mattress moved the tiniest bit as he lay down on the other side.

She was grateful for the blanket wall, but she wanted him closer. He was too far away. "Liam?"

"Hmmm?" the reply was sleepy.

"Hold me?"

He didn't move. A few seconds passed before she heard, "You sure?"

"Please," the word was almost a whisper.

The sheets rustled, and a moment later, she felt his arm go around her abdomen. He pulled her a little closer, the barrier still between their bodies. Even so, she could still feel the warmth and solid wall of his chest against her back. She moved her arm so she could rest her hand on top of his.

Before sleep reclaimed her, the last thing she thought was how right it felt being there like that with him.

Zoe woke to see the room bathed in soft early morning sunlight. At some point, she had turned in her sleep and was now facing Liam. He was still asleep, his arm draped over her middle and his hand on her back. His face was relaxed. No tension, no sadness. Just peace.

Alex's words ran through her mind. Despite her denial that night, she knew her friend wasn't wrong. She was falling for Liam. His vulnerability and honesty the previous afternoon had only made her fall harder.

It was all so new. Feeling attracted to another person was an unfamiliar sensation. Liam's admission made her wonder if he was also experiencing everything for the first time. It seemed nearly impossible for them to find themselves together in the same boat.

The hand on her back moved, and she saw Liam's eyes slowly open halfway. He focused on her face, and a drowsy smile appeared. "You're really here. I didn't dream it," his voice dripped with sleep.

"Yup, not a dream."

"Were you able to get any sleep?" he asked.

She nodded, "I was."

"Good." His eyes closed, and as he drifted off, she heard him murmur, "I sleep better when you're with me."

She let him pull her closer and snuggled against him, feeling his breathing grow deep and even. He was fast asleep, but she was wide awake and didn't feel like getting out of bed was an option. Then again, she didn't want to. It was pleasant lying there in the quiet with him.

Her eyes traveled around the parts of the room she could see from her vantage point. Beside the window stood a tall bookshelf. It was filled with all kinds of books. She wondered if he'd let her browse it. The way he was positioned, she couldn't see what was on his nightstand, apart from the lampshade she could see peeking over his shoulder. Everything was tidy and nice. It was impossible to ignore that Liam was well-off. Maybe that's why he didn't have a job. Maybe he didn't need one.

Normally, people with money made her feel uncomfortable. It was a reminder of just how little she truly had. Liam hadn't ever made her feel that way. He'd been incredibly generous but didn't flaunt what he had.

I'm not good for much. That's what he'd said in her kitchen. He had such a low view of himself. He'd told her he wasn't a good person, and even the day before when she'd complimented his looks, he'd responded in a way that told her he didn't see himself in a good light. She wondered what people had said to him over the years to make him think things like that about himself.

Based on what she'd learned about him, it was obvious they had very different backgrounds, but at the same time, there were some similarities. They'd both been abandoned by their parents. He'd just been left with another family member rather than a virtual stranger. Not that it made the pain of rejection any less brutal. Zoe felt bad because she envied Liam a little. He had been older; he had clearer memories of his parents. Her recollections were little more than images of the man and woman who had left her behind. She didn't even know why. It wasn't something Fred had ever bothered to share with her, and the only time she'd asked, he'd told her to shut up.

After a while, Liam was sleeping deeply, and she slowly slipped out of his arms. He didn't react as she did, so she hoped he'd be able to stay asleep until she returned. She left the bed and ran to the bathroom as quietly as she could. Once finished, she collected her phone from where she'd left it plugged in. She scrolled through her notifications as she returned to the bed.

To her relief, Liam was still asleep. Carefully, she maneuvered herself back into the same position she'd been in before. Holding her phone, she opened her texts to reply to the one Alex had sent.

Dahlia's annoyed with you.

Why?

You haven't responded to her news yet. Will you be home tonight or staying with your boyfriend again?

A. What news? B. Don't know. Probably? C. He's not my boyfriend.

Didn't you get her text?

She opened her texts from Dahlia; there was nothing since Friday night. She texted a screenshot to Alex.

She's moving out. Lily needs her back home.

This is all I've got. What's her news?

Inwardly, she groaned. If Dahlia moved out, they'd need to find another roommate. Until they did, Zoe and Alex would have to pay more rent.

Any idea how soon?

She's packing right now.

Shit. She texted the screenshot to Dahlia.

Alex told me your news. I'm sorry. Your text never arrived. Is everything okay?

It was a few minutes before she received an answer.

I didn't know. Sorry for being pissed. Lily isn't doing very well, so I'm headed home to Cheyenne.

That sucks. I'm gonna miss you. I hope she gets better.

"Bored?"

Zoe glanced up from her phone to see Liam watching her with curiosity. She shook her head, "Just checking in with my roommates." Turning the screen off, she rolled over and placed the phone on the nightstand.

"Everything okay?"

She sighed and, rolling back to face him, "Not really. Dahlia's sister isn't doing well, so Dahlia is packing up right now to move back home. Which sucks for her but also for Alex and I. Rent is about to increase dramatically for both of us. I have to find a job and soon."

He gently rubbed her back, "Any leads?"

"People aren't exactly lining up to hire a high school drop-out. I'm just gonna have to suck it up and beg Fred for my job back. If he hasn't already filled it, that is."

Liam's hand stopped moving, "No."

She swallowed hard, fighting back the tears that threatened, "Yes. It'll suck, but at least I'll be able to mostly cover my bills until I find something better."

He sighed, "I'll help you cover your bills. We'll find you another job. You deserve better than returning to an abuser."

She backed away from him, shaking her head, "No. I'm not going to put myself in debt to you just so I can avoid that asshole."

Escaping his hold she got out of the bed, but stopped when she heard him say, "Zoe, wait."

She turned back and saw he was sitting up, "What?"

"You won't owe me anything."

She rolled her eyes, "Sure, I won't. You realize that every time I'd see you, I'd spend the entire time doing mental math trying to figure out how soon I can pay off what I owe."

He looked at her quizzically, "It wouldn't be a loan. I don't want you to pay me back."

Her stomach tightened as anger began to fill her, "So what, you're just gonna give me the money and expect nothing in return? Do you think I was born yesterday? I may not have a ton of life experience, but I have enough to avoid making naive mistakes like that."

She turned and walked out of the room. The sound of Liam leaving the bed and following her was loud. She wasn't surprised when she heard him behind her, sounding slightly frustrated, "Would you just stop for a minute and listen to me?"

Frustrated, she snapped, "Can you just take me home? Please?"

Several seconds passed before he quietly asked, "Why won't you let me help you?"

Sixteen

Liam

Everything had been going well. At least, that's what he thought. Zoe had seemed okay being with him, and then he offered to do something that just made sense, and she'd gotten angry with him. Really angry. She hadn't spoken to him the entire drive back to her house. When she got out, she slammed the car door so hard he felt like he'd been slapped.

Strangely, he wasn't angry. Frustrated and confused, but not angry.

He was grateful that Dr. Constance had scheduled him for another appointment that afternoon. By the time he reached her office, he'd decided that if Zoe continued to refuse the money, he would just give it to Alex without telling her. She was being stubborn over something stupid.

"Liam, at any point in your life, have you experienced financial insecurity?" Dr. Constance asked after he wrapped up his recap of the events following his last session. He had finished by telling her about the fight.

Confusion filled him, "What do you mean?"

"Have you ever had to pick which bills to pay and which not to pay because the money isn't there for all of them? Have you ever had to live on ramen because it's the only thing your grocery budget will allow for? Have you ever been worried about losing your home because you're behind on rent? What about not going to the doctor because you can't afford it and don't have insurance? When you were a child, did you always have everything you needed physically, like healthy food and a good winter coat?"

He tried to process her list of questions. In his mind, he could see Zoe in her kitchen telling him *Not the first time I've settled for something I don't want. Won't be the last.* It was true. He'd never had to do that. Never had to worry about going without. "Why won't she let me help her? I can and I will. I just need her to let me."

"You said she was worried about paying you back."

"Which I told her she wouldn't have to do. I don't want her to pay me back. I just want to take care of her. What is the point of having money if I can't do something good with it?" His frustration grew, "If we were married, she wouldn't have to want for anything ever again, and we wouldn't have had this stupid fight."

Dr. Constance studied him for a good long while before asking, "Are you planning to propose to her?"

"I shouldn't have said that," he muttered.

"I'm not interested in shoulds. Why did you say it?"

Zoe was all he could think about. The way her hand had felt on his face when he'd cried. The way her voice had sounded when she called him *Muffin*. He could see how bright her eyes had been when she laughed and how they'd flashed when she'd been furious. His voice was rough when he finally admitted, "I love her, and I'd marry her today if she'd let me."

Dr. Constance sat back in her chair, still giving him that careful appraising look, "Liam, I'm glad that you've found someone you connect with and have been able to start opening up to. I think it's wonderful that you care about her so much that you want to make sure that she's safe and wanting for nothing.

That speaks volumes about your character.

"I won't tell you not to propose, but I do think that waiting a bit might be a good idea. As we discussed yesterday, this is all very new for you. Marriage is a huge commitment and not one to rush into because it seems like the best immediate solution."

She offered him a gentle smile as she continued, "Liam, I've been married for thirty-two years. I can tell you from personal experience that marriage comes with all kinds of unexpected challenges. There is no guarantee that something won't happen to empty your bank account. If the main reason you want to marry her is because of this financial situation, then I'd suggest taking a step back and re-evaluating."

"If she's going to insist on being stubborn, I'm just going to give her roommate the money, and then she'll have to be okay with it."

Was it possible that there was disappointment in Dr. Constance's eyes? She actually sighed, "Liam, do you remember when we discussed that consent is clearly important to Zoe?"

He nodded but said nothing.

The doctor leaned forward, "She told you no about the money. If you go behind her back like that, you'll possibly destroy whatever trust she has given you. Is that what you want?"

He glared, "What am I supposed to do? Let her starve and lose the roof over her head?"

Her voice gentled, "Of course not. But right now, it sounds like you're both running on exhaustion and strong emotions. Take a step back and breathe. You could try asking her how you can be helpful. She's an adult. This is her life. You have to let her be the one in control of it. You can be there for her without taking away her independence."

Three hours at the piano, and he didn't feel any better. While he understood what Dr. Constance had said, he was still frustrated. If she was right, his hands were tied. He couldn't do anything to help unless Zoe gave permission. If he just stepped in and took care of things, he might lose her completely. Why did she have to be so damn stubborn?

No new messages were waiting when he checked his phone while reheating the leftover Thai. Should he text her? Was he supposed to wait for her to text him? And if he was, how long was he supposed to wait? He decided to give her until the next morning, and if he still hadn't heard from her, he'd check in.

Drained from therapy, he decided to go to bed early. He quickly made the unpleasant discovery that since he now knew what it was like to have Zoe in bed with him, sleep was impossible without her there. What was he going to do if she was done with him?

Lying in the dark, he stared at the ceiling, memories of the night before playing. Her screams had yanked him from sleep. Fear had radiated from her, but of what, he had no idea. What if she had night terrors again, and he wasn't there to comfort her? *She had them long before you entered her life, and she'll continue having them whether you're there or not.*

He rolled onto his side and watched the numbers on his clock tick by slower than molasses in January. Sleep remained nonexistent. He kept thinking about Zoe. Life had been so much less complicated before he'd met her. Then again, before they'd met, his life had completely sucked. Complicated as things might be, life sucked significantly less with her in it.

By the time one a.m. arrived, he said, "Fuck it," and picked up his phone, intending to text her. No sooner was the phone in his hand than it began to ring. Zoe's name populated on the screen, and he answered immediately, "Zoe?"

"Liam?" her voice was shaky.

He was already out of bed and grabbing clothes as he asked, "Are you okay?"

She didn't immediately answer. There was sniffling from her end, and he paused what he was doing. Sitting on the edge of the bed, he tried again, "Sweetheart, what's wrong?"

In between more sniffles, he heard, "I...can't...sleep."

That got him moving again, "I'll be there in ten. Okay?"

"Okay."

"Figure out if you want me to stay there or if you want to come back here." He pulled his shirt on and headed out of the bedroom, "Do you need me to stay on the phone until I get there?"

She was quiet, and he put his shoes and jacket on while waiting for an answer. His hand was on the door handle when she said, "Wait. No, don't...don't come over. I shouldn't have...called. I'm sorry for waking you up."

He paused and leaned his forehead against the door, "Do you really not want me to come over?"

"I..." There were tears in her voice, and he wished he was there to wipe them all away. "I..."

Her words faded, and when she added nothing else, he told her, "I was picking up my phone to text you when you called. I can't sleep either. So, unless you genuinely don't want me to come over, I'll be there soon."

As he headed toward his car, he heard her say, "Okay," and hang up.

Once he pulled into her driveway, he texted to let her know.

Am I coming in or are you coming out?

I'll be there in a minute.

That sounded like they were headed back to his place. A fact that was confirmed when she walked out of the house with a duffle bag. She got in, dropped the bag on the floor, and turned to him. He was so relieved to see her that he had to stop himself from reaching for her. It was possible she wouldn't want to be touched, and he wasn't sure if she was still upset with him. She was the one who reached out and took his hand. Squeezing it, she said, "Thank you."

He squeezed back, "Of course. Ready to go?"

"Please. Get me out of here."

Zoe was silent for a few minutes, but as they approached his apartment building, she said, "I'm sorry I got so angry this morning."

He glanced at her, "I've been informed that I need to remember that this is your life, and I need to let you be in control of it. That I should've asked you what you'd like me to do to be helpful, not just tell you what I was going to do."

"Whoever told you that sounds awful smart," her voice was a little lighter.

"They are."

"Though, now I'm a little worried about who you're talking about me with," her voice had taken on a hint of anxiety.

He shook his head, "Don't be. She's very discreet."

"You're not making this sound better." There was no question about it; she was definitely anxious.

He pulled into his parking spot, turned off the ignition, and explained, "She's my therapist."

Zoe took in that information, and some of the anxiety melted from her face, "Oh. Okay."

In the apartment, she dropped her bag just inside the bedroom door. She pulled her hoodie off and made a beeline for the bed. Before following her, he detoured to the bathroom to change into his pajamas. He found her curled up, buried under the blankets, when he entered the room. Turning off the light, he joined her. She moved closer to him, resting her back against his chest as he wrapped his arm around her middle to hold her close.

"So, you're in therapy," she said after a few seconds.

"I was going to tell you."

Her hand went on top of his, "What's it like?"

"Awful." He laughed a little, "I suppose that means it's working."

"Do you go every Monday?"

He shook his head, "No. Wednesdays are my normal day. This week has been...an exception."

"How so?"

He hesitated a moment before replying but decided she might as well know. No secrets from her. That's what he'd been promising himself. "I went on Sunday and Monday."

She pointed out, "Sunday was a holiday."

"It was."

"Does she normally see patients on weekends and holidays?"

"No," he answered.

"Then why...?" He felt her shake her head, "Sorry, I shouldn't be making you talk about it."

He pressed a kiss against her hair, "It's okay. I told you to ask me what you want to know."

"That was about your past," she replied.

Why was it so easy to talk to her like this? "I'm in therapy because of my past. You can ask me about whatever; no exceptions. I'll answer. My life...it's been full of keeping secrets. I...I can't do that anymore. Especially not...with you."

She moved in his arms to face him. The room was mostly dark. The streetlights outside gave a small amount of light. His eyes had adjusted enough that he could mostly make out her face. His hand rested against her back. One of hers lifted and pushed his hair back a little before moving down and going against his chest. She studied his face and asked quietly, "Liam?"

"Yes?"

"What am I to you?"

He stared at her. Her eyes were wide open, but it was too dark to get a good read on what she was thinking. He'd told her to ask whatever, and she certainly had. His hand moved from her back, and he lightly touched her cheek. His voice was husky when he finally replied, "Everything."

Seventeen

Zoe

She slept deeply. When she woke, the sun was bright. She felt better than she had in a long time.

The day before had been awful. She'd been so incredibly angry with Liam. By the time he'd dropped her at home, she'd been completely miserable. Considering that he'd told her he had anger issues, she was shocked he'd let her be so mad and hadn't responded in kind. She was relieved because she had no desire to see him angry. *But if we do this, I will. Can I handle that?* That was a question she'd have to answer sooner rather than later.

The rest of the day had been a complete shitshow. By the middle of the night, she'd been at her wit's end. Unable to sleep, her loneliness had been overwhelming. She needed him.

Everything. That's what he'd told her she was. The answer hadn't been what she'd expected. Then again, she wasn't sure what she'd expected. It was strange because when he answered her question like that, she realized that if he had asked her that question, that would have been her answer about him. She'd never believed in soulmates, but the connection she felt with Liam was unlike any she'd ever experienced. There were moments when it seemed they could read each other's minds. They hadn't known each other long, yet somehow, it felt like she'd always known him. Being with him felt like she finally fit somewhere. Like she belonged.

She stretched a little and heard a huff of a laugh near her ear, "Wondered when you were gonna wake up."

"Do I even want to know what time it is?"

"It's still morning if that's what you're worried about," he replied.

Her stomach picked that moment to growl, "I think I need breakfast."

"Preferences?"

"Toast?"

"That's it?" he asked, a note of surprise in his voice.

"I wouldn't turn down applesauce."

Another quiet laugh, "Toast and applesauce. I think I can manage that."

"You do have to let go of me," she informed him.

He squeezed just a smidge, then relaxed his hold, "Fine."

She sat up and turned to watch him. He was looking at her, and she noticed he didn't look nearly as tense and sad as usual. He almost looked...happy wasn't the right word...maybe content?

He quirked an eyebrow at her, "What?"

"You look less miserable than usual."

He gazed at her, "I feel less miserable than usual."

She could feel her cheeks heat and turned away. Sliding off the bed, she retrieved her bag from where she'd dropped it the night before. Placing it on the bed, she dug out clothes for the day. Liam left the room, closing the bedroom door behind him. She appreciated the privacy and quickly got changed.

He was at the kitchen counter when she emerged. Bread, butter, and both strawberry and blackberry jam sat in front of him. He met her eyes, "Afraid I'm out of applesauce, but I can pick some up the next time I'm at the store."

"No worries. Toast is fine." She smiled at him, and he returned her smile. The dimples that formed on his face made her feel weird inside. A good weird. Turned out she liked them quite a lot.

He pulled a plate from the cupboard and a knife from the drawer. As he placed them next to the bread, he said, "I assume you know how to make toast."

She laughed, "Yes, I unlocked the secrets of the toaster many years ago."

Still smiling, he headed to the bedroom. The door shut, and she set about making her breakfast. "Do you want any?" she called out.

The door opened a crack, "Depends. How many people have survived your cooking?"

"To date? All of them. Granted, there haven't been that many who've gotten to experience it."

Her reply was met with a chuckle, "Go ahead and fix yours. I'll take care of mine when I get back out there." The door shut, and she was left staring at the toaster.

While she waited, her thoughts drifted to the day before. She would have to tell him what had happened, and she hoped it wouldn't lead to another fight. He'd seemed much more reasonable at one a.m. that morning than at nine a.m. the previous morning.

The toast popped up, and she buttered it. For a few seconds, she debated the jam but ultimately decided against it, just wanting the comforting flavor of buttered toast. Moving to the table, she saw Liam come out of the bedroom.

While he waited for his toast, he leaned against the counter and looked at her, "How are you?"

She took a bite of the crust, ate it, and then answered, "Okay." Biting her lip, she added, "We need to talk."

He teased, "I thought that was my line."

That made her smile a little, "You're welcome to take it back once we get through my thing."

He watched as she continued eating, a slightly puzzled look taking over his features. His toast popped, and after applying butter and blackberry jam, he joined her at the table, asking, "Do you always do that?"

"Do what?"

"Eat your crusts first."

She glanced at the second piece of toast she was now holding. She'd eaten it so that only the crustless bread remained to be consumed. "I know it's weird. I can't help it. For some reason, my brain thinks that's the correct way to eat bread." He nodded, a contemplative look on his face. It was a little unnerving how he observed her, and she set the piece down on the plate, "What is it?"

"You have very specific ways you do things."

Her brow furrowed, "What are you talking about?"

He ate a mouthful before replying, "On Saturdays, you come into the studio and follow the same pattern every time. Right down to the placement of your coffee and where the microphone is set."

She blew out a breath, "Yeah. It's...I don't know if this'll make sense, but...my brain says I have to do things in very particular ways. Otherwise, I'm doing it wrong."

"Has it always been that way?" the question was more curious than judgmental.

Picking up her toast, she ate a few more bites. She felt very self-conscious as she realized he was watching her eat it in a clockwise pattern. Swallowing, she replied, "I guess so. I can't do it wrong, or I'll..." What made sense in her head suddenly sounded incredibly stupid as she tried to say it aloud.

"You'll what?" Good lord, the man had become quite chatty. She didn't mind, though; she liked hearing him talk.

Her eyes shut. He'd been open with her; the least she could do was try to be just as open. "If I do it wrong...I'll...I'll get in trouble." Her eyes opened, and she gave him a sad smile, "And yes, I do realize how stupid that sounds."

He looked confused, "You'll get in trouble for eating toast wrong?"

She looked away, "Yes. Can we please not talk about this anymore?"

"Okay."

Relieved, she finished off her toast and turned her attention back to him. He was still watching her, and she couldn't quite figure out what that expression on his face meant. Curiosity? Worry? Perplexed? Her mind pulled her back to the thing she had to talk to him about, and she asked, "Did you really mean it about letting me tell you how you can be helpful?"

He nodded, "What do you need me to do?"

Her eyes dropped to the table, and she began to pick at her thumb cuticle. It was one of her nervous go-tos. She realized he had noticed when his hand went over hers, halting the movement. "Zoe, what is it?" his voice was soft.

She stared at his hand and, after a deep breath, relayed what had happened, "Yesterday...yesterday morning. After I got home." She moved one of her hands out from underneath his and rubbed her forehead, trying to disperse the tension that was gathering. Her eyes shut, and she kept going, "When Alex...when he told Dante that Dahlia is moving out...Dante asked him to move in."

The tension was getting more painful, and she winced, "I'm going to have no roommates, and I can't afford my rent right now, let alone take on their shares. And getting new roomies off Craigslist scares me. And...and...I just feel super screwed. I need somewhere to live and..." she swallowed hard, "right now my car is the option. Which I can't handle thinking about...and I know. *I know* exactly how this sounds after our fight yesterday, but is there even the tiniest chance you'd want a roomie until I can find another place? I can't pay much in rent, but I'll do what I can, and I swear I'm really not that bad of a cook and–"

"Yes." He cut her off with one simple word.

Despite his answer, her anxiety was spiraling, "It won't be long, I promise. I'll be out of your hair as soon as I can find a job and a new place...I swear you'll barely notice I'm here, you can put me in a closet for all I care, and...and..."

A finger lifted her chin, and she opened her eyes to see Liam looking at her with an expression as soft as his voice. "I want to notice that you're here. I want you to take up space. I want *you* here." His lips formed the smallest smile, "And if you try to pay even one dime in rent, I'll hand it right back to you."

She could feel her lips trembling, "Are you...are you sure?"

"When do you have to be moved out by?"

"The fifteenth." She sighed, "Are you absolutely sure?"

"Yes."

"You're sure you're sure? I know what a huge ask this is. You can say no. I'll figure out something else, I promise. I feel like I'm invading your life. And–"

"Oh, for fuck's sake," his voice held a hint of exasperation mixed with mild amusement, "Sweetheart, would you just move in with me? I sleep better when you're with me, and it would be much easier if you were here rather than somewhere else."

He'd never asked if he could call her the endearment, and she knew it wasn't the first time he'd done it, but she didn't mind. She liked it, though it did make a funny feeling happen in her stomach whenever he said it. The same funny feeling she got when she saw his dimples.

To her surprise, he'd taken her request for a place to stay in stride. As calmly as if she'd asked him for a piece of gum. Though, what she'd intended to be a brief stay was apparently going to be a bit more permanent. And that should freak her out. It really should. But it didn't.

After they ate and the dishes went into the dishwasher, she retrieved her ancient laptop from her bag and asked for the wifi password, which he quickly supplied. She spent the next few hours submitting applications for any job she might qualify for, though nearly all wanted applicants to have at least a high school diploma.

She didn't even have her GED. High school had stopped being part of her life in tenth grade. Her grades had been abysmal, and she couldn't seem to raise them. Hours would be spent studying, but as soon as she sat down to take a test, everything she thought she knew would evaporate. It didn't help that when she wasn't at school, all her time was spent working. When Fred discovered she was failing all of her classes, he'd strongly encouraged...more like ordered...her to drop out and start working at the shop full-time. *Time to start paying me back.* He'd liked to remind her just how much of a burden she'd been on his life.

Liam was right. She couldn't go back. Fred was abusive. True, he'd never harmed her physically, but the emotional and verbal abuse had been excessive. That was why there were so many specific rules she made herself follow. Even down to how she ate toast. If she didn't follow her rules, she would face even more abuse.

She blinked and realized she'd been staring at the same job posting for at least five minutes while her thoughts wandered. Liam was sitting across the table, working on something on his laptop. She watched him surreptitiously, trying to decide if they were about to do the stupidest thing either of them possibly could.

"You're staring."

He hadn't even looked up. How could he possibly know? "No, I'm thinking. You just happen to be sitting where my thinking stare is focused."

"Oh really?" he still hadn't looked up, and she was tempted to throw something in his general direction to see if he'd catch it or let it bounce off his head.

She stood and stretched. Her head ached a little from staring at the screen for so long. She began to pace the length of the living room. Back and forth, her feet carried her, and her mind wandered back to the problem of her lack of education. She wasn't dumb, despite what Fred had said countless times. Why hadn't she ever tried to get her GED? Why hadn't she even bothered to look into it? It couldn't be that hard to obtain, right?

Returning to her laptop, she did a quick Google search. She sank into the chair, defeat filling her as she saw what the GED required. Tests. She should've known. Well, so much for that thought. Passing one test was next to impossible, and the GED required multiple.

What she needed was a job where she could just tinker all day long. No one to bother her while she fixed and built to her heart's content. Frustrated, she shut her laptop and glared at it.

"Has it somehow personally offended you?"

She looked up and saw Liam was watching her. Shrugging, she replied, "No more than usual."

"How's the job hunt?"

Her eyes returned to the laptop, "They all require qualifications I don't have. I'm submitting applications that are probably going to get ignored because I don't fit the computer's algorithm. I could do the work, I know I could, but I'm never going to get past the filters."

"What kind of qualifications?"

She sighed, "A degree. Literally any degree. Even a GED."

"You don't have your GED?" His voice was laced with surprise.

She shook her head, "Nope. And I just looked up how to get one, and I can tell you right now, that's not going to happen.

"Why not?"

She stood and returned to pacing, "Because tests. Maybe if it was just one, I'd stand a chance, but multiple? Impossible. Completely impossible."

"What happens when you take tests?" He was watching her apprasingly.

"I fail. I always fail. I know the material until I have to sit down and prove it. Then it's just...just gone."

She stopped looking at him, though she could still feel his eyes on her as she moved up and down the room. After a few minutes, she heard him shut his laptop and get up. He passed her and stopped at the piano. "Show me Middle C."

She came to a halt, "What?"

"Middle C. Come here and show me where it is."

She rolled her eyes, "I know what you're doing. This isn't exactly subtle." Still, she moved toward the piano and lightly touched the key she was almost sure was right, "This it?"

"I don't know, is it?"

Annoyed, she retorted, "Seriously?"

He nodded, "Tell me where it is. Don't second guess yourself."

She looked down at the keyboard and concentrated. She'd had it on Sunday. On Sunday, it had seemed so easy. Now, as she looked, she wasn't sure. She shook her head, "I remember it's in the middle, and I'm pretty sure it's one of these three, but I...I don't know."

Sagging in frustration, she started to walk away, but he caught her hand and gently pulled her back. "Look at me."

She did, "I told you. I can't do tests. And I told you that you don't have the patience to teach me. I can't remember one fucking key, let alone more than that."

He gazed down at her, looking strangely unperturbed by her outburst. With his free hand, he put the book he had her use a few days earlier on the music stand. "This isn't a test. You're not gonna to be in trouble if you get it wrong. Can you tell me anything from what I showed you on Sunday?"

She turned her attention to the open page. Something was prickling in her mind. Pointing to an image on the paper, she said, "I don't remember what it's called, but this squiggly thing, you said...you said..." She squeezed her eyes shut, trying to remember, "Middle C and above."

"Good."

Her eyes opened, "Wait, am I right?"

He nodded, "The squiggly thing is called a treb–"

"Treble clef!" she was almost giddy that the words had come to her.

"Correct," he was smiling at her. "We'll take this as slow as we need to. You're smart. You know the material."

Her face fell, and she pulled her hand free of his hold, "You told me about four things on Sunday, and I can barely remember one."

"But you remember that I showed you four different things. With a little help, you already remembered one of them."

She searched his face. He looked far more pleased with her than he really should. "Even if I can kind of remember any of it, the fact remains that if I try to take the GED tests, I'm doomed."

"If you're meant to take them, we'll get you to the point where you can manage it. For now, tell me, out of those three keys you indicated, which one do you think is Middle C?"

"Liam...I can't..." she shook her head.

He looked slightly pensive before saying, "Let's try something." The chair he'd moved from the table was still by the piano. He glanced at it and told her, "Sit there."

She did, and he sat on the piano bench. He held her gaze and touched a key, "This is Middle C."

Her eyes dropped to where he'd placed his finger, and she was confused, "No, it's not."

"What do you mean?"

What was he doing? She reached across him and touched a key, "This is."

"Correct."

Irked, she met his eyes, "You tricked me!"

His smile was lopsided, "Not really. I was just hoping that maybe if you were in the position of teacher, it might trigger something."

"That's sneaky."

He shrugged, "It worked."

Other things started to come back to her, and she shut her eyes, "The lines...they're a...a..." it was right there. She could feel the words in her brain. It was like there was a door that they were waiting to walk through. But the door wouldn't open. It was locked tight. She took a few deep breaths, "There are two...clefs and...and..." Nope, it had evaporated. Her eyes opened as she shook her head in disappointed frustration, "It's gone. Sorry."

"Don't apologize. You're right. There are two clefs. Treble and bass. The lines are a staff."

She tensed, waiting for him to say the words that would remind her why she couldn't do this. The words that would remind her why she shouldn't even try. They were going to come. Her eyes slid shut again, and she waited for him to get it over with.

Except he didn't say anything along those lines. Instead, she heard, "Sweetheart, look at me."

She forced her eyes open and saw he had moved just a little closer to her. Shaking her head, she told him, "Just give up on me. I can't do this."

He studied her, "Are you going to give up on me?"

She was incensed by the suggestion, "How can you even think I'd do that?"

He held out his hand, "Don't give up on me, and I won't give up on you. Deal?"

She stared at his hand for a long time before finally reaching out and clasping it, "Deal."

Eighteen

Liam

Wednesday morning, he dropped Zoe at her house. As the car came to a stop he told her, "Let me know when you're ready to be picked up. I'm usually pretty drained after therapy, so if you aren't up for dealing with me, I'll understand."

Unbuckling, she asked, "You're going to keep going after I move in, right?"

He nodded, "Yes."

"Well, there's no time like the present to get a feel for what to expect. Text when you're done."

"I will."

She grasped his hand for a second, giving it a squeeze, "Good. I'm proud of you for going." Confusion at her words flooded him as he watched her head into the house. It swirled inside him for the rest of the drive.

"How have the last few days been?" Dr. Constance asked as he settled onto the couch.

Anxiety mixed with his confusion. He remembered her reaction to his admission of wanting to marry Zoe, and he was worried about how the doctor would respond when she found out what had transpired in the two days since they'd last met.

"Liam?"

"Why would Zoe say she's proud of me for going to therapy?"

Dr. Constance's head tilted, "You told her you're in therapy?"

He nodded, "A couple nights ago."

"Was that before or after our last session?"

He took a drink of his coffee, "After. Monday night."

Her face was unreadable, "Does this mean you were able to work through the conflict you told me about?"

"She called me in the middle of the night. Neither of us could sleep. I went to get her, and...and she spent the night."

"By spent the night, you mean...?"

The glare on his face seeped into his voice, "Sleep. We slept. That's all we did."

She nodded, "What led to you telling her about therapy?"

"I told her what you had told me about letting her control her own life and...how I should let her ask me for the help she needs rather than making decisions for her. She was worried about...about who I was talking about her with."

"I see. How did she take that information?"

He thought about it, "Okay. This morning, she said she was proud of me for attending therapy."

Dr. Constance jotted something on her notepad, "She sounds very supportive."

"Why did she say it?"

"Obviously, I can't speak for her. If you want her reason, you'll need to ask her. I suspect she said it because she sees that you are actively trying to heal. She knows what you're doing isn't easy but will be worth it in the long run."

He supposed that made sense, but it still felt strange to think Zoe would consider his therapy attendance worthy of praise. His eyes dropped to his hands, "She's moving in with me."

"She is?" He could hear the surprise in Dr. Constance's voice.

He took another drink before relating what had happened, "When she went home on Monday, she found out that not just one of her roommates is moving out, both of them are. She asked if she could move in temporarily so she wouldn't have to live out of her car or get questionable roommates from Craigslist. The way she asked, it was like...like she thought I was going to say no. That I'd find her...an inconvenience."

"So this is temporary until she finds somewhere else to live?"

He slowly shook his head, "I...asked her to...to move in permanently."

Dr. Constance was silent for what felt like an eternity but was likely only a handful of seconds. "She's the one who asked? You didn't say anything to prompt the request?"

He chewed the inside of his cheek, "Yes. Well, kind of. I mean, she was the one who broached the subject and asked. I'm the one who asked for it to be more than a temporary thing."

More notes were written before the doctor looked at him again. Her expression was softer than usual as she said, "This is a huge step for you, Liam. How are you feeling about all this?"

"Good." He didn't even have to think about it.

The rapidity of his reply seemed to surprise her, and she asked, "Are there any other feelings you're experiencing?"

"Relief."

When Zoe got in the car, he realized he didn't feel quite as shitty as he normally did post-therapy. That's not to say he wasn't drained. He was, but not nearly as much as usual. It didn't feel like he would need to spend the rest of the day in bed trying to recover.

When they returned to the apartment, she dove back into her job hunt, and he went to the piano.

The day before, Zoe had asked if she could browse the bookshelf. Fifteen minutes later, she had set a small stack of books on the table by his laptop. He'd looked up from what he was working on as she bashfully requested, "Can you add these to your rotation? Nothing against classical, but it'd be nice to have more variety in there."

Now, he rifled through what she'd picked and pulled one. Opening to a random page, he let himself get lost in the song. He felt himself start to decompress. He wasn't really focusing on what he was playing. Just followed the notes and let them flow. Time became irrelevant. It was just him and the music.

Zoe's voice pulled him out of his bubble. She was singing along from across the room. Just little snippets here and there. If he hadn't already fallen in love with her, that would've been the moment it happened. He was up and moving toward her before fully realizing what he was doing. She looked slightly surprised as he stopped beside her and cradled her face between his hands. Her eyes were wide as she watched him lower his head so his lips hovered just above hers. He asked, "May I?"

"Yeah," the word was breathy and barely out of her mouth when he pressed his lips against hers.

It wasn't a long kiss, but it was soft and sweet. "Okay?" he asked when he broke it and stepped away.

A blissful smile covered her lips. It was far better than her expression after their last kiss. She nodded, "Okay."

For a few seconds, he debated with himself before asking, "Want to go for a drive? I think I need to get out of here."

He drove north, out of the city, and into the country. There was no plan. It was probably a waste of gas, but the drive was what he needed.

As he drove, words started to come out of his mouth, "What happened to Alex, that wasn't...wasn't an isolated case. And he's right, I did jack shit to stand up for him. I let him be...humiliated. I...I..." he swallowed hard, staring straight ahead, "I couldn't have stopped what happened, but I could've said...something."

He kept driving and kept talking. "There was this girl when I was in junior high. She was the perfect little Christian girl. People treated her like she was...she was incapable of doing wrong. She was a senior...and she got pregnant. When..." he could picture what had happened and hated what he was about to say, "when the church leadership was...informed...they punished her. Made her go to every family in the church and...and apologize for her sin."

"Her sin?" Zoe sounded confused.

He nodded, "Premarital sex. She...didn't...wait for marriage. The church wasn't very big at that point, so it was..." he sighed, "it was easy to make her go and beg for forgiveness from everyone."

He couldn't continue, and after several seconds, Zoe asked, "What happened to her?"

"Her boyfriend was a piece of shit, and her parents made them get married. He was awful to her...and he...he..." Liam's eyes scanned the road and saw a place where he could pull off for a few minutes to collect himself. Putting the car in park, he continued to stare out the windshield. "The guy...he shook the baby one night."

"Oh no," Zoe gasped. "Did the baby...?"

She didn't finish the question, but she didn't need to. He nodded, "People in the church...they...they said it was probably a blessing it died. The mom wouldn't...have to deal with her child having...brain damage."

The car was deadly silent. He gripped the steering wheel tightly, "The way people talked...it seemed like most of them believed that it was punishment from God for her...sin." He inhaled sharply, "The casket...was tiny."

At least a minute passed before Zoe asked, "What happened to the mom?"

Shame flooded him as he admitted, "I don't know. She kind of disappeared and would...would only get mentioned if someone was talking about what happens when you sin." He shut his eyes tightly, feeling even worse, adding, "I was just as bad as everyone. I used her as...as an example...when I gave abstinence talks."

"Abstinence talks?" The question didn't sound nearly as judgmental as it probably should have.

"Telling teenagers not to have sex. Making them sign...purity pledges." He opened his eyes and returned to staring out the windshield, "It was easy. I couldn't understand why anyone would...want...to have sex."

"What do you mean?"

He chewed the inside of his cheek. They were in territory he hadn't intended to go anywhere near yet. He wasn't even sure why he'd thought of that girl.

"You okay?" she asked after he remained quiet a little too long.

He leaned his head back against the headrest and stared at the ceiling of the car, "Up until very recently, I'd never...experienced...attraction to another person."

There were a few beats before Zoe spoke softly and haltingly, "I get it. I do. I...I thought something was...wrong...with me."

He was so surprised by her admission that he turned to look at her. She was staring out the passenger side window, and he couldn't see her expression as he assured her, "There's nothing wrong with you."

Her laugh was sad, "I've just felt...broken...and alone."

His voice was gentle as he told her, "You're not broken or alone."

A few seconds passed before she turned to face him with a tear coursing down her cheek, "Neither are you."

Nineteen

It was late afternoon by the time Liam drove back to town. He was silent and stony-faced. The things he'd told her had been hard to hear. He hadn't given details about what had been done to Alex, but based on everything else he'd shared, Zoe could make guesses, and none of them were good.

Liam finally broke his silence at the city limits, "Are you hungry?"

"Yeah."

"Any preferences?"

"Burritos."

A few minutes later, he pulled into line at the drive-thru of a local Mexican restaurant. An establishment known for cheap and filling food when one was drunk at 2 a.m. He glanced at her, "What do you want?

"Green chile burrito with a side of queso." It was her go-to order.

"Drink?"

"Horchata."

His silence returned and only broke when he placed the order. Less than fifteen minutes later, they were on their way back to the apartment with dinner sitting in the bag on Zoe's lap. They ate in silence, and then he returned to the piano.

She jumped as he began playing. He struck the keys hard over and over. It was as if he was pouring every ounce of rage inside himself into what he was playing. He sat stiffly and didn't use a book. Whatever he was playing was something he'd memorized.

This went on for nearly twenty minutes. He played the same thing on repeat. Finally, he stopped and pulled one of the books from the lid. His body was a little less tense, and when he resumed playing, his touch was gentler. It no longer sounded like he was beating the music into submission.

"Sing?" he asked. It was the first thing he'd said since the drive-thru.

She moved from the table and sat in the chair next to him. Looking at the book, she shook her head, "I don't know this one."

His face was still stony, but his voice was less tight, "Pick something you do know."

She grabbed a book from the stack. Though she didn't know the songs well, she was familiar enough with them to manage. She placed it in front of him. He said nothing; just started playing. She did her best to stay with him. He played through a few songs, but then part of the way through one, he came to a sudden stop. Staring at the book, tension radiated off of him. Gently, she placed her hand on his arm, "Liam?"

She wasn't sure what she expected, but him pulling her out of the chair into a near-crushing embrace was definitely not it. Somehow, she managed to free her arms and return the hug. "I'm sorry. I'm so sorry," he repeated in a hoarse voice, clinging to her as if she were a life raft and he a drowning man. She said nothing, just let him hold her.

The embrace lasted a long time, and when he eventually released her, she was able to look into his face. He no longer bore a stony expression. He just looked lost. His lip trembled as he said, "They're going to get worse."

"What are?" She hoped her voice sounded soothing.

"The stories." His eyes shut as he rubbed his temples.

"Headache?" she asked.

He nodded, and his eyes opened, "I need to sleep." Holding out his hand to her as he stood, "Come with me?"

She remembered him telling her he slept better when she was with him. Though she wasn't tired, he clearly was. Nodding, she took his hand and followed him back to the bedroom.

He shut the curtain and got into bed. His arms reached for her, and she let him pull her close. It wasn't long before his body relaxed, and his breathing deepened as sleep claimed him.

So, this was Liam post-therapy. It wasn't as bad as she'd feared it might be, and she knew she could handle it. Fred had been far worse throughout her entire life, and she had never gotten a private piano concert out of it. Not that it had been Liam's best playing, but that was okay. It seemed a healthier way to release the anger than doing something like punching a wall.

Her thoughts drifted to the kiss. It had been completely unexpected but not unwanted. The way he held her face had been so gentle, and the kiss had been tender. He was still cautious, but so was she. They were trying to figure out something most people seemed to have tackled as teenagers. It was awkward and weird and kind of fun. How could it be so many conflicting things? She had no idea; she just knew it was.

They hadn't verbally defined their relationship, but they were definitely in a relationship. Which was also weird. She'd been so convinced that no one would want her as more than a friend she'd long ago given up any hope of being with someone. Navigating these waters was going to be a challenge. The idea of sharing life with another person was intimidating.

She lightly ran her fingers along the back of Liam's hand. This was nice. Peaceful. Safe. Things she'd never really felt like she had.

It was going to be difficult to let him take care of her. She had always figured out a way to manage, to get through. Asking him to let her stay had made her feel weak and helpless. It shouldn't have, and he'd certainly not said or done anything to make her think that he thought she was any of those things. Though Fred had been her guardian, she'd been her own primary caretaker for nearly as long as she could remember.

She didn't need Liam, but at the same time, she did. And she sensed that it might be the same for him regarding her. They were both their own people. They had faced life on their own for a long time, and now they were going to try to be together. Two fiercely independent people trying to make a go of it. It was either going to go exceptional, or they'd kill each other.

It felt like she had just drifted off when movement woke her. Her eyes opened a fraction. The room was dark, and she had no sense of the time. Deciding she might need to put a clock on her side of the bed, she reached for her phone on the nightstand.

"It's a little after five," Liam said from behind her.

Her hand dropped, "A.M. or p.m.?"

"A.M."

She traced the veins on the back of his hand, "How are you feeling?"

"Better than yesterday." He pressed a kiss against her hair and added, "You?"

She thought for a few moments before replying, "Good."

"Good." He sighed, "I'm sorry if I scared you yesterday."

"You didn't."

"You sure?" he pushed.

She laughed quietly, "Yes, I'm sure. Trust me, I've seen way worse. At least you don't put your fist through walls."

He tensed at her words, and after a moment, she heard, "Not anymore."

She wasn't sure she was ready to open that can of worms and simply said, "That's good."

He relaxed a fraction, and they lay there together quietly for a bit. The blanket wall was no longer a complete barrier. It had moved down to their midsections, and she appreciated that it was still there. Even if they were in a relationship, she wasn't sure she was ready for more than gentle hugs and kisses.

"I was thinking," he murmured.

"That's dangerous," she teased.

His tone was wry as he stated, "Hilarious."

She patted his hand, "You love it."

He was quiet a second too long before replying softly, "I do."

She definitely wasn't ready to think about what that extra second might mean and lightly asked, "What were you thinking?"

"Do you have any experience with 3D printers?"

She laughed, feeling weirdly caught off-guard, even though she'd been the one to redirect their discussion. "No. I want to try one out, but the one at the library is always being used by someone else whenever I go. Why?"

"I bought one last year, or rather year before last, but I've...I've never used it."

She shifted and rolled over to look at him in the dim illumination the street-lights managed to get into the room, "Why haven't you? They're so cool!"

He didn't immediately answer. She waited, watching him, and eventually, he sighed, "I was...I was in a really bad place then." His eyes shut, and it sounded like the words were being pulled from him by force, "I didn't...I didn't get out of bed...very much."

She wasn't sure what the appropriate response was and simply said, "Oh."

"I bought it thinking that it might...help me start...functioning again." His eyes opened, but he didn't look at her, "It got here, and the thought of opening the box was fucking exhausting. So, it went in my closet, and I haven't touched it since."

She'd never gotten that stuck in her depression, but she did know what it was like to find simple things impossible because her brain was screwing with her, "Depression sucks, doesn't it?"

He blew out a breath, "Yeah."

She wanted to pull him back from the moroseness she feared was taking over, "We should get it out."

"That's what I was thinking. Seems like it would be right up your alley."

She grinned, "Wait until you see the pile of things I've saved on Pinterest that I want to make!"

That seemed to do the trick, and he chuckled, "Why do I have a feeling I'm going to have to peel you away from it and remind you to eat and sleep?"

"I promise to only get a little hyperfixated," she joked and sat up. "Well, I'm awake, and there are things to make."

Twenty

Liam

He was making breakfast when he heard the growl from the table. Looking over, he saw Zoe sitting with her head in her hands in front the open laptop. He couldn't walk away from the stove, which was a little frustrating at the moment, but he did ask, "What's wrong?"

She didn't look up, but her voice was annoyed as she read, "*Thank you for your interest in this position. At this time, we have decided to move on with other candidates in our search process. We wish you luck in your continued search.*" Standing and stretching, she shook her head, "You don't even want to know how many emails I have sitting there that all say variations of that."

Moving toward him, she rested her back against the kitchen counter and stared at the pan, "It's so dumb. They didn't even interview me. Just looked at my application and decided I wasn't worth their time."

He flipped the pancake, "That's frustrating."

"That's the understatement of the year."

He wanted to tell her she didn't need to keep job hunting, but he kept that to himself. She wanted to find a job. Had been very adamant about that. But it was hard watching her be so discouraged. He slid the pancake onto a plate and handed it to her.

She grinned, "Thank you."

To his surprise, she didn't move back to the table; just began eating right there. He didn't mind, though. He liked having her so close. Pouring more batter into the pan, he added the swirl of cinnamon mix and asked, "Safe to assume you want more?"

She nodded enthusiastically, "Yes, please. They're really good."

He smiled at her fondly. She was so easy to make happy. "So, when do you want to start moving your stuff?"

She shrugged, "There's not that much to move. Mostly it's clothes, and honestly, there's not that many of them. Maybe this weekend? I probably should go pick up the rest of my bathroom stuff before then. That way you won't have to keep sharing your shampoo."

"I don't mind."

"I know you don't, but I do. It makes me feel weird," her eyes dropped to her empty plate.

That confused him, "Why? It's there to be used."

She looked at the stove and watched as he flipped the pancake, "I...I appreciate that. I'm not sure why I feel that way. I just do."

He placed the pancake on her plate, "Okay, I'll take you over to pick that up in a bit. You should probably bring your car over, too. I need to get a parking spot for you."

She groaned, "I wasn't even thinking about that. Is it going to be a pain to take care of?"

He shook his head, "Shouldn't be."

She ate a few bites, and he was watching the batter in the pan when she asked, "You're still sure you want to do this?"

He saw her staring at him with a look that made his heart ache. She seemed so convinced he was going to pull the rug out from under her at any second. Leaning over, he kissed the tip of her nose, "Yes. Tomorrow. Next week. Three hundred years from now. I'll still be sure."

Her eyes were a little misty as she joked, "Fairly certain in three hundred years, we'll both be ghosts."

"Well, in that case, I'm sure I'll want to haunt things with you." Her cheeks turned pink, and she looked away from him. He continued, "Once I get this cleaned up, I'll go talk to the apartment office. I'll let you try to figure out how to put the printer together."

After he'd told her about the printer that morning, she'd been anxious to get it out and start using it. He'd managed to convince her to wait by reminding her she needed breakfast. She'd only agreed to eat first once he promised to make her favorite pancakes. He wasn't about to tell her the other reason he'd decided to have her put the printer together, but if she got suspicious and asked, he wouldn't lie.

He wanted her to be able to reach a point where she felt she could tackle the tests to get her GED, but he knew it might take a while. She wanted to be able to work, and the pile of rejections in her email that morning had served to confirm what they both knew. Without the degree, she would have a hard time finding a job. He knew that it was possible to sell 3D-printed things online, and maybe if she took to the printer like he anticipated, it would be a way for her to make an income.

Would she be mad if she knew that was his thought? Technically, he was helping her without asking first, but surely, since he wasn't actually telling her what she should do with it, that meant he wasn't trying to control things. If she decided on her own that she wanted to try to make a business of it, he'd support her completely, and if she just wanted to play with it for fun, that was fine, too. He wouldn't try to influence her one way or the other.

Taking care of the parking spot was less of a headache than anticipated. When he returned from the office, he found Zoe with the printer parts spread out over the table. She was staring at them, looking ready to commit murder.

"How's it going?"

Her lips were pursed, "I think I know why IKEA furniture leads to breakups."

He was confused, "This isn't from IKEA."

"I know it's not."

He sat down across from her, "What's giving you trouble?"

She sighed, "This thing is not complicated to put together, but I've been fighting with the damn Allen wrench for at least twenty minutes, and it's making me want to scream. I don't get it. I've put stuff together that's way more difficult, but right now, you'd think I'd never seen a tool in my life."

He chuckled, "Maybe you need a break. Want to go get your stuff? I've got your parking spot figured out."

She pushed back from the table, "That sounds like a plan. You're probably right. I'm too frustrated right now, and if I step away, it'll probably go together like magic when I get back."

Before they left, he showed her the spot. When he pulled into her driveway, she told him, "You can go back. I won't be too long."

"You don't want help?"

She snorted, "Carrying shampoo? No, I think I'm good. If it'll make you feel better, you can help me carry stuff from the car to the apartment."

He looked at her with bemusement, "Alright, you know how to reach me if you change your mind and want me to come back." She reached for the door handle, and he added, "I'm going to run to the store. Any food requests beyond the applesauce?"

She paused and thought momentarily before shaking her head, "Nope, get whatever."

He watched until she was in the house before he pulled away. Driving to the store, he decided he should ask her to make a list of things she liked to eat and things she abhorred.

He'd been home a few hours when Zoe texted that she was back. He hurried out to meet her. She gave him a sheepish look as he saw what she'd brought back and told him, "I kinda got started and couldn't stop. There's not much left in my room, so I guess that's good."

Even though she'd brought a fair amount of things, he realized she didn't own very much if that was the majority of her belongings. They made quick work of moving everything inside, and Zoe set about putting things away.

He leaned against the bedroom door frame, "I would've come back to help you."

She shrugged as she hung up things in the closet, "It's not a big deal. It wasn't anything beyond my capabilities to handle."

Why won't you just let me help you? He bit back the question. She was letting him help her, just not as much as he'd have liked. Still, he sensed that asking for and receiving help wasn't something she was very comfortable with.

She buzzed around, putting things away, and then sat on the edge of the bed, looking around. "All I've really got left is my bed, dresser, and everything in it. It's not a big dresser, so it should fit in here fine, but I have no idea what to do with the bed. My mattress is shit. It should probably just get thrown away unless you're planning to send me back to the couch. In which case, I'll need it."

He gave her a very pointed look, "Toss the mattress."

"I don't know, you might change your mind if I start sleep fighting," she joked.

He lifted an eyebrow, "Is that something you do?"

She laughed, "Not that I know of, but I've never had anyone around to let me know if I do."

He'd been right. The break had helped, and Zoe put the printer together with little trouble. She did enlist his help to hold things so she could place some of the screws. He enjoyed watching her work. Completely focused, there was a look of peace on her face. It was a shame that places wouldn't even interview her. If they could see her working, they'd realize what a loss it was not hiring her.

There were things he wanted to ask about her past, but she hadn't given him carte blanche to ask anything and everything, which meant that for the present, he had to put together the pieces based on things she would say.

Her comment that morning about not punching holes in the wall had hit a little too close to home. Back before everything truly went to hell, his anger would get so wildly out of control he would violently destroy things. There had been holes in walls and doors that he was completely responsible for. He'd hated that was how he reacted, but he couldn't handle his anger. Hadn't even known how. It was just this overwhelming force that took over him. Growing up, he'd only been told not to get angry without being given any suggestions on how to deal with the red-hot fire that burned deep inside. It was as if everyone thought not being angry was a simple matter of just deciding not to be.

One of the first therapists he'd tried had been the one to suggest that he play piano when the anger got to be too much. The therapist hadn't had anything else useful to say, but that one recommendation had been quite helpful. He knew the anger wouldn't ever truly be gone, but making music had proven to be a far healthier outlet than his previous destructive ones.

Had Fred put holes in the wall? Had he beaten Zoe? Liam wasn't sure how he'd handle it if he learned that Fred had laid a single finger on her.

"Liam?"

He blinked and focused on Zoe, "Yes?"

She was watching him with curiosity, "You looked very far away just now. Everything okay?"

He shouldn't ask her. He really shouldn't. And yet he found himself doing that exact thing, "What did Fred do?"

"Are you sure that's a conversation you want to have right now?" she asked after a very long time.

He shook his head, "I shouldn't have asked that."

"Why did you?" She didn't look or sound mad, so he hoped that meant he hadn't trespassed too far over a line.

"You don't have to tell me if you don't want. This morning, when you mentioned punching holes in a wall? I...I know that kind of rage all too well. Did he do that?"

Twenty-One

Zoe

She didn't want to talk about it. However, if they were going to live together, she knew she should. She wasn't sure she'd ever be able to tell him everything, but she could at least tell him some of it.

Her mind filled with an image of being dropped off at Fred's as a little girl. He was a big guy, and to her terrified five-year-old eyes, he was a hulking ogre. "I don't know why my parents left me with him, let alone why he agreed to take me in the first place. He clearly didn't want me. I couldn't make him happy, no matter how hard I tried. And god, I tried."

The way Liam was looking at her was too much. Embers burned within his eyes that spoke of both the rage he was holding back and deep sadness. She couldn't stand it. Stepping away from the table, water bottle in hand, she began to pace, staring at the floor, "He never hit me, but he'd throw things...Yell...that kind of thing."

Taking a drink, she tried to keep going, "I don't remember a lot of what happened. It's all just kind of a blur of awful. And...yeah, there were walls that ended up with holes from him. I was twenty-six when I finally saved enough to move out. I think that was the first time I breathed since I was five."

She could feel the anxiety squeezing her chest tightly. Her breathing grew shallow. She didn't want to think about that asshole anymore. "I'm...I'm sorry...I just can't. Not right now."

Her feet came to a sudden stop as she found Liam standing right in front of her. She hadn't even realized he'd gotten out of his chair. Her eyes bore holes into the floor as she heard him say, "I'm sorry. I shouldn't have...I shouldn't have asked."

She shook her head, "No, it's okay. Well...maybe not okay, but I know I should tell you about this stuff."

Taking a step back, she looked up at him. Distress filled his face. She tried to give him a comforting smile, "I'm not upset with you, I promise."

His stare was intense, and after a few moments, he told her, "My anger...I know it's an issue...but I swear to God I'll never do to you what he did. I don't want you..." his lips were trembling as he tried to form the words, "I don't want you to worry...about that. I don't...don't want you to be...afraid."

She could see how scared he was that she'd think he'd do anything like that to her. Inside, she really wanted to believe he was telling the truth, but she wasn't naive enough to believe that. She believed he would genuinely try not to turn his anger on her. Uncertainty filled her because she honestly didn't know what she'd do if he did. They should probably talk about that. Instead, she stepped closer and slipped her arms around him, dropping the water bottle on the floor.

A moment passed before he returned the embrace. She rested against his chest and listened to the beating of his heart. His cheek was against her head, and one of his hands moved up, pressing his fingers into the back of her neck.

"We're both a little messed up, aren't we," she murmured.

"Just a little."

Late that night, she was curled up against his side, her head resting on his chest and her arm across his abdomen. His arm held her loosely. He was fast asleep, but sleep evaded her. Thinking about her past with Fred had left her unsettled. It was easier to leave those memories buried where they couldn't hurt her.

She wished she could be as strong as Liam. He was willing to face his shitty past, willing to let her ask anything and everything about it. God, he must trust her an unbelievable amount. She'd never betray that trust, but she had absolutely no idea what he saw in her to make him decide that he should.

Liam wasn't in bed when she woke. It was the first time in days she'd woken up alone. She didn't like it. Not one bit.

Opening her eyes, she looked at the clock. 6:20 a.m. Her hand felt under the covers. His side was still slightly warm. He couldn't have left that long ago.

The sound of the bathroom door caught her attention, and she rolled over. He walked into the bedroom, toweling off his hair. He was only wearing pajama pants. His bare chest was on prominent display, and she couldn't look away. She'd known that she'd eventually see him like that but hadn't been prepared for it quite yet. She also wasn't prepared for how much she liked it. Her hands itched to explore the smooth skin.

If he was embarrassed, it didn't show. He simply looked at her and asked, "Did I wake you?"

Slowly, she shook her head, 'N-no. I...I just woke up."

He took the towel back to the bathroom before heading to the closet. Less than a minute later, he emerged, pulling on a T-shirt. She felt an unfamiliar wave of disappointment that was unnerving. Her thoughts were out of control. *Take the shirt off. Please. I would really, REALLY like it if you took it back off. Just leave it off. You don't need it.*

Her body was growing hotter, and alarm coursed through her as her legs clenched against nothing. She'd never experienced such a visceral reaction to another person. No matter how attractive she might find someone, she'd never actually felt attraction. People were like art in a museum. She could see them, appreciate their beauty, and move on. She'd never felt more.

Liam sat on the edge of her side of the bed. Stroking her hair, he asked, "Did you sleep okay?"

"Meh," she replied with a shrug, hoping she sounded less hot and bothered than she felt.

Anxiety gripped her. What was she going to do? They would be sharing a bed for the foreseeable future. Maybe that wasn't such a good idea. Sleeping next to him, knowing what he looked like half-naked and how it affected her? Nothing good could possibly come from that.

Secretly, she hoped he would kiss her.

Secretly, she hoped he wouldn't.

"Want to go back to sleep, or should I start breakfast?"

Did the man really have no idea what he was doing to her? "Um...breakfast would be good."

He kissed her temple before getting up, saying, "I'll get it started."

Oh, he'd definitely gotten something started.

As soon as he left, she ran for the bathroom and locked the door behind her.

What the hell was happening to her? She looked at the tub. A shower would help. It had to help.

The ache between her legs was growing more powerful, and she groaned. This wasn't okay. It wasn't the first time she'd been aroused, but in the past, it had always been a random, abstract thing. Something easy to deal with.

She turned on the water and stripped while she waited for it to warm up. It didn't take long, and soon, she stood under the cascading water. Massaging in shampoo, she suddenly thought about how it felt when Liam's fingers had been in her hair. She imagined what it would be like if he were in the shower with her, what it would feel like if he were the one working in the shampoo.

It was a slippery slope because once she started picturing that, she found herself thinking about how he had looked fresh out of the shower. His dark, nearly black hair, so wild after being toweled dry. She'd seen it that way before, but not combined with his naked chest. And, of course, thinking of his hair only made her think about his full lips. The ones that had started kissing her more and more frequently. Tender, cautious touches that always ended far too soon.

What would sex with him be like? Would he even want to have sex with her? Maybe he didn't want more than hugs and kisses. Maybe sex wasn't something he'd ever want. She'd certainly never wanted it before. Her knowledge of the topic came solely from movies, books, and the internet. She could form a vague idea of what being together would be like but really had no idea what to expect.

Her hands roamed her body. She'd get this worked out, and then she'd be able to be around him without it being too difficult. But when he looked at her, would he know what she'd done? Would he be disgusted? Would he know the direction her thoughts had gone? It was a little eerie how he seemed to intuit what was going on in her mind.

Her fingers wandered lower, finding their destination between her legs. She pictured his eyes. Those dark eyes that said far more than he ever verbalized. She loved his eyes. She loved how he treated her, like she was special and delicate. Two things she knew she wasn't.

She loved him.

The sudden realization of the truth about her feelings made her gasp sharply as she found relief. To her distress, it wasn't anywhere near as much relief as she needed. She still wanted him. Desperately.

How would she face him?

The rest of the shower was a quick affair. Her mind raced the entire time. She was in love with Liam? When had that happened? She'd known she had a crush on him. Known that she wanted to live with him. But love? That was a whole other thing. It was far too early to be in love with him. They needed more time to get to know each other.

She chastised herself. He seemed to be attracted to her, and he didn't mind taking care of her. But he wasn't in love with her. At least, she was fairly certain he wasn't.

I'm going to live with a man that I'm in love with. A man that probably doesn't love me.

The thought hurt, and it was all she could think about as she turned off the water. Everything suddenly felt so much more complicated. Her feelings were impossible to ignore, but she didn't dare tell him. If she so much as gave a hint of how she honestly felt, it could ruin everything. If he knew...Oh god, if he knew. Would it push him away? The thought of him retreating because he thought she was too needy and clingy was too much to bear.

Living together was a bad idea.

But she didn't have anywhere else to go.

Wrapped in her towel, she sank onto the edge of the tub. She was glad the exhaust fan was running. Hopefully, it would mute the tears that had begun to fall.

He couldn't love her. People didn't love her. Some liked her. Most tolerated her. But none loved her.

Twenty-Two

Liam

A gnarled finger caressed the girl's pale face. The pointed nail a sickly yellow, only a shade or two darker than the old man's skin. The girl was clearly terrified.

Zoe was clearly terrified.

The old man was gone, but Zoe was still there. Frightened and angry. Furious. "You knew," she seethed with flashing eyes.

Liam felt sick, "I...I..."

His eyes flew open. He was in his bed. Safe in his apartment. Zoe was fast asleep, curled up against his side. His heart was racing, and he was sticky with sweat. He felt gross both inside and out. He needed a shower. Desperately needed to wash it all away.

Turning his head, he saw it was almost six. Looking back at Zoe, he was relieved to see she looked like herself. This wasn't the Zoe from his dream, yet it was.

He held her a little tighter. *I won't let it happen again. I won't let it happen to you.*

Shower. It was a necessity. He might be able to extricate himself and get back before she woke up. She'd be none the wiser.

The water was scalding. He scrubbed until his skin felt raw. It made no difference. The ickiness would always be with him.

Defeated, he turned off the water and grabbed his towel. He dried off and stepped onto the bathmat. On his way to the bathroom, he had grabbed clean underwear and pajama pants. Dressing, he began to towel dry his hair. He hadn't grabbed a shirt, but Zoe would still be asleep, so he didn't need to worry about her seeing him.

Returning to the bedroom, still drying his hair, he very nearly froze as he met Zoe's eyes. She was on her side, definitely awake, and staring right at him. It took everything in him to look and sound nonchalant as he asked, "Did I wake you?"

She answered in the negative, and he set about finding a shirt. He could feel her eyes on him as he moved around the room. Something about the look he'd seen in her eyes told him she didn't find him completely repulsive. It gave him a strange feeling. Self-conscious and yet, at the same time, pleased.

Overall, it was an uneventful day. Zoe submitted more job applications and faced an inbox filled with even more rejections. When she'd had enough, she turned her attention to learning how to use the printer.

She was very quiet all day, and when they went to bed, she curled into a tight little ball of tension. He spooned her and asked, "Do you want to talk about it?"

"Hmm?"

"Whatever it is that's bothering you?"

She yawned and told him, "It's nothing. Just tired. Been a lot in less than a week."

He couldn't deny the truth of that statement. Rather than dig for a better answer, he simply said, "Okay," and softly kissed the top of her head.

Saturday morning, she still wasn't herself. She did seem a bit better once they got to the studio, but after the broadcast, she pulled back in on herself. He struggled against the feeling that she was pushing him away. Dr. Constance would probably tell him that he needed to step back and examine the whole situation before jumping to the worst possible conclusion.

That night, she curled back into the tight ball. They proceeded to have a re-enactment of the previous night. She still claimed she was tired from the week. Again, he let it go, though he wondered if that was a mistake. He settled for another kiss against her hair, hoping she'd be better in the morning.

He wasn't sure how long he'd been asleep when the sound of crying woke him. Coming to, he realized that Zoe wasn't in his arms like she had been when he fell asleep. His eyes flew open, and he sat up a little, looking for her. Relief settled over him as he saw she was still in the bed. Confusion mixed in because she was at the edge, as far away from him as she could get, without falling off the mattress. Her body was still curled into a ball that was shaking and sniffling.

"Zoe?" He reached out and lightly touched her shoulder. She didn't respond. Her entire body was tense.

Scooting closer, he wrapped his arm around her middle and held her. Thinking it might be her night terrors, he softly told her, "It's okay...you're not alone, sweetheart...I'm here..."

"I know," came a small, weepy voice.

Surprised, he asked, "You're awake?"

She sniffled, "Yeah."

"What's wrong?"

"Nothing." Except it came out "Nuh-ing."

He sighed, "It's not nothing. What is going on?" If possible, she tensed even more but said nothing. "Is it because of what I asked the other night? I'm sorry, sweetheart. I'm so sorry. I never meant to upset you."

She shook her head, "It's...not."

"Then what is it?" He couldn't keep the worry out of his voice.

She was quiet for a long time, and he waited as patiently as he could. Eventually, he heard, "I'm...I'm just tired. It's been...a lot...fast."

It had barely been a week since their New Year's Eve kiss. Two weeks since she lost her job. On top of which, moving in together had come about very suddenly. Both of their lives were going through massive changes. He nodded, "It has."

"And this is...new...and I don't know...if I can..." her words trailed off as she started shaking more.

Shit. "Is it too much?"

"I...I don't know."

"What will help?"

She didn't move or say anything for nearly a minute before she uncurled and rolled over to face him. He watched wordlessly as her fingers reached up and lightly ran along his jaw. She sniffled and giggled, "You're scratchy."

"Is that helping?" he teased, trying not to think about how the touch affected him.

He wasn't prepared for her to move and suddenly press her lips against his. Not prepared, but not unhappy. He pulled her closer, and his hand moved up her back and into her hair. She broke the kiss with a gasp, "Liam."

"Sweetheart," his voice was ragged to his ears. Her hand was pressed against his jaw, and he leaned into her touch. "Are you trying to distract me?"

She laughed, but it was a very breathy sound. "Why would you think that?"

At least she wasn't crying anymore. He pressed a kiss to her forehead, "I don't know. You tell me."

"Are we...are we going too fast?" her voice was soft and hesitant.

He was quiet for a moment, then released his hold on her and moved so he could turn on the lamp. Turning back, he looked at her. She stared at him with wide eyes. He tried to figure out what to say. Too fast? Considering he was about five seconds away from proposing flying to Vegas and getting married, he was probably not the best person to answer that question. "Do you think we are?"

"It...feels like we've gone from zero to sixty...in almost no time."

He sat up and lightly tugged at her, "C'mere." He wrapped an arm around her shoulder and gazed down at her, "So what if we're moving fast? I don't care."

"Really?"

"Really." He nuzzled her, "Is that what's been bothering you?"

She leaned against him, "Do you feel like there's all these confusing feelings just swirling around inside?"

Her head was right beneath his, and he rested against her. "It's a lot," he admitted.

"You have to...to tell me if I'm too needy. I..." her voice was teary again, "I don't want to be a burden."

He stiffened, disconcerted by her request, "Why would you even think that?"

She shook her head, "Just promise you'll tell me."

He sighed and sat up straighter. Lifting her chin so she was looking at him, he said, "You are not a burden. Do you understand me?"

She gave him a sad smile and moved out of his hold. Lying down, she murmured, "Go back to sleep."

He turned the light off but didn't lie down immediately. His fingers stroked her hair. She drifted off while he did that. He stared down at her sleeping silhouette and contemplated her words.

Earlier in the week, when she'd asked to move in, she'd made that comment about how he could just toss her in a closet, that he wouldn't even notice she was there. She seemed to have it in her head that she needed to make herself as small and unnoticeable as possible. Combined with her comment about how she couldn't make Fred happy, he thought he was starting to get a clearer picture of things. She genuinely thought that no one wanted her. Especially not him. What would he have to do to convince her he'd meant everything said? That he'd meant it when he told her she was everything to him?

Twenty-Three

Zoe

"Where are we going?"

Liam's eyes didn't leave the road, but she saw the corners of his mouth twitch as he replied, "Do you really want to know? We're almost there, after all."

It was mid-morning on Sunday, and over breakfast, he suggested they get out of the apartment and do something. After the middle of the night crying session, she was feeling worn down to the bone emotionally. "Is it going to involve many people?"

He'd shaken his head, "Probably not, and if there are too many, just tell me, and we can go somewhere else."

Now, they were almost to the edge of town, and she was still clueless about what he was planning. "Not even a hint?"

The car turned a corner, "We're here."

She didn't even try to hide the delight in her voice as she took in t, "Seriously?"

He navigated the car into a parking spot and teasingly asked, "So I should turn around and leave?"

"Don't you dare!" she swatted playfully at his arm.

"Ow."

She laughed as he turned off the ignition. Quickly, she got out of the car, and he met her on the sidewalk a few moments later. Reaching out, she caught his hand with hers. He looked down at her, slightly surprised, and laced his fingers with hers. Hand in hand, they walked toward the entrance.

She had no idea how he had guessed this would be the perfect place to bring her. She'd always wanted to visit, but it had never been an option. Walking into the building, he pulled out his phone and squeezed her hand before releasing his hold, "Need my hand for a sec."

Unwillingly, she let go and followed him to the front desk. He held out his phone to the woman working, and she scanned it. "Enjoy," she beamed at them.

He reclaimed her hand, and they stepped away from the desk. They walked down a short hallway and passed through double doors that led to an immense glass structure. Immediately, they were hit with a wall of humidity, but Zoe didn't mind. Her eyes flitted around, taking in the beauty. The deep green of the leaves. The stunning bright reds and blues, yellows and purples of the blossoms. She halted, inhaling deeply. The scent of the flowers filled her, and she sighed happily.

"You hate it?" He joked.

Eyes misty, she looked up and shook her head, "No, it's...it's perfect. How did you know?"

"I didn't. It was a guess. Thought you might find it peaceful," he told her tenderly, teasing no longer in his voice.

She pulled him forward to wander among the flowers, "I do. I love plants."

Slowly, they meandered down the path, and to Zoe's relief, only a few other people were there. It was easy enough to keep their distance. Liam didn't seem to mind that she kept stopping to take photos of different plants with her phone.

A stream had been built to run throughout the complex, and at certain points, it would drop down in little waterfalls. She paused, watching one of the falls, "I've always wanted to see this place. It just never happened. No one else was really interested." Her eyes moved up and sought his. He was watching her with a look as tender as his voice had been. She stretched on her tiptoes and kissed his cheek, softly saying, "Thank you."

He pressed his lips to her forehead, "You're welcome." As she relaxed from her stretched position, he added, "I know things have been overwhelming. I hope this helps."

She felt more peaceful than she had in a long time and nodded, "It does, it really does. How long can we stay?"

"As long as you want, though I think they'll probably kick us out once they close for the night." The teasing glint had returned to his eyes.

They resumed their wandering, and she saw two women attempting a couple's selfie. It didn't seem like it was going well, so she let go of Liam's hand and hurried over, "Want me to take your picture?"

They grinned at her. The woman holding the phone handed it over, saying, "That would be great! Thank you."

Zoe took several pictures and handed the phone back, "I think I got a few good ones."

Liam had walked up while Zoe was taking the photos. She took hold of his hand, and they turned to continue their walk when they were stopped by one of the women asking, "Want us to take your photo?"

Zoe looked up at Liam, and he gave her a small shrug. Turning to the women, she handed over her phone after opening the camera app. "That'd be really nice. Thanks."

Dropping Liam's hand, Zoe snaked her arm around his back. His arms went around and pulled her close.

"Oh my god, you two are precious!" said the woman taking their photo. After a few seconds, she returned the phone to Zoe, "You should look up blue butterflies. I think I read somewhere they're a sign of good luck."

"Thanks," Zoe stammered. Looking at the screen, she browsed the photos. They were better than she'd anticipated. She'd never been very photogenic, but with Liam, she looked okay. In fact, she liked how she looked with him. There was something about the image that was just right. Her eyes lit on a small part of the photo, and the woman's statement suddenly made sense. Looking up at him, she said, "There are butterflies!"

He quirked an eyebrow, "What are you talking about?"

"Don't move." Holding up her phone, she rapidly snapped more photos of the butterfly perched on his shoulder. Its vibrant blue wings drew her closer, but she moved too quickly, and the insect fluttered away. She watched it for a few seconds, then held her phone out to Liam, "It liked you!"

He shook his head, "Why do I have a feeling you're going to hang this up on the fridge?"

She laughed, "I hadn't thought about that, but now that you mention it..." He rolled his eyes, but she could tell he wasn't irritated. She smiled softly to herself. He was getting easier to read.

A little while later, she pulled him over to sit on a porch swing. Across from the swing, the stream opened into a pond with lily pads floating on top. Pink and white flowers were in full bloom. Liam let go of her hand and put his arm around her. She rested against his side and let the scent of flowers and the sound of running water fill her. Sighing with contentment, she moved a little to glance up at him.

The look on his face made her feel strange. It was the kind of look she wore when looking at something precious. She found it hard to keep looking at him and returned her gaze to the lily pads. His hand gently ran up and down her upper arm. Reality pulled at her, but she tried to resist. She didn't want to think about the fact that whatever was between them wasn't going to last. It couldn't.

Feeling his lips on the top of her head, she was yanked from her spiraling thoughts. Glancing up again, she saw he was still watching her with that same look. It was the one he'd had in the middle of the night when he'd told her she wasn't a burden. She chewed the inside of her cheek. Was it possible he really believed that? The way he talked, he made it sound like he didn't think they had an expiration date.

"You're going to fill the apartment with plants, aren't you?" he asked.

She grinned, "We should stop so I can pick up The Fab Four when we leave."

"The Fab Four?"

"My succulents. John, Paul, George, and Ringo."

He laughed, "You named them?"

She nodded, "Of course. It was probably my imagination, but they seemed happier when I played the Beatles. Hence the names."

Dimples on full display, he told her, "We'll stop on the way home."

They stayed at the conservatory until Zoe's stomach started growling loudly. Leaving to find lunch, she told him, "We are definitely coming back here."

"I assumed you'd want to, especially since we didn't go out into the garden."

She nodded, "Figured there wouldn't be much growing out there right now. Plus, it's a little chilly."

The car passed through the front gate, and he asked, "Where am I going?"

"Surprise me."

They ended up at a burger place. "How worried do I need to be that you'll put pineapple in everything?" he asked when she took her first bite of the burger topped with the fruit.

After swallowing, she shrugged, "It goes with everything."

"Does it, though?"

She considered the question, "Well, maybe not everything, but most things are improved by it." She took another bite, "Like this burger, which is delicious."

A few minutes passed, and he asked, "Anything else you want to pick up other than your plants?"

"Might as well pick up the rest of my clothes." She toyed with a fry, "I'm not sure how we're going to move my dresser. It's not that big, but definitely won't fit in your car."

Finishing his burger, he told her, "I'll rent a truck."

Alex's car was in the driveway when they arrived at the house. As Liam parked, she told him, "Let me go check with Alex. Make sure he's okay if you come in." Liam's face was pensive, and she rested her hand on his arm, asking, "What?"

He turned off the ignition, "I need to talk to him."

"You sure you want to do that today?"

He nodded, "Yeah, if he's open to it."

"Okay, I'll ask. Wait here."

She found Alex in the kitchen. When he saw her, he grinned, pulling her into a tight hug, "I've missed you. It's been weird not seeing you every day!"

Laughing, she replied, "It's good to see you too."

His face grew serious, and he searched hers, "Is everything alright? Is he treating you okay?"

She nodded, "He's been great. You don't need to be worried, I promise."

He sighed, "I just don't want you to get hurt."

She gave him another hug, "I appreciate that. It really is going good, I promise." Stepping back, she stared at her friend, "He's out in the car. Is it okay if he comes in?"

Alex hesitated before nodding, "I guess so."

"He wants to talk to you."

She watched Alex's face pass through various emotions before he said, "I'm not sure if that's a good idea."

Remembering how Liam had talked that day in the car earlier in the week, "I...I think he genuinely regrets things. If you're not up for it today, I'll tell him. Okay?"

Alex sighed, "If he's wanting to apologize, I'm not sure I can forgive him."

She considered that and nodded, "No one's asking you to. Just listen to him. If it's too much, send him to my room or back to the car."

Several seconds passed before Alex finally nodded, "Okay."

Twenty-Four

Zoe

She left Liam in the kitchen with Alex and went to her room. "Hi, boys," she greeted her succulents as she closed the door. "Ready to go to your new home?"

She stopped in front of her dresser and debated how to handle it. Maybe they should just leave everything in the drawers and move those separately? That seemed a good plan, so she began to remove them. She pulled out her underwear drawer and decided that was one she'd rather not have on display. It wasn't that Liam wouldn't see her underwear at some point. He probably already had since she'd thrown them in her laundry basket.

He'd probably seen her underwear.

She paused, the full weight of the thought hitting her. It hadn't occurred to her that he'd seen them, even though her laundry basket was in clear view. Maybe it was because she knew he hadn't seen her *in* her underwear, and that's why it hadn't been something she'd thought about before.

The sound of Alex's raised voice drew her attention. It was tempting to open the door a crack to hear what was happening, but she resisted the urge. This was between the two men. If either of them decided to tell her what happened, that would be fine, but she wouldn't violate their privacy.

She wondered how Liam would be the rest of the day. He'd been so relaxed all morning and through lunch. She liked seeing him like that. It was very likely that he'd go home and play the piano for the next several hours. She was proud of him, both him and Alex. What they were doing took courage. They might never be friends again, but hopefully, they'd at least be able to be around each other without so much tension between them.

Drawers all pulled out and on her mattress; she looked around the small room. It was bittersweet saying goodbye. She'd be back before the fifteenth, but this would probably be the last time she'd be in here like this. Sinking onto the floor, she sat cross-legged.

A soft knock sounded at the door, and it opened to reveal Liam. He stepped inside and shut the door behind him. She watched as he moved closer and sank onto the floor facing her. He was not as tense as she'd anticipated. "Okay?" she asked softly.

He nodded, "As okay as can be."

"That's good."

He reached out and took one of her hands between his. They nearly enveloped hers. His eyes looked to where they were joined. "I'm proud of you," she told him after several seconds. "I know that wasn't easy."

"No," he sighed, "it wasn't, but it was necessary."

"Yeah," she acknowledged.

He didn't add anything else, and she found herself talking after a little while, "This has been my home since I moved out of Fred's. I think I knew that I'd have to move out at some point, but it always seemed like this far-off, someday-type thing. I thought that when the three of us went our separate ways, it would come with more...warning."

She felt him squeeze her hand, and then he looked at her. Gently, he tugged until she scooted closer so they were sitting side-by-side facing each other. He let go of her hand, and his arm moved so it ran along her upper back to where his fingers landed, cradling the back of her neck. His other arm went around her lower back. She smiled at the embrace. Her fingers touched his hair gently, and she told him, "I've never been alone with a boy in my room before."

A lopsided smile appeared on his face, "Oh, really?"

She wound a lock around her index finger, "Well, I guess Alex has been in here, but I'm not really counting him."

"Why not?"

She leaned in a little, resting both hands against his jaw, "I didn't want to kiss him."

They were getting better at this she decided, as she felt him react to her pressing her lips against his. She could feel the fingers on her neck flexing, and his other arm moved a little higher on her back, pulling her even closer. Her eyes slid shut, and she just let herself feel.

The kiss broke eventually, though she wasn't sure who pulled away first. They were breathing a little hard, and his eyes shone as he gazed at her. She slipped her hands around his neck, and he embraced her tighter. They remained like that for a while, not saying anything, just intimately sharing the space together.

When she let go, he released her. She sat back and met his eyes. He wasn't quite as relaxed as he had been that morning but was less tense than when he'd entered the room. Softer. One of his hands moved up and stroked her hair. "Take as long as you need. We're not in a hurry."

For a moment, she wasn't quite sure what he meant, possible answers running through her mind. She put two and two together. He wouldn't rush her to leave and head back to the apartment. "Thanks," she glanced around and back to him, "I think I'm ready to go."

They untangled from each other, and he helped her stand. She glanced at her bed, "What do you think? Should I toss everything in garbage bags or leave it as is? Which would be easier for getting back to the apartment?"

He thought about it, "Just leave them as is."

He didn't even react to the underwear drawer, leaving Zoe more at ease. They returned to the apartment and put the drawers on the floor where the dresser would soon live.

She hadn't been wrong. Liam went to the piano and played for over an hour. He didn't attack the keys quite as aggressively as she'd anticipated he might.

Curled up on the end of the couch closest to the piano, she used her phone to pull up a book she'd been reading. Listening to the music, she tried to get sucked into the story. It was a sweet romance that had become one of her favorite reads. It had served as a good escape over the past few years.

She couldn't focus on the book for some reason. Her eyes scanned the page but took in no information. Liam was still playing, and she tossed her phone aside to turn her attention to him. She wasn't sure what he was playing, but it was quite beautiful. His fingers danced gracefully across the keys, and it was mesmerizing. Watching him, she felt the swirl of emotions inside settle a little. She still felt mixed up, but suddenly, it wasn't quite so overwhelming.

He's not Fred. He's not my parents. Over and over, those words ran through her brain. She studied his face. The man she saw wasn't the same as the man in all those photos online. The stern, angry face that had glared at cameras years earlier was gone. Not that he didn't still look stern sometimes or glare, because he did. But the anger didn't live on his face anymore.

"Pick something," he told her without looking in her direction as he finished the piece he'd been playing.

She slipped off the couch and walked a few feet to the piano to pull from the stack of books. Opening to the song she wanted, she set it in front of him.

She watched his eyes scan the page, and a small smile formed on his lips. He positioned his fingers on the keyboard, and the song began. She moved a few feet behind where he sat.

Knowing he couldn't see her, she felt freer and let herself sway and spin to the music. She sang the lyrics she could remember as she danced. Eyes shut, she was alone in her own little world.

The song came to an end, and she slowed to a stop. Eyes still shut, just breathing. Waiting. For what, she wasn't quite sure.

Music started again, but this time it wasn't the piano. Liam must've pulled up something on his phone. She heard him get up from the piano bench, and his footsteps approached her. Fingers tapped her shoulder, and she turned, opening her eyes to look up at him. Soft Liam was there, fully on display. He held his hand to her, "May I have this dance?"

She gave him her hand, and his free arm wrapped around her back, pulling her close. They didn't exactly dance. Mostly, it was just holding each other and swaying.

It was perfect.

Twenty-Five

Liam

"What are you doing?"

He didn't look up. Teeth holding the Sharpie lid, he ordered, "Stay still."

She laughed, "Just tell me what you're doing."

Mildly exasperated, he took hold of her hand, "You are not staying still."

"Maybe you should tell me what you're doing."

Holding her still, he began to write on the back of her hand. The first joint of each finger got a number. When he finished, he let go, moved to her other side, and repeated what he'd already done. Recapping the Sharpie, he said, "Finished."

She studied her hands, "Is there some reason you think I've forgotten how to count?"

He shook his head, "This isn't for counting."

"Alright, I'll bite. What is this?"

He placed the opened book on the music stand. "I thought this might help you visualize things better."

They'd managed to get her through some of the basics. She seemed to have a good grasp on notes and rests, and over the last few days, she'd struggled with her memory a little less. It was time to have her use the piano. He watched as she looked from the page to her hands and back to the page. She looked at him perplexed, "Seriously, Liam, what is this?"

"We're only gonna worry about your right hand for now."

"I need to be worried about my right hand? What about my left? Do I need to worry about it too?"

He looked at her, trying to hide his amusement, "You finished?"

She leaned over and kissed him on the cheek, "Okay."

He huffed out a laugh, "You will not distract me."

"No, of course not," she said innocently. Batting her eyelashes at him, she added, "Explain numbers to me."

It was so tempting to kiss her senseless, but he restrained himself and told her, "Put your thumb on Middle C."

She did, and then he showed her the placement of her hand on the rest of the keys. The next twenty minutes were spent walking through how the numbers correlated to what was on the page. She seemed to be grasping it, and he went as far as teaching her the five keys her fingers were sitting on. He could tell when she stopped focusing. Rather than trying to force her to continue, he told her they were done for the day.

"I get why you put numbers on one hand, but why both?"

He sat back in the chair, "So that you'll keep seeing it, and the image will get lodged in your brain. You'll need to know it eventually anyway."

She got up from the piano bench and went to the kitchen, returning a few moments later with a drink. Sitting cross-legged on the couch, she asked, "Are you going to be reapplying the numbers every time they start to fade?"

He moved from the chair and sat beside her, "Probably."

She laughed, "If I actually get a job interview, they're gonna see that and think

I'm a weirdo."

He smiled at her, "They'll be thrilled to know you're learning a new skill."

She took a sip of her drink. When she put the cap back on the bottle, she leaned her head sideways against the back of the couch and stared at him. "So."

"So?"

"I live here."

He quirked an eyebrow, "I assumed you'd figured that out, given that all your belongings are now here."

It was the January fifteenth. Her house keys had been returned, and they were officially living together.

"I want to ask you something," she told him after a few moments of deliberation.

"Anything." He studied her face. Whatever it was she wanted to ask, it was something she wasn't certain about approaching. It was tempting to push, but instead, he held his tongue and waited.

She picked at the bottle's label and finally said, "It's about your past."

He nodded, "What is it?"

A few seconds passed before she asked, "How did you meet Jonas?"

He'd known he would have to tell her at some point. It was probably best to talk about it now rather than wait until some undetermined point in the future. "Do you know what a church elder is?"

She shook her head, "An old person?"

He smiled slightly, "No, but good guess. In some churches, they're called deacons, but as far as I know, it's all basically the same thing. They're the men who govern the church."

She made a face, "Is it just men? Women don't get to be elders?"

"Women get to be elder's wives," he cringed as the words left his lips.

"So, it's just a bunch of men deciding things for everyone. Great. Doesn't sound misogynistic at all." She looked a little disgusted.

He huffed out a laugh, "Welcome to Church 101. There are churches where the women get to be the elder or deacon instead of just being the wife, but I've not been involved with them."

"So, was Jonas one of the elder things?"

He shook his head, "No, but I probably wouldn't have met him if not for one of the church's elders. When I was thirteen, one of the elders came to Mark insisting that Jonas be brought in to speak. Mark wasn't thrilled by the idea, but the elder was one of the wealthiest men in the church, and there was a building project looming."

Standing, he walked to the kitchen to refill his coffee cup. He continued, "Jonas came and spoke on a Sunday morning, and there were special services all week where he continued to speak." He sighed and leaned against the counter, staring at his now full mug, "I could tell pretty early on that Mark didn't like Jonas. The thing was, Jonas was nice to me. He genuinely seemed to take an interest in me. I didn't sense that he feared me the way other people seemed to. I quickly realized that I had a golden opportunity. I could piss Mark off without him being able to do anything about it. If he showed publicly that he had an issue with Jonas, that would rankle the elder who was obsessed with Jonas's teachings."

Picking up his cup, he walked back to the couch. Zoe watched him, and as he sat, she asked, "What exactly do you mean when you say he took an interest in you?"

Liam considered how to answer. After a few moments, he said, "Jonas is very skilled at picking up on a person's strengths and weaknesses. He offered me unsolicited praise for things that everyone else seemed to take for granted. By the end of the week, he informed me that he could see I had a capacity for greatness, and he wanted to help me become what he knew I could be."

A harsh laugh escaped his lips, "I know how that sounds now. But back then...I felt like everyone only tolerated me because...because I was Mark's nephew. Any compliments I received felt hollow. I...I never knew if they actually meant it or if it was just what they felt they had to say because of who I was." He took a drink and added, "So, Jonas walked into my life, and he didn't give a shit about what Mark thought. He told me things I wanted to hear. I assumed that he meant all of it. There was no reason for him to lie. He wasn't interested in currying favor with Mark."

He ran his free hand through his hair, "Mark told me to keep my distance, and I didn't. After he left, Jonas began emailing me under the guise of being a mentor. I told him Mark didn't think I should be in contact with him, and he asked me if I agreed with Mark. I told him I didn't, and he suggested we communicate privately, leaving Mark out of the loop."

Zoe shook her head, "You were thirteen when all of this happened?"

"Yeah."

She chewed on her nail briefly before saying, "That kind of sounds like grooming."

He was slightly surprised by her choice of words and shook his head, "No, it wasn't like that."

"An adult told you to keep it secret that you were in communication?" She fixed him with a very pointed look, "Liam, if it was your child and an adult did that to them, what would you call it?"

"It *wasn't* grooming," he insisted, feeling agitated. There was something about what Zoe was saying that felt a little too close to the truth, and he didn't like it. He shook his head, "It couldn't have been."

She reached out and took his hand gently. Looking up at him, her voice was soft as she asked, "Have you told Dr. Constance about this?"

"No."

"Maybe you should."

"How have things been?" Dr. Constance asked as he settled onto the couch Wednesday morning.

"Good," he replied without offering anything more. Zoe's words from Sunday had been stuck in his brain for the last few days.

"Care to expand on that?"

He wasn't ready to dive into what had been bothering him and instead said, "Zoe's officially moved in."

Dr. Constance took a moment to drink from her water bottle, then asked, "Are you still feeling good about this?"

He nodded, "Yes. I like having her there. It's nice...being together. I'm definitely sleeping better than I ever have."

The doctor smiled, "I'm glad to hear that. Does she seem to be adjusting fairly well?"

"I think so. She's not having too many bad nights." Her night terrors hadn't stopped, but they were happening less frequently.

"Good."

He fell silent, and his eyes dropped to his hands. At least a minute of silence passed before he said, "Zoe said something on Sunday that..." he shook his head, "I can't stop thinking about it."

"What did she say?"

He recounted the conversation and ended with, "She suggested that Jonas had been grooming me. But that can't be right."

Dr. Constance finished writing some notes and looked at him. "Why do you think it wasn't?"

"He wasn't trying to have sex with me," Liam replied flatly.

She shook her head, "Liam, do you understand that grooming isn't specifically tied to sex? It can be non-sexual. You've told me before that Jonas used you. And now you tell me he began developing a relationship with you when you were a minor, under the guise of being your mentor, and encouraged you to keep it secret. What was his goal in being your mentor?"

Liam was quiet for a long time before replying, "He said it was God's plan for him to hand the ministry over to me when he was ready to retire."

"Did you want to take over the ministry?"

He shook his head, "No."

"Why did you go along with it?"

Her questions weren't asked with judgment. He knew she was trying to get him to see the entire picture. Shame and anger were warring inside as he admitted, "Jonas...he made me feel special. I wanted to...to make him happy, and if taking over for him was what I had to do...I was going to."

Twenty-Six

Liam

It had been months since he'd last been in such a dark mood. As he left therapy, rage consumed him. He wanted to crush something. Wanted to feel it fall apart in his hands and watch it hit the ground completely decimated.

He'd been so convinced Dr. Constance would tell him Zoe was wrong about Jonas. Instead, she'd agreed with Zoe. His anger burned hot. Could he really have been so blind?

Sitting in his car, all he wanted was Zoe. Wanted her in his arms. Wanted to hear her telling him it was okay. He stared at the parking lot, unable to bring himself to drive home. He didn't want her to see him like this. She had enough to deal with without adding a rage-filled monster to that list. If she saw him like this, she might be so frightened that she'd decide living in her car was preferable to being with him.

His body grew chilled. He sat there a long time, knowing he needed to leave but unable to make himself. It felt like he was being pulled back into the gaping maw of the dark pit that had held him prisoner for such a long time.

A knock at the car window made him jump. Looking up in surprise, he saw

Dr. Constance standing there. He opened the car door, and she knelt a little to look at him. Her eyes were worried as she told him, "Come back inside, Liam."

He shook his head, voice tight, "I'm about to go."

"You've been out here almost two hours. Come inside and get warmed up."

He knew she wouldn't take no for an answer and silently followed her inside. Back on the couch, he took the mug of hot tea that she handed him. "Drink that," she instructed.

He made a face. He hated tea. "I'm fine."

She sighed and sat across from him, "Who are you trying to convince?"

The warmth of the cup was pleasant. He stared down at the tea bag floating in the water. Despite the warmth, he could still feel the anger pulsing through him. There had been a time when he would've thrown the cup as hard as he could against the wall. He'd be lying if he said the temptation wasn't still there. *And what would that accomplish?* He sighed in frustration and forced himself to sip the leaf water.

He didn't look up but knew Dr. Constance was watching him. A few minutes passed, and his phone dinged. He pulled it out and saw a text.

Just checking in.

His shoulders slumped as he read the message. What was he going to tell her?

"Liam, is that Zoe?"

He nodded, "She expected me home almost an hour and a half ago."

"Why didn't you go home?" Dr. Constance's voice was gentle.

He started shaking, and not because he was chilled. Setting the cup on the table beside the couch, he clasped his hands tightly and stared at the floor. His head was beginning to pound. "I couldn't." He buried his head in his hands, "I don't want...to scare her."

"Would you be okay with it if I talked to her? I don't think you should drive right now, and I know you don't want her to be worried."

He held out his phone with Zoe's number on the screen. Dr. Constance took it and told him, "I'm going to step out for a few minutes, and then I'll be back, okay?"

A shrug and slight nod was all the response he could give.

When Dr. Constance returned, she placed the phone on the couch, saying, "Zoe's on her way."

His head jerked up, "She is?"

"When I talked to her, she asked if she could come see you. She cares about you quite a lot. Is this okay?"

The moment she'd said Zoe was coming, relief had filled him, helping some of the anger to disperse. Zoe knew he was in a bad place, and she was still coming to him. He nodded.

His head dropped back to his hands, and he shut his eyes. Time passed slowly. After a while, there was an unfamiliar noise, and Dr. Constance said, "I'll be back shortly."

Less than a minute passed with him being alone. The door opened, footsteps drew near, and he heard, "Can I sit here?"

He opened his eyes and raised his head. Zoe stood there, looking at him, eyes filled with compassion. He stared at her for a few seconds, then nodded. She sat next to him, and after a moment, he reached for her. Without hesitation, she let him pull her into a tight embrace. The angle was awkward, but she didn't complain. Simply held onto him almost as tightly as he was holding her.

They sat like that for a long time, and he began to calm down. Slowly, he started to let go and looked at her. She lifted a hand and tenderly pushed his hair out of his eyes. Her fingers slowly trailed down the side of his face. "Want to go home?" she asked softly.

"Yeah."

The rest of the day passed without incident. He got home and went to the piano, where he spent several hours playing until his fingers ached. Zoe didn't crowd him, but she didn't leave him alone, either. Late afternoon, as he finally backed away from the instrument, she told him, "I'm going to make something to eat."

He sat on the couch while she busied herself in the kitchen and found himself turning the tv to that stupid cartoon dog show. It really wasn't stupid, but he felt stupid for needing something so childish.

After a little while, Zoe brought him a bowl of pasta and joined him on the couch with her own. They ate quietly, and when finished, she took the bowls back to the kitchen and cleaned up.

When she rejoined him, he reached for her. She nestled against him. One episode ran into another. He didn't let go. They would have to talk about what had happened, but that would have to wait.

It grew dark outside, and Zoe lightly patted his arm, "I promise I'll be right back, but I really need to pee."

He let her go, and she hurried out of the room. Getting up from the couch, he stretched and realized how thirsty he was. He got a drink and stood at the counter for a few moments. He didn't feel as bad as he had at the end of therapy. Zoe's quiet company had been soothing.

She returned, and he noticed she'd changed into her pajamas. Flannel pants and an oversized t-shirt. It was a good look for her. Then again, pretty much everything was a good look for her. She stepped close, her gaze searching as she asked, "How are you feeling?"

He wrapped his arms around her, pulling her close. Kissing the top of her head, he sighed, "Okay. Not great, but better than I was."

Her arm went around his back, "That's good."

He rested his head against her, "Thank you…for coming and getting me."

"Of course."

"And for feeding me."

She giggled, "I made sure to leave out the pineapple."

He groaned, "You put pineapple in pasta?"

She shrugged, "It's not nearly as weird as you think."

"Sure it's not," he replied with a quiet laugh.

When they went to bed, Liam could not get comfortable. Before Zoe, he'd always slept without a shirt, but that had stopped as soon as they started sharing a bed. Mostly, wearing a shirt hadn't bothered him, but as he lay there, it felt like it was strangling him. He could feel every centimeter of fabric scratching against his skin. All he could think about was how he wanted to tear the shirt off and set it on fire.

Frustrated, he finally asked, "Zoe?"

She was curled up beside him, but he was fairly certain she wasn't asleep yet. Something that was confirmed when he felt her nod and heard, "Hmm?"

"Is it…going to bother you if I take my shirt off?"

In reply, she backed away and said, "No."

Relieved, he sat up, ripped off the shirt, and hurled it onto the floor. "Thanks," he told her as he laid back down.

She yawned as she replied, "Sure," and scooted closer.

He froze as she snuggled against him, her arm and head coming to rest on his naked chest. A shiver ran through him at the feel of her skin pressed against his. To his horror, his body began to quickly respond to the intimate contact, and he knew he needed to get away from her. He stood from the bed.

"Liam?" he heard her sleep-drenched voice speak his name. It did nothing to help the rapidly growing situation.

"Go to sleep. I'll be back in a few minutes," he told her, voice raspy. Before she could say anything more, he made a beeline for the bathroom and locked himself in. Turning on the exhaust fan and shower, he hoped that was enough noise that if Zoe were still awake, she wouldn't think anything more than a shower was happening.

Stripping off his remaining clothes, he stepped under the spray of water and pulled the curtain closed. Quickly, he was soaked, and he braced one hand against the shower wall. Eyes shut, he tried to relax.

He wasn't sure he'd ever been so turned on in his life. It wasn't the first time he'd felt aroused because of Zoe, but this was unlike those other times. This time he didn't just want her, he desperately needed her. He needed to be as close as possible to her. Consuming her. He'd never do anything without her permission. He might be a monster, but he wasn't that kind of monster.

He'd seen the work of those kinds of monsters, and it sickened him.

He sighed in frustration. It had been a beyond shitty day, and all he wanted to do was make love to the woman he loved.

And that wasn't an option.

He wasn't proud of what he proceeded to do, but at least he'd be able to clean up and return to the bedroom with Zoe none the wiser. And just to be safe, he'd sleep in a shirt for the foreseeable future.

Twenty-Seven

Zoe

"L iam?"

"Hmm?"

"I love you."

Liam's eyes went wide. A moment later, he broke out in that broad, dimpled smile that always gave her butterflies. He pulled her close, "I love you, sweetheart. I love you so incredibly much."

The dream was clear in her mind when she woke the next morning. She yawned and rubbed her eyes. The room was full of sunlight. Her eyes focused on Liam. He was gazing at her with eyes crinkling at the corners from the smile that filled his face. Relief coursed through her. He must be feeling better than he had the night before. "Hi," she said with another yawn.

He cupped her cheek and leaned in, giving her a tender kiss. "Hey."

Something had shifted in him overnight. He was more relaxed. Confident.
"Wait..." Something was niggling at her brain as she felt the fabric of his shirt, "Didn't you...?"

"Didn't I what?"

She shook her head, "Must've been another dream. Weird."

Bemused, he asked, "Another dream? How many did you have last night?"

She smiled, remembering how his bare chest had felt against her in the dream. Remembering how he'd responded when she told him *I love you*.

"That smile would say they were good."

"Yeah," she sighed happily. Happiness that lasted for all of five more seconds as she fully woke up and realized that was all they had been.

Dreams.

Her face fell, and she tried to turn away before he would notice, but she didn't quite succeed. "What's wrong?" he asked her, and when she didn't look back at him, his fingers went against her cheek to move her head to face him. "Zoe?"

Dream Liam had told her he loved her. Not real Liam. She could feel the tears beginning to collect. Her eyes shut tightly, "It's fine." Unfortunately, her shaky voice only added to the evidence she was lying.

"Sweetheart?"

The endearment was too much. She pulled away and got out of bed. Going to the dresser, she started taking out clothes for the day. "Need the bathroom, or am I good to take a shower?" she asked, forcing her voice to sound brighter than she felt.

"You can shower." She jumped and spun around to find he was close enough to touch. He stared down at her, perplexed, "What's wrong?"

She swallowed hard and tried to convince her eyes to keep the tears back. Turning away, she replied, "Just need a shower."

"Zoe."

She ignored him and went into the bathroom, locking the door between them.

The tears had already begun to fall, but she managed to get into the shower before the floodgates burst. Sinking to the floor of the tub, she hugged herself and sobbed. Great gasping inhales and exhales.

The dreams had been so real. For weeks, she'd been trying to push her feelings down where they would be easy to hide from Liam. It was getting harder every day. She couldn't tell him. Absolutely could not tell him. What if he didn't return her feelings? She wanted to believe he did, but if she had read everything wrong...that would make things even more painful.

It would ruin everything.

By the time she turned the shower off, she'd managed to get her emotions under control. She was fairly certain that she'd be able to keep the truth buried and able act like herself once she left the bathroom.

Dressed and hair still damp, she unlocked the door. Returning to the bedroom, she found Liam waiting for her. He was sitting on the edge of the bed facing the door. She did her best to smile, "Shower's free."

"C'mere," he held out his hand to her.

She hesitated a second before stepping closer and taking it, "Yes?"

"Tell me the truth." His face was as serious as his eyes.

She gave him a quizzical look, "About?"

He pulled her a few inches closer, "You're not fine. Tell me why."

She leaned forward, dropped a light kiss on his lips, and began to back away, "Don't worry about it."

He didn't let go, and she had to stop moving. His eyes held hers, and she was unable to look away. He drew her closer again and lifted his hand to rest against her cheek, "Don't tell me not to worry about it."

The feel of his hand on her face had its intended effect. She leaned into the touch and sighed, "I'm serious, Liam."

"So am I, Zoe. You're the one who told me you love me. So, don't tell me not to worry about it. Tell me what's wrong."

His words sank in, and she froze. It took a few seconds to find her voice, "I...I did?" He nodded, and her brain exploded. It hadn't been a dream? "You said you love me," she murmured.

He nodded, "I did."

Her lips trembled, "You love me?"

His smile was dazzling, "I do."

Their faces were inches from each other. She searched his eyes to see if there was anything there to tell her that this wasn't actually happening. Liam's eyes were honest. She only read love in those dark depths. "I thought I dreamed it."

"Is that why you were upset?" he asked.

She began to nod, but before she could say anything, his lips pressed against hers. His hand moved away from her face and up into her hair. His other arm wrapped around her, holding her close.

This kiss was different than the others. It was more alive, far less cautious. Hungry, but a hunger that she could tell Liam was keeping a tight reign on. His head was tilted up, meeting hers. She gazed down at him briefly before her eyes closed as the kiss deepened.

He began to laugh, and the kiss broke. Baffled, she asked, "What?"

"I'm just wondering what else you *dreamed*." He held up the hand that had been in her hair seconds earlier to make air quotes around the word *dreamed*.

She pressed her lips to his forehead before stepping back, "Wouldn't you like to know?"

He stood up and pulled her back into an embrace, "I asked, didn't I?"

She laughed and quickly ducked out of his hold. Leaving the room, she said, "Be good, and maybe I'll tell you."

"I'm holding you to that," he called out after her.

In the kitchen, she pulled a bowl from one cupboard, grabbed cereal from another, and milk out of the fridge. Setting everything on the counter, she paused as realization slammed into her.

Liam loved her.

He knew she loved him, and he hadn't responded in any of the ways that she'd been so scared he would.

She loved Liam McPherson, and he loved her.

"Are you trying to use telekinesis to fill the bowl?"

Speaking of Liam McPherson, he stood on the opposite side of the counter, staring at her with amusement. She blinked a few times and shook her head, trying to feel less wibbly wobbly. "I...uh...I..." Words were not working with her.

He was just so damn happy. It took her breath away, and she wasn't sure what to do with that. He beamed at her, walked around the counter, and picked up the box, "Tell me when."

She reached for the cereal, "I can do it."

He held it just out of reach, "Sure you can."

She went up on her tiptoes, trying to grab it, and he held it even higher. "That's not fair!"

He kissed the tip of her nose, "Dunno, seems pretty fair to me."

Jumping, she barely grasped one corner of the box and tried to wrest it from his grasp. To her annoyance, he went up on his tiptoes and pulled it even further out of her reach. "Liam! Give it to me!" she squealed indignantly.

He stepped back, "Tell me about your other dream,"

"You think this qualifies as being good?"

He smiled that infuriatingly adorable smile and shrugged, "Depends on your definition of good."

Her eyes did a quick scan of her surroundings. Before he could fully realize what she was doing, she'd scrambled on top of the counter nearest where he was holding the box up. Reaching out, she managed to get hold of it...right as she lost her balance.

The box crashed to the floor as Liam reached out to catch her before she went crashing to the floor as well. Her momentary panic quickly shifted to surprise as his arms went around her. Somehow, he managed to maneuver her, so one arm was under her knees, and the other was around her back. She looped her arms around his neck and shakily told him, "Th-thanks. You can put me down now."

He raised an eyebrow, "That sounds like a terrible idea."

It really did, but she still shook her head, "I'm too heavy. You're going to hurt yourself."

Instead of saying anything, he rolled his eyes and pressed his lips against hers for a few seconds. She sighed happily into the kiss, and when he broke it, she stared at him with slightly disappointed eyes. He was still smiling at her. It had to be a new record for the length of time Liam McPherson could smile. A mischievous light entered his eyes, and he told her, "I'll put you down on one condition."

She had a pretty good idea of what was coming but still asked, "What?"

"Tell me about the other dream."

"Fine," she didn't sound nearly as exasperated as she tried to.

He looked a sight too pleased with himself at her reply and moved with her still in his arms so his back was leaning against the counter, "Go ahead."

"It's really not that big a thing. You don't want to hear about it."

He chuckled, "You do realize the more you say things like that, the more intriguing you're making this."

She could feel her cheeks growing warm. She buried her head in the crook of his neck as she mumbled, "You weren't wearing a shirt."

"I see," his voice dripped with amusement and a note of something else she couldn't quite put her finger on.

She sighed, slightly annoyed, "It was just a dream. Now put me down."

Her feet went on the floor, and she knelt to pick up the box. To her relief, it hadn't popped open when it landed. At least there wasn't a mess to clean up. Standing, she moved back to her bowl. Before she could start filling it, arms went around her shoulders. His chest was against her back, and his chin rested on her head, "You sure that was a dream?"

She nodded, though she was doubting it more and more by the second, "Yeah."

"Really?"

She managed to move so she could turn and look up at him. Her cheeks were still warm, and she was surprised to see his were slightly pink. She bit her lip as she admitted, "I'm...I'm not sure."

His smile had softened, and he kissed her forehead before telling her, "Good instinct. Go with that. Now," his eyes shifted from her to the cereal components on the counter, "Is that really what you want for breakfast?"

What exactly was he implying? "Do you have a better suggestion?"

He nodded, "Want some French toast? I need to use up the last of that loaf of bread."

Twenty-Eight

Liam

By the time he turned the shower off, guilt and shame threatened to suffocate him. He was such a hypocrite. How many times had he stood up and told groups of students that masturbation was a sin? While he sincerely doubted most of them had taken his words seriously, that didn't change the fact that he'd stood there and had the audacity to say it.

Leaving the bathroom, he pulled a t-shirt from his closet and returned to bed. Zoe was barely awake, and she immediately glommed onto him. He held her loosely, a little relief mixing with his otherwise turbulent feelings. She clearly had no idea what had happened in the shower.

He stared at the ceiling, disappointed in himself. It had been a phenomenally shitty day.

"Liam?"

"Hmm?" he looked at her and saw she was watching him with eyes as sleepy as her voice.

She smiled dreamily, "I love you."

He heard her words, but for a heartbeat of a second, they didn't fully click.

Once they did, joy overwhelmed him. He held her tighter and poured every ounce of love he could into his reply, "I love you, sweetheart. I love you so incredibly much." Her eyes slid shut at his words, and he watched as she drifted off in his arms, lips still curved in a smile.

It wasn't such a shitty day after all.

Zoe was all smiles as he kissed her forehead while handing her the plate of French toast. He resisted teasing her about the fact she thought she'd dreamt what had happened the night before. There would be time enough for that later. This morning, he was just going to enjoy being with her. He joined her at the table with his plate. After she'd eaten a few bites, she told him, "I'm going in to record this morning. Want to come with?"

She'd been going two or three times a week since moving in. He'd gone with her nearly every time. The studio staff were surprised to see him so frequently but thrilled to see Zoe so often. He enjoyed seeing just how much they loved her. They seemed to see her the same way he did. The way he hoped he'd be able to help her see herself someday. "Sure. When do you want to leave?"

Her eyes were on her phone, "Looks like booths are available at eleven. Want me to go ahead and sign us up?"

He nodded, and they returned to eating. As he watched her, it occurred to him that there was a whole pile of things they needed to discuss. He wasn't sure how to approach that particular conversation. It felt like everything in their relationship had been done out of order. They'd moved in together before figuring out where they stood with each other. Started sleeping together without discussing boundaries. They would have to have the conversation soon, but maybe not today. They just needed a nice, peaceful day after the last several weeks.

After breakfast, they collected Zoe's car from the lot at Dr. Constance's. Not long after, they headed to the studio. Once they finished recording, Zoe spent twenty minutes talking with Will. It had started with him asking her about a few upcoming dates to see if she could cover live reads, and then they just talked about whatever. Liam stood a few feet behind Zoe, listening to the animated conversation. When she finished, they headed for his car.

Turning the ignition on, he asked, "Do you want to go home immediately?"

"Not necessarily. I'm not really up for sorting through even more rejection emails right now. Why?"

He glanced at her, "I want to stop somewhere, and we can grab lunch after if you want."

She nodded, "Sure."

Ten minutes later, he parked at the entrance of a storage unit complex. Leaving the car, he told her, "You should come with."

She looked surprised but left the car and followed him inside without question. He led her down to one of the units and unlocked the padlock. Pushing the door up, the unit's contents sat before them. He hadn't been to check on them in almost a year.

"What is all this?" Zoe asked.

He leaned against the door frame, "Stuff I haven't really wanted to deal with. Honestly, I should've gotten rid of it ages ago, but I just never got around to it. See anything you want to take home?"

She looked around, and her eyes lit upon a few boxes, "Who's Ariadne?"

"My grandmother. She died before I was born."

Zoe stepped closer to the boxes and opened one. They were the kind of boxes that held clothes on hangers. Looking into it, she said, "These are gorgeous. She had good taste.”

“Do you want them?”

She lifted a black and red dress and studied it, “Not sure if it’ll fit.”

“You can take it home; if it does, I’ll come back and get the rest for you to go through.”

She hesitated briefly before asking, “It won’t be weird for you if I’m wearing your dead grandmother’s clothes?"

He chuckled, “Why would it? It’s not like she’s got much use for them anymore.”

She placed the dress back in the box and closed the top. Her hand rested on it for a few moments. Picking it up, she carried it to the entrance, “Let’s take this one.”

“Anything else?”

She shook her head, “I don’t think so. Was there something you wanted to grab?”

He nodded and moved past her. Though he wasn't completely sure where his quarry was, he had a general idea of where to start his hunt. Roughly fifteen minutes later, he found it. Opening it, he quickly checked to ensure his memory hadn’t failed him.

They took the boxes back to the car. The clothes went in the back seat while he put the other box in the trunk. Zoe hadn’t asked him about it, and he was glad. She’d find out about its contents eventually. He never should’ve put that particular box in storage, but he hadn’t thought he’d ever need what was inside. Thankfully, his stupidity hadn’t come back to bite him in the ass.

“Lunch?” he asked as he pulled out of the parking spot.

“Sure.”

“What do you want?”

“You can pick,” she replied.

He drove a few blocks before parking in front of a restaurant. Turning the car off, he asked, "This okay?"

She nodded, "Sure. I've never had Greek before."

Once they placed their orders, they sat in the booth facing each other. Zoe took hold of one of his hands. She held it while her free hand explored the lines covering his palm, "What do you know about your grandmother?"

He smiled at the question. When it came to talking about his family, his grandparents were a subject he didn't find painful to discuss. "My grandfather said she was the most intelligent and beautiful woman he'd ever met. He also said that the fact she agreed to go out with him was scandalous."

Zoe's eyebrows went up, "How so?"

"She was the daughter of a senator, and he was her father's bodyguard. He was also five years younger than her. They started dating secretly and eventually eloped. When she got pregnant, their secret relationship became public knowledge. He said that it might have cost her career."

"But it didn't?"

He shook his head, "Didn't have a chance to. She died in childbirth, and he was left alone to raise my mother and Mark. I don't think he ever really got over her death."

"That's so sad," Zoe sighed.

It really was. He could remember the look on his grandfather's face when he'd talked about Ariadne. Though Liam had been very young, the image of the man's grief had left a permanent impression. He'd never understood how his grandfather could still be so deep in mourning decades after she had died. Now, though, as he looked at Zoe, Liam finally understood.

They carried the boxes into the apartment. He placed the one he'd grabbed on the top shelf of the closet. Zoe opened the clothing box, began pulling items out, and laid them on the bed. She hadn't been wrong; his grandmother had good taste.

Zoe studied them, her fingers lightly trailing over the material. She paused on one dress with fabric that shifted from dark purple to light blue. She picked it up after a few seconds and disappeared into the bathroom.

He wasn't sure if she was okay with him staying in the bedroom while she figured out if things fit, but she hadn't told him she wanted to be alone, and he was very curious to see her in the dresses. A minute passed, and the door cracked open, "Um, can you zip me up?"

Walking to the bathroom, he saw her open the door wider, with her back to him. The zipper was partially zipped, but the last several inches were hanging open. Carefully, he took hold of the zipper and finished its journey. Stepping back, he watched as she turned to look in the bathroom mirror before facing him.

She took a few steps toward him and spun around, letting the skirt fly out with a gentle swishing sound. Grinning at him, she said, "I love it! I can't believe it fits!"

He stared at her, unable to respond, barely able to breathe. She was so incredibly beautiful. The dress might have been made for her; it fit that perfectly. His heart hammered in his chest as he watched her sway with the skirt softly moving side-to-side.

Zoe's face fell after a few moments of him not responding. She sighed, "Do you hate it? Was I right about this being too weird for you?"

He managed to unfreeze and shook his head as he stepped closer. Holding his hand out to her, she took it. He spun her out and pulled her back into his arms. She giggled at the move, and he kissed the top of her head. She took a step and turned to look up at him. His voice was rough as he met her eyes, "It's not...too weird. You..." he swallowed hard, "You're gorgeous."

Her cheeks turned pink, and she went up on her tiptoes to kiss his cheek. She stepped back and looked down at the dress, "No idea when I'll ever have reason to wear this," her eyes looked to the bed, "or any of the rest of them. But this is honestly the prettiest thing I've ever had on, and I don't think I can bear to get rid of it."

He made a mental note to take her on plenty of dates that would allow her ample opportunity to wear the dresses.

She let go of his hand and walked to the bed. Picking up another one of the dresses, she carried it to the bathroom and hung it on the shower curtain rod. She returned to the doorway and turned her back to him, "Start the zipper for me?"

He wasn't sure that was a good idea. The sight of her was doing things to him and helping her get out of the dress wasn't going to help matters. *I can do this. She's trusting me to behave. I can behave.* Steeling himself, he made a point of not touching her skin as he pulled the zipper down to approximately where he thought it had been when she had asked for help earlier.

She shut the bathroom door between them, and he raced for the relative safety of the kitchen. Downing half a bottle of water, he mentally kicked himself. He was better than this. After all, he wasn't some horny teenager who couldn't control himself.

"Liam?" Zoe appeared wearing a yellow dress covered in embroidered pink flowers.

"Need help?" he asked, making his voice sound as normal as possible.

She shook her head, "Nope, zipper's on the side on this one." Stepping around the counter, she did another spin, laughing in delight. "Do I look okay?"

He nodded, not trusting himself to speak. She was still smiling as she bounced back to the bedroom. As she tried on the remaining few dresses, he held it together. To his relief, the rest had zippers on the side, so he was able to keep his distance. There was no doubt in his mind that they would need to have that talk soon. Very soon.

Twenty-Nine

Zoe

She sat cross-legged on the couch, crochet hook in hand, yarn ball in her lap. Alex had taught her the basics of the craft while they were roommates, and while it wasn't something she was very skilled at, she'd found a blanket pattern that was easy and didn't require remembering how to do several different types of stitches.

Liam sat on the other end of the couch, watching her work. She'd told him he could put something on to watch, but he'd shaken his head and sat quietly for the last half hour.

It had been a beautiful, perfect day. She was still stunned by the clothes. Honestly, she'd never been much for dresses. Leggings and sweatshirts were her go-to wardrobe. When she'd slipped on that first dress, it had fit like a glove. It had been shocking when she looked at herself in the mirror. She almost looked pretty. The dress certainly made her feel lovelier than she'd ever felt before.

Liam's stunned reaction to seeing her had made her worry, but then he'd told her she was gorgeous. He was being kind, but she still treasured the compliment. He'd gotten a little weird as the afternoon had passed. With every dress she tried on, he'd seemed to try to put more space between them. She wasn't sure how to interpret that.

She focused on the yarn, trying hard not to skip a stitch. She didn't want to have to frog it if she didn't have to. Frogging was a nightmare because she never seemed to catch her mistakes until she had to frog multiple rows. "You okay?" she asked without looking up.

"Hmm?"

She paused her work and lifted her eyes to meet his. He was staring at her intensely. He'd been looking at her that way for the last several hours. Something was definitely on his mind, but she had no idea what. "Seems like you've been thinking very hard about something."

There were a few seconds before he slowly began to nod, "Yeah."

"Want to talk about it?"

He pinched the bridge of his nose, releasing a heavy sigh. "Want to? Not really. But I think we probably have to."

He was so serious it was hard not to feel alarmed. "Okay, should I be worried?"

"No."

"I'm gonna need a little more to go off of than that," she gently teased when he offered nothing more.

He swallowed something invisible, "I know."

They were getting nowhere fast. She picked up her work again, thinking that maybe if eye contact weren't involved, he'd find it easier to talk. One row finished, and she started another before he finally said, "We've never really...talked... about boundaries."

She shook her head, "No, we haven't."

"We need to."

Oh. Not looking up, she asked, "What kind of boundaries?"

He was quiet for at least thirty seconds before replying, "Physical."

It took everything in her to keep her hands moving and her eyes glued to the yarn creation, "Yeah...we probably should...discuss that." *Especially since I already know how your bare chest affects me.*

His voice was a little rough as he told her, "I...I promised you that nothing would happen that you don't want. I meant that." There was a brief pause before he added, "I will never do anything you aren't okay with."

"I appreciate that," she replied softly.

"You're going to have to tell me what is and isn't okay." His voice grew tighter as the sentence finished.

Pausing her work, her hands lowered to her lap, and she finally met his eyes. His face was pinched with tension. She chewed the inside of her cheek, trying to figure out how to respond. "How detailed of a list are you looking for?" she wondered how red she was turning as she asked the question.

"I'll leave that up to you."

She squeezed her eyes shut and took a few deep breaths, trying to get her thoughts into some semblance of order. Forcing her eyes back open, she put it as simply as possible, "Hugs and kisses, yes. Sex, not yet." She immediately dropped her focus to the work in her hands, and she waited to see what he would say.

"Okay." A few beats passed before he asked, "Do you...want me to sleep on the couch?"

Her head snapped up. Confused, she shook her head, "Of course not. Why?"

She watched his Adam's apple bob as he swallowed nothing. He ran a hand through his hair and moved restlessly, "I don't...want you to be...uncomfortable."

Her hand clamped over her mouth, but it was too late. The laugh had already escaped. "Sorry, I didn't mean to laugh. Why would I..." her words trailed off as she belatedly understood what he was implying. "Oh, um..." she shook her head, "No, I don't want you...on...the couch. Do I need to move to the couch?"

He slowly shook his head, "I'd...I'd rather you didn't."

They both slept better with each other than they ever had alone. She wasn't eager to give that up. Thinking about the situation, she finally offered the only solution she could think of that didn't require sleeping apart. "We've got the blanket wall. We can make that a little bigger if we need to."

"You sure?"

She nodded, "It's worked so far."

"You need to...to tell me if you change your mind."

That made her smile, and she leaned the side of her head against the back of the couch. She gazed at him fondly, "I will."

He was still tense, "I swear to you, I won't do anything."

She set her work on the coffee table. Moving close, she reached for his hands. Holding them with hers, she looked up at him, "I know you won't. I trust you."

Her words seemed to relax some of his tension. His gaze softened, and he leaned forward, resting his forehead against hers. "I love you," he said in a low, quiet voice.

"I know," she murmured. "I love you too."

His eyes slid shut as he relaxed a little more. She gently pressed her lips against his. The touch lasted only a moment, then she sat back, and he lifted his head, eyes open and holding hers once more. She squeezed his hands, "You're going to have to tell me if something is too much. Okay?"

He nodded, "Okay."

Wall firmly in place that night, she curled up against him, saying, "You don't have to wear a shirt if you don't want to."

He tensed slightly and told her, "It's not so much a matter of want as of need."

She had a pretty good idea of what he meant and wasn't up to digging more into that statement to see if her suspicions were correct. His hand stroked her hair gently, and she sighed at the touch. "We'll be okay, won't we?"

A few moments passed before he replied, "I think there's a decent chance we will be."

She yawned, sleep already beginning to pull her under, "That's good."

The next morning, she faced another few emails, all containing the same *Thanks, but no thanks* reply to her applications. The feelings of rejection were long past the point of getting old. She stood from the table and ended up beside the stove where Liam was making eggs.

He looked at her, "Good news?"

She shook her head, "Nope. Even fast food places are turning me down. Apparently, I'm not qualified to flip burgers."

He leaned over and dropped a light kiss on her head, "You're overqualified for flipping burgers."

She looked at the egg mixture in the pan, "I think if I see one more rejection email today, I'm going to scream."

He stirred the mixture, beginning to scramble it, "I want to ask you something, and you don't have to answer if you're not up to it."

"Shoot."

"Why did you drop out of high school?"

She rolled her head from side to side, stretching her neck, "You want the short answer or the long one?"

"Whichever you feel like giving."

She watched as he finished the eggs and portioned them out on the plates. He handed her one, and she took it. She opened the fridge and pulled out the ketchup.

Liam followed her to the table, and she laughed at the face he made as she dispensed the ketchup on her eggs. Finished, she held the bottle out, "Want some?

"What do you think?" he looked at the offered bottle with a slightly sick look.

She laughed more and quickly returned the bottle to the fridge. Back at the table, she tackled her eggs and began talking. "I couldn't pass my classes. I worked my ass off, and it was all for nothing. No matter how hard I tried, the tests always ruined everything. I'd do all my homework, all the extra credit, and then I'd flunk all my tests. Fred found out I was failing, and he thought my time would be better spent working at the store."

Liam's eyes narrowed, "He made you drop out?"

She shrugged, "Kind of. I already knew I was going to have to retake tenth grade, and I was still probably going to fail. No one wants to be a sophomore forever. He saw my grades, pointed out that I owed him for pretty much every-thing and I might as well start paying him back rather than wasting my time on something I couldn't do."

"You were in tenth grade?"

She could see the anger in his eyes. Reaching over, she lightly patted his hand, "Hey, it's okay."

His hand was clenched in a tight fist, "It's not."

She shook her head, "No, it's not, but I can't change the past. I can either be okay with it or let bitterness eat me alive. I know which option I'd rather stick with." He didn't say anything, so she continued, "Yes, I was in tenth grade. School sucked for me so much, it was almost a relief not having to go anymore. I'm not dumb. I like to learn. But I definitely did not thrive at school."

He fist relaxed, and the anger lessened in his eyes, "I know you're not dumb. I'm sorry no one tried to help you succeed."

"That would've been nice," she acknowledged a little wistfully. Brighter, she joked, "When I figure out time travel, I'll go back and make sure I survive high school." Eating a few more bites of egg, she told him, "And that's pretty much all there is to tell. Any questions?"

He swallowed and told her, "I don't suppose you'd consider letting me go tell Fred exactly what I think of him."

She shook her head, laughing at the idea of what he was proposing, "Don't waste your time. It wouldn't change anything, and I'd rather you not end up with a broken nose."

His brow furrowed, "I thought you said he didn't beat you."

"He didn't. But I've seen him get in plenty of fights with other people. That's something I'd rather you avoid if at all possible."

Thirty

Liam

"How are things in your world this week?"

He was relaxed on the couch and smiled at Dr. Constance, "Really good."

She returned his smile, "You certainly look like you feel that way. Things are going well with Zoe, I take it? It's been a month since she moved in, right?"

"Almost a month and a half, if we're counting when she started staying with me." Warmth filled him, thinking about his beautiful girlfriend, "And yes, things are going well."

"Do you have plans for Valentine's?"

Valentine's Day was a little less than a week away. "I have plans, but I'm not sure if they're going to be good enough."

He filled her in on what he was thinking. She listened and told him, "That sounds lovely, Liam."

He grew a little more serious, "I just want to make her happy."

"That's very thoughtful."

He was quiet for a little bit, thinking. Finally, "She's never asked about that night, and I know she must've read about it. I need to tell her about it, but I just haven't been able to."

"Why do you think that is?" Dr. Constance was studying him with that unreadable expression he'd gotten used to.

"I've been...having more dreams about it," he admitted. It was true. The dreams were happening nearly every night. Zoe told him he was sleeping restlessly, but he hadn't been able to bring himself to tell her what he saw when he was asleep. He rubbed at his forehead, "I...I don't want her to..." His hand moved to the back of his neck, and he massaged the area.

When he didn't continue, Dr. Constance prompted, "Don't want her to what?"

He swallowed a sip of his coffee, "I just remember when it happened. The questions. I know...*I know* how my answer sounded to...to everyone. I was telling the truth, and everyone assumed I was lying."

His body tensed as he remembered how people responded to him. The way they looked at him. They despised him almost as much as he despised himself. "I don't want her to..." He sighed, "I don't want her to hate me."

Dr. Constance considered that and, after a few moments, began talking, "From what you've told me of what happened, I can understand why people responded the way they did. Would you say that people reached that conclusion knowing the whole story?"

He shook his head, "No."

"Do you think Zoe knows more of the story than others?"

He thought about what he'd told her and slowly began to nod, "Absolutely."

"Do you trust her?"

"Yes," he barely had to think about that answer anymore.

"Assuming she knows the version of what happened that night that everyone else does, do you think she'd be willing to be with you if she believed that was the full story?"

He shook his head, "I'd hope not."

"Liam, based on what you're saying, it appears she's waiting until you're at a place where you're able to tell her about it. If you're not ready, that's okay."

As soon as he walked in the door after therapy, Zoe ran across the room and threw herself into his arms. She held him tightly for a few seconds and beamed, "Guess what!"

He gave her a quick kiss, "What?"

She broke the embrace and grabbed his hand, dragging him across the room to where her laptop and phone sat. Picking up the phone, she tapped the screen a few times and held it out for him to see. Her Venmo was open, and he saw the balance was larger than $0. He looked at her curiously, and she was vibrating with excitement as she told him, "People are actually watching the live stream and sending me tips!"

"That's great," he told her earnestly. It really was. She'd been so down about the overwhelmingly negative response to her job applications that she had finally decided to take a break from applying. It had been her idea to start streaming the 3D printer while it worked. So far, she'd been doing it for two weeks, and this was the first time she'd seen any financial response.

She bit her lip, "I know it's not much, but it's something."

"It was a good idea. I'm happy for you."

She searched his eyes, "You really are, aren't you?"

"I really am," he replied as he kissed her forehead.

She put the phone down, "That's it for my news. How was therapy?"

He moved toward the piano, "It was fine. She seems to think I'm doing better."

As he sat down on the bench, Zoe wrapped her arms around his shoulders and gave him a quick kiss on his cheek, "I agree."

"What am I playing today?"

She moved to sift through the pile of books that now sat on the table beside the piano. It wasn't long until she held out two, "Here you go."

He smiled a little, looking at her picks. Placing one of the books on top of the piano, he opened the other and placed it on the music stand. "Will you sing?"

She gave him a little nod, "If you want me to."

"I always want you to." They had the same exchange every time, and he hoped one day she'd no longer feel the need to ask.

Usually, when he got home from therapy, he'd play aggressively for a bit before calming down enough to play gentler. This time, the opposite happened. As he started playing, it went smoothly. Zoe's voice soothed him. But the longer he played, the more agitated he grew, and he began to attack the keys with ferocity.

Maybe it was minutes. Maybe it was hours. He really wasn't sure how much time had passed when he surfaced from his rage playing. As he lifted his hands from the keys, he felt Zoe's hand on his shoulder. Meeting her eyes, he saw the concern on her face that was echoed in her voice as she asked, "What's wrong?"

He turned to her, his heart aching at the thought of what he had to do. Of how she'd respond when he was done. He wasn't sure he was ready to tell her about that night, but he wasn't sure he'd ever be ready.

Standing, he walked to the couch and sat down. She followed and sat a few feet away. Close enough that he could reach for her if he wanted but far enough away not to make him feel crowded. He had no idea how she knew to do that, but he was grateful she did.

He studied her face. He loved this woman. Trusted her with his everything. She deserved to know the truth about what had happened. If she chose to believe him, that would be a relief. But if she didn't...if she walked away after hearing it...he'd have to let her go. It would destroy him, but he'd do it. He'd never force her to stay with him.

She tilted her head to the side and looked at him, worry very present in her eyes, "Did something happen at therapy?"

He swallowed hard and forced himself to start talking, "When you looked me up, did you read about the night everything went to hell?"

She was quiet for a moment, seeming to search her memory, "The night with the police?"

"Yes."

She nodded, "Yeah."

"You've never asked me about it."

Sadness mixed with the worry, "No, I haven't."

"Why not?"

"I wasn't sure you were ready to talk about it. What I read...it sounded awful."

He sighed, "It was." Closing his eyes momentarily, he breathed, trying to organize his thoughts.

His hands were balled into tight fists, and he felt Zoe gently place her hand on one of them while she said, "You don't have to tell me if you're not ready."

He opened his eyes, "Dr. Constance said something similar. Unfortunately, I don't think there's ever going to...to be a good time to talk about it." Zoe nodded, and he dove into the story when she didn't say anything more.

"I wasn't supposed to be there that night. But I was behind on some work and had locked myself in my office to try to get caught up. I...I realized I was missing some paperwork, and the last place I'd seen it was Jonas's office."

He took a few deep breaths before continuing, "It was late, and I didn't think anyone was in the building. I had the key for Jonas's office. It wasn't the first time I'd had to retrieve something after he'd left for the day. I went up there and...and the door was open a crack."

A sick feeling gripped his stomach as he remembered the dread he'd felt approaching that door. It had been so strange. There had been no reason for the dread. Jonas had probably been in a hurry to leave that night and forgotten to lock his office. Pushing the door open, Liam had frozen at the sight in front of him.

Anxiety gripped him as he remembered the girl's terrified eyes. The way she'd stared at him helplessly. The eyes that haunted his dreams. He couldn't stop his voice from shaking with anger as he said, "She was fifteen, Zoe. Fifteen. She shouldn't have been there. He shouldn't have been there with her. All I knew was that I had to get her away from him."

Zoe's hand was still on his, and he stared down at it. "I lied. I told her there was a call for her. A family emergency. Jonas was...I don't think he'd known I was in the building...The way he looked at me...he knew I was lying. But he was...distracted enough that the girl was able to get away. I got her to my office and called the cops."

Angry tears were trickling down his cheeks. Zoe moved a little closer and, with her free hand, wiped away a few of them. "I think it's okay that you lied. You got her out of there."

He shook his head, "It wasn't enough...you saw the articles. You've seen the numbers. Everyone... Everyone asked the same damn question." He sighed in defeat, "I told the truth, and no one believed me."

She was still sitting there, still touching him. Her eyes filled with sorrow, "The articles all say you said you didn't know. There was never any other information. What didn't they include?"

He didn't immediately answer. His fist slowly unclenched, and her hand slipped into his. Her hands weren't the smallest, but compared to his, they looked downright delicate. He held it, swiping his thumb across the back, and forced himself to answer her question. "People who supported Jonas's ministry, they would send their kids to be interns. Every few months, the interns would move back home, and we'd get new ones. There was this promise that being an intern with us would mean things like job offers with politicians who were of like mind and guaranteed entry to certain colleges. Most of these kids had been homeschooled, and it was too good of an opportunity to pass up."

Looking up at her, he shook his head, "When I graduated college, Jonas gave me my job. He...he wanted to have me take over for him when he retired. I thought everything was on the up and up. I didn't really want to be his successor, but..." he sighed and shook his head, "he'd been so good to me. I just wanted to repay him.

"There were always rumors about the interns. Both boys and girls, but especially the girls. About Jonas's...behavior." He grimaced, "I noticed that he did seem to take... interest ...in the interns. Maybe it was inappropriate, but I wasn't sure. I confronted him, and he *explained* it to me." He couldn't keep the bitterness out of his voice as he remembered that particular conversation.

His stomach twisted into knots, and his mouth was suddenly dry. He squeezed Zoe's hand, stood, and walked to the fridge. "Do you need a drink?" he asked.

"I'm good. Thanks," she replied.

Water in hand, he returned to the couch. He consumed a third of the bottle before asking, "Do you need me to stop? Is it too much?"

She shook her head, "You can keep going if you're up to it."

He remembered how Jonas had looked at him when he'd told the older man what he'd been hearing. That look that he'd always read as being kind and caring but had later realized was calculating and manipulative. "He told me that the rumors were nothing more than the whispers of Satan trying to destroy the good work he was doing for God. He said he was mentoring the interns the way he had mentored me. He asked," Liam sucked in a breath as the hideousness of what he was about to say coursed through him, "He asked if I thought that our interactions when I was a teen had been inappropriate."

He shook his head, his voice shaking again, this time more with pain than anger, "I believed him. I fucking believed that bastard, and I have no idea how many people he hurt because I turned a deaf ear to the rumors." The tears had resumed. Hot and wet, they fell from his eyes, "If I had just...just looked into it a little further...instead of taking his word...it's my fault. It's...all...my fault."

Agony coursed through him, and Zoe reached for him. He pulled her to himself and wrapped his arms around her. "I know..." he couldn't pull himself together and heard how weak his voice sounded. "I know how...how it sounds. I know why people think I was...covering things up."

"Oh, Muffin," she said softly, and he couldn't stop the choking laugh at hearing her use the nickname. "Can you loosen your hold, just a little?" she asked after a few more moments.

He did, and she sat back just far enough to be able to look at him. Her hand raised and rested along his jaw. He searched her eyes. There was no hate there. Nothing that said she found him disgusting or even a little monstrous. She held his gaze for a long time before saying, "Jonas spent years turning you into someone he could use. You were a lonely, angry kid, and he took advantage. Of course, you believed him when he told you that bullshit. You trusted him, and he used that trust for his own sick purposes."

She wiped away a few more tears, "When you found that girl, you didn't leave her there. You got her out. If you were really covering things up, you wouldn't have called the cops. When you learned the truth, you didn't take Jonas's side. You didn't protect your abuser. If you were truly as bad as everyone tried to paint you, you wouldn't have done any of that."

Thirty-One

Zoe

The car headed north of the city. She watched Liam as he drove them to an unknown destination. Well, unknown to her. He knew exactly where he was going and he seemed both nervous and excited about wherever it was.

Her hands smoothed the fabric of the dress. She wondered if she would ever feel completely comfortable dressed up. This was the first time she had opportunity to wear one of Ariadne's dresses out in public. Liam was taking her to dinner for Valentine's Day, and he'd promised it would be nice but not unbearably fancy. She'd warned him that fancy places made her incredibly uncomfortable, and he'd promised that he wouldn't take her somewhere that would make her feel like that.

She drank in the image of Liam next to her. Dressed in all black, he looked smart and sophisticated. She wasn't sure how someone could look that good and say she was gorgeous. But Liam did fairly regularly, and he was never mocking her. He always said it in a way that told her he genuinely believed what he was saying.

Maybe he needed his eyes checked.

He glanced over at her and smiled, "Just a few more minutes. It's not that far."

She nodded, "Okay."

His eyes returned to the road, and she kept watching him. The previous Wednesday, he'd finally told her his side of what had happened when he'd called the police on Jonas. The story had been heartbreaking, but after hearing his side of things, she felt she had a better grasp on the events. She'd been worried that talking about it would be too much for him, that it would push him into a dark place, but so far, he'd been okay. He was a little down but could still get out of bed and function. He was still playing piano and smiling. She'd take the win.

The car turned from the highway and onto a road that wound through a wooded area. She kept shifting her gaze from him to the scenery and back to him. It was a beautiful area, and that was saying something, considering it was still winter. When the trees had leaves and everything was green, she suspected it would be breathtaking.

She heard the sound of the blinker, and the car slowed. After a few seconds, Liam turned onto a graveled road that she soon realized was a long driveway. It went around a corner and opened to reveal a two-story house built into the side of a small hill. The exterior was made up of logs, and the roof was hunter green, covered with solar panels. It was beautiful.

Liam parked the car in front of the house and turned to her, "We're here."

Outside the car, she looked at the place, "Where exactly are we?"

Rather than answer her, he walked to the door and unlocked it, pushing it open, "Come on."

A little hesitantly, she followed him inside. He led her up to the second floor, which turned out to be the main living area of the place. She looked around curiously. The place was empty and didn't look like anyone had lived there in years. It was incredibly dusty, and had an odd sour smell. The kind of smell that places took on when no one had lived there in a long time.

"What do you think?" Liam was looking at her with nervous expectation.

She thought about the question and did another survey of the room. "Needs some TLC, but it's nice. We aren't going to be in trouble for being here, are we?"

He shook his head, "We won't. Do you like it?" If anything, he was getting more nervous.

She nodded, "Yeah." Curiosity growing, she asked, "Liam, what is going on? Why are we here?"

He swallowed hard, "Would you want to live here?"

His question made no sense, "What are you talking about?"

He raked his fingers through his hair, and his hand went to the back of his neck. The anxiety radiating off him could probably have powered a small town for a day. He took a deep breath, "My lease is up in March. I can renew or...or we can move here."

She was feeling more confused by the second, "Are you wanting to rent this place?"

He shook his head, "This is my house."

"What do you mean this is your house?" Was the man having a stroke?

"I own it," he replied simply.

He owned it? "Are you saying you bought this place?"

He shook his head, "No."

She braced her hands on her lower back and stared up at him, trying to figure out what the hell was going on. "Okay, back up because none of this is making sense."

He stuffed his hands in his pockets and looked incredibly sheepish as he finally explained, "This was my grandparent's house. I was six when my grandfather died. He left Mom and Mark some money, but he left me everything else, including this place."

His words took several seconds to sink in fully, and she felt a little faint once they did.

"Zoe? Are you okay?"

She took a few steps away from him and said, "I...Give me a minute..." Her feet started moving, and she walked through an entryway into the kitchen and dining area. The back wall had a sliding glass door that looked out into a backyard. She barely took in her surroundings. Just unlocked the door and managed to get it to move after a few hard pulls. Stepping out onto the back porch, she slid the door shut. So much was starting to make sense. She'd never asked questions about his financial situation, and he'd never offered any information. She knew he wasn't lacking, but that was about it. Apparently, his grandfather had made sure Liam was set for life.

Pulling her jacket tight around herself, she looked at the yard. At the woods that formed the back edge of the property. It was so quiet. Peaceful.

It was overwhelming.

It was too much, right?

Liam was offering to move her here. He wanted to make a home with her here. He was seeing a future that included her, and as she stood there, she began to picture what that future could be. She'd never given much thought to the future. It never seemed like something that would be worth thinking about. Tears started sliding down her face as she realized just how much she wanted that future with him.

The door slid open behind her, and she heard footsteps. Liam suddenly stood before her, eyes full of worry as he took in her tears. He shook his head, "I'm sorry...I...I didn't mean to upset you...I thought–"

She put her fingers on his lips to get him to shut up. He stopped talking, but his eyes didn't leave hers. "I'm not upset," she managed to get out.

Stepping closer, she wrapped her arms around him and rested her head against his chest. He held onto her and quietly asked, "Sweetheart?"

She took several deep breaths, leaned back, and wiped away a few tears. Nodding at him, she said, "Yes."

"Yes?" he didn't look like he was processing what she was saying.

Her lips formed a smile, and a few more tears fell as she told him, "Let's move."

He looked as stunned as she probably had a few minutes earlier. His hands raised and cradled her face, "You sure?"

Her own hands reached up to encircle his wrists, or at least as much of his wrists as her smaller hands could manage, "Yes."

His head lowered, and his lips pressed against hers for a few seconds. When the kiss broke, she saw that relief had replaced the nervousness. Her stomach picked that moment to growl loudly, which made her begin to laugh through the tears that were finally slowing down.

"Dinner?" he asked, amusement joining the relief.

"Yes, please," she smiled up at him.

By the time they finished dinner and returned to the apartment, some of the shock had started to wear off. As she joined him in bed, she found herself puzzling over something. Liam was sitting up with a pillow against his back, book in hand. He lowered the book and looked at her as she asked, "Why?"

"Why what?"

She lay down, looking up at him. He reached over and stroked her hair. "Why are you living here if you have that place?"

He closed the book and set it on the nightstand before turning his attention back to her. She watched as he seemed to debate how to answer her question, but finally, his face cleared, "It's a house for a family. I didn't want to be there alone. It felt wrong."

"You want a family?" she asked quietly. They hadn't discussed that sort of thing before. It was one of those future-type things that she'd never give much consideration.

He turned the lamp off and laid down, pulling her against his side. His lips pressed against her forehead, "*You* are my family."

Thirty-Two

Liam

The rest of February was spent cleaning the house, and they began moving things in slowly. He was still going to therapy every Wednesday. Dr. Constance kept focusing on what she called the progress he was making. He could almost believe what she was saying. In just a few months, he felt like he'd started becoming a completely different person. Better. Healthier. Happier.

He was pleased with the progress he saw Zoe making at the piano. He'd always wondered if he had what it took to teach. Secretly, he'd dreamed of teaching kids to play, but that had never seemed like it was in the cards. Teaching Zoe had forced him to get creative to help her learn. When she struggled to make sense of whole notes versus half, quarter, and eighth, he'd pulled out Legos to help her visualize. To his amazement, it had worked.

Early in March, he had a doctor's appointment. He wasn't worried. It was a regular check-up. He had a family history of intestinal cancer, so he'd made a point of making sure he stayed on top of check-ups. They drew blood for routine lab work at the appointment, and Dr. Wanda told him she'd call with the results in a few days.

It was an ordinary Thursday. March ninth. He was making lunch when his phone rang. He propped the phone up between his shoulder and neck.

"Liam?" Dr. Wanda asked.

"I'm here. Lab work back?"

"Yes." Her voice sounded a little off. A prickle of concern ran through him.

"Is everything okay?"

"Liam, there are some levels that are a little concerning. Have you been feeling okay?"

He paused, "Yeah. I feel fine."

"Would you be able to go in tomorrow to get an ultrasound? I want to get a look at your abdomen. The sooner, the better."

He nodded, though the doctor couldn't see it, "I can do that."

"Good. I'll send the order in, and you should receive an email with instructions of where to go."

After he hung up, he returned to making food, trying to tell himself not to worry. He was young and healthy. He felt perfectly fine. The lab results were probably just a fluke.

The front door opened, and Zoe returned from the studio, "I'm back!" A few seconds later, arms went around his middle, and she inhaled deeply, "That smells so good!"

He looked down to see her grinning up at him. Still stirring, he gave her a quick kiss. "Recording go okay?"

She nodded and stepped away to pull plates from the cupboard, "Yup. Finished another book. Will said that at this rate, I'm going to run through everything they have waiting to be read, and they're going to have to find more for me."

She kept talking, and he was only partially listening. He should tell her what Dr. Wanda said, but he didn't want to worry her. It wasn't something to worry about. The doctor was just being cautious, covering all bases. It was going to be fine.

"Liam?"

He blinked and realized Zoe was staring at him, "Sorry, you were saying?"

She shook her head, "What's going on with you? You're extra distracted."

He turned the stove off and portioned out the food onto the plates, "I don't want you to be worried."

"About?"

He followed her to the table, "The doctor called right before you got home. My lab results came back."

Zoe cut her chicken and asked, "Were they not okay?"

He shrugged, "She's a little concerned about some of them. I have to go in for an ultrasound tomorrow. I'm sure it's nothing."

Zoe took in what he said and nodded slowly, "Okay. How are you feeling?"

"I feel fine. Perfectly normal. Honestly, there was probably something that went weird with the lab tests. I'm sure the ultrasound will come back completely fine. Promise me you won't worry?"

She ate a bite of chicken and replied, "I can't promise that, but I'll do my best not to worry too much until I know if there's something to actually worry about."

"There won't be," he reassured her. She nodded, but he could tell she wasn't convinced.

"Huh."

That's not what I want to hear right now. Liam looked toward the ultrasound tech, Elena. She was staring at the screen with an odd look on her face. "Is everything okay?" he asked.

She pushed a few buttons on the keyboard, then removed the device that had pressed against his abdomen and wiped away the gel. As she did that, she replied, "I can't interpret or diagnose what I'm seeing." She lifted her hand and turned the screen toward him, "But I can show you what I'll be sending to the doctor to be interpreted."

Her fingers pointed to an image on the screen, "That's your right kidney." She tapped a key and pulled up a different image, "This is your left kidney. As you can see, it's a bit bigger than your right one."

A bit bigger was an understatement. The left kidney was easily double the size of his right. She turned the monitor back to face her and began typing, "We're finished. You can go ahead and head out. I'm sending this to the doctor right now, and you should hear something back in a little bit."

He nodded and sat up. Walking to the door, he told her, "Thanks."

She looked up and smiled, "You're welcome. Good luck."

Halfway home, his phone started ringing. He pulled into a parking lot as he noticed the number was Dr. Wanda. "Hello?"

"Liam, I just got your ultrasound results back. Did you see what they captured?"

"Yeah," he replied.

"I want you to go in and get a CT scan. We need a better view of that left kidney. Are you able to go back and get that done today?"

"I can," he informed her.

"Good. I'll send the order, and you should be good to go. We'll talk once I have that result, okay?"

"Okay."

The call ended, and he stared at his phone. There wasn't something wrong. There couldn't be something wrong. Things were too good. Life was finally not a complete shitshow. He needed to tell Zoe what was happening and didn't feel it was the kind of thing he should relay via text. A quick detour home to fill her in, and he'd head back to the imaging center.

Zoe was sitting at the piano when he walked into the apartment, her fingers moving a little clumsily on the keys. She looked up as he appeared and hopped off the bench. Moving to him, she gave him a quick hug, "Everything look good?"

He wrapped his arms around her and held her tight. Resting his cheek against her hair, he inhaled, breathing in that coconut-ginger scent he'd grown to love.

"Liam? Everything is okay, isn't it?" he could hear the tinge of worry in her voice.

Sighing, he eased his hold and gazed down, "I'm not sure. I have to go back and get a CT scan."

He could see the anxiety that flared in her eyes as her body tensed. Her voice was soft, "Why?"

"One of my kidneys is a little bigger than the other one. Dr. Wanda thinks it needs to be checked out further." He kissed her forehead and let her go, "I'm headed back right now. I don't think I'll be gone all that long."

Zoe nodded slowly, "Okay."

"Try not to worry. I probably just have a kidney that's a little weird."

She gave him a shaky smile and teased, "Makes sense. You are pretty weird."

He grinned, "Yup." Leaning in, he kissed her before heading to the door, "I'll be home soon."

They injected him with contrast. He lay on his back while the machine made mechanical noises, taking images of his insides. His mind raced. Over and over, he told himself there was nothing wrong. He was fine. He was healthy. This was a lot of fuss over nothing. Absolutely nothing.

When the tech finished, Liam was sent on his way. "Your doctor should have the results in a little bit. Good luck."

Why did people keep wishing him luck? The words were starting to feel like a curse instead of encouragement.

He'd just parked in the apartment's lot when his phone rang. He answered, and Dr. Wanda began to talk, "Liam, I just got your CT results."

Something about her voice told him that maybe it wasn't all a lot of fuss over nothing. "What's going on?"

She filled him in on the situation, and after giving a few instructions, she ended the call. He sat there for several minutes processing what she'd said. Tried to figure out what he was going to tell Zoe. Finally, he knew he couldn't put it off any longer and headed for the apartment.

Zoe was changing the filament on the printer when he walked in. "Just a sec, let me finish this," she told him without looking up.

He sat on the couch and watched her. After a minute, she was done and joined him. Her face fell as she looked at him, "What is it?"

Reaching out, he tucked a loose curl behind her ear, "Dr. Wanda called right as I was parking."

"And?"

He took her hand and looked into her eyes. She could handle this. He knew she could. They would get through this. It could be so much worse. Still, he was dreading telling her. "It's a tumor. It's too attached to remove without taking the entire kidney."

Her face went pale, "You're going to have surgery?"

He nodded, "Yeah."

"How soon?"

"I'm waiting for the surgery scheduler to call, but Dr. Wanda is hoping to have it done by the end of next week."

Zoe chewed her lip, "That's...soon."

"It is."

They sat there in silence for nearly a minute, staring at each other. Finally, she squared her shoulders and nodded, "Well, alright then."

"Are you okay?" he asked.

She smiled, "I'm not the one who has to have major surgery. Are you okay?"

He rolled his eyes, "It's not major surgery."

She snorted, "They're removing an organ. Pretty sure that qualifies as major surgery."

Before he could say anything, his phone rang. It was the scheduler. A few minutes of conversation passed, and then he hung up and turned his attention back to Zoe. "Thursday, the sixteenth. I have to be there at five a.m."

She nodded slowly, "That's a week from today."

"It is."

She squeezed his hand, "I guess I know what we're doing next Thursday, Kidney Boy."

He raised an eyebrow, "Kidney Boy?"

"Would you prefer Kidney Man?"

He laughed, some of his anxiety dissipating, "I think I actually prefer Muffin."

She glanced around the room, "I guess we should get as much moved as we can before then. I doubt they'll want you doing much lifting after surgery."

He nodded, "Yeah, Dr. Wanda said something along those lines." He'd already hired movers to deal with the furniture and the piano, but plenty of smaller things still needed to be taken to the house. Standing up, he let go of her hand, "Back to packing?"

She nodded, "Back to packing."

Thirty-Three

Liam

The clock on the nightstand read 3:47 a.m. He'd barely slept and had spent the last hour wide awake, staring at Zoe's sleeping form. Thinking. He'd been thinking about one thing for a few days.

If he died in surgery, what would happen to her?

He needed to ensure she wouldn't lose everything if he were gone.

She was sleeping deeply, and he thought he could get out of bed without waking her. Once she was that out, she didn't wake easily. Slowly, he started to move, and she didn't react at all. It took him a bit, but finally, he was out of bed. Pulling the blanket up, he put it over her shoulders before heading to the closet.

As quietly as he could, he shut the door and turned on the light. Reaching for the box on the top shelf, he pulled it down and set it on the floor. Kneeling, he opened it and began to dig. He knew exactly what he was looking for, though he hadn't planned on needing it for several months. The plan had been to retrieve it by Zoe's birthday, but the looming surgery had sped everything up.

Of course, it had fallen to the very bottom of the box.

He pulled it out and set it aside. Quickly, he refilled the box with the other things he'd removed. If everything went okay on Thursday, he'd give her those things after. If it didn't go well, she'd find them eventually. Standing, he placed the box back on the shelf before kneeling to retrieve the item he'd left on the floor.

A knock at the door made him jump. "Liam?" came the sleepy voice from the other side.

Damn. He thought he'd been quiet. Slipping the item into his pajama pant pocket, he turned the light out and opened the door. Zoe was standing there looking more awake by the second. "Are you okay?" she asked, her voice less sleepy and more concerned.

She'd been worrying about how he was doing for days. No matter how often he reassured her he was fine, she didn't seem to believe it. He nodded, "Sorry, I didn't mean to wake you."

She shrugged, "I woke up thirsty, and when I got up to get a drink, I saw the light from under the closet door."

He followed her as she walked to the kitchen and filled a cup with water. She leaned against the counter, took a few sips, and asked, "Can't sleep?"

His hand slipped into his pocket. This wasn't how he'd planned to do it, but his kidney clearly had other ideas.

"Liam?" She was watching him with curiosity.

He moved around the counter and faced her, "Do you have plans today?"

She laughed, "This is what you're asking at 4 a.m.?"

He nodded, "Today and tomorrow. What are your plans?"

"Same as always. Going to read. Running the livestream. Probably driving out to the house with some boxes. Why?"

He stepped closer, eyes fixed on her. There was no doubt in his mind regarding what he was about to do. Kneeling, he looked up at her, "You know I love you."

Her brow furrowed, "What are you doing?"

"Zoe, you've changed my entire life. You...you've made it so much better."

"Liam, are you okay?" She felt his forehead with her hand, checking for a fever.

He caught her hand, "I didn't plan to do it like this. I want you to know that. I was going to wait. I was going to make it special."

"Do what?"

"Sweetheart, I love you so much. I...I can't face surgery knowing that if something happens to me, you won't be taken care of." He held the item from his pocket, "What's mine is yours. Everything that I have. Everything that I am. Marry me?"

She froze. A solid five seconds passed before she moved. Her eyes scanned his face, seeming to try to figure out if this was some kind of elaborate prank. When she didn't say anything, he could feel himself begin to tremble. His voice cracked a little with the last word, "Please."

Still, she said nothing, and his heart clenched. Was she going to say no? "I know this is fast. I...I'm sorry...I just can't–"

His words were cut off as her hand pulled out of his grip and her lips crashed into his. She sunk to the floor with her arms looped around his neck. He wrapped his arms around her and held her for the few seconds the kiss lasted. She was the one who broke it, and leaning back, she stared up at him with bright eyes that shined with tears, "Yes."

Elation filled him, "You will?"

She gave him another small kiss and nodded, "Of course."

He crushed her to himself in a tight embrace. After a few seconds, she began struggling, gasping and laughing, "Can't...breathe!"

Unwillingly, he loosed his hold and gazed down at her. She was going to marry him. He was so unworthy of her, and she was willing to tie her fate to his permanently.

She giggled, "So, why did you ask me about my plans?"

His brain was sluggish, but it caught up after a few seconds, "Want to fly to Vegas?"

"Like, today?" Her brain was struggling to catch up as well, it seemed.

He nodded, "I'm serious. I want to get married before Thursday. Depending on what tickets are available, we can get married today or tomorrow."

She bit her lip, "Are you sure?"

He nodded, "I've been sure for months."

Her eyes went a little wide, "You have?"

"Mm-hm."

She ran her fingers down his face and along his jaw. "You're crazy," she said softly.

"About you," he replied. He leaned forward and rested his forehead against hers, his voice serious. "Please? We can have a ceremony and all that later if you want. But I need to know that you'll be okay if the worst happens on Thursday."

A few seconds passed before she nodded, "Okay. Let's go to Vegas."

He realized she hadn't even looked at the ring yet. She'd been staring at him the entire time. Moving his arm, he held it out to her again, "If it doesn't fit, we'll get it resized."

Her eyes dropped to the silver band. The setting was two small flowers. One sat above the other a little to the side. Little diamonds made up the petals and the center of each flower. Zoe held out her hand, and he slipped it on her finger. "It's beautiful," she murmured as she looked from it back up to him.

"You like it?"

She nodded, "I love it."

"I can get you something different if you want," he offered.

She rolled her eyes, "No, thank you. I'm quite happy with this."

His heart was full, "Good."

Their flight didn't leave until that evening. Zoe was happy about that. While they waited to board, she told him, "This means we can get married on Pi Day!"

"Pi Day?"

She smiled, "Tomorrow is March fourteenth. Three fourteen. It's the first three digits of Pi."

"You're such a nerd," he teased her.

"And you love it."

He kissed the crown of her head, "Yes, I do."

It was a three-hour flight, and to his surprise and relief, the seat next to the aisle was empty. Zoe took the window seat, and he sat in the middle. She became anxious as they sat down and gripped his hand tightly. "Sorry, never been in a plane before."

He squeezed her hand, "It's okay. I'm not going anywhere."

She grinned at him shakily, "You better not."

Take-off went smooth, and she relaxed a little once they were in the air. She looked at her ring and back at him, asking, "When did you buy this?"

He shook his head, "I didn't. It's my grandmother's."

Zoe's face went soft, "You gave me your grandmother's ring?"

"Yes."

She leaned her head against his shoulder, "Thank you."

They arrived at the hotel late, and he crashed hard. When he fell asleep, Zoe was sitting in front of the window staring out at the city, looking amazed. When he woke, she was still sitting there. He got up from the bed and went over to her. She looked up at him, and he smiled, "Have you slept at all?"

She bit her lip and shook her head, "Too much to see. The Sphere is bizarre. I couldn't really look away."

He leaned down and kissed her, "Still want to get married?"

She nodded, "Yup. You?"

He grinned, his voice teasing, "Nope, totally changed my mind."

She stood up, laughing, "Too bad. This is happening, Kidney Boy."

He pulled her into his arms and leaned her back a little before kissing her deeply. "Good."

She locked herself in the bathroom for nearly an hour. When she opened the door, her back was to him, "Zip me?"

He stepped closer, smiling as he saw she was wearing the purple-blue dress. The zipper moved easily, and then she spun around to face him. His breath caught as he looked at her. Her sapphire hair was down, and loose curls framed her face. She'd applied a little bit of makeup. Not much, but enough that it made her hazel eyes pop, and her lips look even fuller than usual.

She moved her hands down the skirt, flattening it a little. Looking back up at him, "This okay?"

"You're perfect," he murmured.

She smiled gently, and her eyes ran up and down him, "You look good."

"Not as good as you."

She rolled her eyes and looked away, "Puh-lease."

He lifted her chin and stared down intensely, "You are the most beautiful woman I've ever seen."

Her eyes were the tiniest bit sad at his words, "You're very kind."

He sighed, "Sweetheart, you're gorgeous inside and out. I wish you could believe that."

She closed her eyes as his words sunk in. Opening them, she smiled, "So, how are we doing this?"

It took him a moment to realize what she was asking. After a few seconds, he replied, "Breakfast first or wedding?"

She considered the question and told him, "Wedding, then breakfast, I think."

Taking hold of her hand, he led her to the door, and they headed for the chapel.

It was shockingly easy to get married in Vegas. He knew that, in theory, but it wasn't until they were actually there, doing it, that he realized just how easy it was.

Standing at the altar, he gazed down at her as they went through the cookie-cutter ceremony. It wasn't the wedding he wanted to give her. She deserved better. She deserved to be on a beach or in front of mountains, not in some cliche wedding chapel in Vegas. He swore to himself that he'd make it up to her.

"Do you take this woman to be your lawfully wedded wife?"

He smiled at Zoe. He'd made a lot of mistakes in his life. Trusted the wrong people. Hurt people. He wouldn't do that to her. He'd spend the rest of his life, no matter how long or short it might be, making sure she never felt worthless or unloved. There was no doubt in his mind that this was who he was supposed to spend the rest of his life with. Things wouldn't be easy, he knew that. But he didn't want to face the future with anyone else by his side. They would be together, and that was what mattered. With confidence, he answered, "I do."

When the officiant asked Zoe the question, she stared up at Liam. A few seconds passed as she held his gaze. With a serene smile, she said, "I do."

Thirty-Four

Zoe

They were married.

Halfway through breakfast, she froze. Her fork was stuck in mid-air with a piece of sausage on it.

Wife.

She was a wife. She had absolutely no idea how to be a wife.

"Zoe?"

Her eyes met Liam's. He was gazing at her with fondness and a little curiosity. She was his wife. He was her husband. Liam McPherson had married her.

Zoe McPherson.

She officially had a new name if she wanted it (which she really did). A new husband. A new everything.

Less than four months earlier, she'd been alone. Completely alone. Trying to figure out how to make it through one more day. Trying to make the best of the hand life had dealt her.

It was Liam, leaning across the table and stealing the bite of sausage off her fork that shook her out of her frozen state. "Hey!"

He shrugged, "It was getting cold."

Just for that, she reached across to his plate and stole a strip of bacon. She began to chew it, and her thoughts continued to swirl around chaotically. One rose to the top of all the others, and she abruptly lost her appetite. Setting the remainder of the bacon on her plate, she stared at the half-eaten breakfast.

Married people had sex.

She and Liam were still sleeping with a blanket wall between them. Sex was this thing that had been out there as a thing they'd get to...eventually...at some point in the future. Not that she didn't want to have it with him. She did. But every time she thought about it, it got more scary to consider actually trying. Liam hadn't brought it up again after their discussion about boundaries. He'd left it completely up to her.

But now they were married. Was he expecting that she was going to be ready to go up to the room and have sex? The thought filled her with panic. She wasn't ready. She couldn't do it.

Her hands began to shake, and Liam took hold of them. "What's wrong?"

She couldn't look at him, afraid that he'd be able to read the reason for her panic in her eyes. "I just need sleep," she managed to get out, voice shaky.

"Okay," his voice was soft. Minutes later, they were at the elevator, and not long after, they walked into the room.

Her panic was getting worse. Breathing grew shallow. Her teeth began to chatter. Wrapping her arms around herself as tightly as possible, she dashed into the bathroom and shut the door. Sinking to the floor with the door behind her, she began to rock back and forth, still hugging herself. Hot tears streamed down her face, and she felt like she was choking on them.

There was a soft knock at the door, "Zoe?"

She was trembling. Her husband was on the other side of the door. Possibly with all kinds of expectations that they had absolutely not discussed. She'd married him without thinking about any of the things she should've. The tears fell faster. What was she going to do? What if he was angry when he found out she wasn't ready?

There was no piano in the room. The piano was hundreds of miles and several states away. If he couldn't play out his rage...Memories of Fred's fist going through walls popped into her brain.

Oh god, what had she done?

"Sweetheart, please. Tell me what's wrong." Liam's voice came through the door. He sounded worried. How long until that worry turned to anger? "I'm not mad. Please let me in."

He wasn't going to want her when he knew. He was going to leave her. Would he even make sure she got back home, or would he just leave her in Vegas? She'd be alone. Unloved. Homeless. What the fuck had she been thinking?

"Please, Zoe," he pleaded.

Just get it over with. Let him in, and let him end things. She choked out, "Okay." Scrambling back as far from the door as she could, she managed to wedge herself under the sink vanity as the door opened. Pulling her knees up and hugging them to her chest, she stared at the tiled floor and prayed that she wouldn't get some awful bacterial infection from sitting there.

Liam was in front of her within seconds. He sat down quietly, and she couldn't look at him. Couldn't bear to see his eyes as he realized what she couldn't do. She didn't want to watch the love die in them.

"What do you need?" he asked.

She couldn't answer. Love was finally in her life. She finally knew what it was to be truly loved and cherished, and it was about to be extinguished.

Her voice shook as she managed to get out, "I...can't..."

When she didn't add anything more, he asked, "Can't what?"

Just get the words out. Get them out and brace for the inevitable. "I...I...can't...havesex."

The bathroom was silent except for the sound of her hysterical sobbing. She was tensed. Waiting. It was coming. He was going to–

"Oh, sweetheart, I didn't even think...I'm so sorry..." he murmured.

"I can't...I'm...I'm not...ready..." the words came out with desperate gasps for air. "And...I...I know...I have to do it."

"Zoe." His voice was soft and firm. He didn't sound mad. "Look at me."

Still braced for the worst, she squeezed her eyes shut and forced her head up. It took a few seconds before she could open them and meet his.

He held her gaze, his own eyes still full of so much love. He held out a tissue box, and she pulled one out and wiped at the tears that wouldn't stop falling. Gently, he told her, "It's okay, I promise."

She shook her head, "I'm...your wife."

He nodded, "And I'm your husband."

"We're supposed...to..." Her head dropped, eyes focused on the floor.

A few seconds passed before he said, "And we will when we're both ready."

Her head was aching from the tension created by her panic, "I...don't know...when I'll be."

"I'm not sure I'm ready either," he admitted after a few moments.

Her head snapped up, "What?"

He looked sheepish and raked his fingers through his hair, "I...I want to..." he huffed out a laugh, "you have no idea how much, but...but I'm not sure I'm ready."

Her panic began to ease at his words, "Really?"

He gave her a weak smile, "Really."

She felt better when she woke up several hours later. By the time her panic attack had calmed, Liam almost had to carry her to the bed. He'd tucked her in and sat beside her, stroking her hair while she fell asleep.

Blinking a few times, as she came to, her eyes focused on him. He was staring at his e-reader, and as she started to move, his eyes shifted from the tablet to her. "Hey," he said gently.

"Hi."

"Better?"

She nodded, "Yeah."

"Good."

It was still bright outside, "What time is it?"

He glanced at his tablet, "Four."

She groaned, "I slept all day?"

"You were exhausted."

Sitting up, she looked at him. Relieved, she saw the love was still there in his eyes. "I'm sorry for my panic attack."

He shook his head, "I'm sorry. I was so fixated on making sure everything was okay before surgery I didn't even think about telling you not to worry about that."

"When do we have to be at the airport?"

"6."

She was ready to go home but was disappointed she'd slept through her opportunity to see Vegas. "Guess we won't get to go sightseeing."

He shook his head, "Not on this trip, no. But we can come back if you want. Now," he shifted the conversation, "You want to get something to eat before we have to leave?"

She grinned, "You know me so well."

They got back to their apartment in the wee hours of the morning. The trip had been a whirlwind, and now that they were home, Zoe was suddenly facing the fact that in a little over twenty-four hours, her husband would be going under the knife. Going to Vegas had let her put that out of her mind for a little over a day.

They went to bed, and Liam drifted off. Zoe stayed awake, watching him. In theory, the surgery should be fine. He was healthy enough that there was little reason to be concerned. Unfortunately, there was no guarantee that she would ever see him alive after they rolled him to the operating room. Her mind was filled with horrifying visions of some doctor coming out and telling her, "We did everything we could, but he didn't make it."

She couldn't sleep because if she slept, she'd miss out on time to be with him. To see him. Touch him. Sleep would steal away a few precious moments, which might be all they had left.

Eventually, despite her best efforts, sleep won, and she drifted off. It wasn't good sleep, though, and when Liam started to move, she came to suddenly.

Sunlight lit the room, and Liam was watching her with a smile. He stroked her hair, "Morning, Mrs. McPherson."

His words filled her with warmth, "G'morning." She moved closer and gave him a quick kiss.

He squeezed her and said, "It's almost nine. I need to get up for therapy. You can go back to sleep."

"Sounds good." She yawned, "Have fun at therapy."

He chuckled, "Oh, I'm sure Dr. Constance will only have a small heart attack when I tell her about this last week."

Zoe giggled and watched through half-shut eyelids as he got out of bed. Sleep claimed her again. This time, it was a little more restful, but not much.

Liam downed a disgusting beverage late that afternoon and disappeared to the bathroom. The sounds she heard were impossible to ignore. She knew the colon cleanse was necessary, but it sounded incredibly unpleasant.

Eventually, Liam reappeared and collapsed on the couch, "That was a really shitty experience. Pun intended."

She snorted, "I'm not jealous."

His head rolled to the side and he grinned, "No? You don't want to share this experience with your husband?"

She shrugged, "I had to hear it. Pretty sure that's enough experience sharing for two days into our marriage."

He chuckled, "Fair." His voice grew serious, "Zoe, I hate to do this, but I have to. If...if things don't go well tomorrow, there's a folder in the safe. It has everything you'll need to know."

It was a grim thing to think about, "Thank you for telling me."

"Hopefully, you won't need that information for a very long time, but just in case..." He sighed as the sentence trailed off.

She nodded, "Just in case."

They didn't sleep. They sat on the couch, watching TV, Liam holding onto her. She was determined to remember how it felt. Remember the way his voice sounded when he spoke to her. Remember the soft touch of his lips on hers.

At 4:30, they got in the car and headed for the hospital. Time suddenly slammed into fast forward. Too soon, he was gowned and in the hospital bed.

They took blood to run last-minute labs, and then it was just a matter of waiting.

She sat beside him, gripping his hand tightly, staring into his eyes. Now that they were here and the surgery was imminent, it was all too real. She was terrified.

"Hey, it's gonna be okay." He told her gently.

She wanted to believe that. Wanted to believe that in a few hours, it would all be over, and he'd be back smiling at her.

People filed into the room. They introduced themselves as the surgery team, and Zoe knew she should be paying attention, but it was all a blur. They were going to take Liam away. They were going to cut him open and remove part of him, and she might never get him back.

"Okay, well, that's pretty much it. Time to kiss your husband, Mrs. McPherson." One of the women in scrubs told her.

Zoe stood, still holding Liam's hand, leaning her head down to rest against his. He held her gaze, and she kissed his lips softly. When she pulled away, she quietly told him, "Come back to me, Liam McPherson."

He grinned, "Always."

"I love you," her voice was barely a whisper.

He lifted his free hand and rested it against her cheek, "Love you, too, sweetheart. See you in a few hours."

A final squeeze of the hand and she forced herself to let go of him. Stepping back, she let the team whisk him out of the room. She watched until they were gone.

Feeling slightly shaky, she left the room. The older woman from the desk looked at her with sympathy. She held out a piece of paper, "Mrs. McPherson, here's the instructions so they can keep you updated during the surgery."

Zoe forced herself to move and take the paper. "Thanks."

The woman pointed at doors that led out onto a terrace, "If you want, many people like sitting out there while they wait."

The appeal of fresh air drew her, and Zoe nodded gratefully, "Thank you."

Outside, she found a bench to sit on. It was a mild day, and she was perfectly comfortable in her hoodie. Looking at the paper, she followed the instructions so that updates about Liam's procedure could be texted to her. One of the last lines on the paper gave her pause. It stated that if there were problems during the procedure, a care team member would come to notify her in person.

She sat on the bench and looked around. A water feature was in front of her, and she watched the water cascade. There were a few plants, but it was too early in the season for the flowers that she was sure would be there later in the year.

A notification arrived, informing her the procedure had begun.

She texted Alex and updated him. He'd offered to come and sit with her, but the hospital had recently reinstated Covid restrictions because there had been another surge of the disease. She wasn't allowed to have anyone there with her.

Time drug. She received an update roughly every twenty minutes. Alex texted with her, and it helped make the time pass. She hadn't told him that she'd eloped. That needed to be a face-to-face conversation. Hopefully, he wouldn't hate her.

Nearly two hours had passed when a young woman in scrubs walked out onto the terrace. Zoe had seen a few other hospital employees wander through while she'd sat there. On their break was her assumption. Another text arrived from Alex, and she was answering it when she heard, "Mrs. McPherson?"

She looked up, and her heart clenched. The woman in scrubs was standing a few feet away. She looked at Zoe gently and said, "It's your husband."

Thirty-Five

He's dead. He died. He's gone. I'm never going to see him again. She could feel the tears accumulating as the horrible thoughts overwhelmed her with despair.

The young woman smiled, "Your husband is doing fine. They're closing right now, and then he'll be in recovery. Sorry, I hope I didn't scare you. The texting system is being a little screwy right now. We wanted to make sure you knew what was happening."

Zoe was glad she was sitting down. She was fairly certain her legs would've already given out. Liam was alive. "When can I see him?" she asked.

"Unfortunately, due to the Covid restrictions, we can't let you back into recovery, but as soon as they move him to his room, you'll be allowed to see him. When they finish closing, the surgeon will want to talk to you."

Zoe nodded, "Okay."

"If you want to come back into the waiting area, they'll come get you in a few minutes."

Zoe got to her feet a little unsteadily and followed the woman back into the building. Minutes ticked by before the surgeon she'd seen earlier appeared and called her back to a room.

She wished desperately that someone else was there with her. She heard what he was saying but was having trouble keeping up. Liam was fine. The surgery had gone well. He'd need...it was something about rechecks. She wasn't sure what that would entail. Results would be in...tomorrow? Her head ached as she tried to keep up.

Finally, the surgeon told her, "I know this is a lot. Don't worry; we'll give you a printout with all of this information, and it will also be available on the patient portal. Do you have any questions?"

"He's okay?" She knew he'd already told her that, but she was still so incredibly scared.

He nodded, "He's okay. I'm sure he'll be thrilled to see you."

And then the surgeon was gone, and she was alone again.

More waiting.

She found the cafeteria and got something to eat. Liam had left her his debit card and told her to get whatever she needed or wanted.

Time was passing even slower than it had while he had been in surgery. She ate slowly and doom scrolled. The woman at the desk had told her it would be at least two hours before Liam would be moved to his room.

Eventually, she made her way to the floor where Liam was supposed to be. Stopping at the desk, she told them who she was. The man working nodded and made a phone call. It was a quick exchange, and he told her, "They're still getting his room ready. We'll let you know when you can see him."

Great. More waiting.

An hour passed, and they hadn't told her she could go back.

Another hour passed, and she stared at the clock in desperation. Due to the Covid restrictions, the hospital kicked visitors out at six, and it was nearly five. Taking a chance, she went back to the desk and asked, "Have they moved him into his room yet?"

The man gave her a quizzical look, "Who is it you're waiting to see?"

She could've screamed. She very nearly did. Instead, smile plastered on her face, she said, "Liam McPherson. He's supposed to be getting moved in from recovery."

"Okay, let me check."

Another phone call and the man looked at her, "Room 407. Go on back."

She barely thanked the man before she sped through the doors to the rooms. Her eyes scanned the numbers, and a sign pointed her in the right direction. She reached room 407, and the door was shut. Knocking, she waited. Joy flooded her as she heard the bark of a very familiar, very grumpy voice, "What?"

Opening the door, she stepped inside, and all her terror, all her anxiety melted away. Liam was propped up in bed, looking paler than usual, but it was him. He was there. He was alive. The annoyed look on his face faded as soon he saw her. He held out his arms. She shut the door and ran to him.

"Careful," he murmured, voice a little tight, as she leaned in to hug him.

She was as gentle as could be as she kissed him. Sitting on the edge of the bed, she stared at him, holding his hand, unable to stop touching him. "You're okay," she said on repeat.

He grinned and winced. She squeezed his hand, "Are you in a lot of pain?"

"A bit. They gave me some stuff, but I don't think it's doing much. I thought you went home." He was so alert and speaking so clearly that she had to agree about the meds.

Surprised, she replied, "There was no way I was leaving without seeing you. I've been waiting for them to let me. Did you just get back here?"

Perplexed, he shook his head, "I've been here for nearly two hours. I would've called, but I realized I have no idea what your phone number is, and you had my phone with you."

Frustration filled her, "I'm so sorry. They told me that they'd let me know when you were back. I've been sitting in the waiting area for ages. I should've gone back and re-checked with the desk sooner instead of waiting so long." Digging in her bag, she pulled out his phone and handed it over.

He looked at the screen, "You didn't happen to bring a charger, did you?"

She took one out and looked around. Finding an outlet near the bed that wasn't red, she plugged it in, and he handed her the phone. Once on the charger, she set it on the table right by his bed within easy reach.

He started moving around, and she grew alarmed, "What are you doing?"

"I just need to get up and walk."

She nodded, "Okay, let's call the nurse."

He glared, "I'm fine. I can walk."

She returned his glare, "I know you think that, but you shouldn't get out of bed without letting the nurse know."

"Don't be ridiculous." He was getting very annoyed.

Trying to keep in mind that he'd just gone through major surgery, she softened her voice, "Please call the nurse. Do it for me? I'll feel better if you check with the nurse before getting up." All she could picture was whatever painkiller they'd given him kicking in mid-walk and him collapsing. He'd probably take her down with him, and then they'd both be in the hospital.

"Fine," he growled. He pushed the button, and after a short wait, the nurse responded. He told her that he needed to go for a walk.

"Okay, I'm on my way."

Liam was still glaring as Zoe moved closer and kissed his temple, "Thank you."

He grunted in reply, and she resisted the urge to laugh.

Someone knocked at the door, pushed it open, and the nurse entered the room. She looked to be a little younger than Zoe, and she was tiny. The nurse smiled at her, "I'm Dakota, Liam's nurse. You must be his wife."

Zoe nodded, "I'm Zoe."

Dakota stepped closer to the bed and looked at Liam. He was trying to get up, but she stopped him. "Let me deal with the catheter before we have a mess on our hands."

Liam glowered but let the nurse do her work. As Zoe watched, she thought about the fact that Dakota was even less likely to survive in one piece if Liam collapsed. This was a disaster waiting to happen.

Liam was up, and after a momentary wobble, he headed for the door. Zoe walked on one side and Dakota on the other. They moved slowly, but he was pretty steady on his feet, which she hoped was a positive sign.

"It's really good that you're already up and moving so well," Dakota commented.

Liam glanced down at Zoe and muttered, "I told you I was fine."

Dakota wouldn't let them take a very long walk, and though Liam protested, by the time they got him back to the room, he sagged into the bed, looking completely exhausted. Dakota got everything hooked up and said, "I'll be back to check on you in a while. If you need anything, just push the button." She stopped at the doorway, "And do not get out of that bed without me being here. Do you understand?"

"Yes," he grumbled.

Dakota pulled the door shut, and Zoe was alone with Liam. A tray of food had been delivered while they were out of the room. She looked at it, "You think you can eat something?"

"I'll try."

She maneuvered the table with the tray on it so it was in front of him. She sat on the edge of the bed on the opposite side of the table. He made a face, looking at the food. She thought it looked surprisingly good, considering it was hospital food, but she hadn't been the one who spent hours under anesthesia.

He picked up the fork and began to pick at the chicken. After a few bites, he shook his head, "You want the rest? I can't eat anymore."

"You sure?"

He nodded, "Yeah. I have no appetite. And given your propensity for forgetting to eat, I have a feeling you haven't eaten anything all day."

It was true. She did forget fairly often, though it had been happening less since moving in with Liam. He made sure she was eating on a regular schedule. She grinned, "You'll be pleased to know I fed myself lunch."

He raised an eyebrow, "Actual food or candy?"

"Actual food. I promise."

He leaned back against the pillows, looking slightly less grumpy, "Good. I was worried."

She picked up the fork and began to eat, "You really didn't need to. There wasn't much else to do other than eat and wait."

He chuckled, but a yawn broke up the sound. She finished the food quickly and glanced at the clock. She had fifteen minutes until they were going to kick her out. Liam's eyelids were growing heavy. Moving the table back so it was beside the bed instead of over it, she moved closer to where he was propped up. She took hold of his hand. He lifted it to his lips, pressing a kiss to the back.

She reached up and gently stroked his hair, letting her fingers linger a little against his face. He smiled at the touch, and his eyes were almost shut. She squeezed his hand, "I'm going to go home, okay?"

"'kay."

"I'll be back in the morning."

He nodded, and she could tell he was almost asleep. Standing, she leaned down and gave him a tender kiss. His free hand reached up, and his fingers pressed lightly against her neck. She broke the kiss and looked at him. His eyes were barely open as he told her, "Love you."

"Love you, too. Go to sleep, Muffin."

His eyes closed completely, and he mumbled something that sounded an awful lot like, "Yes, ma'am."

His hold on her hand loosened, and she finally let go. She placed one more light kiss on his forehead and whispered, "Good night."

Leaving the room was hard to do. She stood in the doorway and watched a few seconds more before making herself pull the door shut between them.

"Zoe?"

She let go of the door handle and looked toward the voice. Dakota was standing a few feet away, "Yes?"

Dakota stepped closer, "I just need to verify we have the correct phone number for you in case we need to reach you in the night."

Zoe's stomach clenched, "Is that likely to happen?"

Dakota smiled, "We just want to make sure all our bases are covered."

Zoe noticed the nurse was avoiding actually answering the question. Too tired to press, she rattled off her phone number, and Dakota nodded, "Good, looks like we're set. Is he still awake?"

"No, he just fell asleep a few minutes ago."

"Good. Did he eat anything?"

Zoe shook her head, "Not really. Few bites of chicken. I'm the one who finished it."

Dakota grinned, "I won't tell. You headed home?"

Zoe nodded, "Yeah."

"Have a good night. We'll take good care of him for you."

Thirty-Six

Zoe

She had barely been home five minutes when she grew overwhelmed by loneliness. The place was nearly empty. Almost everything had been moved to the house. Furniture, a few items of clothing, and toiletries were nearly all that remained. Without Liam there, the place felt big and vacant.

She sank onto the couch, completely exhausted, but she wasn't sure she could sleep. This would be their first night apart since New Year's Day.

What if the hospital called in the middle of the night? What if he went into cardiac arrest and they couldn't resuscitate him?

It was too much. If she had to face the night alone, she'd never get to sleep. She sent Alex a text.

> Is there any chance you guys can come spend the night? I don't think I can handle being alone tonight.

> Send your address. We'll be there in a little bit.

Relief filled her. Alex and Dante would make sure she was okay. They'd take care of her if something awful happened.

Twenty minutes later, there was a knock at the door, and peering through the peephole, she saw the guys standing there. As soon as they were inside, they pulled her into a tight hug, and she instantly felt better.

She wasn't sure how Liam would feel about her letting anyone else into the apartment, but surely he'd forgive her when he knew the reason why. The men looked around curiously and landed on the couch.

Smiling wearily, she said, "I know you just got here, but I need to try to sleep. Will you be okay? The remote is there. Help yourself to whatever's in the fridge."

They assured her they'd be fine. She started to walk to the bedroom but stopped when Alex took hold of her hand. Looking down, she met his eyes, "Yes?"

He held her hand up and looked at the ring, then back to her, "Is there something you're not telling us?"

Oh yeah. She'd momentarily forgotten that they didn't know. She bit her lip, "We kinda got married."

"WHAT?!" Both men yelled the word in unison.

Alex shook his head, "What the hell do you mean you *kinda got married*?"

She pulled her hand out of his grasp and stepped to the recliner. Sinking into it, she filled them in. "Monday morning, he proposed, and we flew to Vegas. Got married on Tuesday. Flew back that night."

Both of them stared at her in shock. Dante was the first to say anything, "Why?"

"He was worried about the surgery. Worried that if he died on the operating table, I wouldn't legally be his wife, and he wanted to make sure I'd be taken care of. He was planning to propose on my birthday, but with the surgery..." she shrugged.

Both men exchanged a look before Alex said, "That's surprisingly logical and decent. Still a little pissed off that you said nothing before now."

She smiled apologetically, "I'm sorry. It just happened so fast. We'll probably have a party or something in a few months."

"Good," Dante nodded.

She yawned, "I really need to try to sleep. Okay, if I leave my phone out here? Answer it if it rings? I'm worried the hospital may call, and I'll sleep through it." Alex held out his hand, and she handed him the phone. "Thank you."

He nodded, "Go sleep. Don't worry."

She got some sleep, but it wasn't good. She woke trembling from a dream of shopping carts chasing, surrounding, and trapping her. An hour ticked by before she drifted off into another rough sleep, clutching Liam's pillow tight to her chest.

When she woke again, her eyes landed on the clock. 10:15 a.m. She bolted out of bed. Visiting hours at the hospital had started at eight. She'd planned to be there as soon as they'd let her in.

Rushing around, she put herself together and went to the living room. Dante and Alex were still on the couch, watching Netflix. They smiled at her. "Get some sleep?" Alex asked.

She nodded, "A little. Massively overslept, though. Did the hospital call?" They shook their heads, and she felt relieved.

"Liam texted you a little bit ago. I replied. I hope that's okay." Alex informed her.

Picking up her phone, she opened the texts and saw the exchange.

They're sending me home today. I should be released by 11.

This is Alex. Zoe's asleep. I'll tell her as soon as she wakes up.

Is she ok?

She asked us to come over & spend the night. Didn't want to be alone. Think she was worried the hospital would call in the middle of the night.

Thank you.

She looked at the time. 10:36. She would have to dash if he was getting discharged by eleven.

I'm so sorry. Just woke up. I'm headed out now & will be there as soon as I can.

Breathe and eat.

I promise to do one of those. See you soon

Slipping her phone into her pocket, she looked at the men, "I'm so sorry, I need to get to the hospital." They were already standing, and they pulled her into another group hug. "Thank you so much for being here," she told them.

They let her go, and Alex grinned, "Anything for you, Mrs. McPherson." He made a face, "Gonna be weird getting used to calling you that."

"Stick with Zoe." she grinned.

"I think I will," he replied.

They walked with her to the door, and Dante handed her a cello-phane-wrapped item. She glanced at it and saw it was an Uncrustable. "You need to eat something," he informed her.

Grateful, she took it, "Thank you."

Before they went their separate ways in the parking lot, they told her to text if she needed anything. She ate as she drove. Liam would have to forgive her for the crumbs. He had a rule about eating in the car, but she decided this qualified as an exceptional circumstance.

Parking wasn't as much of a nightmare as she'd been worried it would be. She raced from the car to his room. The door was open, and Liam was sitting on the edge of the bed, his bag of belongings sitting beside him. He smiled as she skidded to a halt in front of him. Giving him a quick kiss, she sank onto the bed, "Gimme a sec.'

He nodded, "Catch your breath."

"I'm so sorry. I meant to be here hours ago. Any idea when they're going to discharge you?"

He held out a stapled pile of papers to her, "They already did."

"Without me here?" Frustration flooded her. The way things had been handled was annoying. She should've been there. They'd actually trusted that hopped up on painkillers he'd be enough with the program to know what they were telling him?

"There are a few prescriptions that they sent to the pharmacy for me. I'm supposed to go home and sit." He glowered.

She laughed a little, "Am I going to have to tie you to the chair?"

"No," he grumbled.

Having caught her breath, she stood, "Ready to go home?"

He nodded, and she held out her hand to him. Gripping it, he stood slowly and took a moment to steady himself. "Do I need to get a wheelchair?" she asked.

That was something discharged patients were supposed to use, wasn't it?

He glared, "What do you think?"

She picked up the bag of belongings and grinned, "I think that if you fall, you're going to take me down with you, and we'll both be stuck here even longer."

"I won't fall," he promised.

"You better not."

The walk from his room to the car took far longer than it would've normally. By the time she got him to the vehicle, she could tell he was ready to sit. Getting him inside turned out to be a small challenge. He winced and gasped as he slowly maneuvered into the seat. Climbing into the driver's side, she looked at him, "Need help with the seatbelt?"

"Do I have to wear it?" She knew he was worried about the incisions. The seatbelt would likely be quite painful if it hit him wrong.

She sighed, "Unfortunately, yes. If we get pulled over, we'll be in trouble if you're not buckled. I promise to drive careful and avoid all the potholes."

He steeled himself. Reached for the belt, pulled it across, and clicked it into place. Through gritted teeth, he told her, "Let's just get home."

True to her word, she made the ride as comfortable as possible. She kept checking on him and could see he was miserable. Fortunately, the hospital wasn't that far from the apartment. As soon as she'd parked, he had the seatbelt undone and was sighing in relief.

The trek to the apartment was as slow as the one at the hospital. Inside, Liam didn't even fight her; he just sank into the recliner. She set about trying to make him comfortable. Brought pillows out from the bedroom and placed them as he instructed. Handing him the remote, she asked, "What else do you need?"

He yawned, "Water?"

She filled the cup from the hospital. He took it and gave her a weary smile, "Thanks. Sorry, I've been such an ass."

She kissed his forehead and replied, "You get a pass right now because I know you're in pain."

His hand raised before she could stand up, and his fingers landed on the back of her neck, pulling her back down so he could fully kiss her on the lips. When the kiss broke, he grinned, "That's better."

She reached out and gently ruffled his hair, "You're ridiculous.

Stepping away, she picked up the discharge papers and sat on the couch, reading over them. They were going to have to keep the incisions clean while they healed. He wasn't allowed to lift anything over ten pounds for a few weeks. No strenuous activity. Easy walks. Hydrate. Take the pain medication. She scanned the document and found the directions for the prescriptions and where to pick them up.

"When did you take your last pain pill?" she asked.

He thought for a moment, "About twenty minutes before you got to the hospital."

"Good. That gives me time to get to the pharmacy and pick up your meds without worrying you're going to be in excruciating pain."

He shrugged, "It's not like they'll actually do anything."

She rolled her eyes, "I know that's what you think. Take them for me? It'll give me some peace of mind."

He huffed out a laugh, "If it'll make you happy."

"It will," she stated.

Standing, she asked, "Are you going to be okay alone if I run to get your meds, or do you want me to see if Alex or Dante can come over?"

He shook his head, "I'll be fine. Probably going to sleep."

She grabbed her purse, "Promise you'll behave while I'm gone?"

"You're so worried," he teased.

"You're the one who didn't want to wait for the nurse to come undo his catheter. I think I'm well within my rights to be worried." She gave him a very pointed look and moved closer to give him another quick kiss. "I'll be back soon. Text if you need anything."

Friday evening, Liam was in the recliner. Zoe handed him his next round of pain meds right as his phone began to ring. "It's Dr. Wanda," he said as he picked it up.

Zoe sat on the edge of the couch, watching Liam's face and listening as he said things like, "I see," and, "I understand." His face was unreadable, and she could feel her anxiety spike.

The call was only a few minutes long, and when he hung up, she asked, "Everything okay?"

He sighed, "Good or bad news first?"

She picked at her thumbnail cuticle, "That sounds ominous. Bad first, I guess."

"Pathology finished their exam. The tumor is cancerous."

Cancerous. Cancer. An ugly, scary word. She pictured Liam, bald and frail, lying in a hospital bed. "Does that mean you're going to have to go through chemo?"

He shook his head, "It hadn't metastasized, and they're fairly certain they got it all. Dr. Wanda said the borders where they made the cuts were all clear. I just have to go back and get checked every six months for the next five years to make sure I'm still good."

"No chemo?"

"No chemo," he reassured her. "Apparently, if you have to have cancer, kidney cancer is the one to have."

That made her laugh. Relaxing for the first time in days, she felt a wall of exhaustion crash into her. Yawning, she said, "I need sleep. Want anything before

I hit the hay?"

He shook his head, "Go to bed. I'll be fine."

Stopping beside him, she kissed his forehead, "I'm so glad you're home."

He reached up and guided her lips to his, saying, "Me too, sweetheart. Me too."

Thirty-Seven

Liam

"How are things?" Dr. Constance asked.

"Good," he nodded. "Getting used to the house. It's nice to be all moved in." After a month of living there, it was really starting to feel like their place. Like home.

"And being married?"

He hesitated a few seconds, "Overall, it's good. We're happy." And they were. It wasn't a lie. There was just one little fly in the ointment.

Dr. Constance picked up on it and asked, "What aren't you saying?"

"I'm...I'm having...trouble," he admitted.

"How so?"

Was there a more embarrassing subject to discuss? He couldn't immediately think of one. He took a drink of coffee and said, "Last week, Zoe told me she's ready...she wants to have...sex."

"How do you feel about that?"

"Great." He nodded, "Honest. I was happy when she told me. But..."

Dr. Constance prompted him after a few moments, "But?"

His eyes dropped to the floor, "We started making out. It got...heated. I...I was enjoying it...until...I wasn't."

"What were you thinking when you stopped being able to enjoy it?"

That was the worst part. He'd been ready to do it. They'd been so in sync, or at least as much as they could be. Honestly, it'd been pretty clumsy, but it had been fun and felt good. And then his stupid brain had gotten in the way and ruined everything. "All I could think was...we were doing something bad. We were going to get...in trouble."

"Liam, was there anything you were doing that was illegal?"

He looked up, confused, "Of course not."

"Was consent an issue?"

He shook his head, "No."

"You and Zoe are both adults, correct?"

He almost laughed, "Of course. She's twenty-eight."

Dr. Constance was silent for a moment before asking, "Can you tell me what you mean by getting in trouble?"

Therein was the problem. The question he couldn't answer. He shook his head, "I don't know."

"That's okay. Let's back up to the other thing you said. Can you tell me more about thinking you were doing something bad?"

Exasperated, he exclaimed, "I don't know, okay! And god, I wish I did." His eyes squeezed shut, and his voice became much smaller as he added, "I want her so much."

Zoe was in the backyard and headed for the house when she noticed him coming up the driveway. As soon as he reached the top of the stairs, she was there waiting for him, wrapping him in a comforting hug.

He returned the embrace and kissed the top of her head before he let go and stepped toward the piano. She followed a few feet behind, "How was therapy?"

In answer, he proceeded to pound on the keys for an absurdly long time. The piano tuner was going to have his head. She'd been less than pleased the last time she'd worked on the instrument and had practically begged him to be gentler.

"Liam?"

He jumped as he felt Zoe's hand on his shoulder. She never interrupted him during his rage playing. Something had to be wrong, and he immediately stopped and looked up at her, "What?"

Her eyes were fixed on something outside the window. His head swiveled, and he saw what she was looking at.

"Why is there a sheriff's vehicle in our driveway?"

He was already up and headed for the stairs, "Hell, if I know."

The officer was knocking when Liam yanked the door open. Two minutes later, he'd shut the door, and the vehicle left. Leaning his back against the door, he opened the envelope he'd been given. His eyes scanned the document. What he read was unexpected and unwanted. Icy fingers of dread clutched at him, and the paper slipped from his fingers and drifted to the floor.

Zoe had been sitting at the top of the stairs, but now she slowly came down, moving as though she was worried she might spook him. She stopped a few feet away from him, "What is it?"

"A subpoena," he managed to get out.

She knelt and retrieved the document. She shook her head as she read over the contents, "What the hell?"

He stared at her, "I have to testify." He had no option. There was no avoiding the summons.

She looked up at him, and he finally thawed enough to reach for her. She let him hold her tightly. He'd always known it might happen, but as the years had passed, he'd started to hope it never would.

"You won't be alone," she said gently, "I'll be there with you."

He stiffened, "I don't want you anywhere near any of this. I don't want him to even know you exist."

She sighed, "I appreciate that, but if they're calling you as a witness, they'll probably find out about me. Don't lawyers have to do research on their witnesses?"

Defeated, he sagged a little more against the door and admitted, "I don't know."

She took a step back, and he unwillingly dropped his arms. Meeting his eyes, she took hold of his hands, "I will be there. The entire time. I will sit in the courtroom the entire time you're on the stand. And then we will come home."

He shook his head, "I can't ask you to do that."

She smiled sweetly, "Muffin, I'm your wife. I may not know much about how to be a wife, but I know what *for better or worse* means. You have to go sit and get asked questions about a really shitty thing. You will not do this without me. You will not have to face that asshole alone."

The subpoena completely threw off the rest of his day. Criminal charges were being pressed against Jonas, as they should be. Given Liam's role in what had happened, it was no surprise that he'd received the summons.

By bedtime, it was almost a relief to have something to distract himself with. Granted, the thing that was distracting him was the other problem that had screwed up his day.

They'd gotten rid of the blanket wall a few weeks earlier, and sleeping with his wife had gotten so much better yet so much worse. Once he'd mostly healed from the surgery, things had started to progress physically between him and Zoe.

It started with making out. They'd been making out a lot. He was fairly certain that there was no part of the house where they hadn't made out like teenagers.

Making out was great. He loved it. He loved having her in his arms, feeling her respond to his touch. Loved hearing the little noises, the gasps and sighs that would come out of her. It was like magic.

Things had grown much less chaste. Their clothes stayed on, but that didn't mean they hadn't touched each other nearly all over. And a few days earlier, his hands had finally gone under her shirt, and it had driven him a little crazy feeling her skin under his hands like that.

And then his stupid, stupid brain had turned into a world-class asshole. He'd let go of her almost instantly, and she'd looked so hurt. Like she thought he found her undesirable. Which was the furthest thing from the truth. He had tried to reassure her it wasn't her. Tried to tell her how much he wanted her. She'd told him it was okay, that they'd just slow down.

He didn't want to slow down, but until he figured out what the fuck was wrong with him, they didn't have much other option.

Even Dr. Constance had told him that taking things slower might help.

Already in bed, he watched Zoe come out of the bathroom, pulling her hair into a low ponytail. She hit the light switch and slid into bed next to him. Lying on her back beside him, she stared at the ceiling. One thing that had been a pleasant surprise for her had been the skylight over the bed. On a clear night, like the one they were looking at, they could see hundreds of stars twinkling far above on the black sheet of night.

"How are you?" she asked in the darkness.

"I've been better," he replied after a few seconds.

She sighed, "Today kinda sucked, didn't it?"

"Yeah." No kinda about it. It had definitely sucked.

He moved one hand out from under his head and maneuvered it so he was holding her. "I've been thinking," he said after a minute.

"That's dangerous," she teased.

He smiled. This particular bit of banter came up frequently. Lightly squeezing her, he retorted, "Hilarious."

"You love it," she giggled.

He rolled onto his side, and she looked at him as he leaned in, "I love you." He kissed her tenderly but backed away before it could devolve into another make-out session, "Anyway..."

"You were thinking," she interjected.

He nodded, "You never got a honeymoon."

She laughed, "You're saying that caring for your post-surgery grumpy ass wasn't my honeymoon?"

He let out a pained laugh, "God, I hope not. I can't believe you still want to be married to me after that."

"Oh, believe me, there were moments when I was yelling at you for lifting too much where I wondered when I'd lost my damn mind."

He grinned, "I didn't overexert myself. I was careful."

"Sure you were," he could hear the eye-roll. "You are so incredibly stubborn."

"Takes one to know one." he shot back.

"So, anyway, this honeymoon you mentioned..." she steered the conversation back onto course.

"Where do you want to go?"

She rolled onto her back and stared up at the sky. He gazed at her, wondering what she was thinking. "Where do you want to go?" she asked after a little bit.

He shook his head, "Nope, this isn't about me."

"I mean, it is. Honeymoons are for the couple, not just half of the couple. Last time I checked, this particular couple is made up of you and me."

He lightly touched her cheek, tilting her head back to look at him, "I appreciate that, but I want to know what you want."

She moved closer, voice suggestive, "You want to know what I want?"

He sighed, "You know what I mean. Where do you want to go?"

She was quiet for a few seconds before inquiring, "When are you thinking of taking this honeymoon?"

"After I have to testify. I need something to look forward to."

She nodded and looked back up at the sky, "That's a good idea." He waited and, after a while, began to wonder if she was ever going to answer him. Eventually, she asked, "You know what I've always wanted to do?"

"What?"

"Just get in the car and drive. Go see stuff. I've never really seen the mountains. Never seen the ocean. Honestly, I'd really like to visit a tourist trap just for the hell of it." She sighed wistfully, "There's just so much I haven't seen."

It was a good answer, "Any particular direction you have in mind?"

"West."

He propped himself up so he could look down at her. Gently caressing her cheek, he hovered over her lips and, before kissing her, said, "West sounds good."

Thirty-Eight

Zoe

She scanned the trunk's contents, "I think that's everything." Looking up at Liam, she asked, "Anything else you can think of?"

"No," He shook his head, raised his hand, and pushed the trunk lid down.

He moved silently to the passenger side of the car. She ran to the house and checked the doors to ensure they were locked before joining him. She'd be driving the first leg of the trip. Possibly more. Liam wasn't doing the best and hadn't fought her when she'd cautiously suggested that maybe he shouldn't be driving, at least not for the beginning of the trip.

With one last look at the house, she turned on the ignition and headed down the driveway. Liam's decision to take the honeymoon trip right after testifying had been a good idea. She hoped that getting out into nature would start providing some healing.

They'd gotten home two days earlier, and he'd spent those two days at therapy. Dr. Constance had agreed that the trip was a good idea, and he was scheduled for remote sessions.

"You can put some music on if you want," Zoe told him when they'd been on the road for a few minutes. "I've got a giant playlist downloaded on my phone."

He said nothing as he reached for the phone sitting in the center console. Not long after, music began playing from the car's speakers. She kept her eyes on the road but glanced over to check on him as often as possible.

The lost look on his face hurt her heart. It had appeared after he'd been questioned by that weasel Hiller. Throughout the grilling, Liam held it together, looked, and spoke clearly and professionally. But from her seat in the back corner of the courtroom, she could tell that he was holding on by a thread.

His testimony had taken two days, and she was fairly certain the only way he'd managed to get through it was the keyboard and headphones they'd bought and taken with them (the one currently in the trunk). He'd gotten back to the hotel after the first day and spent hours playing. Then he'd gone to bed and held her tightly. After that first day in court, he'd barely spoken. He talked on the stand. Off the stand, when she could manage to coax him to say anything, he was monosyllabic.

After a little while she said, "I think I want to grab some coffee when we hit Sioux City. That okay?"

"Sure."

She reached over and lightly squeezed his hand, "Thanks." Returning her hand to the steering wheel, she kept heading north on I-29. They still had at least an hour before they'd hit the small city at the border of South Dakota.

The list of things that she wanted to see was long. They would easily be gone for a few weeks. As soon as she'd known when they'd be leaving, she'd gone in to talk to the studio staff. She knew being gone meant Saturdays would need coverage. To her relief, everyone had been incredibly compassionate. She hoped it hadn't been difficult to find coverage, and when she'd expressed concern, they'd told her not to worry about it.

Outside the car, trees and hills whizzed by. Inside the car, happy music played from the speakers. She bounced along to the beat and sang. Liam always seemed to like hearing her sing, and she hoped it might help now.

When they reached Sioux City, her eyes scanned the sides of the interstate, and when she saw a sign indicating Starbucks, she took the exit. Liam wordlessly entered the order on the app. Waiting in line at the drive-thru, she asked, "We're about an hour out from our first stop. Need to stop and take an actual break, or are you good for me to keep going?"

"Keep going."

Not quite an hour later, she pulled into a parking spot. Out of the car, she stretched, and Liam joined her after a few seconds. Silently, he took hold of her hand, and they walked to the building.

Before she'd started looking up places to put on her list, she had no idea South Dakota had a music museum. She knew they had to stop as soon as she ran across it. It absolutely screamed Liam to her.

They wandered the exhibits. She made little comments and tried to crack jokes, but every time she'd look at Liam, he'd still have that lost look on his face. He didn't seem angry and held her hand as gently as ever. It had been five days since the last time she'd seen him smile, and she missed it. She'd gotten so used to his smile and laugh that she'd forgotten what he'd been like when they'd first met. He'd changed so much in the months they'd known each other.

Jonas and Hiller were not going to win. She wouldn't let them. They had done a number on him in less than forty-eight hours. She was glad she'd insisted she go with. Who knew what condition Liam would be in if she hadn't? It would take time and patience, but her Liam was still in there. She was sure of it.

"Oh my god, I love it!" She squealed as they stood across the street from the strange structure. The facade was covered in a mural made up of corn cobs. She'd always wanted to see the Corn Palace. Wasn't interested in going inside, just wanted to see what it looked like. It was as amazing and weird and absurd as she had anticipated.

Taking out her phone, she snapped a few photos. As she finished, she looked up at Liam. For the first time in days, he had a different facial expression. Perplexed was the best term she could come up with. The sight of it filled her with relief. This was a good sign. Stretching up on her tiptoes, she kissed his cheek. His eyes shifted from the building to her, and he asked, "You love it?"

She exuberantly nodded and laughed, "It's just so magnificently weird." He nodded but said nothing else. She held out her phone to him, "Picture time."

He took the phone from her. When she'd started planning the trip, she'd told him she wanted them to take selfies together to document what they'd seen. He hadn't been thrilled but had agreed to her request. Having the longer arms, he was in charge of actually taking the pictures.

Standing with their backs to the building, she held onto him and smiled as he snapped the photo. He returned her phone, and she looked at the picture, "Looks good." In truth, it didn't look that good. He looked pained in the photo, but she wasn't about to complain. He was complying with her request and she'd take the win.

All along I-90, spanning most of the width of South Dakota, were countless billboards advertising her next planned stop. They proclaimed things like *Free Ice Water* and *Homemade Pie.* Many of them also listed how many miles there were left to go. At one point, she laughed, "For what they've spent on advertising, this place has got to be amazing."

They reached the small town of Wall mid-afternoon. Zoe's body was starting to ache from the hours of driving, but she wasn't about to mention that to Liam. She knew he'd feel like he had to take over the driving, and she wasn't going to let him. After Wall, they had less than an hour before they'd reach their stop for the night. She could manage that.

Wall Drug wasn't just a wide spot in the road. It was huge. Most of Wall was taken up by the attraction. As she drove past it, she was overwhelmed by how many people were there. And the more people she saw, the more anxious she grew. She couldn't handle that many people. With a glimpse at Liam, she felt crestfallen, seeing he was back to looking lost. She gently asked, "Hey, can you take some pictures, just so I have evidence that this place exists? I don't think I can handle the crowds."

He picked up her phone, and as she drove slowly, he took some photos. Zoe drove back to the interstate, and they continued west. When they reached the hotel in Rapid City, she was glad she hadn't tried to add one more stop to the day.

After checking in, they carried a few things from the car to the room. While Liam set up his keyboard, she opted to take a shower. Hopefully, the hot water would untangle some of the knots that had formed from sitting in the car so long.

The shower helped, and when she re-entered the main part of the room, Liam was still at the keyboard. Due to the headphones, she couldn't hear what he was playing, but watching his fingers, she quickly figured out he was playing scales. Scales were usually a good sign. He didn't tend to attack the keys as hard when he played them. Playing scales seemed to be his version of Linus's security blanket.

They brought him comfort, though she wasn't quite sure how. He'd started teaching her how to do them, and she found them aggravating. But there was a consistent, repetitive motion to them that she suspected he found soothing.

She dug out her e-reader and curled up on the bed to try to read, but her eyes kept traveling to her husband. Hiller had been downright vicious. Liam remembered the lawyer well from when he'd worked for Jonas. He had warned her that Hiller would be an ass. In the days leading up to giving testimony, Liam had run through every possible scenario of things Hiller might throw at him. The one thing he didn't think of was, of course, the one thing Hiller went after like a rabid dog.

The blonde man had sneered at Liam. Had asked questions that were clearly loaded with plenty of extra meaning that Liam understood but was lost on pretty much everyone else. Hiller had asked things that were completely unnecessary. Things that the prosecutor had objected to, but Judge Gladstone had overruled time and time again. Liam had done well; he hadn't been obvious about looking at her, but she'd been able to tell every time he had. Zoe had kept her eyes fixed on Liam, her hand making the *I Love You* sign that she tried to hold discreetly, but not so discreetly that he wouldn't be able to see it. They had agreed beforehand to the sign. Whenever it got to be too much, he could look to her, and she would be there, making it.

The scales stopped abruptly, and Liam pushed a button on the keyboard while yanking off the headphones. He stood and stretched. Turning around, he met her eyes. He didn't look quite as lost as earlier. He sat on the edge of the bed, facing her. Taking hold of her hand, he stared down at it, tugged gently, and she moved closer. He pulled her into a hug, and they sat that way for a minute.

When he released her, she reached up and lightly ran her fingers along his jaw. He sighed and leaned into her touch. She rested her hand against his cheek and asked, "How are you?"

His head moved, and he pressed a soft kiss into her palm. He seemed to be trying to formulate words. She waited, and he finally said, "I'm sorry...I know I'm not much fun."

It was the most words he'd strung together in days. She kept her voice and smile soft, though inside, she was doing an overjoyed happy dance, "That's okay. You don't need to be. I can be enough fun for both of us."

He didn't smile. That had been too much to hope for, but it was only the first day of their trip. He leaned forward and kissed her quickly before standing and saying, "I'm going to shower."

"Want me to order something for dinner?" she asked as he stood.

He nodded, "Get whatever."

The food arrived a little after he'd finished showering. Dinner was a mostly silent affair. When they finished, she was so tired she told him, "I think it's bedtime for me."

Turning off the lights, he got into bed next to her. He spooned her, holding her tightly against his chest. His lips feathered a few kisses against her hair. Held securely, she started to drift off, but his voice pulled her back momentarily. "Thank you for not making me deal with crowds," he murmured.

She squeezed the hand against her abdomen, "You're welcome."

"I'll try to be better tomorrow."

"It's okay if you're not," she replied. All she cared about was that he was talking to her again. She yawned as she added, "Love you."

"Love you, too," was the last thing she heard before sleep finally won.

Thirty-Nine

Liam

5 Days Ago

"Mr. McPherson, what did you do on March fourteenth of this year?"

Liam stared at Hiller trying not to show his confusion. *Keep answers brief and to the point.* "I got married."

"I'm sure we all congratulate you, Mr. McPherson. Can you tell the court where you got married?" Liam knew Hiller well enough to know that there were absolutely no well wishes in the man's words.

"Las Vegas."

Hiller nodded. The look on his face told Liam that the rat of a man had something up his sleeve, and there was no way to stop it. "I see. How long had you and your wife been together before you got engaged?"

"Objection, Your Honor. Relevance." The prosecutor glared at Hiller.

Judge Gladstone asked, "Counsellor, what is the reason for this line of questioning?"

Hiller's smile made Liam's skin crawl, "I'm simply establishing the witness's character."

The judge nodded, "I'll allow it."

Fucking hell. Had Jonas paid off the judge? Liam tried to keep his face unreadable, and when Hiller answered the judge, Liam's eyes flashed to the back corner where Zoe was sitting with her hand in the pre-agreed-upon sign. She hadn't looked away the entire time. It was helping. He was glad she'd insisted on being there.

Hiller turned back to him, "How long had you and your wife been together before you got engaged?"

Liam considered the question. He knew what he was about to say would play right into Hiller's plan. It was rapidly becoming clear what the lawyer was trying to do. "Two and a half months."

Hiller's smile grew. He had Liam right where he wanted him. "And how long were you engaged?"

"A little over twenty-four hours."

Hiller smirked, "My, you were eager, weren't you."

Present

The hand holding his squeezed, and Liam blinked, looking at the immense rock formation before them. He'd gotten lost in the memory of Hiller's abominable line of questioning. Zoe was beaming up at him as she enthused, "Isn't it amazing?!"

He nodded wordlessly. She looked so incredibly happy. He couldn't believe she'd spent two days in the courtroom listening to the examination from hell and was still perfectly content to be right there with him.

She held out her phone, "Selfie time."

Taking the phone, he angled it so they were both in the photo with Devil's

Tower visible behind them. After a moment, he handed the phone back, and she nodded happily before going up on her tiptoes to kiss his cheek, "Thank you."

In truth, he didn't quite understand what she found so appealing about the really big rock, but she'd been adamant they had to see it. He wasn't about to mention his confusion. She'd been put through the wringer. The least he could do was let her see all the things she wanted to see. No matter how bizarre they might be.

They continued walking the trail. She swung their connected hands and started talking, "Alex made me watch Close Encounters like a year ago. He made mashed potatoes and had a contest where he, Dahlia, and I had to recreate Devil's Tower the way the one guy in the movie does."

The image of the three friends making the mashed potato replicas was a little amusing. He very nearly smiled. And then he remembered Hiller's sneer, and he was right back in the seat in the courtroom with Jonas staring at him with that sickening smile.

Jonas had looked even older and more twisted than Liam had remembered. Then again, he hadn't seen the man in nearly three years. He'd foolishly hoped he'd never see the bastard again.

"Hey, look up there!" Zoe's voice broke in again.

"Huh?" He blinked in confusion at being yanked back to the present.

She pointed, "Up there. I think it might be a hawk....maybe an eagle?"

He followed her line of sight and saw a bird high up in a tree, "Hawk, I think."

She pulled her hand free and pointed her phone at the bird. A few seconds later, the photo had been taken, and she reclaimed his hand with hers.

Back at the car, he looked at her. Really looked at her. She had raccoon eyes again. He knew she wasn't used to the elevation change, and it wouldn't be good if she got sick while driving. Where they were headed would require alertness. She'd never driven in the mountains, and he wasn't sure it was a good idea to let her try, at least not yet. He held out his hand, "Keys."

She hesitated and searched his face, "You sure? I'm fine."

He nodded, "You need to get a feel for the mountains before you drive them."

Still, she hesitated, "Are you absolutely sure you're up to it? I promise I'll be careful."

"I'm sure."

Finally, she placed the keys in his outstretched hand. He adjusted the seat and the mirrors, and soon, they were back on the road.

Heading northwest toward the Montana border, he reminded himself of his promise to her that he would try to be better today. He needed to attempt conversation. If he asked a question, Zoe would likely be able to carry on talking for a while. He liked hearing her talk; it helped push away some of the darkness. "Have you thought about what I asked?"

"What you asked?" she sounded slightly confused, which made sense considering his vague question.

"About ADHD."

"Oh." She was quiet for a few seconds before continuing, "I don't know. I mean, would it really make any difference if we knew? If I do have it, it's not like it's suddenly gonna be fixed just because some doctor diagnoses me."

For months, he'd been growing suspicious that she had ADHD and possibly OCD. Things she would say and do only served to confirm it to him. Early in their relationship, he'd started looking up information about things he would notice. Teaching her to play piano had made him more convinced that he was on the right track. But he wasn't a doctor. He couldn't say for certain that's what was going on.

Right before he'd gone to testify, he'd finally broached the subject to her. He'd updated his health insurance and added her to it. Once the new cards arrived, he'd given her one and asked if she'd ever considered that she might have ADHD. She'd stared at him with confusion, "ADHD? I'm not nearly hyper enough to have that."

He'd explained what he'd found in his research. Women with it were often left undiagnosed until they were adults because they didn't typically present the same way little boys did. "I'm not telling you to get diagnosed. I just want you to know that if you want to get checked out, you have my full support." he'd told her and left it at that.

Eyes on the road, he said, "I'm not suggesting that it would be fixed, but if you do have it, they would be able to help you manage it."

She sighed, "And by manage, you mean doping me up with meds until I can't function."

He shook his head, "From what I found, if they go the med route, they give stimulants. The idea is to keep you from turning into a zombie." Talking was starting to get a little easier. "I can show you the Reddit threads if you want."

She hesitated a moment before replying, "I don't know. I need to keep thinking about it."

"Okay."

She put some music on, and he listened to her sing along to all kinds of pop music. He was slightly surprised by all the metal covers she'd put in the playlist. That was unexpected. Nearly an hour passed when she suddenly paused the music mid-song and asked, "Can we stop somewhere? I need to take something for my head."

The elevation must have finally caught up to her, and he pulled over as soon as he could. She went to the trunk and dug out the ibuprofen from her bag. Climbing back in the passenger seat, she took the pills and shook her head, "I don't know what's wrong with me."

"Elevation sickness," he informed her as he pulled back onto the road.

"Wait...that's a real thing? You weren't just screwing with me?"

"It'll get better," he promised.

"Is this why you wouldn't let me drive?" she asked.

He nearly smiled as he replied, "I suspected it might hit."

She groaned, "Well, this sucks."

In Billings, they stopped at a burger place that Zoe had read reviews of online. She was adamant that they had to try the milkshakes. They ate at the small restaurant, then got back in the car, milkshakes in hand. He'd decided that his no food-in-the-car rule wouldn't work well for a road trip. Zoe liked to snack too much, and he wasn't about to tell her not to eat. It was good seeing her not look so hollow all the time. That said, as soon as they got home, he would be deep cleaning the vehicle.

Zoe was a little quieter as they continued toward Gardiner. She hadn't turned the music back on, and he suspected her head was still bothering her. When he felt his thoughts beginning to wander back to the courtroom, he pulled over again.

"Everything okay?" she asked as he turned off the ignition.

He nodded, "Need to clear my head."

He leaned against the car hood and stared at the scenery. The Yellowstone River was not far from where he'd parked. Zoe joined him and started taking pictures. After a few minutes, she leaned her back against his chest, and he draped his arms over her shoulders. She clasped his hands with hers.

"It's so pretty out here," she murmured.

"Mm-hm."

"You were right. I probably shouldn't be driving right now. Some of those steep grades would've been a little much for me with how I'm feeling."

He kissed the top of her head and straightened back up. This was nice. Good.

Safe. Jonas couldn't get him here. Hiller couldn't poke at him, trying to provoke an angry outburst. Liam had been so certain he'd finally escaped them, and the moment that subpoena had shown up, it was like the universe was saying, *You'll never be free.*

Some of Jonas's victims had been in the courtroom. Liam had recognized most of them. He shuddered, remembering how they had stared at him the entire time he was on the stand. There had been so much pain in their eyes. So much anger. *You could have stopped this. You let this happen to us.* And when Hiller had asked about Liam's marriage, he could've sworn there had been hate in those victims' eyes. Hate he absolutely deserved. *You don't deserve to be happy. You let our lives get ruined and walked away scot-free.*

"Liam?" Zoe's soft voice broke in. She had shifted in his arms and was looking up at him.

He kissed her forehead, "Ready to get back on the road?"

She didn't move. He could see the gears of her mind working, and finally, "He was wrong, y'know."

"Who?"

"Hiller."

Oh.

She held his gaze, saying, "You aren't impulsive. You don't make rash decisions."

He closed his eyes and shook his head, "Eloping in Vegas with my girlfriend of less than three months would say otherwise."

"No." Her voice was surprisingly sharp, and his eyes flew open to meet hers. There was an intensity there he wasn't used to. She told him, "If you had died on the operating table and we hadn't been married, I would've spent the rest of my life knowing that I never got to be your wife. If all I'd gotten were two days of marriage, that would've been better than not being married at all."

She sighed, "It wasn't rash or impulsive. You were looking out for me. You were making sure I wouldn't have to face living in my car if you died. Even Alex and Dante agree it was decent and logical of you."

By the time they reached the hotel in Gardiner, he was exhausted. Surprisingly, he was also feeling a little better. Zoe's words had been an unintentional pep talk. They'd helped pull him a little more out of his head. After they checked in, they went to the room, and Zoe immediately pulled a chair up to the window to stare at the river that flowed right below the hotel. He was reminded of Vegas and how she'd sat up all night to watch the city.

Lying on the bed, he asked, "Is it okay if we wait until tomorrow to go into the park?"

She turned to look at him, "Yeah. I don't really want to get back in the car for the next several hours."

He watched as she turned back to the window and heard her ask, "Think we'll see any bears?"

"I hope not," he replied with a yawn.

They did see bears, but to his relief, they were at a sanctuary specifically for bears and wolves. Zoe was enamored with the giant creatures. Fortunately, they didn't encounter any roaming wild in the park.

He hadn't expected Yellowstone to be as stunning as it was. Zoe was in love before they even got into the park proper, and once they were inside, she was beyond overjoyed. Her happiness was infectious and drew him back from the dark a little more.

The second night they stayed in Gardiner, he found his thoughts returning to something he hadn't thought about since the subpoena had arrived.

Sex.

That night, he took off his shirt when he went to bed. It was the first time since that semi-awful night months earlier. Zoe had seen him without his shirt plenty of times at this point. When his incisions had been healing, he'd had to remove it so they could be cleaned.

When he got into bed, Zoe curled against him, and he felt her fingers lightly run over the longest incision scar. "They're healing well," she murmured.

"I had a good nurse."

She laughed, "Damn right you did."

Moving up a little, she kissed him, and when she broke the kiss, he wasn't ready for her to stop. He pulled her back and started to kiss her again. It was the first time they'd made out in weeks, and he hadn't realized how much he'd missed it until he had her in his arms again. She responded eagerly, and it grew feverish.

She was above him, and her hands were tangled in his hair. His hands were running up and down her back. Breathing became heavier, and he rolled her onto her back, positioning himself above her. She giggled at the move, but it was a breathy, gaspy giggle, and it only made him crave her more. He kissed her hard. Ravenously.

He trailed kisses down her throat, and she gasped more. In one of their previous make-out sessions, he'd discovered a spot at the base of her throat that seemed to drive her crazy when he kissed it. He reached the spot, and she squealed and writhed beneath him. Stopping to catch his breath, he looked up at her in the semi-darkness. His voice was rough as he told her, "I want you so fucking much."

She grabbed his face and pulled him back to resume their make-out. For the first time in weeks, he was happy.

How dare you be happy.

He froze as the thought came to him unbidden. Suddenly, he saw the victims and their haunted eyes. A bucket of ice water might as well have been dumped over him. He pushed away from Zoe and sat up with a heavy sigh, "I'm sorry."

She joined him and turned on the light, "What happened?"

He shook his head, his voice sounding as broken as he felt, "I can't do this."

"Did I do something wrong?" she asked, her voice trembling slightly.

He shook his head and stared dejectedly at his hands.

A second passed, and then she moved closer. Leaning her head against his bicep, she asked, "This okay?"

"Yeah."

She took hold of one of his hands and held it with both of hers, "Want to talk about it?"

"No."

She pressed a kiss to his arm, "Okay. Want to try to sleep?"

He wasn't sure he could sleep but nodded and laid back down. Zoe turned the light off and resumed her previous position against his side. He held her and sighed wearily, "I'm so sorry, sweetheart. I do want you. Please, believe me; I want to do this. I just...can't...right now."

She didn't immediately reply, but after a little while, he heard, "We'll figure this out, okay? I'm not going anywhere. I promise."

Forty

Liam

"Where are you today?"

He looked at the image on his laptop screen. It was strange not being in the same room as Dr. Constance. "Montana. Right outside Yellowstone."

"That's a beautiful area. My husband and I were up there a few years ago for our anniversary," she told him.

"I think Zoe's in love with it," he mused.

Dr. Constance smiled, "I'm sure she is. I know I fell a little in love with it. Speaking of, where is she right now? Is she there with you?"

He shook his head, "There's a little bookstore with a cafe a few blocks away. She'll probably come back with a pile of books."

"You look like you're doing a little better than the last time we spoke. How are you feeling?"

He sighed, "I'm not sure. Mixed up."

She nodded, "Are you able to differentiate any of the feelings, or is it all one giant mish-mash?"

He considered that for a bit, "Yesterday was the best I've felt in weeks. But...last night..." He groaned inwardly, remembering the disaster that had been their most recent attempt at sex.

"What happened last night?"

He rested his elbows on the table and leaned his head against them. "We tried again."

"I see. Was this the first time since the subpoena arrived?"

He nodded miserably, "I...I couldn't...do it."

"Liam, when you say you couldn't do it, what does that mean?"

He was confused, "Exactly what I said. I couldn't do it." What didn't she understand? He hadn't been able to have sex with his wife. How did this need clarification?"

"I understand that. Is it okay if I ask some questions that are a bit more in-depth?"

He sighed, "I guess."

"When you think about sex, what does that look like?"

He felt like he was about to burst into flames at the thought of having to discuss this. But he wanted to be able to have sex, and if this was what he had to do, it's what he would do. Gritting his teeth, he replied, "Kissing...touching each other...penetration. Sex."

To her credit, Dr. Constance looked completely unruffled. "I see. Are you able to experience arousal?"

"Yes," Why couldn't one of those earthquakes Yellowstone was known for hit and swallow him whole?

"Have you talked with Zoe about what she's expecting when it comes to sex?"

He shook his head, "It's just sex. We should be able to figure it out."

"Let's put a pin in that for a minute and return to last night. What was happening when you were unable to continue?"

He thought back. It had started so good. He wasn't sure what had happened.

"We were making out, and I just...just couldn't keep going."

She nodded, "What were you thinking about?"

How dare you be happy.

He raked his fingers through his hair, forcing himself to remember the exact moment that thought had entered his head. "I...I was happy. And..." he sighed, shook his head in defeat, unable to continue.

"Liam, do you believe that you are safe when you talk to me?"

He slowly nodded, "Yeah."

"Is there something I can do to make it easier to discuss this?"

He thought for a moment, "Can we turn the camera off?"

"Just go to audio, you mean?"

"Yeah."

"Yes." The image went black, and he heard her voice through his headset, "Is this better?"

It was. It was so much better. "Yes."

"Now, are you able to talk about what you were thinking?"

Not having the doctor staring at him was a relief, and he relaxed a fraction, "I told you that some of Jonas's victims were at the trial."

"Mm-hm."

"The whole time I was on the stand...they were...they were staring at me. I let their lives be ruined and they just stared at me. I could see how much they despise me. And when...Hiller started asking about my marriage...I could see the hate. I let their lives be ruined, and I...dared...to be happy." The words felt like they'd been ripped from him, like a tooth being extracted without anesthetic. Tears slipped past his eyelashes. "I...keep...I keep seeing their eyes."

There was silence for a few moments before Dr. Constance gently asked, "Liam, have you talked to any of the victims since everything came to light? Have they verbally told you that they hate you? That they blame you for what happened? That they think you shouldn't get to be happy?"

He shook his head and wiped his eyes, "Not verbally, but...but I could see it. And...and I know it's my fault."

"Liam, are you the one who did those despicable things to them?"

He shuddered. How could she even ask such a thing? "NO!"

Dr. Constance's voice remained calm, "Who did those things?"

"Jonas."

"That's right."

His stomach twisted angrily. What was she trying to say? "He wouldn't have been able to do that stuff if I hadn't ignored the rumors."

"Liam, before you went to work for him, how many years had Jonas had his ministry?"

"A few decades."

"And when did the ministry start taking on interns? Did that start before or after you went to work for him?"

"Before." He was feeling more and more confused. What did any of this have to do with anything?

"Liam, have you looked at the list of victims who have come forward so far?"

He thought for a few seconds, "Yes."

"Did they all come into Jonas's world after you went to work for him?"

"No. Some of them were interns before I ever met Jonas."

There was a long pause before she said, "Liam, if you're comfortable with it, I would like to turn the visual back on. I want to tell you something, and I think it would help if you could see me. After, we can turn it off again if you want."

He hesitated but then acquiesced, "Okay."

The image of the doctor filled his screen again. The unreadable mask was gone. She was the most earnest he'd ever seen her. She held his eyes with such intensity he couldn't look away. "Liam, Jonas is an abuser. He has a very long list of victims, and those are the victims that we know about. He's been hurting people since before you were born.

"What he did? That was him. That was not you. You've told me that when you discovered the truth, you immediately helped the victim and called the police.

"You did not commit those acts of abuse. Jonas did. You confronted him when you first learned of the rumors. He lied to you and used the trust you had given him to hide behind so he could continue his abuse.

"I can't say whether the other victims hate you. Unless they verbally tell you to your face that they do, you're operating on assumptions. Do you believe that Jonas's other victims deserve to be happy?"

What an odd question, "Of course they do."

"Do you believe that you are one of Jonas's victims?"

He stared at her for a long time before saying, "I...I don't know."

"What do you think separates you from Jonas's other victims?"

He felt a headache forming, "I didn't stop him."

"Liam, you did stop him."

He shook his head, "Too late."

"Liam, you stopped him. You saved his future victims from him."

When Zoe returned from the cafe, he was sitting quietly in the chair, staring out the window. He heard her come in and drop something on the bed. Seconds later, her arms went around his shoulders, and she kissed his temple, "Hey."

He reached up and gently took hold of her hands, "Hey."

"How was therapy?"

"A lot."

A few seconds passed, and she asked, "What do you need right now?"

He turned and looked at her, "Want to go find some geysers? Watch the earth blow up for a while?"

She grinned, "You had me at geysers."

The cloud of steam blew high into the air. Liam felt like he was watching a visual representation of how he'd felt all his life. He didn't say much, just walked the boardwalk, hand in hand with Zoe. What Dr. Constance had told him would take him a while to process. She seemed to believe that he was just as much of a victim of Jonas as all the people the man had hurt so badly. Liam wasn't sure how he felt about that.

As long as you continue to take responsibility for things Jonas did, he's still hurting you.

But he was responsible, wasn't he?

It was all his fault, wasn't it?

They paused on the boardwalk because Zoe wanted to take photos. She handed him the phone, and he took a picture of her kissing his cheek. He returned the phone. She looked at the picture and smiled, "You don't look as pained in this one."

He glanced at the image that still filled the screen. She was right; he didn't look quite so miserable as he had in the selfies from the past few days.

When they returned to the hotel, he found himself thinking about the other thing Dr. Constance had told him.

Zoe was sitting on the bed, crochet in hand. He sat in the chair, watching her. "I have a question."

She looked at him, "What's up?"

"What are your expectations when it comes to sex?"

Forty-One

Zoe

Her hands froze as she processed his question. After a few seconds, she put her work down, "I mean, it's sex."

He nodded, "Right, but what are your expectations?"

This was a very weird line of questioning. "That we'll have it?"

And that was the thing that finally made him laugh. At first, her hackles went up, but she quickly realized he wasn't laughing at her. Amused, he said, "Apparently, that's not the answer Dr. Constance thinks I should've given her."

"What else would you say?"

He shook his head, "I have no idea." He grimaced while adding, "She emailed me resources."

Zoe's face felt hot as she said, "Oh, um...that was nice of her...I guess?"

"It's homework."

She tried and failed to stop her giggles as she asked, "Is this solo homework, or are you allowed to work with a partner?"

He flushed, and an embarrassed laugh escaped him, "I guess it depends on if my partner is interested in giving me a hand."

"Oh god, this is awful," she burst out laughing, collapsing onto the bed as the laughter consumed her. She kept laughing; it grew wildly out of control, and she could feel tears on her face. Breathing was difficult, and sitting up was impossible. "Can't...breathe...Ow..." she clutched her side as it cramped. "Ow...ow!"

When it finally calmed, she was able to sit up. Liam was watching her with a very amused look that immediately softened her. His broad smile was on full display, complete with dimples. She hopped off the bed, walked over, and hugged him. "I've missed your smile so much."

He returned the embrace. Things felt better. The world had righted itself a little.

The next day, they headed even further west. She felt weepy watching Yellowstone disappear from view. It had been beautiful beyond anything she had expected. "Can we come back?" she asked, craning her neck to catch one last view.

Liam didn't take his eyes off the road, but he did reach over and squeeze her hand, "Absolutely."

They hadn't tackled the homework yet. They would, but she wasn't sure when. He had forwarded it to her, and she had taken a peek. Enough of a peek to know that she might be in way over her head. She thought she was fairly knowledgeable about the topic, but there was a big difference between reading something in a novel and doing it in real life.

It was intimidating.

She watched out the window as I-90 took them to the edge of Montana and then into Idaho. It felt like they barely had gotten into Idaho when they were already at the Washington border. By the time they reached the hotel in Spokane, she was ready to be out of the car.

As they settled into the hotel room, she looked around, "Did you not want the keyboard?"

He shrugged, "I think I'll be okay tonight."

She studied him. When she'd returned to the hotel after he finished therapy the day before, he hadn't been playing. He'd been very contemplative the rest of the day until their slightly awkward sex conversation, but he hadn't used the keyboard. She couldn't decide if this was a good thing.

As they were preparing for bed that night, she hesitated before going to the bathroom to change clothes, "Um...is it okay if I change out here?"

Liam eyes widened, "Do you want me to go in the bathroom until you're finished?"

She swallowed hard and shook her head, "Not if you don't want to."

"Are you sure?"

She wasn't, not really, but they were married after all. Had been for a few months. They'd been sleeping in the same bed for even longer. If they were ever going to manage to have sex, she was going to have to be okay with him seeing more of her body than what wasn't covered by her leggings and sweatshirts.

Even if she did change in the same room with him, that didn't mean she had to look at him while doing it. Turning her back to him, she took a deep breath, pulled off her shirt, and immediately replaced it with the t-shirt she'd been sleeping in. Before she put her arms through the holes, she quickly undid her bra and dropped it on the floor.

Okay, she'd survived that. She took a moment to breathe before slipping off her leggings and quickly pulling on her pajama pants. Steeling herself, she turned and found that Liam had also changed into his pajamas. Shakily, she told him, "That...that wasn't so bad."

He gave her an encouraging smile, "That's good."

She crawled into bed and admitted, "I'm not sure I'm up for anything else tonight. Sorry."

He sat and kissed her quickly before turning out the light, "That's okay. We'll get there, beautiful."

She stared at the ceiling, "I'm really not, y'know. Maybe we should schedule you for an eye exam when we get home."

The light turned on. Liam sat up and looked down at her. She could see sad frustration in his eyes. "Why do you do that?" he asked.

"Do what?" She was confused. She hadn't done anything.

"Talk down about yourself."

She rolled her eyes, "I don't. I'm being realistic. I've lived in this body for twenty-eight years. I have a pretty good idea of how it looks."

"You have a distorted view." The sharp words were out of his mouth, and regret instantly filled his face as he hurried to soften them, "I just mean, you don't see yourself..."

She sighed and sat up, "Are we really going to do this right now?"

His voice was soft, "I just...hate hearing you say something that...that isn't true."

"And you think I like hearing you do it? At least I'm being honest about myself," she snapped.

"When have I done that?" he asked.

Her frustration grew, "You say things are your fault when they clearly aren't. You told me that you're not worth much. I fucking hate hearing you say that shit."

He was quiet for a long time, and she finally said, "I don't want to fight."

"I don't either."

They stared at each other for a moment, seemingly in a stalemate. Liam reached out toward her hand, and she let him take hold of it. He looked at her, "You really have no idea what just looking at you does to me, do you?"

Makes you want to gag? She bit back the response and just shrugged.

He swallowed something invisible, "The first time I met you...I...I was stunned. I wasn't prepared to be in that booth with someone so beautiful."

She shook her head, "Don't say that."

"Would you like me to have Dr. Constance pull up her notes from the session I had the Wednesday after I met you? I will if that's what it will take to get you to believe me."

"You told her about me?"

He nodded, "I did."

Perplexed, she asked, "Why?"

"Because I'd...I'd never been attracted to anyone before I met you, and I didn't know how to...handle it." His eyes dropped to their hands, and he shook his head, "I couldn't even figure out how...to talk to you."

She wasn't sure what to say to that.

"Do you remember me telling you I met with Dr. Constance on New Year's Day?" He was still staring at their hands.

"Yeah."

"I don't think I ever told you why."

She shook her head, "Nope. You don't have to if you don't want to."

He blew out a shaky breath, "After we kissed...I was terrified I'd fucked everything up."

"What?" she stared at him, stunned.

"The way you looked at me...when you asked what we were doing. You were so...upset...and I was so...in love with you." His eyes dropped again.

"You were in love with me?"

He nodded, "You were the first person I let in my apartment. You...you were the first person I let touch my piano. And when you sang while I played..." He shrugged and looked up, "That's when I knew...you were it."

She was stunned. Those had been such little things. Barely anything. Tiny little moments that she was sure he'd completely forgotten about. "I didn't know," she admitted.

"I know."

Liam fell asleep long before she did. After he'd told her about when he fell for her, he'd grown less talkative and eventually fallen asleep. She lay beside him in the dark and listened as his breathing grew deep and even.

She had no idea what he saw in her. He talked as if she was this amazing, gorgeous person. All she could see when she looked at herself was the hopeless woman who hadn't even graduated high school, who had stuck with a shitty job for way too long because there hadn't been anything better to hope for.

She was nobody and had come from nothing. And yet he never let her feel like that's what he thought.

It was confusing.

The next morning, she changed in front of him again, though she did ask him to turn around while she changed her underwear. She still wasn't ready for him to see her entire body.

When they got back on the road, her mind raced as fast as the scenery out the window. Were there other couples that struggled this much with the physical side of a relationship? There had to be, right? They couldn't be the only couple in all of space and time that had gone through this.

"You okay?"

She turned to look at Liam. He was still handling the driving. Ever since his most recent therapy session, he'd been better. The darkness he'd been pulled down into hadn't held on quite as tight as she'd been afraid it might. He was talking, smiling, even laughing.

"Just a lot on my mind."

"Want to talk about it?" he asked.

She shook her head, "Not right now. Want me to put on music?"

"If you want."

They crossed the border into Oregon. Music played, and sometimes she sang along. Eventually, they passed through Portland. And they kept driving.

She was in a funk, and she had absolutely no idea why. After the night before, it seemed like she should feel the exact opposite way.

It's because he talks like you have worth. And you know better.

The thought smacked her upside the head, and she turned to the passenger window, trying to hide the tears she couldn't hold back.

Hopefully, the music was loud enough to cover her sniffles. She was trying so hard to keep him from knowing anything was wrong. He needed her to be bright and happy. It helped to keep balance. He was the dark and she was the light, that was how it had been from the beginning. She couldn't be dark when he was already dark.

She squeezed her eyes shut as tightly as possible and prayed that she'd be able to get back to normal by the time they reached their destination.

"You said you've never seen the ocean. Well? What do you think?"

His voice broke through her cloud. She opened her eyes and looked forward. Stretching out as far as she could see was an immense, unending body of water. How was it possible for there to be that much water all in one place? "It's...big," she managed to get out.

He chuckled, "You're not wrong."

She felt even smaller than she had before opening her eyes. Insignificant.

The car pulled into the hotel parking lot, and Liam said, "I'll be back."

She didn't look at him, just nodded. He disappeared into the front entrance, and she told herself to pull it together before he returned from check-in. He'd had such a bad few weeks and was only just surfacing. He did not need her dragging him back down.

Forty-Two

Liam

She'd been crying for over an hour and trying to hide it from him. He pretended he hadn't noticed. Something was bothering her. Something he couldn't figure out. And he hated it.

Returning from check-in, he found her in the car, staring straight ahead at nothing. Her eyes were red, and she jumped in surprise when he opened the car door. She got out and immediately wrinkled her nose in disgust. "What the...it smells like dead fish."

"Funny thing. The ocean smells like fish," he teased, hoping to make her crack a smile.

She just shook her head, "All those scented things they label with names like ocean breeze...all lies. I should've known."

He chuckled, but she didn't react. They unloaded a few things from the car and went to the room. Leaving the suitcase by the bed, she went to the window and stared at the ocean. "It's just so big," he heard her murmur.

He stepped closer, "Want to go down to the beach?"

She shrugged, and her voice was flat, "Sure."

Holding her hand, he led her from the hotel to the beach and the water's edge. She stood in her flip-flops, letting the little waves wash over her feet. Her eyes were fixed on the water, and he watched as the tears started again.

Should he still pretend he didn't see them?

He felt ill-equipped to handle whatever was going on in her head. She needed someone like Dr. Constance, but he had a feeling it wasn't the moment to suggest therapy.

She started walking, and he fell into step beside her. They didn't talk, just walked. He remembered a few days earlier when she'd swung their joined hands happily, and his heart ached at how limp she now felt.

Maybe she was just tired? It had been a lot of driving in a short amount of time. He was so tired; he just wanted to go back to the room and sleep, but it really seemed like she needed to be outside breathing fresh air. Even if it did stink like dead fish.

He watched as she wiped her sleeve across her face, trying to remove the tears. He'd seen her down before, but this felt different.

Looking away from him, she stopped and said, "I think I want to go back to the room."

"Okay," he led her back to the hotel.

In the room, she slipped under the sheet and curled into a tight little ball. He joined and tried to spoon her, but she scooted away to the edge of the bed. "Not right now," he heard.

"Okay. I'm here if you want me," he told her gently.

He took a small nap, and she was still curled up at the edge of the bed when he woke up. Getting out of bed, he grabbed a rice cake and started eating it. She didn't move, and he decided she must be asleep. He hoped that sleep would help whatever was wrong.

Sitting on the bed, he tried to read, but his eyes kept drifting to his wife. He'd been awake nearly an hour when she stirred and sat up, her back to him. She went to the bathroom, and when she returned, she gave him a weak smile that looked a bit too forced. "Sorry, guess I just needed a nap."

He nodded, "I did too."

She wandered to the window and looked out. "It's not what I expected."

"Hmm?"

"The ocean. It's big and stinks and is freezing. But I think I love it? Does that make any sense?"

He joined her, "Not really."

Her laugh sounded off as she muttered, "Like everything else."

"Zoe?"

"Yeah?"

He tried to figure out what to ask that wouldn't push her too much, finally settling on, "What's bothering you?"

She shook her head and didn't look at him, "Just tired."

"This seems like more than tired."

"How would you know?" there was an edge to her voice that he wasn't prepared for.

Leaning against the wall, he studied her, "Well, I did spend the better part of a year barely leaving bed, so I'm not exactly unfamiliar with depression."

"I'm not depressed," the edge had lessened, but not by much.

"It's okay if you are."

She shrugged, "What do I have to be depressed about? My life is pretty damn great." And then she was pressing her face into his chest, and the tears were flowing again. She grasped his shirt and balled it into her tight little fists. Cautiously, he began to rub her back. She didn't balk at his touch, which he took as a good sign.

She wept as if every tear she'd ever bottled up had suddenly broken free, and when it seemed like she had no tears left, she cried even more. He did his best to be as comforting as possible, but he wasn't sure if it was enough.

Eventually, she did run out of tears. She looked up at him and relaxed her hold on his shirt. Sniffling, she said, "I think I ruined your shirt."

He remembered her saying that on Christmas Eve and replied similarly to how he had then, "Pretty sure it takes more than tears to ruin a shirt."

The smile that graced her face was wobbly, but it was real. He felt slightly relieved. She ran her hand along the front of his shirt, trying to flatten the spots where the fabric had been bunched in her hands. Her voice was shaky as she held his gaze, "I don't think I'm okay. And I don't know why."

He tucked a strand of hair behind her ear, letting his fingers linger, "That's okay."

She sniffled, "It's okay that I'm not okay?"

"Mm-hm."

"I'm sorry."

He shook his head, "Don't be."

"But you need me to be," she insisted.

"I need you..." he considered his next words carefully, "to be you. Okay or not."

She shook her head, "We can't both be depressed at the same time."

He offered her a small smile, "If we are, we are. At least we'll be able to remind each other to shower more than once a month."

She began to laugh. It wasn't the strongest or fullest laugh, but like the smile, it was genuine.

"Liam."

He groaned and barely opened his eyes. The room was still mostly dark. "What time is it?" he mumbled.

"4:30."

"In the morning?" he squeezed his eyes shut.

Her voice was brighter than the night before, "It's 6:30 at home."

He sighed and opened his eyes to see her propped up, looking down at him, "You're not going back to sleep, are you?"

She shook her head, "Nope. Let's go to the beach."

"Right now?"

"Mm-hm."

Slowly, he sat up, "Fine, but only because I love you."

She leaned over and kissed him, "Thank you."

His brain was not fully functioning yet, and he sat there trying to wake up while she got out of bed and turned the light on. He watched as she began to change out of her pajamas. Her back was to him, so he didn't see that much and closed his eyes when she asked him to. He was pleased she had started trying to get comfortable changing around him. It was a struggle for her, and he was doing his best not to make it more difficult for her than it already was. He wished he could tell her how much he liked seeing her body, but he didn't think that would be the wisest move after their fight. Even if he couldn't tell her yet, he still let himself enjoy watching his gorgeous wife.

She turned back to him once changed and looked surprised, "Are you okay?"

"Still trying to wake up," he replied. *And frankly, sweetheart, I'd much rather sit here and watch you be mostly naked than get up and change.*

The situation between his legs was doing nothing to help matters. He tried to distract himself by asking, "How are you feeling this morning?"

"Not great, but better than yesterday, I think," she replied after a few moments.

"That's good."

"You?"

"Hungry," he replied, wondering if she'd sense the extra layer the word contained.

She did not. "I don't think the breakfast thing opens until six."

"That's okay. I can see exactly what I want." He was getting freakishly bold; it had to be the fact he was still not quite awake.

She froze briefly as she finally pieced together his meaning, "Um...want me to grab you something from the fridge?"

Never mind. She'd pieced together nothing.

He held out his hand to her, "C'mere."

She looked perplexed but moved closer and took his hand. He pulled her on top of himself. A squeak escaped her mouth, and she looked down at him, "Is there something you would like?"

He reached up and toyed with a dark brown curl. She'd dyed it before he went to testify. It had been her idea. He hadn't wanted her to, but she'd been worried that her non-traditional hair color choices would reflect poorly on him. He missed the more colorful hues she normally wore. Gazing at her with longing, he spoke, voice husky, "You."

Uncertainty clouded her face, and she rolled off him, "I...don't think...I can. Not right now."

Now he knew how she'd felt when he'd had to stop things. She'd always let him and never forced him to continue. Sitting up, he told her, "That's okay."

"You sure?" She looked pensive as though she thought he might change his mind.

"Sure," he nodded. "Let me get changed, and we'll go."

Forty-Three

Zoe

The sky was a grey overcast. It was a little after five in the morning, and the beach was almost empty. The waves rolled in, cresting in a spray of white. They walked along the water's edge, hand-in-hand. She needed to talk to somebody. Liam was wonderful. He let her talk and rage and cry, and he never made her feel bad for doing it. But she needed more. And that made her feel awful. Guilty. Like she was somehow not appreciating the good things she had.

She paused and looked at the big rock formations out in the water. "It really does look like a haystack."

"Mm-hm."

They resumed walking, pausing occasionally for her to crouch down and pick up a shell or rock that she'd wash off and tuck in her hoodie pocket. Her nose had finally adjusted to the smell, and she was no longer finding it overwhelming.

Her thoughts drifted back to what happened right before leaving the hotel. Liam had wanted her. Really wanted her. And she just couldn't respond in kind. It was so frustrating. Why was it that as soon as one of them was ready, the other couldn't follow through? It was just a matter of kissing and then sticking the penis in the vagina, right? That's what sex was. It wasn't rocket science.

She loved him. She trusted him. She wanted him. And he seemed to feel all those things about her. So, what was the problem?

Why was this so much easier for everyone else?

"Zoe?"

She glanced up, "Yeah?"

He looked a little nervous. Seemed to be debating something. She could see the conflict on his face, but finally, he said, "If you ever want to talk to Dr. Constance or someone else...It doesn't have to be her...You know that I'm fine with that, right?"

"I know." She knew he wasn't a mind reader, but he had this weird ability to sense the path of her unspoken thoughts. How could they be so in sync about so much and yet be unable to have sex?

Stopping again, she turned to watch the waves, "I probably should. The idea of it, just...I don't know...it's intimidating."

"Do you want to sit in on one of my sessions?"

Surprised, she looked up at him, "That's your time."

He shrugged, "I could talk to Dr. Constance. I don't think she'd have a problem with it. Maybe it won't be so intimidating if you see what it's like."

Actually, that would be really nice. It would definitely help her decide if that was the kind of thing she was looking for. "I don't want to make it weird for you."

He looked slightly amused at her words, "Does this mean you'd be okay with me asking her?"

She chewed her cheek for several seconds. It might be good. Dr. Constance had certainly helped Liam. Maybe she could help Zoe make sense of her unexplainable depression. Slowly, she nodded, "Yeah...if you really are okay with it and she is...I...I think I'd like that."

When they returned from their walk, Liam called Dr. Constance's office, and not long after, an email filled with forms arrived. Zoe would be allowed to be part of his next session, but Dr. Constance wanted the paperwork filled out beforehand. And since Liam's next session was the following morning, Zoe spent a few hours filling everything out.

The following morning, Zoe sat beside Liam in front of the open laptop, waiting. She was nervous. What was going to happen? She'd met Dr. Constance once, and the older woman had seemed nice. What if she wasn't nice during the session?

"Try to breathe," Liam told her as he snagged her hand.

"She's going to think I'm insane," Zoe grimaced. She was relieved he was holding onto her. Maybe it would help her survive the next hour.

"No, she's not."

Zoe started to say, "Maybe this is a bad idea," and got as far as *is* when the doctor's image filled the screen.

"Good morning," the older woman said, "Liam, Zoe, it's good to see you."

Zoe raised her hand in a small wave, "Hi."

"Are you still in Yellowstone?"

"Canon Beach, Oregon," Liam replied.

"That's quite the trip you're taking. It sounds wonderful. Are you having fun?" There was only kindness in the woman's voice, no judgment.

Liam didn't immediately answer, and Zoe tried to sound bright as she said, "It's good."

"That's good," Dr. Constance nodded. She looked at Zoe and asked, "How are you feeling, Zoe?"

Zoe glanced from the screen to Liam and back to the screen, "Um, just ignore me. This is Liam's time."

Liam squeezed her hand, "It's okay. You can talk."

She looked at him in surprise, "But..."

"You need to talk. I can wait. Go ahead if you're up to it."

She looked back to the screen. Her index finger began to pick at her thumb cuticle. It would probably be bloody by the time the session was finished, but she couldn't stop the movement.

"Zoe? Do you want to talk about something?" Dr. Constance wasn't nagging, just gently nudging her.

Zoe's eyes dropped, and she sighed, "I don't know what's wrong with me."

"Can you explain a little more about what you're experiencing that makes you feel that there's something wrong with yourself?"

Zoe was quiet for a few seconds, then said, "I...um...I don't know. I just feel...dark. And I keep crying, and I don't know why." Her words picked up speed, "I usually know why I feel depressed, but I don't know why I am right now. And I feel like I'm ruining everything. And I don't know why." As if to illustrate her point, traitorous tears dropped from her eyes. She wiped her arm across her face, "See? I can't stop crying. Something's wrong with me."

After a moment, Dr. Constance spoke, "I'm sorry you're feeling this way. That must be very frustrating. I want you to know it's okay to be feeling this way."

Zoe shook her head, "No, it's not! We're good. Things are good. I'm just fucked up in the head."

Dr. Constance didn't flinch at Zoe's words. Instead, she said, "Zoe, I want you to do something for me."

Zoe wiped her arm across her eyes again. The stupid tears made her look even weaker in front of the woman. "What?"

"Walk me through the big events in your life from the last several months."

Zoe blinked at her, "Like, how many months?"

Dr. Constance considered that, "Six months? Is that too much?"

"What do you mean by big events?"

"Things that have had a profound effect on your life."

Zoe did a mental backtrack, "Um...six months...I mean, I quit my job, but I'm not sure that counts. I...uh...I moved in with Liam. Let's see...got married...I think that's pretty much it."

"How long were you at your job?"

"Since I was a kid. Fred started making me work at the store pretty much when I moved in. I was...five...so that's..." she squeezed her eyes shut and did the calculation, "twenty-three years."

"That's most of your life, correct?"

Zoe nodded, "Yeah."

Dr. Constance wrote some notes before asking, "How many times have you moved in the last six months?"

"Two."

"Would you consider Liam's surgery and diagnosis and him going to testify to have had an effect on your life?"

Zoe blinked in surprise, "Of course." She wasn't sure why the doctor was asking these questions. She must have already known all this from talking to Liam.

"Zoe, in the last six months, you have experienced at least seven high-stress life events."

Zoe shook her head, "Not really, I mean maybe some of them were a little stressful...but it's not that big a deal."

"Every single one of those events, both good and bad, has quite a lot of stress attached to them. Just going through one or two in a year is enough to cause a wide variety of emotions and even physical health changes. You've been through many more than that and in only six months. It's perfectly understandable that you are feeling the way you are."

Zoe sighed in defeat, "So, there is something wrong with me."

Dr. Constance shook her head, "This is not about something being right or wrong. You are experiencing emotions due to several high-stress situations, and your brain and body are trying to work through that stress. Does that make sense?"

She thought about it. It made sense, but it didn't. "I don't know," she admitted.

Dr. Constance smiled at her gently, "That's okay. Take some time to think about it. If you want, we can talk more soon. If you'd like, I can email you some resources on things to try that can help you manage these emotions."

"Like the sex homework?" The words were out of her mouth before she thought about it, and her hand immediately clapped over her mouth.

She knew she was blushing as she heard the soft huff of a laugh from Liam. Dr. Constance, to her credit, didn't laugh. Just kept that patient, gentle smile and nodded, "Something like that." There was silence for a few beats before Dr. Constance asked, "Since you brought up the sex homework, as you call it, do you want to talk about it?"

Zoe worried her thumbnail between her teeth, "I...I'm not sure. We...haven't..." her words trailed off. She looked at Liam for help.

He took the hint, "We haven't really looked at it yet."

Zoe braced for the doctor to yell at them and was surprised when the older woman said, "That's okay. This is something that's going to take time. Have things progressed in that area otherwise, or are they still the same?"

Zoe was convinced her face was on fire as Liam admitted, "It's about the same."

"Have you talked about it?"

"Kind of," Zoe managed to get out.

"Do you feel comfortable telling me what you mean by that?"

Zoe's eyes dropped to her thumb that she was back to picking at, "Um...he asked me...my expectations."

"That's good. Were you able to express those to him?"

Zoe's shoulders slumped, "I'm not sure what expectations I should have. We're just supposed to have sex." Her tears started again, "And we can't."

Forty-Four

The sky above was an unnatural blue. She wasn't sure she'd ever seen the sky that particular shade; didn't even know the sky could be that color. On both sides of the road, there was just desert as far as she could see. Miles and miles of tan. Just like the ocean, it was unfathomably big. It felt like her eyes were playing tricks on her when she looked at it. It didn't seem real.

They'd driven from Oregon to San Francisco to see the Golden Gate Bridge. After, they headed east on I-80 toward Utah. She wanted to see the Great Salt Lake, and after, they were planning to drop south to the Grand Canyon.

They were taking their time. It wasn't necessary to hit everything in one trip, but nothing was stopping them, and they certainly had no pressing reason to get back home immediately. She felt incredibly spoiled. Liam hadn't been bothered by her elaborate travel plans and had even suggested a few stops along their route.

He was driving again. She was astonished by how well he was doing. Since Yellowstone, he'd not only slipped back to being the Liam she knew, but something she couldn't quite pinpoint had shifted in him. He didn't seem so deeply under the cloud that was always with him. He talked more than ever, laughed deeply, and was just so incredibly alive. Whatever had happened in the session he had with Dr. Constance in Gardiner, it must have been some kind of breakthrough.

"So, homework?" he broke into her thoughts.

They still hadn't touched the sex homework. They also hadn't tried to have sex again. Making out had become a more frequent activity again, but it was all over the clothes touching, and there was something weirdly hesitant about it.

"Now?" she asked.

"If you're up to it, we might as well. Not much else to do for the next several hours."

She pulled her email up on her phone, "I'm not sure I'm up to getting through all of it right now."

He nodded, "That's okay. I don't think that's a requirement. The hardest part is just going to be getting started. We can take it one piece at a time and stop when we need to."

She smiled. He was speaking so much clearer. The last few days, she'd noticed far fewer pauses when he spoke.

Tapping on one of the documents, she watched as it loaded and quickly skimmed it. "Do you think it matters where we start with these questions?"

"Go for whatever seems easiest."

None of these seem easy. She debated for a few minutes and finally picked one. "Okay, initiating. Who should initiate and how? Like, is there some word or something that would be a good indicator?"

"I assume that means we're not supposed to just make a guess and hope the other person is on the same page?"

She laughed, "Apparently not."

"Damn it," he joked. A little more seriously, he added, "Do you always want me to initiate, or would it be easier for you to be the one making the first move?"

"I...I'm not sure. That seems a little...I don't know...unbalanced? Does that make sense?"

He thought about it briefly, then nodded, "Yeah. So, either of us can?"

She mulled that over, "Sure, but it's okay to say no, right?"

"If you say no, it won't go any further. I promise."

She nodded, "Thanks. Um...I guess that means we have to figure out how..." She wet her lips and tried to get the words out, "how to let each other know."

The car grew quiet and stayed that way for a few miles. Liam eventually broke it with, "I don't suppose *wanna fuck?* would work?"

"Oh god," she groaned, and an anxious laugh escaped her. After a few deep breaths, she added, "Well, I guess we wouldn't have to worry about it being misinterpreted."

"If you misinterpret that, we may need to have an entirely different discussion about your understanding of the English language," he teased.

She was glad Liam was driving because he couldn't easily look at her and see how incredibly bright red she was at the moment. She asked, "What if we're not...y'know...at home? I...I just don't know if that would be the most...appropriate...thing to say in public."

"Would grabbing your ass be considered inappropriate?"

She buried her face in her hands, "Okay, I'm just going to curl up and die right now."

He laughed, "To be fair, you do have a really cute ass that is fun to grab."

"Just let me out right now so the vultures can end it all," she tried to sound serious but couldn't stop laughing.

"Sweetheart, vultures are scavengers. They're not interested in living things."

"Fine. Maybe the coyotes would be interested."

With a grin, he informed her, "Also scavengers. Maybe try a rattlesnake."

She looked at him, amused and curious, "You seem so much more...comfortable...talking about this than I am."

He laughed softly, "I'm not sure *comfortable* is the right term."

"You're saying you don't want the earth to open up and swallow you right now?"

"That would make having sex significantly more difficult," he joked.

She giggled, "I guess so."

"Maybe we could have a code word?" he offered after a few more miles.

She nodded, "That could work. Any ideas?"

"It would need to be something that wouldn't raise suspicion, but also not a word we use all the time."

"Like something we could put into a sentence that would sound perfectly normal?"

He nodded, "Exactly."

"Pineapple?" she suggested.

"I said a word we don't use all the time."

She grinned, "Pineapple pizza?"

He let out an exaggerated sigh, "You're impossible."

"Just one of the reasons you love me."

He squeezed her hand quickly, "Just one of them. Alright, let's come back to this one. We don't have to figure out the word this very minute."

"Okay."

"Want to keep going, or do you need a break?" he asked.

"Break would be good."

An hour later, they had stopped to get gas and stretch their legs. They swapped seats, and Zoe took over driving. A few miles along, Liam asked, "Want to tackle another question?"

"Are you just wanting to see how red I turn?"

He laughed, "I won't deny that I'd enjoy seeing that. Couldn't really watch you while I was driving. It's only fair, y'know."

She groaned and rolled her eyes but nodded, "Fine. One question. And I'm allowed to ask to stop if it's too much."

"Okay." He was quiet for a few minutes while he browsed the options, and she heard, "Huh."

"What?"

He didn't answer immediately, and she finally said, "Just tell me."

His voice was hesitant, "I'm not sure you want to do this one."

Inwardly, she groaned, remembering some of the things on the list and dreading what had caught his attention. Taking a deep breath, she told him, "It's okay. We're going to tackle them all at some point. Tell me what it is and if I'm not ready, I'll say 'next'. Fair?"

At least two miles passed before he finally broke the silence, "Sex toys. Pro or con?"

"Okay, that's not so bad."

"You want to talk about this one?" he sounded surprised.

"Why not?" She was a little surprised that she didn't feel any of the awkwardness about the subject that she'd felt about the previous. It seemed like this was the one that should make her wildly uncomfortable.

"I just..." he left the sentence unfinished.

She shrugged, "Just cause I'm a virgin doesn't mean I'm unfamiliar with the subject. I mean, I've got a vibrator."

"You do?" he sounded completely dumbfounded.

She nodded, "You've seen it. How is this a surprise?"

"I have?"

She laughed, "Yeah, I keep it in my nightstand. You're telling me you didn't notice it when you grabbed my ibuprofen out of there a few weeks ago?"

"You...have...a...vibrator."

She glanced at him and saw he looked like his brain had melted. "Does this bother you?"

"I...no, not...I..."

She had to remind herself not to laugh and asked, "Are you telling me that you're thirty-four and have never masturbated?"

The car went deathly silent and stayed that way for at least five miles. Eventually, she broke the silence, "Liam? Does this bother you?" When he still said nothing, she asked, "Do we need to take a break for a while?"

"This is the thing you're comfortable talking about?" he didn't sound upset, just baffled.

She shrugged, "I'll admit that compared to the first question, this one definitely is the more difficult. I don't know why this doesn't bother me."

"I just didn't think that you..." his words trailed off again.

"Have had an orgasm?" she supplied after a few seconds.

The word dangled in the air between them for a long time. She sighed, "So, it does bother you."

Another two miles passed before he finally said, "No, it doesn't bother me."

"Really?"

His voice was a little lower and quieter when he replied, "I thought you would be upset if you knew...that I had..."

She glanced over and reached for his hand, "I'm a virgin, not an idiot. Plus, you take some absurdly long showers. I kind of assumed."

He groaned, "You noticed?"

"Again, not an idiot."

He sighed, "I'm sorry."

Now she was confused, "For what?"

A few more miles passed before he explained, "I was taught it was a sin. I feel so ashamed every time, and it used to be that I just needed to...release. But since you...I just picture you. I'm sorry."

She saw a place to pull over and put the car into park. Turning to him, she said, "You don't need to be sorry."

"I don't?"

"And I don't think it's a sin. Why would it be?"

He rested his head against the headrest and stared at the ceiling, "Because."

"That's a dumb reason."

He shook his head, "It's this whole thing about resisting temptation...not stealing pleasure...from my mate."

She managed to catch the laugh before it sounded and said, "If it's okay, I'd rather you never call me your mate ever again. That's just very weird."

To her relief, some of the tension in his voice faded, "I was always told it was wrong...and I taught people that it was wrong."

She considered that for a bit, "I mean, if you're not doing something illegal while you do it, doesn't really seem like it's wrong."

He tilted his head and looked at her, "You're not disgusted by me?"

She laughed a little at that, "No. Are you disgusted by me?"

He shook his head, "No."

"Good." She turned back to the wheel and resumed driving.

The car was quiet for a while, and then he laughed, "I can't believe you have a vibrator."

She glanced at him, "I can't believe you didn't notice it."

"The only thing in your drawer was the ibuprofen, one of those weird back massager things, and a bag of chocolate. There wasn't a vibrator in there."

She laughed, "Oh, my sweet summer child, please think about what you just said."

It felt like an eternity before she heard the realization in his voice as he said, "Oh."

"And there it is."

More miles passed, and he asked, "Did you bring it with you?"

All the awkwardness suddenly crashed into her, and she bit her lip, "Um...I'm not sure if I should tell you."

"Well, that's a yes if I ever heard one."

When she said nothing, he gently asked, "Break time?"

Sighing in relief, she nodded, "Yes, please.

Forty-Five

Zoe

They were seven hours into their twelve-plus hour trek. It had been almost two hours since they had tackled the sex toy question. Liam was driving again, and Zoe had been alternating between watching him and watching the scenery.

"Up for another question or need to wait a while?" he asked.

"Sure." She pulled up the list again and glanced through it. "You saw the list. Anything else stick out to you that you wanted to discuss?"

He didn't immediately answer, and that made her suspect that there was something that he was thinking about and hesitating to bring up for some reason. She gently squeezed his shoulder, "No matter how awkward it is, we should talk about it."

Another few miles went by while she waited, and finally, he asked in a slightly strained voice, "Oral?"

She was very grateful he was driving because that was one question she wasn't ready for him to watch her while discussing. Taking a deep breath, "Alright. So...that's definitely a thing."

He laughed softly, "It is."

The car grew quiet and stayed that way for a few minutes. She broke it with a nervous giggle, "This is dumb. We're married. We can talk about this."

"Yes, we can."

"It still feels awkward," she admitted.

He chuckled and glanced at her, "Yes, it does."

She worried her thumbnail between her teeth for a moment before saying, "I'm not sure about it, to be honest."

He nodded, "May I ask why?"

"It's...um...a whole bodily fluids thing."

"Bodily fluids thing?"

She groaned, "This isn't getting less awkward."

He reached over and squeezed her hand for a moment, "Do we need to put a pin in it?"

"It's not gonna be any less awkward if we wait until later."

"No, probably not."

She took a few deep breaths, "I keep...keep thinking about the fact that's..." *Just say it. I just have to say it.* "It's gross. That's where pee is...and even if it's clean, that's all I'll be able to think about...and I just don't think...I...can...swallow." Her face was on fire, and she sank back into the seat as far as she could, wanting to disappear.

At least he didn't laugh. He didn't say anything. Not for a solid eight miles. Finally, "We don't have to do it if you don't want to."

"Are you sure?"

He nodded, "I'm not going to ask you to do something that disgusts you. If you feel that way, then it won't be something we try."

Relief filled her, "Thank you." But almost as soon as she said it, she grew worried, "Are you going to be upset if we don't?"

"I don't think I could enjoy something if I know you're not enjoying it."

She melted a little at his words, "That's very sweet."

"I do have a question, though."

"What's that?"

He took a deep breath, "Are you going to want me to do it to you?"

She shook her head, "I don't think so."

"Would you be open to revisiting this subject later on?"

She stared out the window, "We can, but don't hold your breath that I'll change my mind."

"I won't."

Neither of them spoke for a while. Eventually, he said, "I have a question."

She glanced over at him, "Okay."

"You seem really uncomfortable letting me see your body. Why is that? You know I think you're gorgeous. Is there something that would help make you more comfortable?"

"Oh boy," she blew out a breath, "I'm not sure I can give you a quick or easy answer."

He turned his head toward her momentarily, "I don't want easy, and at the moment, we're not lacking for time."

Her laugh was anxious, "No. No, we are not." She sighed, "I am trying to get more comfortable, I really am."

"I know you are."

She looked out the windshield, watching the road, thinking. Trying to figure out how to explain and have it make sense. "There's a few things that come to mind about why I'm so uncomfortable, and I'm not sure if you'll understand."

"Try me."

"Well, for one thing, I have to protect myself."

He glanced at her, "Do I make you feel unsafe?"

She shook her head, "No. Trust me, we wouldn't be together if you did."

He was silent for a few moments. His voice rough when he asked, "Did you have a Jonas in your life?"

"Not exactly." She sighed, "Fred had some friends. Well, no, that's not really the right term. I don't think he actually has any friends. But these guys, they would come over to the house and...they weren't good guys."

There was silence for a few minutes, and then Liam took an exit and pulled into a truck stop's parking lot. Driving toward an empty part of it, he put the car in park and turned to her. His face was dark, voice tight, "What did they do to you?"

She shook her head, "Liam, it's okay."

"No, it's not," his eyes were the angriest she'd ever seen them.

Making her voice as strong as possible, she told him, "I need you to calm down. Can you please do that for me?"

He closed his eyes, and she watched him take several deep breaths. Looking at her again, he said, "Okay, this is about as calm as I'm going to get. What did they do to you?"

She picked at her thumb cuticle. It hurt, but she couldn't stop. "Physically? Not really anything. There were some...unwanted hugs, touches on my arms, that sort of thing. But nothing that went beyond that. I just...I caught a few of them trying to...to spy on me." She swallowed a small lump that formed in her throat at the memory, "I...I told Fred after one of the times, and he...he told me it was my fault."

"Fuck." Liam growled the word out. His hands were clenched into fists, and his lips formed a tight line.

She sighed, "It didn't happen as much when I started wearing really baggy clothes."

"But it still happened?"

"Yeah."

She watched as he unbuckled and exited the car, "I need some air."

Fast as she could, she got out and hurried to him, "Liam, I'm sorry."

He met her eyes and shook his head, "You have nothing to apologize for."

"But you're upset."

He nodded and swallowed something invisible, "Yeah, I am."

She stepped closer and slipped her arms around his waist, resting against his chest. After a few seconds, his arms went around her. "I didn't want to upset you," she said softly.

He sighed, "It's a good thing we are several hundred miles away from that bastard."

She stepped back and looked up at him, "You have to promise me you won't go after him. Please!"

He shut his eyes, and she watched as his jaw rolled, "I won't, but the thought of him letting that happen. It just...I..." His eyes opened, and his hands moved from her back to cradle her face, "Sweetheart, it was not your fault. You know that, right?"

She nodded, "I do."

"Do you believe that?"

Her smile was sad, "As much as I can."

Zoe took over driving since Liam was still too upset. She should've guessed he'd have a reaction along those lines, given his history with Jonas. "Liam?"

"Yeah?"

"I really appreciate that you haven't tried to rush me to get comfortable. It's just gonna take time."

He was quiet for a few seconds before asking, "What can I do to help?"

"Hand me my drink, please?" She held out her hand.

He laughed as he gave it to her and said, "Not quite what I meant, but there you go."

She took a sip and handed the cup back, saying, "I know it sucks, but I just need you to keep being patient with me. I'm trying. I really am."

He squeezed her shoulder, "I can definitely do that."

For a while, they didn't talk. Zoe had him put on some music and sang along loudly while she drove. Nearly half an hour passed that way, and then the music paused between songs. She heard, "Do you want kids?"

This was something they should've already talked about. She'd known it but kept putting it off. Liam had obviously decided they should stop avoiding the conversation. A few seconds passed, and she replied, "Honestly?"

"Yes."

She shook her head, "I don't know. What about you?"

"I'm not opposed to it."

"So you do?"

She felt his fingers tuck a loose curl behind her ear before he said, "I think you'd make a good mom."

"That's sweet, but I really don't know. I'm sorry. I never thought I'd be in a situation where it would be a possibility."

"Okay."

Looking over at him, she saw he didn't look upset anymore, and to her relief, he didn't look disappointed either. Returning to look at the road, she realized something, "I'm not on birth control. Should we use something or just leave it up to fate?"

"Do you want to?"

She rolled her eyes, "That's not very fair answering a question with a question."

He chuckled, "No, I suppose not." A little more seriously, he added, "I will do whatever you are most comfortable with. You want to leave it up to fate, we will. You want to do everything possible to stop it; that's what we'll do. Does that work?"

She nodded, "Yeah." Softly laughing, she teased, "Should I be worried that you're being so agreeable?"

"Try getting me to eat pineapple pizza and see how agreeable I am," he joked.

By the time they reached the hotel, they were so exhausted they collapsed into bed and slept until late the next morning.

When Zoe woke up, Liam was lying on his side, watching her. She yawned and smiled, "Mornin'."

He reached out and ran his fingers alongside her face and down her neck. The touch sent a shiver down her spine. She shut her eyes and sighed, "That's not fair, y'know."

"I don't know, seems pretty fair to me," he teased softly.

She felt his lips on her forehead and then her temple. He continued feathering kisses down her cheek and finally pressed a soft kiss to her lips. As the kiss broke, she opened her eyes and met his. She lifted her hand and mirrored what he'd done. He took hold of her hand, raised it to his lips, and kissed her open palm.

He released her hand, and she rested it against his cheek saying, "I don't want to get up."

"Then don't."

She laughed, "Pretty sure I can't stay in bed all day."

He kissed her forehead again, "Says who?"

"Um...people?"

"Sweetheart, we're on our honeymoon. People expect us not to leave the bed at all."

Butterflies fluttered in her tummy, "But we...have stuff...to do."

He moved even closer, eyes suddenly hungry, and grinned mischievously as he stroked her cheek, "I can think of stuff to do."

She didn't know what happened. The butterflies panicked and flew away. Her entire body went stiff. Liam's eyes softened, and he backed away a few inches, "Hey, breathe."

She sighed in frustration, "Why is this so hard?" Exasperated, she apologized, "I'm sorry. I just keep fucking this all up."

He shook his head and held his arm open, "Come here." When she hesitated, he added, "Nothing's gonna happen. I'm just gonna hold you, okay?"

Slowly, she moved toward him and let him wrap his arm around her. He pressed a kiss to her hair and said, "You're not fucking this all up."

Her voice shook a little, "I know Dr. Constance said...there's nothing wrong with me...but I feel like there is. We're supposed to..." her words trailed off as she burrowed into his chest.

He was quiet a long time before saying, "We've been trying to force this to happen without either of us being fully ready. What if we just stopped trying?"

His words stirred her panic, and she pushed away from him. She wrapped her arms around herself tightly and stared at him with anxiety, "What do you mean? Don't you want to anymore?"

He shook his head, "Of course, I want to. I just don't think we're going about this right."

Her panic eased a little, "Then what do we do?" She felt like a broken record as she told him again, "We're supposed to..."

He smoothed back her hair, "When have we ever done what we're supposed to? Aren't you tired from all the pressure we've put on ourselves over this? I know I am."

She sagged against him feeling weirdly relieved, "I really am." After a few seconds, she laughed softly, "Have you always been this smart?"

He chuckled and wrapped his arm around her again, "If I were smarter, I would've figured this out a few months ago."

Forty-Six

Zoe

"**N**eed help?"

Zoe turned to see Liam standing a few feet away with the cart. He'd been resupplying in the grocery department before they left Salt Lake to head to Arizona. She bit her lip, "I'm not sure you can."

"You don't want me to tell you what I'd like to see you in?"

She glanced around at the sleepwear racks ranging from modest to downright scandalous, "That seems slightly dangerous."

He chuckled and stepped next to her, "Alright. Show me which ones you like."

Waving her hand at a rack, she told him, "Just some shorts and a tank."

"Get the black."

She laughed, "Out of all the colors sitting here, you want me to go with black?"

He shrugged, "You'll look good in black." Quietly, in her ear, he added, "You'll look good in nothing at all."

Her entire body flushed at his words. She quickly moved to take the black options and dropped them in the cart. He followed and told her, "I'm not going to apologize."

She giggled, "Good."

They checked out and got back on the road, headed south. It had been two days since they'd agreed to stop with the pressure, and things were already so much better. They had both relaxed, and things had started to feel more fun. Liam had grown very playful, and the things that he'd started saying...well, there wasn't much subtlety, that was for sure. It didn't bother her, so maybe that was a good sign? That morning, she'd decided it might be time to try sleeping in something other than baggy pants and shirts. *Might* being the operative word. She wasn't sure if she'd actually be able to make the switch before they got home.

"Hey, let's pull over at that marker," she said.

The car crossed to the other side of the road. Liam parked and turned off the ignition. Zoe hopped out and went to the sign. She got excited as she read what it said, and by the time Liam was beside her, she was bouncing on her heels. He looked down at her in curious amusement, "Yes?"

"It's a ghost town!" She felt giddy.

"Obviously, you're uninterested in driving down to it," he joked.

She laughed, "Please? Can we?"

His eyes scanned the sign, and he nodded, "Sure, it's not that far."

They returned to the car and headed down the dirt road leading to the town-site. The dirt road was slightly treacherous, but they made it in one piece. There wasn't much to see other than the small graveyard enclosed with a locked fence. Hanging from the fence was a sign that listed the names of those buried there. The town's remains were in a valley, surrounded by large red and grey-striated rock formations. It served well for their selfie background.

She looked at the picture and grinned, "I think this is our best one yet!"

He was behind her with his arms wrapped around her shoulders. "I think you're right," the feel of the words against her neck sent a shiver through her. He placed an open-mouthed kiss at the base of her neck, and she sighed. Her legs felt like jelly, and she began to wobble. One arm moved to be around her abdomen, and he kept her from losing her balance.

He pulled back and straightened up. "Okay?" he asked as she steadied.

"Yeah," the word was a little breathy.

They returned to the car, and as they headed back up the dirt road, Zoe sat with her head tilted against the headrest so she could watch Liam.

"You're staring," he mused a few minutes later as they pulled back onto the highway.

"I just really like you," she sighed blissfully.

A few seconds ticked by, and he asked hesitantly, "You do?"

She laughed, "Of course I do. Did you think I didn't? You like me, don't you?"

"I adore you," he murmured, the words giving her goosebumps.

"But do you like me?" she asked.

He nodded, squeezing her leg right above her knee, "I like you."

Liam surprised her once they got to the hotel. So far, he'd rented regular rooms, but since this was their last big stop on the trip, he'd rented the honeymoon suite. "Are you disappointed?" he asked as she looked around the room.

Turning, she grinned at him, "Incredibly."

He set the luggage down and moved toward her, "Well, we'll have to do something about that, won't we?"

She giggled as he took hold of her. He dipped and pressed a kiss to her lips. She was slightly lightheaded as he brought her back up from the dip. He grinned, "Better?"

"I'm not sure," she laughed.

"I see," he replied, pulling her close for another kiss. Breaking it, he asked, "How about now?"

Laughing harder, "Still not sure."

She squealed as he gently pushed her back onto the bed. Leaning over her, his hands sunk into the mattress, and he kissed her a third time. He trailed kisses down to the base of her throat, "And now?"

"This place is definitely improving." she returned his smile. Reaching up, she grasped his neck and pulled him back for another kiss. His body pressed against her, pushing her down into the mattress. She gasped at the feel of his weight. Something inside her felt deliciously good, but suddenly, she clenched and froze. "Liam," she breathed out in a ragged voice.

"Yes, sweetheart?" he murmured.

"Stop."

He paused for a moment, then moved off her. "Too much?"

She nodded, biting back the apology that longed to fly from her lips. That had been something they'd agreed to the day before. No apologizing for asking for what she needed and wanted. So far, she'd had about a twenty-seven percent success rate.

They stood at the edge of the Grand Canyon's South Rim, looking down.

And down.

And even further down. "That is quite the hole," Zoe said.

Liam chuckled, "Shocking, that's not how the Park Service advertises it."

Zoe grinned up at him, "They really should. It's short and sweet and to the point."

He kissed the top of her head, "Just like you."

Her lips pursed, "I'm not short!"

"Sweetheart, you are."

"You're a giant. You make everyone look short," she joked.

Liam rested his arm on her shoulder and leaned against her, "Nah, you're just short. You make a great armrest."

She rolled her eyes and moved closer. His arm went around her shoulders, and hers went around his middle. She sighed happily, "It really is beautiful."

"Yes, you are," he said as he kissed her temple.

"You think you're so smooth," she teased.

"I must be. How else would I have gotten you to fall in love with me?"

How else indeed? She turned a little and looked up at him. Stretching up, she aimed for his cheek, but at the last second, his head turned, and his lips met hers. The kiss only lasted a few seconds, far more chaste than many of their recent kisses. She settled back down and rested her head against his chest. His hand gently rubbed her upper arm, and she thought back to her life before Liam had walked in and upended it.

Less than a year ago, she'd been so incredibly lonely. She'd used the little hope she had to get through the days. It was what got her through those long, unbearable shifts where Fred made her feel worthless. She sighed, "Thank you."

"For?" he sounded a little confused.

She squeezed him, "Everything."

That evening, when they got ready for bed, Zoe dug out the shorts and tank from the Target bag. She studied them. After a few seconds, she pulled the tags off and tossed them in the trash. Returning to look at the flimsy sleep things, she debated. Was she really ready to do this? As always, she kept her back to Liam as she began changing.

She could feel his eyes on her. Would she ever get used to the way he watched her? His gaze was adoring, which was the only reason she'd been able to handle it. Her t-shirt off, she picked up the tank and hesitated. It wasn't going to be as easy to remove her bra once the tank was on. Tucking the tank under her chin for a moment, she undid the bra and let it fall to the floor. The tank slid on, and she changed into the shorts.

Climbing into bed, she finally met Liam's eyes. He probably hadn't seen all that much; her back had been to him, after all. But it had been the first time she'd taken the bra off without a shirt to hide under. Now, she was wearing clothes that did absolutely nothing to hide her body. The tank clung to her, highlighting every single curve. Her husband's gaze was pleased and hungry. Really hungry. A little startled, she realized she felt just as hungry gazing at him. His naked chest drew her eyes, but then she found herself looking up at his dark hair that was filled with loose curl. It had grown longer. Wilder. It was very tempting to ask him to keep growing it out. That, combined with the facial hair he'd been letting grow at her request, created an incredibly handsome image.

She lay on her side, looking at him, pulling the sheet up to her waist. Liam reached out and stroked her hair. His head lowered to hers, and he kissed her tenderly. Her hands slipped up and began to wind themselves into his hair. She loved how soft it felt wrapped around her fingers.

His arms moved and wrapped around her, pulling her tight. She felt his tongue run along the seam of her lips, and she opened her mouth, letting him in. With only the thinnest cloth as a barrier between them, she could feel him so much more than ever before. The moan that slipped from her only seemed to encourage him to press against her even more, taking and giving everything. She gasped as she felt his lips leave hers and trail down her throat.

"Please," she breathed out, though she was having a little trouble figuring out what she was asking for. Her brain felt foggy. Fragmented. The heat that filled her abdomen was drawing most of her focus.

He paused and looked up at her, "Please what?"

She giggled breathlessly, "I don't know!"

His lips found hers again, and she smiled into the kiss. It just felt so fucking good. One of his hands moved from her back to her side. As their tongues tangled, she was vaguely aware that his hand was slowly moving toward her chest. She gasped as he began to massage her breast. The heat was growing, and she felt a rush of wetness between her legs. Clenching her thighs together, she broke the kiss. Breathing heavily, she stared into Liam's ravenous eyes.

This was new. Until now, they'd touched each other's bodies but avoided three certain areas. Her breasts were one, and between their legs were the other two. For a moment, it felt amazing, and then her body went into lockdown. Despite the glazed look in his eyes, Zoe could see that Liam picked up on what was happening, and his hand left her chest.

Still holding her, he eased back a little, putting a few inches of space between their bodies. "Do we need to stop?" he asked quietly.

Her body was screaming mixed messages. *Yes. No. Please keep going. Please stop. Please...please...*Why couldn't she figure it out? Why was she flooded with panic over something she wanted so much? Her voice shook a little, "I...I'm not sure..."

He completely loosed his hold and backed away, "Okay."

She moved toward him, "I don't want to stop, but I...I can't seem to keep going." Traitorous tears gathered, and she blinked rapidly, hoping to stop them. A few escaped, and Liam lifted his hand to cup her cheek. His thumb wiped away the salt water.

They lay that way for a bit. Staring at each other, she could see Liam's mind was working, seeming to puzzle something out. Finally, he said, "I have a thought."

"What's that?"

Her tears had stopped, and he moved his hand back to her hair as his eyes searched her face, "God, you're beautiful."

She smiled bashfully. It wasn't easy to hear the praise, but she tried convincing herself to believe him when he said things like that. Someday, she might be able to hear him compliment her and not have to perform mental gymnastics to convince herself that he actually meant it. She laughed a little, "That's your thought?"

"Just one of them," he mused. "But, no, that wasn't the main thought."

"Tell me."

He was quiet. What could he possibly be thinking that would make him so hesitant? She touched his hair again, saying gently, "Just tell me. Please."

He chewed at his lip, "Do you want to try something?"

She eyed him with curiosity, "What kind of something?"

He was still hesitating. Finally, he asked, his voice rougher than she'd ever heard, "Would you let me watch you?"

Confused, she blinked at him, "Watch me?"

He nodded, "I won't touch you if you don't want. I just...I want to watch you come." He blew out a ragged breath, "Please?"

It clicked in her brain. The thought left her slightly breathless, but she couldn't resist teasing, "Is this because I told you about the vibrator?"

He looked as bashful as she felt, "It's not the only reason."

She studied his face. What he was asking for...it was such an intimate thing. To her surprise, she didn't hate the idea. It seemed like it would be far easier than what they had been possibly heading toward. She'd be able to control what was happening to her own body. That was appealing. Weird. But definitely appealing. It was the whole being watched thing that she was uncertain about.

Finally, she decided, "The lights have to be off. I...I don't think I want you to touch me while I...do...that. And...I don't want to be the only one...doing...y'know..."

He quietly laughed, "It's only fair if I can't touch you."

She took a few deep breaths and held his gaze briefly before leaving the bed. Feeling slightly unsteady on her feet, she took a moment to adjust before walking to her suitcase. She retrieved the tool and pressed the button to ensure the charge was still good. A little shakily, she returned to the bed. He'd been watching her the whole time, and as she joined him, his gaze fell to the lilac silicone in her hand. She knew she was blushing furiously at how he looked from the toy to her and back to the toy.

Taking a few deep breaths, "Lights?"

His lust-filled eyes met hers, and he hesitated only a moment before moving to switch the lamp off. The room grew mostly dark. There was a red glow on the ceiling from the smoke detector, and the numbers on the alarm clock gave everything else a weird green glow.

Liam lay on his side, facing her, leaving plenty of space between their bodies. She pushed the button and felt the vibration start. Lying on her back, staring at the ceiling, she shut her eyes tightly and told him, "I...I don't know...how long this will...take. When I'm...alone...it goes pretty fast usually. But...I don't know..."

"Go at whatever speed is most comfortable," he told her softly.

She shut her eyes. Okay. They were doing this. She could do this. Moving the vibrator down under the waistband of her shorts and underwear and placing it on the spot between her legs, she sucked in a small, sharp breath as it made contact. Trying to clear her mind and just go with the feelings it created, she let the sensations roll through her. At least she attempted to. Feeling Liam's eyes on her, even in the dark, made everything a little more difficult.

She shuddered as something deep inside her tightened. The heat, which had cooled a little, grew even hotter than before. Her breathing was shallow and rapid. Thinking of Liam, she wondered if this was really what he wanted. Did he actually want to see her like this? Could she even come in front of him? And if she could, would he be disgusted if he saw her completely undone?

His ragged breathing caught her attention, and she opened her eyes to look at him. In the dim light, she saw he was watching her through half-closed eyes. The movement of his shoulder drew her attention, and she followed the line of his arm to where it disappeared under the sheet. Despite the barrier, it wasn't hard to see what was happening.

Her eyes returned to his, and she could not look away. Tapping the button, the vibrations increased, and she felt herself start to shake a little as her hips moved, pressing hard against the buzzing silicone. She was on fire. A throaty sound escaped her, and out of the corner of her eye, she noticed his arm was moving faster.

There was something that settled in the air between them. Something thick that made everything feel more intense. Their eyes locked on each other. She felt herself arching as she tapped the button again, and everything became stronger. Deep inside, it tightened to an unbearable point, and an animalistic cry escaped her as it all became too much. Her legs clamped around the tool, and she shook hard as a few waves crashed into her. Curling in on herself as the last one ebbed away, she removed the toy from her body and shut her eyes, trying to regain her bearings.

The sound that came from Liam pulled her back to the moment, and she blinked open in time to see him experience his own release.

They lay there for nearly a minute, panting hard and staring at each other. They were still Liam and Zoe. That said, with what had just happened, they suddenly looked just a little different to each other. Zoe knew they had just crossed a line from which there was no return. The feeling that coursed through her at that knowledge was overwhelming, but to her relief, it wasn't scary. It was right.

Everything was right.

Forty-Seven

Liam

I t was still dark when he pulled into the parking spot back at the South Rim. Zoe wanted to see the sunrise, and he wanted to watch her see the sunrise. As they got out of the car, his thoughts continued to drift back to the night before. To what they had done.

He hadn't been sure she'd agree to it. It was a huge step for both of them. But he had wanted to see her. Wanted to watch as reason completely abandoned her and feelings took over. It had been hard not touching her, but the way she'd held his gaze had been more than enough to fuel the flames inside himself.

She'd been so incredibly gorgeous in that moment. The way her mouth had opened and the sounds that had escaped her had only made her more breathtaking. He knew that no matter how much time went by, he would never get tired of seeing her like that.

Once they had cleaned up, they'd laid quietly, softly touching each other. No pressure, no trying to take things further. Just being gentle with each other. Talking in low voices. Her musical laugh rang out frequently. It had been perfect. She was perfect. It overwhelmed him that she could be so wonderful and manage to see something in him that she thought was worth her time and energy.

They took a seat on a large rock at the canyon's edge. She curled against him, looking east as the first streaks of dawn cut through the black of the night sky. Even he had to admit that watching the sun begin its journey was incredible. Shadows receded as light hit the ancient stone formations.

A thought occurred to him. Squeezing her, he slipped off the rock and knelt before her. She glanced away from the sunrise to look at him with curiosity, "What's going on?"

He held her hand and said, "This is how I wish I could've proposed to you."

She laughed gently, a soft look on her face, "I dunno, your four a.m. proposal was pretty memorable."

He stroked her cheek, "You deserved better. You deserved so much better. I wish I could've given that to you."

She placed her hand over his, "It was perfect. I wouldn't trade it for anything."

He chuckled, "Zoe?"

"Yeah?"

"Stay married to me?"

She leaned forward, and as the sun rose above the horizon, she said, "Yes." Her lips met his for a moment, and when she moved back, he resumed his seat beside her. Arms around her, he held on as they watched day fully push the night away.

The next day, they headed northeast toward the Arizona-Utah border. He'd been the one to suggest doing a drive through Monument Valley, and Zoe had been excited by the idea once he filled her in on what it was. They didn't watch many Westerns, but something was intriguing about seeing the rock formations that showed up in so many movies and TV shows.

Desert flew by as they drove. Zoe had taken the first leg of the trip, and they would swap when she got tired. A little over an hour into their trek, he asked, "Want to do more homework?"

Not looking away from the road, she nodded, "Sure."

He scanned the list of questions and found himself thinking back a few days to the conversation that had left him so angry with Fred and his cronies. She hadn't answered one of the questions he'd asked. "Is it okay if I ask something not on the list?"

"What do you want to know?"

"Is there something that will make you more comfortable when it comes to letting me see your body?"

She glanced at him, "You already asked that."

He nodded, "But you didn't really answer it."

A mile passed before she acknowledged, "Guess I got a little distracted by how upset you got."

"Fair." He asked, "Any thoughts on this?"

"It's just a very daunting thing, y'know?"

He remembered watching her take her bra off without hiding under her shirt to do it. From the angle he'd watched her, he hadn't been able to see more than the smallest bit of one of her breasts. He longed to see what they actually looked like. Then again, he longed to know what all of her looked like, completely free of clothing. "So, how do we make it less daunting?"

He watched as Zoe kept her eyes on the road, her fingers flexing on the steering wheel. "I'm not sure."

"Okay," he nodded. "So, can you tell me why you're not sure?"

She burst out laughing, "You sound like Dr. Constance. She'll be so proud."

He joined in the laughter, "She'll be thrilled."

She sighed as her laughter faded, "The things I think when you ask that...I don't think they'll make sense outside of my head."

"Try me. Tell me one of them."

"You sure?"

He reached over and squeezed her shoulder, "Sure."

A few miles passed before she replied, "I...I don't want to gross you out."

It was so absurd that he very nearly laughed. Stopping himself just before the sound escaped, he gently told her, "I could never find you gross."

"You don't know that," she said softly.

He shook his head, even though she wasn't looking at him, "Why do you think I might be grossed out? Do I gross you out?"

He was not prepared for her to be the one to laugh as she replied, "If I ever get grossed out by you, we should get my head examined."

"I'll remember that," he assured her.

She moved her head side-to-side in a small stretch. Her voice was more serious when she said, "I need you to promise you're not going to get upset again."

That didn't bode well. A prickle of unease ran through him. "I can't promise that. But I will do my best to stay calm." That was the most he could do, and he hoped it would be enough.

She didn't immediately say anything. Another mile disappeared in the rearview mirror. "My whole life I've...I've been told plenty of times what I look like. How...ugly...how disgusting..."

He stared at her in disbelief. Before he could say anything, she added, "What I see when I look in the mirror...it's not pretty. And I know you're going to say I'm wrong, that I have a distorted view of myself...but the truth is that's honestly what I see." She sighed heavily, "I just don't know why you seem to see something else."

"Who told you that?" his voice was low, but he tried to keep the edge out.

She shrugged, "Everyone. Kids at school. Fred. Take your pick."

He saw red and forced himself to remember to keep breathing. Zoe was opening up to him, and he didn't want her to shut down because of his temper.

"I'm sorry," he said simply.

"It's okay. I got used to it. Kind of had to. I figured, if enough people thought that...it must be true," her voice was sad.

"They were wrong."

She shook her head, "I don't know."

"Zoe, they were wrong," he insisted.

She didn't reply, and he decided that if she didn't add anything more, he'd drop the subject for now. Nearly fifteen minutes passed before she said, "You probably think I should talk to Dr. Constance about this."

"Do you think you need to?"

She sighed, "Maybe."

They drove through the famous landmarks and stopped multiple times because Zoe wanted to take photos. When they completed the seventeen-mile loop, Liam took over driving as they headed for Albuquerque.

"I have a question," Zoe asked after they'd listened to music for a while.

"More homework questions?" he asked with amusement.

"Not really, just something I've been wondering about."

He nodded, "What is it?"

"What did you want to be when you grew up? Like, if all the things that happened hadn't happened and you could've done what you actually wanted to."

The question surprised him. He knew the answer without even having to put much thought into it. "I wanted to teach."

"Really? What did you want to teach?"

"Beginning piano."

She was silent for a few seconds before asking, "Is that why you wanted to teach me?"

He nodded, "I was curious to see if I actually could."

She patted his arm, "You're a good teacher. Even if I am a terrible student."

He laughed softly, "You're not a terrible student. I like teaching you. It makes me get creative."

"Why only beginning piano?" she asked after a few seconds.

He thought about it, "It's hard to learn an instrument. Some people it comes to naturally. I was lucky like that. But I remember seeing kids get so discouraged because they would want to learn, only to get stuck with a teacher who was rigid and unwilling to try to make it a better experience. The kids would end up hating it and give up. If they'd had a better teacher to start with, maybe they'd have stuck with it."

He shook his head, "If I hadn't picked it up so easily, I would've been one of those kids. My teacher was a terror. We'd butt heads constantly, but somehow I managed to survive lessons with her without losing my love for playing."

It was quiet briefly before Zoe said, "You should do it."

"It?"

"Teach kids. You'll be good at it. Let's face it, you've proven to be far more patient than I ever expected. Kids need that."

He sighed, "I can't."

"Why not?" came her surprised question.

He gripped the steering wheel tightly, "What parent in their right mind would trust me with their child?"

They were both exhausted by the time they reached Albuquerque. Liam sincerely doubted there would be a repeat of their first night in Arizona. He was very surprised when Zoe began to change for bed and didn't turn her back to him. She didn't look at him, but she didn't try to hide herself either.

It was insanely hot.

He stayed perfectly still, watching her, resisting the urge to move toward her. That would probably spook her, which was the last thing he wanted. This was such a huge step, and he wasn't about to do anything to discourage her.

When her shirt was off, she stood there in only her leggings and bra. He could feel himself start to grow hard at the sight. She undid the bra and let it fall to the floor. Moving fast, she had the tank on before he had a chance to fully appreciate her breasts. Swapping leggings for shorts only took a few more seconds, and then she crawled into bed beside him.

Zoe looked at him with wide eyes as he reached for her. She was tense, and he felt himself deflate a little. There definitely wouldn't be a repeat of that night. He suspected that just letting him see more of her had been as much as she was up for. He kissed her forehead, "Relax, we're not going to do anything."

"Thank you," her voice sounded small, but he did feel some of the tension leave her. They fell asleep not long after.

Forty-Eight

Liam

S tanding outside the car, Zoe looked around and squealed, "I love it!"

He gazed at her fondly, "Of course, you do."

"It's Roswell. This is history!" she enthused.

"Well, you wanted to see a tourist trap. This might be the ultimate one," he informed her.

She laughed and pulled him toward the UFO museum. Even though he considered this the stupidest stop on their trip, he wouldn't say that. Wasn't going to steal away the joy that the ridiculous place was bringing her.

She looked at everything, and he looked at her. She took photos of everything, and he took photos of her. After they returned to the car to head north, she laughed, "This is the absolute dumbest place I've ever been to, and I'm so glad we came."

"Do we need to drive out into the middle of the desert and stay up all night so you can watch for UFOs? Get the full Roswell experience?"

Amused, she replied, "No, I think I'm good." Her tone shifted, "I've loved this trip, but honestly, I think I'm ready to be home again. It'll be nice to sleep in our bed and not be living out of a suitcase."

He quirked an eyebrow at her, "Sure you don't want to add a bunch more stops to the itinerary?"

"I'm sure. We can always hit the rest of the United States on the next trip. Another big, exhausting road trip."

He chuckled, "I'll be very curious to see how you intend to drive to Hawaii."

"Listen, we just need to make a few modifications to the car...train a whale...it'll be great!"

Late in the afternoon of the next day, the car came to rest outside their front door. Liam watched as Zoe climbed from the car and stretched. Getting out, he mirrored her movements with his own aching body. It would be at least a week before he'd be ready to even consider getting back in the vehicle.

Zoe went into the house before he did, and by the time he caught up to her, she was lying on the bed, flat on her back. He looked down at her with amusement as she said, "Oh my god, it's even better than I remembered."

It was tempting to crawl on top and kiss her, but instead, he laid down beside her and let out his own sigh of relief, "It really does feel good."

She rolled onto her side and smiled, "Thank you. It was a good honeymoon."

He returned her smile, "It really was." A shadow passed over her face, and he looked at her quizically, "What is it?"

She sighed, "I'm sorry."

"For what?" confusion filled his voice.

She rolled onto her back and stared up at the skylight, "We didn't have sex."

He reached over and gently turned her face toward him, "No, we didn't, but we did other stuff, and that was pretty great. And even if we hadn't, it still would've been a good trip. No apologizing, okay?"

Zoe was still working on getting more comfortable with letting him see her body. She continued facing him while changing but wouldn't meet his eyes. He always watched her but never tried to push what was happening to be more. As the days passed, he realized her movements were getting the tiniest bit slower every time.

One morning, a week after they got home, Zoe had been showering, and he realized he needed his phone charger. Retrieving it from the nightstand, he turned to walk back to the living room when he froze as the bathroom door opened. Zoe stood there wrapped in a towel.

His eyes went wide at the sight. He'd now seen her much more naked, but there was something about knowing that she had absolutely nothing under the towel that definitely did things to him. To his surprise and relief, she didn't seem very bothered by seeing him there. After a few seconds, she moved to the dresser to retrieve clothing. He couldn't look away and asked, "Do you want me to leave?"

She shrugged, "Up to you. Dr. Constance would probably say you should stay if I'm comfortable with it. I think it fits under that whole exposure therapy thing she said I've unknowingly been doing when I've been changing."

"Are you comfortable with it?"

She turned back to him, underwear in hand, and considered the question. "Kind of? If you could close your eyes right now, that would really help. I'll tell you when you can look."

His eyes slid shut at her request, and less than a minute later, she said, "Okay, we're good."

Opening his eyes, he saw the towel was gone, and she was dressed in her bra and panties. He very much would've liked to see her take the towel off, but he wasn't going to complain. She was making progress, and that was the important thing.

That night, they tried what they'd done in Arizona. She still didn't want to be touched while they did it, but they held eye contact the entire time. If anything, it was far better than the first time. After, he held her. They talked about anything and everything until the wee hours of the morning when they both drifted off. Over the next few weeks, that was how they would be intimate.

Life fell into a routine. On Wednesdays, they would go to therapy. His session would be first, and Zoe's would be second. After, they would spend the rest of the day recuperating. Therapy still wasn't easy for him, but after the session in Montana, he finally could see that he was making genuine progress. Zoe was having a harder time, but she was still in the early sessions. Dr. Constance had agreed that ADHD seemed very likely and had scheduled Zoe to see someone else to get an official diagnosis and treatment.

During the week, Zoe would go in to record, and on Saturdays, they both would spend two hours in the booth reading the news. Zoe still maintained that the live news reads were her favorite part of the week, and Liam had come to feel the same. There was something truly fun about spending time with his wife while doing something that helped so many people.

Given the chaos of their spring, Zoe hadn't gotten to plant the vegetable garden he knew she wanted. He watched her make plans for it, and she informed him that she'd be planting it the next spring. He was thrilled at the thought of having the fresh ingredients. They'd invested in a few hydroponic planters to tide her over until she could plant a full garden. She had filled the yard with as many flowers as she could. It wasn't unusual to find her sitting outside surrounded by the plants, book in hand.

They'd been brainstorming ways to make his dream of teaching a reality. Zoe had come up with a few ideas she thought would ease parents' worries. The ideas were good, but still, he hesitated. Believing that anyone would be willing to trust him with something as precious as their child seemed outside the realm of possibility. Especially since Jonas's trial had served to remind the world that Liam existed. His testimony was public knowledge, and he'd encountered a handful of things online written by people who again questioned his honesty. There would always be those who would believe the worst of him.

On clear nights, Zoe would pull him out to the yard to lie down and stargaze. They could see the stars through the skylight, but she loved seeing the sky without barriers. Unbeknownst to her, he was planning a trip to Alaska so that she could see the Northern Lights. He couldn't wait to see her face when he told her. It was going to be a good birthday present.

Every day, he found himself a little more in love with her. He was completely overwhelmed that she was there, loving him as much as he loved her. Some mornings, he would wake up and momentarily panic that it had all been some glorious dream, but then he'd feel her in his arms, and that made everything better.

Life was good.

Forty-Nine

Liam

It was late on a Thursday afternoon, four weeks after they got home. A summer thunderstorm rolled in. Once it moved on, Zoe took her hammock camp chair out to the porch to watch the clouds.

He was at the piano, but he was distracted. His eyes kept drifting to his wife. Dr. Constance had suggested the chair to help with Zoe's anxiety. It had arrived at the beginning of the week, and she'd practically lived in it ever since.

Leaving the piano, he made his way to the back porch. Opening the screen door, he walked to her, watching her body being rocked by the chair. Stopping behind her and looking down, he smiled. She looked so peaceful, so incredibly happy. "Hey," she said sweetly.

"Hi."

"You didn't have to stop playing."

He chuckled, "There's something else I want to do more."

She batted her eyelashes, "And what would that be?"

He leaned down, "You."

"Oh really?" she laughed softly, a faint dusting of pink touching her cheeks.

He nodded, "Really."

A few seconds passed, and in the distance, there was a roll of thunder. He moved in front of her and leaned forward. Placing his hands where the frame held up the arms of the chair, he gazed at her hungrily. She didn't look away. His voice was low as he requested, "Let me make love to you. Please, sweetheart?"

She didn't immediately reply. More thunder rolled, sounding a little closer. A few raindrops fell, and she nodded, "Okay."

They went back inside, bringing her chair in so it wouldn't get rained on. He took her hand and led her back to the bedroom. They stopped at the edge of the bed, and she looked up at him. He could see a little anxiety on her face and caressed her cheek with his fingers. "If you need us to stop, we will," he told her.

In reply, she moved her hand up to the back of his neck and pulled him down to meet her lips. The kiss was soft and slow. His hands took hold of her sides. Later, they could have something wild and crazy. Right now, he wanted to take his time. Make it as good as he could manage for her. Hopefully, not leave her disappointed.

The kiss broke, and his hands moved to the bottom of her tee. His eyes held hers, "May I?"

She took a few deep breaths and nodded. He raised the shirt over her head, dropping it on the floor at their feet. He sat on the edge of the bed, and she was in front of him. The bed sat low enough that she was taller than him. He enjoyed the change of being the one looking up with her looking down. Her fingers lightly brushed against his skin as she pushed his hair back. She leaned down and placed a small kiss on his forehead. He shut his eyes for a moment as the sensation of the touch washed over him.

Rain began to lightly patter against the house. It was growing darker outside, and there was another rumble of thunder. Closer than before.

He opened his eyes, and his hands moved to her back. To where her bra was clasped. His fingers took hold of the fabric, and he again asked, "May I?"

She shut her own eyes for a moment. Opening them, she looked down at him anxiously, "Promise you won't be disgusted?"

"I promise."

She let out a shaky breath and nodded, "Okay."

He went to unclasp the bra, and to his annoyance, it did not come apart easily. His annoyance quickly turned to frustration as he found himself in the cliche of not being able to undo a bra.

"Liam, stop."

He looked up, and to his relief, there was amusement on Zoe's face. She laughed a little, "Let me turn around."

Once she did, he was able to see what he was doing, and the bra came undone easily. He turned her back to face him, and the bra was still loosely held in place. Reaching up, he moved one of the straps down from her shoulder and then repeated the move with the other. He began to slide the bra down, and after a few seconds, gravity took over. It landed on the floor, joining her shirt with a soft sound.

For weeks, he'd been getting glimpses of her naked chest, but always from several feet away. Now, he was barely a foot from her breasts, and he gazed at them hungrily. She liked to joke that she had just enough boob to make it necessary to wear a bra but not enough to make it really worthwhile. As far as he was concerned, they were the absolute perfect size. For several long moments, he admired them.

Hands on her sides, he pulled her just a few inches closer. Looking up and meeting her eyes, he did one of the things he'd been fantasizing about. He licked one of the tight pink buds and then the other. Zoe shivered at the touch, and he felt her fingers move into his hair. She pushed her chest forward, and he almost laughed at how easy she was making this for him.

His lips closed around one nipple, and he sucked. One hand splayed against her back while the other lifted to her other breast. His thumb brushed the nipple. She tensed at the touch, her hands gripping his hair a little tighter, and a moan came out of her that thrilled him.

The rain had started falling a little harder, and there was a flash from the lightning outside.

Kissing her nipple, he backed up and looked at her, trying to gauge how she was doing so far. "You still okay?"

The reply she gave was not what he anticipated. She stepped closer, and her lips found his. As their kiss deepened, he continued to brush his thumb across one of the now-hard nipples. Curious, he stopped the movement and began to roll it between his thumb and index finger.

The kiss broke as she gasped out, "Oh god!"

He smiled at her, "Do you want me to stop?"

She moved closer, climbed on top, and straddled him. "Don't you fucking dare," she ordered as she ground against him.

Another time, he would let her run things. In fact, he very much looked forward to letting her take charge, but that was not what was going to happen this time. He lifted her off himself, stood, and laid her back on the bed. Stripping her and covering nearly every part in kisses was something he'd fantasized about many times.

His hands went to the waistband of her shorts. Hooking his fingers around it, he pulled and was rewarded by her lifting her hips so that the shorts would slide off easier. They hit the floor, joining the growing pile of discarded clothing.

She was almost completely naked. It was longest, uninterrupted view he'd had of her body. Reaching for her panties, he hesitated as his fingers came in contact with the fabric. Looking up at her, he asked, "Yes?"

She searched his face, seeming to debate whether she was ready to let this happen. Finally, she took a deep breath and nodded. "Yes," she said softly as she lifted her hips again so he could remove the final piece of clothing.

It hit the floor, and he paused, drinking her in. She was breathtaking, whether she believed it or not. Her breathy giggle caught his attention, and he met her eyes, "What?"

"You're wearing too much clothing," she managed to get out between giggles.

He smiled at her, "Oh, am I?"

"You really are," she responded as she struggled, trying to sit up.

He lightly pushed her down so she was on her back again. His hands went to the bottom of his tee, and he tossed it away. Stripping out of the rest of his clothes, he lay on the bed beside his wife. They stared at each other. This was the first time they'd both been completely naked in front of each other.

Lightning lit up the room. Several seconds later, thunder clapped far above them.

Zoe laughed, and he looked at her with curiosity. "Yes?"

"Sorry...I swear...I'm not laughing at you," she managed to get out.

He reached for her, and she let him pull her close. Pressing his lips to her forehead, he said, "Kind of seems like you are."

She nestled her head into the crook of his neck, her laughter calming a little, "I'm really not. It's just...We're here. We're naked. And after...after how freaked out I've been...this is just not quite as...awkward...and scary as I expected. For some reason, my brain finds the whole thing hilarious."

He smiled at her words. With all the anxious apprehension she'd been feeling about this, it wasn't the most surprising thing that it had led to such an emotional response. At least she was laughing and not crying.

"I do love you," she said, a little softer.

Moving so he could look at her face, "I love you, too."

He proceeded to completely cover her in kisses, leading her to gasping and giggling, squealing and writhing against him. Tickling her, he was rewarded with even more laughter and breathy claims of, "That's not fair!" They touched parts of each other that had previously been off-limits. The more they touched, the more things intensified. Despite his intention to go slowly, things definitely got faster.

They both seemed to be suffering from some brain fog. Words got less intelligible, and touches grew clumsy. When she took hold of him and stroked a few times, he realized that if she continued, it would all be over very fast. He pulled her hand away. "I want to be in you," he murmured.

Another clap of thunder sounded, and this time, it shook the entire house. Rain pounded on the roof.

Zoe looked at him through heavy-lidded eyes and, after a moment, nodded, "Okay, but I think we need lube."

Retrieving the container from the drawer in her nightstand, he used it and then moved so he was above her, poised at her entrance. He leaned down and kissed her, "Tell me if it hurts."

She gave him a small nod, and her eyes widened as he tried to push inside. "Fuck," he growled as he realized she wasn't just tight; she was completely tensed. There was no way he was going to be able to get in.

He backed away as he realized she had tears in her now anxious eyes. Laying down beside her, he slowly ran his hand up and down her side. She curled into a ball, and a few tears escaped. He held her against himself, moved his hands to her back, and gently told her, "It's okay, sweetheart."

She was shaking, and he heard, "I'm s-sorry."

As much as he wanted to be buried deep inside her, as much as he was literally aching for it, he wasn't about to try to accomplish that at the present moment. He shook his head, "You don't need to be."

"B-but...we...you...I don't know why...I can't relax..." her words were choked with sobs.

Moving one hand away from her back, he wiped at her tears, "We'll figure it out, but not right now, okay?"

"I'm just ruining this." Her words made him chuckle, and he instantly regretted it as he felt her tense even more. She weepily pleaded, "Please...please don't hate me."

He moved her chin so she was looking at him. With all the love inside, he told her, "I don't hate you. I'm sorry for laughing. You're not ruining this. I love you."

"Please don't be angry...I just can't..." She buried her face in his chest.

He resumed rubbing her back, "I'm not mad. I promise. This is just going to take time. Besides, we have managed to make a lot of progress today." His words produced a teary laugh from her, and he felt some relief at the sound.

While the storm crashed and boomed around them, they held onto each other. This wouldn't be the day when it would happen, nor would the next day. But a few days later, with a lot of time and patience, he finally found himself buried deep inside her. She gazed up at him with shining eyes. "Okay?" he asked, nuzzling against her.

She smiled sweetly and nodded, "Okay."

They tried to find a rhythm, but things were still clumsy. That didn't matter, though; it felt good being together. The way she contracted around him was everything, and when he finally came, he felt the closest, the most connected he ever had to her. It had taken time to get there, but the sweet smile and soft declarations of love she rewarded him with made it all worth it.

Fifty

Liam

A Few Months Later

The lesson had finished. Asher hopped off the piano bench, running to the kitchen to get the cookie and 3D-printed frog Zoe had promised him. Liam watched the little boy with fondness. Asher was primarily non-verbal, struggled with anger, and had a natural gift for the piano. Liam saw a lot of himself in the six-year-old.

There was the sound of gravel crunching outside, and Liam said, "Asher, your dad's here."

The little boy came out from the kitchen with the rainbow-colored frog in his hands, staring at it with fascination while he moved all the different articulated joints. Liam collected the books off the piano and herded the small child down the stairs. Asher's adopted father, Javier, met them at the door.

Asher went running for the car, and Liam handed Javier the books.

"How's he doing?" Javier asked.

Liam grinned, "Really well. He's picking things up fast. I'm probably gonna have to find something a little more challenging for him soon."

Javier smiled, "That's great. I'm so glad this is working out." He paused and asked, "Any chance you want to take on more students?"

"Certainly. Know someone who's looking for a teacher?"

"Friend of mine. She's a single mom with three kids, and one of 'em has been driving her nuts because they want to learn. She can't really afford lessons. Okay, if I give her your info?"

"Here you go," Zoe said as she came down the steps and handed Javier a container of cookies and Liam's business card.

Javier took the items and thanked them. He headed for his silver car and waiting son. Liam shut the door and followed Zoe back up the stairs. She returned to the kitchen while he walked around, turning off the cameras.

The cameras were there for the parents. If a parent wanted to check in on the lesson at any point, all they had to do was log on and see what was happening in real-time. They'd set it up so the parents always got a new password at every lesson. So far, he only had two students, but word of mouth had started to spread.

He was finally doing what he'd always wanted to do and was putting his grandfather's money to good use. Liam had never told Zoe exactly how much Nathaniel King had left him, but it was safe to say that he and Zoe would never be able to spend all of it. They had discussed it, and he had decided on two things. First, he wanted to teach kids who wouldn't have an opportunity to learn otherwise, and he would never charge them for piano lessons. He didn't want cost to be a barrier to learning. Second, he had begun reaching out to some lower-income public schools in the area and anonymously covering the cost of replacing and fixing instruments, tuning pianos, and providing instruments to kids who needed them.

Once the cameras were off, he wandered to the kitchen, where Zoe promptly stuffed a cookie in his mouth. He was still the primary cook in the house, but lately, Zoe had discovered the joy of baking. She didn't make regular cookies, though. Every batch was some unexpected flavor experiment. He dutifully tried each batch, and to everyone's relief, she had more hits than misses.

Chewing the latest experiment, he was confused. Swallowing, he looked at his wife, who was bouncing up and down excitedly. "Bacon and chocolate?" he asked.

She nodded, "Maple bacon and chocolate."

He thought for a moment, "The consistency is...weird. Not bad, but I can't quite figure out..."

She was beaming, "They're pancake cookies!"

He laughed, "I did not know that was a thing, but yeah, that's definitely like eating a pancake."

She glanced at the cookies on the rack, "They didn't call for the chocolate, but I wanted to use up the rest of a bag and figured it couldn't be too weird of a combination."

He pulled her close and kissed the tip of her nose, "Nope, not too weird at all. Then again, I'm not sure anything will ever be as weird as those pickle cookies you made. After that, everything else seems normal."

She grimaced, "Yeah, the pickle ones were disgusting. I still get nauseous thinking about them."

Nuzzling her, he teased, "I can't believe you saw that recipe and thought it was a good idea in the first place."

She shrugged, "You never know what's actually gonna taste good. I've watched enough of that Dylan guy on TikTok to know you can be pleasantly surprised by some weird ingredient combinations."

The timer rang, and he released her so she could remove the cookie sheet from the oven. As he leaned against the counter watching her, he found himself marveling for the umpteenth time that this woman was willing to build a life with him. He thought back to the first time he met her. How very different their lives had been. How very different he had been.

Zoe turned from placing the sheet on a trivet and gazed at him with curiosity, "What's that look for?"

He held out his arms, and she stepped into his embrace. Looking down, he asked, "Know what this weekend is?"

"Veteran's Day?"

He laughed, "That and?"

She shook her head, "Sorry, I got nothin'."

"Do you remember a year ago this weekend when this guy subbed, and he kept breathing in the microphone?"

She grinned, "Oh yeah, he was a mess. He also drank his coffee loudly in my ear. I remember thinking how incredibly unhappy he was. Wonder what happened to him."

"I heard he got married."

She laughed, "Good for him. I hope he's very happy and that he loves his wife very, very much."

He pulled her tight against himself, "I heard he does. I hope his wife is very, very happy."

Zoe batted her eyelashes at him, "I bet she is. Do you think he is?"

Liam leaned down, and before he kissed her, he hovered over her lips and replied, "I know for a fact he is."

The End

Acknowledgements

Tom: You love me in a way I didn't think anyone ever could or would. You know me better than anyone else. I love you. And, if you're reading this, please know I have absolutely no idea what I want for dinner.

Lindsey: The list of things I have to thank you for is far too long for this section. So, I'll keep it short and sweet. Thank you for being the biggest cheerleader ever, for letting me bounce every crazy story idea off of you, for the listening ear, and all the TLH & RKB discussions. I am forever grateful for you!

Aunty Ellen: I love you. Thank you for reading this and being so encouraging!

JR: You have been endlessly encouraging.

My Beta Readers: Thank you for being willing to read this.

Tory: Thank you for all the encouragement, for always being excited over my little writing victories, and for the advice! I cannot wait to buy my book from Sower Books!

RTBS (Bekka, Cami, Ryan, & Michael): Thank you for all the love and encouragement and adopting me as the office cat.

The therapists I've worked with over the last six years: Thank you for helping me on my journey of working through my past and treating my ADHD/Depression/Anxiety.

Everyone on AO3 that has read my little flights of fancy over the last two years. I don't know that I would've ever been brave enough to do this without all the love and encouragement you've given me. Thanks and Hugs from Mannaberry

Coming Soon

Love in N Scale

Demisexual Romance + Model Railroad
Coming late 2024/Early 2025

About the Author

Beth Hope currently lives in Omaha with her husband, dogs, and cat.

Find her online...
Blog: http://ne2nd.com
Instagram: https://www.instagram.com/mannaberry/
TikTok: https://www.tiktok.com/@memary84